CROWN OF DARKNESS

BEC MCMASTER

LOCHABER PRESS

"A dark romance **perfect for fae lovers**… This is the exact kind of fae fantasy romance I've been craving. It's **dark, it's romantic**, and it is very, very fae…" —**Kate**

"MUST READ fantasy romance… Bec McMaster has painted a **delightfully dark** and sinister world of the fae, the seelie and unseelie and an **enchanting tale of forbidden love** and fated mates."—**Arial**

Kiss Of Steel—Georgia RWA Maggies Best Paranormal Romance 2013

Heart Of Iron—One of Library Journal's Best Romances 2013 and nominated for RT Reviews Best Steampunk 2013

Forged By Desire—RITA Finalist Paranormal Romance 2015

Of Silk And Steam—RT Reviews Best Steampunk Romance 2016 and SFR Galaxy Award winner

Mission: Improper—#1 Amazon Steampunk Bestseller

To Catch A Rogue—RITA Finalist Paranormal Romance 2019

Nobody's Hero—Two-time SFR Galaxy Awards winner

The Last True Hero—Dark Paranormal PRISM winner 2018

Hexbound—Historical Fantasy PRISM winner 2017

Soulbound—Historical Fantasy PRISM winner 2018 and overall PRISM Best of the Best

Promise of Darkness—Finalist in Fantasy, PRISM Awards

CONTENT WARNING

Please note: This is a content warning for self-harm in Chapter 32. I don't believe it is overly graphic, but I respect the right of each reader to decide whether to read that particular chapter.

PROLOGUE

The first earsplitting shriek of abandonment echoes in the air as the baby wails.

The princess stares down at the child, the one she loves so dearly, and every inch of her trembles. This is not what she wants for it, but she cannot keep it. Not without risking its life. And she has already risked too much. The only answer she has is this.

A moon-drenched forest.

An old, hollow stone that has been used for this purpose for eons—an altar to the Old Ones.

And the silence, broken only by the baby's quiet sobs as it stares at her face, its lower lip trembling as if it knows its fate.

"I'm sorry." She falls to her knees, tentatively touching its soft face.

The night steals away its features, but she knows them as well as her own. Those green eyes, so alert, even from the moment of its birth. An old soul, this one. The thatch of black hair is different from the gold of her own, but the soft pillow-shaped curve of its mouth mimics hers, and she cannot help tracing those little lips with her finger.

She never knew love like this until the baby's birth.

"This is for your own good," she whispers. "I must keep you safe, no matter what it costs me. I must protect you. I love you, my little one."

And so I must give you away.

Pressing one last kiss to the baby's smooth forehead, she forces herself to stand, ignoring those whimpering cries even as her heart bleeds.

Shadows draw closer, as if sprites linger. The golden, unblinking eyes of demi-fey watch from the woods, curious and playful. And the baby wriggles fat, chubby arms, tearing free of its blankets.

She should go.

She needs to go.

But she cannot leave the child alone until she knows it is safe.

Hiding in the nearby trees, she tries to steel herself against the whimpering cries. It needs to cry if it is to be found. Old Mother Hibbert can hear the sobs of abandoned babies from a thousand miles away, and it is she the princess wishes to attract.

Minutes trickle past. It's growing late, and she must be away before the sun rises. The child screams now, full-throated sobs that might attract any manner of predators.

"Please," she whispers, clenching her fist around the hilt of her sword in desperation. "Please, come. Please take this child."

Eerie blue-white lights gleam through the trees. Will-o'-the-wisps? Or something else?

The princess freezes.

And sure enough, the sound of bells tinkles through the trees on the heels of the glittering lights.

Relief slams through her. *Thank all the gods.*

An enormous reindeer draws the ancient sleigh, lichen clinging to the hairs under its chin, and breath steaming from its nostrils. A hooded figure hauls on the reins until the reindeer pauses.

"Here now," the old woman calls. "What have we here?"

The princess draws back, pressing her spine against the tree so as not to be seen. Slowly, she peeps around the other side of the tree, to where a spill of moonlight falls on the altar and the child.

"Oh, look at you, my poor, poor sweet," whispers the old hag, stooping to pick it up. The baby's cries grow louder, but she tucks its wrap tightly around it and rocks it in her arms. "Now, no more of that, no more. Old Mother Hibbert is here."

The baby snuffles and whimpers. It is but days old.

And the princess's heart quivers in her chest as she watches another cradle it close, when she has known the feeling of it in her arms. *This is for the best. It has to be.*

But her yearning betrays her.

A stick cracks beneath the toe of her boot as she leans forward.

"Who's there?" Old Mother Hibbert snarls.

The princess freezes.

The old hag cradles the baby with one arm, the other falling to one of the knives sheathed at her waist. "Aye, I can hear you breathing now, you little creeping wretch. Come out and let me see you."

There's no help for it. She cannot afford to let the old crone flee in fright.

She steps around the tree, her hands held in the air.

They stare at each other, and the hag puts the baby back on the altar, her nostrils flaring as she draws a knife.

"No, don't! Please take it," the princess begs. "I know I shouldn't have stayed, but I just wanted to make sure the baby was safe."

"Is this a trap?" the hag demands, her head turning this way and that. "Come forth, you bright and shining wretches, and meet my iron. I shall cut thee and rend thee and boil thee in my cauldron."

"No! No, it's not a trap." The princess takes a step forward, then hesitates when the blade swings back her way.

"I can smell the stink of your power, girl. Why does a child with royal blood lie on this altar?"

"Because those in power will kill it if they know it survived the birth." She bites her lip. "It was never meant to be born alive. It was... a curse of fate. Please. Please take the baby. They'll kill it otherwise."

Old Mother Hibbert's nostrils flare, the tip of her knife slowly lowering. "You ask a great boon of me, Daughter of Maia. I can sense the twist of prophecy all around the child. This will only end in bloodshed and tears."

"I will come for it in twenty years," she promises. "I will bear the burden of its fate. I promise once. Twice. Thrice." The shiver of winds whisper through the woods as Blessed Maia hears her oath. "Just give the baby time to grow and prosper, far away from these lands. Just let it have a chance. I will do anything to protect it. Anything."

The hag looks down, though her brow softens as she

4

looks upon that little face. "There are Shadows on its soul. It bears the taint of the Unseelie and worse, far worse." Then she looks up. "Twenty years," she says coldly. "I will protect this child and return it to you in twenty years. And you will owe me a boon of my choice."

"I will owe you a boon," she whispers, though she knows she risks everything in promising the Unseelie creature her soul—without limits.

But some prices are worth the cost.

"Then away with you. Before you are followed or found." Old Mother Hibbert tucks the baby to her chest and turns to the sleigh.

Bright green eyes blink open as the baby stares over her shoulder, and the princess swallows. Hard.

Something flutters to the ground as Old Mother Hibbert leaps onto the sleigh and sets the baby among her furs. Grabbing the braided leather, she sneers at the princess before she slaps the reindeer's rump with the reins.

And then the hag is gone, and the baby along with her in a jingle of bells and soft sobs.

And as the princess rushes to see what Old Mother Hibbert dropped, she can't stop the tears streaming down her face.

It's a little bootie.

And she can still feel the baby's warmth as she curls the tiny knitted sock to her chest.

CHAPTER 1

Iskvien

I wake with a gasp, still reaching for the child.

The image of it vanishes like the remnants of a tattered dream, my hand closing over nothing. My heart feels like it's going to thunder through my ribs.

Sheets sigh, and then Thiago rolls toward me, sleep sloughing off him the second he catches a glimpse of my face. "What's wrong, Vi?"

I swear I can feel that knitted bootie in my hand, though I've never seen that forest before. Nor that altar. "Nothing."

"I thought we were done with secrets?" Thiago teases lightly, though there's an intensity to his eyes I can't hide from. He kneels over me, then slowly reaches down to brush my cheeks. They're wet, and we both know it, but I turn my face away.

"I'm fine. It was just a dream."

I've been having them for weeks, though they're always different.

"The baby?" he asks.

Collapsing back on the sheets, I scrape my shaking palms over my face. I can never see its face, but it always looks like him in my mind's eye. "It's probably a reminder." The words taste sour in my mouth. "Probably a gift from the Mother of Night, urging me to find the Crown of Shadows."

Darkness hoods Thiago's eyes. "That bitch is not having our child."

I'll wear the cost of the bargain I made with her, no matter what I do. Tossing the sheets aside, I drag my robe on and cross to the bathing chamber. "I know."

We've both discussed this ad nauseum in the last three months, as we recovered from my mother's attempted execution.

Thirteen years ago, I fell in love with my enemy. My mother, the Queen of Asturia, couldn't bear to see me happily in his arms, and so she struck a deal with him. To avoid war between our kingdoms, he could have me for three months and then he must return me. Each year I would spend the winter by his side, and the rest of the year at my mother's court.

If, at the end of thirteen years, I chose him forever, then Mother would be forced to relinquish all hold over me—and surrender all claim upon the disputed border lands that lie between our kingdoms.

If I chose her, then Thiago would be executed.

Thiago agreed to her demands. How could he not? He believed in my love and told me that he'd thought a little patience would be worth it in order to avoid war and still have me.

Only, when the time came for my mother to return me, she revealed a malicious little twist in the game.

She'd cursed me to forget him.

For thirteen years he's spent every winter winning my heart all over again, and I can barely remember any of it.

To save Thiago's life and break the curse my mother laid upon me, I made a bargain with one of the Old Ones who walked this world before the fae arrived. The Mother of Night fractured the curse that stole my memories, but in return, she insisted that I bring her the Crown of Shadows within the year.

If I fail, then my firstborn child will belong to her.

Unless there is no child.

It's the promise I made with Thiago. Until the Mother of Night overturns her own bargain, we can't risk making a baby together. I've been timing everything and drinking bitter nettle tea until I want to gag, and Thiago managed to locate some sheathes, but....

I can't stop seeing her smile the moment we made that deal.

They say she can only see the hearts and souls of those before her—not the future—but her smile chilled me to the bone, and I don't think I've been able to warm myself ever since.

"No child, no bargain," I say softly, looking into the mirror of the bath chambers.

Behind me, Thiago leans one broad shoulder against the doorway, his dark green eyes locked on me intently and his arms crossed over his chest. Every inch of him is carved muscle and olive skin. Tattoos darken his chest and they shift and swirl, little eyes blinking from within monstrous wolfish faces as though they're watching me. One of them trails down the hard-packed muscle of his abdomen, luring my gaze. Thiago must have stopped to haul a thin pair of loose gray trousers from the floor, because it vanishes behind the linen.

But there's evidence I'm not the only one whose gaze lingers.

He'll hold me and kiss me and chase the bad dreams away if I let him, but in this moment, it's not comfort I seek. I want action. We've been trying to trace any hint of rumor about where the Crown of Shadows was last seen, and so far we've found nothing. Three months. Three months of nothing, with only nine months until I must produce the crown.

How prophetic.

"What was it this time? A maze? A set of cliffs?"

"Old Mother Hibbert took the child," I say, turning the faucets on and splashing water over my face. The shock of it steals through the numbness. "A princess left it in the woods for her to find." I can't help giving a bitter smile. "The baby had your eyes."

Thiago stills. Every inch of him is leonine with grace, but there's a coiled violence within him. "My eyes?"

His voice warns me.

"Yes. Why?"

"Maybe it wasn't just a dream," he murmurs, stroking his hand across his knuckles. "Some fae can pick the thoughts from others. And while my wards are impenetrable, you're the one person I might lower my defenses against."

His words slowly penetrate as I turn the faucet off. "You mean, I'm picking up on your thoughts?"

"Or memories."

"You were left on an altar in the forest?"

I remember the day he told me of how Old Mother Hibbert takes all those lost and abandoned babies and raises them in Unseelie.

Thiago crosses the room toward me, wrapping his arms around me from behind. He presses a kiss to the back of my neck. "Yes."

"You wouldn't remember it." He was just a baby, and no matter how strong his magic is, there would have been nothing to hold onto.

I can't be seeing his memories.

His dark lashes obscure his eyes as I turn in his arms. "It was the first nightmare I ever had. A recurring one. One of the other children told me that my mother had cast me to the forest for the wolves to eat, and that's what I dreamed of for months. I would cry and wriggle, but I could never escape. I was too little. Helpless. And then the wolves come."

I rub his knuckles, trying to chase away the shadows in his eyes. "He sounds charming."

"We weren't all friends." His voice roughens. "Old Mother Hibbert takes all that she finds. Not all of them are babies. The older ones are the ones that struggle with it the most, because they can remember their fae parents leading them out to the forest and tethering them to the altars. I don't blame him for being angry. He made my early years miserable, but I can't even remember his name now."

The bristles that line his jaw spike roughly against my hand as I stroke his cheek. "What was it like?"

11

Thiago softens into my touch and sighs. "Hectic. Loud. Cold. Old Mother Hibbert had over a hundred of us there in her hut—"

"A single hut?"

His lips kick up wryly. "It's not the kind of hut you could imagine. The inside is bigger than the outside, and there are chambers burrowed into the walls and tunnels. It's a labyrinth, and sometimes the walls and doors changed. Sometimes rooms moved. Sometimes the hut even moved, though it did so mostly at night, and we'd only notice when we woke and found ourselves in a new part of the forest." He stares blankly into the mirror. "It was cold though. Always cold. And there was never quite enough food."

I hate that he spent his childhood this way.

"Sometimes the foraging parties wouldn't return," he admits in a lower voice. "Old Mother Hibbert would ring the bell when that happened, and we'd all have to return to our rooms and hide under our beds. She'd lock the doors and ward the hut, and we had to be silent. So silent. If we didn't make it back in time—" He exhales sharply. "There are many creatures who hunger for fae flesh in Unseelie. And children are the most vulnerable. Old Mother Hibbert tried to protect us as best she could, but over a dozen children vanished every year. It was... a nervous upbringing."

I step into his body and wrap my arms around him. Thiago stiffens, but then he slowly relaxes into the embrace, his callused hand coming up to stroke the ripple of my spine through my nightgown.

He's been there every step of the way for me.

It's only right that I return the favor.

"I wish that I could take that away for you." And maybe this is the reason I looked into his eyes that long-ago night of Lammastide and saw the other half of my soul.

We have both been lonely.

We have both been lost.

I always thought I was the broken one, but maybe he's broken too? Maybe our jagged edges can meet in the middle and somehow… fill each other up.

"Pain is what shapes you," he murmurs, cupping my face and tilting my chin up. His gaze falls to my lips. "I would never give up a single moment of suffering, a single step in my path, because it all brought me here. To you, Vi."

This prince. I don't deserve him.

But my tongue, as always, won't say what I want to say. "Even if I make deals with eldritch creatures?"

Thiago's gaze falls to my lips. "Keeps life interesting."

"Mmm." The way he's looking at me. "I feel like you're trying to make life interesting yourself…."

It's easier to steer the conversation away from those things best left avoided.

"Do tell?" His voice is like molten honey as he lowers his head. "Perhaps you would prefer to make a deal with me?"

"What kind of deal?"

"The kind where—"

A sharp rap comes at the door, breaking us apart.

Even after all these months, I still feel like someone is going to catch us together and I should feel guilty about it. But that was only the poison my mother whispered in my ear. This wicked prince was my husband and lover long before I remembered it.

And while I still can't recall the day we first met—the first time we kissed, the first time we made love—I refuse to let my mother inhibit this moment. She stole my memories from me, but she won't steal *him*.

Thiago laughs under his breath, as if my guilt flashes across my face. "Later," he promises. And then he goes to answer the door.

Because the only reason someone would knock on the bedchamber of the Prince of Evernight when they know he's with me is if something has happened.

"TELL ME." THIAGO SINKS INTO THE ENORMOUS THRONE-LIKE chair at the head of the table in his council chambers.

In this moment, he's no longer merely my husband.

He's the Prince of Evernight. The Lord of Whispers and Lies. The Master of Darkness. And the most dangerous male in the south. Clad in black leather like this, with only a hint of the darkened tattoos that ripple over his chest peeking out of the opening of his shirt, you could be forgiven for thinking of him as a mere warlord. But there's something about the firm set of his shoulders and the regal tilt of his head that makes it clear he rules every inch of this castle.

There's no sign of the dark wings that belong to his true form—he's mastered the art of shifting between his Seelie and Unseelie forms so well that even I wouldn't know they exist, if not for the fact that sometimes he'll slip into his natural form when we're in private.

And this far south of the wall, where the Seelie rule, he cannot afford to let others know he's not entirely one of them, even though my mother has long suspected.

The word "Unseelie" is a dangerous weapon this far south.

I circle the room and sink into the seat at his side as the rest of Thiago's court grimace at each other. Thalia—Thiago's cousin—had been the one at the door, and she'd hauled him away to discuss something urgent while I dressed, so I'm as much in the dark as anyone else.

Two of his finest generals, Baylor and Eris, are both dressed in leather as they scowl at the table. Thalia reclines like some lady of the manor, though her green eyes are watchful, and Finn, the last remaining member of Thiago's hand-picked court, leans back in his chair at the end of the table, tossing grapes in the air and catching them as if he doesn't have a care in the world.

One chair remains empty at the end of the table.

It's where Baylor's twin brother, Lysander, should sit—though since my sister put an arrow in him six months ago, there's been no sign of him. I'd thought him dead, though Baylor assures me that he and his brother can't *be* killed. Not with the Grimm still alive.

"Adaia's roused her border lords." This comes from Baylor, who is enormous, his shoulders straining the breadth of plate leather and tendons cording in his powerful forearms. I've seen him wield a six-foot-long broadsword when he trains with Eris, and he swings it as deftly as though it weighs five pounds.

With long blond hair, golden eyes that gleam like a wolf's, and a firm mouth that's never seen a smile, he's more than earned his title. Every single one of my mother's generals swallow a little when they know they're facing The Blackheart across the field of war. Centuries ago, he served the Grimm—one of the Old Ones who was locked away in a prison world during the last wars—and he's not entirely fae.

But he's not the most dangerous creature in the room.

No, that honor belongs to Eris, who leans back in her chair with her boots kicked up on the table and her dark brown hair braided in furrows across her scalp, to where it tumbles in a gleaming sheaf down her spine. "They're staging at Caer Luwyn."

"I thought there'd been no sign of the Asturian armies gathering?" Thiago asks sharply.

"There wasn't." Thalia reaches across the table to steal a strand of Finn's grapes. "They appeared in a cloak of mist and all of a sudden."

"Opposite Eidyn." Thoughts race in my husband's eyes.

It's a terrible place to stage for an invasion. The western marshes are just as likely to swallow half my mother's troops. And Eidyn will give us the better ground. No Asturian force has ever taken the keep.

Eris tosses her gauntlets on the scarred table. "Thalia's spies tell us there's a sea of gold and red marching north to join the first wave."

I knew it was coming—my mother promised us war, after all—but after months of inactivity, there was a little kernel of me that hoped she might have come to her senses.

A foolish desire, for I know her best, after all. But it's amazing what manner of hope you can conjure when you wish for something hard enough.

War.

It won't just be two powerful kingdoms angling at each other. This will drag the entire Seelie Alliance into ruin.

Because I chose to love an enemy prince.

"Vi?" Thiago turns to me, and I blink out of the reverie. "Yes?"

"You know your mother best. You know her forces. What do you think?"

"How many?" I ask, for the border lords—whilst fully aware of the danger they're in—are barely loyal to Adaia. Once upon a time they belonged to the Kingdom of Evernight, and then there were long years where they sought to reign over themselves, until my mother slew their leader and brought them under her umbrella.

I've visited the border keeps, and while they don't dare speak of freedom, I've heard the songs their bards play and seen the looks on their faces as they listen to "The Last Stand of Lord Balrogh."

If they could rule themselves, they would.

"Twenty thousand," Baylor tells me grimly. "They're marching under Thornwood's banners."

Twenty thousand. "That's the north and the west." But only half my mother's armies.

"Thornwood's as tough as old boots," Baylor says. "He won't be easy to break."

"That depends," Eris mutters, "on whether he's digging in and waiting for us to come to him or marching across the borders. If he comes for us, then we'll crush him against the Firenze river."

"We start staging at Eidyn," Thiago says, using a golden rod to push little brass figures across the map toward the border. "But we don't move. Let Queen Adaia make the first gambit."

I pace around the table as they argue about the best course of action.

Three months. Why the three months?

Why would she wait that long?

My mother knew there was a possibility I might have regained my memories in time and chosen Thiago at the Queensmoot three months ago.

She came prepared to slaughter us all then and there, and when the choosing didn't go her way, she murdered one of the fae queens of the Alliance and declared war on both my husband and Prince Kyrian of Stormlight.

She would have had her armies ready to march three months ago.

So why did she hesitate to send them west?

"There's something we're missing."

"Vi?" Thiago holds up his hand and the room falls silent.

I tell them my theory.

"So you think the Asturian army on our ass is merely a distraction?" Eris asks, leaning forward in her chair. "For what?"

"I don't know. It's too obvious for my mother. Adaia knows her border lords are fickle. She knows the might of Evernight's armies equals her own. She murdered the Queen of Ravenal, and with Ravenal at her heels, she can't turn her entire focus upon us."

Thalia's lashes lower. "My little birds haven't mentioned any disturbance from Ravenal."

She's not only Thiago's right hand, she's also his

spymistress, though I only learned that fact two months ago.

I consider the map again. A little circle of enemies surrounds the Kingdom of Asturia. "Ravenal to the south of her. Evernight to the north. And Stormlight holding the seas."

It's a trio of knives at her throat. My mother never does like to be backed into a corner.

"But she's not alone. And Aska is not her only ally." My gaze slides north, to the edge of the map. Thick dark trees carved of pure ebony are placed there, and several scarred castles and ruins peak from their depths. The wild lands of Unseelie hide all manner of creatures, and few among the Seelie Alliance know the true depths of the lands.

"Mother was working with Angharad." The witch-queen rules the Unseelie, and if you bring her into the equation, it changes the dynamics quite significantly.

Because now it's not a small island of two kingdoms desperately trying not to sink, but an enormous crashing wave of Unseelie poised to flood into the Alliance kingdoms.

And Evernight suddenly becomes the piece between the wolf's jaws.

My heart sinks.

"It's Angharad. It's got to be Angharad."

If Unseelie rises against us, then Evernight will be crushed.

"Surely your mother wouldn't invite Angharad to invade," Thalia says. "It's one thing to be working with her, quite another to offer her the Alliance kingdoms on a gilded platter. Once Angharad gains a single *toehold* in the south she'll never be removed."

Thiago leans over the map, making swift decisions behind those devilish eyes. "Eris. Send Gwydion to Eidyn and give him command of our border armies. Send Noaz north with several companies to guard the borders we share with Unseelie. If Angharad strikes down from Unseelie, she'll come through Mistmere. She won't be able to get through the mountains in the north of Evernight."

"*Gwydion?*" Eris demands. "And *Noaz?*"

If there's anyone who can hold Angharad at bay, it's Eris of Silvernaught.

"You're both with me," Thiago tells her coolly. "Vi and I have a rendezvous to attend."

"Where are we going?" I ask.

Thiago squeezes my shoulders, then presses a kiss to the slope of my neck. "I have news of my own. Your mother wants to meet with us. She has a gift for us."

"A gift?" My stomach drops. I know all about Mother's gifts. "No. We don't want to meet her. We don't want anything she can give us. This is a trap. She's—"

Thiago reaches out and places something metallic on the table before removing his hand.

A golden ring rattles before it slowly settles into stillness. It's thick enough to grace a man's finger, and the sigil is that of a howling wolf.

"Xander," Baylor blurts, shoving to his feet.

"Yes. We finally know where your brother is. Adaia said she's willing to talk peace. In exchange for Lysander. Vi is right. Eidyn isn't the danger. It's a distraction." Thiago slowly straightens. "You have your orders. And only today to fulfill them. We leave at dawn."

CHAPTER 2

Andraste

Sometimes I think the silence is the worst.

It's a time when you're alone with your own thoughts, your eyes blinded to the world, and nothing but the incessant *drip-drip-drip* of water in the distance offers any respite from the horrors of your memories.

Pain can be ignored. Pain is nausea twisting your stomach. Numbness flooding through your hands. Pain is an old friend, and maybe my mother thinks she can use it to break me, but she doesn't know the truth.

I'm not afraid of pain.

But silence is the whip that breaks my soul.

Silence. Loneliness.

Memory.

The look in my sister's eyes as she realized I'm the one who betrayed her is my least favorite memory, but it's the one that keeps playing in my head, over and over and over.

I try to shift on my toes, and agony flares through my shoulders like a pair of knives driven deep. The chains around my wrists remain stoic, and though I've tried, I know they're anchored to the ceiling above me and nothing I do will shift them.

I will endure.

I will not scream.

I will not beg.

It's not my first time in the oubliette. Nor will it be my last.

And somehow, that thought makes me want to laugh.

Or cry.

Because I don't know how long my mother will leave me chained here, and I don't know what condition I will be in when she finally allows me to go free.

It takes me a long time to realize I can hear footsteps.

I tilt my head in the darkness, my heart suddenly racing. I don't know how long I've been hanging here—time means nothing in the ever-present dark—but surely this is not long enough? I spent months in these chains when I fought for my sister's freedom the first time. Months that broke me.

This could only have been… maybe weeks?

Maybe it's not freedom that beckons. Maybe it's torture. Mother will never dare whip the crown heir, but there are other ways to torture a body. Or a soul. And they don't have to even leave a bruise.

I tense as keys rattle in the lock and the door squeals open. Everything sounds so fucking loud after the silence.

But then there are no further sounds, and I know that someone watches me, even if I can't see them, and maybe that's worse….

Heat flares, and I turn my eager face to it even as my abdomen tenses.

"You're a mess," Edain says coldly.

Not him. Anyone but him.

My heart's in freefall, my throat closing over as if to contain a startled gasp. But I don't dare let him see it.

I tilt my chin, trying to shift the blindfold, but all I catch a glimpse of is his boots. "My apologies, my lord." My lips feel too dry, and they mangle the words, but I continue. "I seem to have misplaced the servants."

My stepbrother stalks closer, and my cold skin yearns for the heat of his torch, even as I grind my teeth together.

"Surely you're not here to bring my meal." My stomach growls at the thought, shockingly loud. "Nor my bath."

The clink of sound tells me he's set the torch in the wall. "Your mother is still furious with you, so I would try not to be so witty when you're brought before her."

My heart skips a beat. "The Queen wants to see me?"

"Would I be down here for any other reason?"

And there it is.

I never quite know if he enjoys taunting me or if he's merely stating a fact, but Edain being Edain, I'm fairly certain he's mocking me.

I don't know what my mother was thinking when she brought him into her court.

Though I can imagine.

I was young when my mother married his father, Reynar, and barely eighteen when Reynar died in a hunting accident. They say Reynar's beauty stole my mother's tongue the first time she laid eyes upon him, and she had to have him for herself, regardless of his wife or young family.

And Reynar, perhaps wise enough to see a path to power, tempted her and wooed her for years, before he finally succumbed to her bed.

Before the sun rose, my mother vowed to marry him, and jokes still linger about the size of the prince consort's cock.

For years, Reynar was all she could see. He came from the Far Isles, and left a family behind to become her consort. I was ignored, as step-children often are—he had no use for me—but I do remember my mother constantly cajoling him to bring his son to court.

"We will show the Alliance that we are a family to be reckoned with," she had said once, when I was allowed to brush her hair. *"No more of these nasty rumors about your previous wife.... I will not suffer them to be heard."*

Reynar unleashed a dangerous smile upon her. *"Let Letithia keep the boy. It's safer for him to stay in Akiva. And I would not want to divert my attention from you. Not even for my dearest son. You are my sun. You are my heart. Let it not know another."*

Safer, always safer.

From the lies and vicious rumors that circulated about a handsome young fae male stolen from his faithful wife.

I remember the day it all changed.

There was a masked ball at court to celebrate my seventeenth birthday and a strange minstrel came calling, wearing nothing but black. He won the court with his voice, and my mother was delighted.

"Reveal yourself," she cried, *"for your beauty must echo the gloriousness of your voice and we must know it."*

I will never forget that moment—the horrible breathless feeling in my lungs as the stranger lifted his hands to slowly lower his mask. It felt like Fate trailed her frozen fingertips down my spine.

The stranger threw back his shining black hair, the mask in his hands, and every fae at court sucked in a single breath.

For the promise of his father was more than generously bestowed on the son.

"*Father,*" Edain said, a dangerously mocking smile on his face as he nodded to his adversary.

Reynar froze, a brief flash of horror flirting through his eyes as Edain turned toward Mother.

"*And my dearest stepmother,*" Edain purred, as he went to one knee and kissed her hand.

I don't know why he came to our court—whether it was to strike vengeance into his faithless father's heart, or whether it was tear them apart—but the second my mother laid eyes upon him, she could not look away.

"Andraste?" There's no sign of his sneer now. Merely something rough I can't identify.

And I'm left scrambling to remember what he asked me.

"Perhaps you're here because you enjoy seeing me in this state." I turn on my toes, and agony flares through the right arch of my foot. I've been balanced like this for far too long. "Or perhaps you're here because my mother sent you to do her bidding, like her favorite little pet. I guess we'll find out."

He laughs under his breath. "I almost missed your insults. And yes, I guess you'll find out."

Hands toy with my wrists, and the heat of his skin warms mine as he stretches up to unlock me. After so long without comfort or warmth, I can barely resist leaning into him, even though I'm fairly certain I stink, and though the servants have doused me with buckets of water every now and then, my skin feels grimy.

"Have a care, my lord. You might soil your robes. I'm still covered in blood and dirt from the Queensmoot."

He pauses, and I wonder at the hesitation, before his hands turn the key in the lock. "If you think dirt and blood concern me, then you're most mistaken."

I tense for the inevitable. My chains start loosening, feeling flooding into raw, bloodless fingers.

I'm finally allowed down from my toes, but my feet have spent too long arched into agonizing points. They're not prepared for my weight.

As my arms fall, my body collapses like dead meat, and a scream escapes me, regardless of intent.

Somehow, I don't hit the cold stone floor.

Firm arms catch me and draw me into an embrace, and I barely have the breath to protest. Everything hurts. *Everything*. My right arm is a blaze of agony, and I fear I've dislocated the shoulder.

"Easy" comes a gentle whisper.

I cling to him, quivering from shock as blood rushes back into my starving limbs. And to think that only moments ago, I was saying that pain would not break me.

"Shush." There are hands on my back, rubbing firmly enough to steal my attention away from my arms and feet.

Oh, gods…. I don't even have the strength to care if my mortal enemy is the one consoling me. No doubt I'll pay the price for this later, but right now, I don't care.

I can't feel my fingers or move my arm. I clutch at it uselessly, trying to ease the weight of it, and then Edain sets gentle fingers to the socket.

"This might hurt a little," he says. "On the count of three. One, two—"

He gives a sharp jerk, and I scream as the arm is shoved back into the socket. *Mother of mercy.* Trembles shiver through me. I think I'm going to be ill, but the last thing I want to do is vomit on his shoes.

Not in front of him.

I grind my teeth together and fight the urge, swallowing down the pain.

Pain is life. Pain is an old friend.

But it doesn't feel like a friend now. It feels like a bitter enemy stealing the strength from my veins.

"You've been here for weeks," Edain says. "So sit on your ass until you've got your feet beneath you." He slips a waterskin from around his shoulder. "And I'll pretend I didn't see your knees quiver."

He's being kind.

Edain is being kind.

Which means this is bad.

"Who are you? Because I'm fairly certain you're not my evil stepbrother." I have to work out what my mother has planned. It could be anything, it could be—

My mind shies away from that thought, because I don't dare betray myself, even in the privacy of my own head.

"I'm the male who's been forced to deal with a furious queen for the past month. What in the Underworld happened at the Queensmoot?" he growls, unscrewing the lid from the water skin.

Nothing else matters. My dry mouth salivates, and I grab at the skin.

He lets me drink, though he takes it away far too quickly.

27

"You'll make yourself ill," he murmurs.

I don't care.

I just want more water.

"In a minute," he says, and I realize he's stroking my hair back off my face. "Tell me what happened at the Queensmoot?"

So that's to be the price of his kindness.

I laugh, a dry, rasping sound. "My sister broke the curse Mother placed on her. She remembered her husband at the last second and then unleashed some kind of magic upon Mother. They drove us back."

"I'm not talking about your sister." His gentle touch is on my face again, though his eyes are as hard as ice. "Why were you sentenced to the oubliette?"

I bow my head.

"Please. Please! If there's any part of you that ever loved me, please stop this."

It doesn't matter how many times I close my eyes, I see Vi begging me for help. "Because I dared ask for mercy. It was killing Vi. I couldn't—"

You don't admit your weaknesses to an enemy.

I shut my mouth.

Curse it. He's caught me at a bad moment.

"Mother blames me for what happened," I say instead and lift my head to meet his gaze.

His lashes shield his merciless blue eyes. "She does, though she won't speak of it. I wondered why she held you accountable."

"How angry is she?" There's no more strength left in me. I lean my head back against his thigh.

He laughs under his breath. "Angry enough to burn the fucking castle to the ground. I think you need to forget about your sister, Princess, and concentrate on keeping your own head. One daughter's betrayal is enough. Two might tip her over the edge."

"I thought you'd enjoy that. You'd be the one to reap the rewards. Perhaps she might even name you heir."

He freezes, and his eyes are glacial as he looks at me. "You know nothing of what I wish for, but let me assure you—your mother would have my head if I even thought to place myself on a throne."

"You're ambitious. I know that. Perhaps she'll give you a duchy. She'll need a strong vassal without me at her side."

"It sometimes amazes me that you've spent the past seventeen years living with me, and yet, you truly understand so little of me."

I do?

My eyes narrow.

"I'll save you the breath." Slipping my arm beneath his shoulder, he helps me to my feet. "Time to stand, Andraste. You've had your moment of respite, and now you need to show the court some of that *fuck you* attitude I always see in your eyes."

"I'm being summoned before the court?"

Not like this.

Not with my hair tangled and blood still staining my clothes. I can't reveal an inch of weakness.

"You're being summoned before the court," he says grimly. "Your mother has need of you."

"Why?"

Edain heads for the door, leaving me wobbling behind him like a newborn foal. "Because we're going to war, Andraste. Let us hope your sense of mercy has died a swift

29

death in the oubliette. Because the enemy we face is your sister and her husband, and your mother has a trap planned."

"*Trap?*"

There's only one thing Mother can mean by that.

I have to stop her.

But do I dare?

I force myself to take a step toward the door, and I don't fall flat on my face, which is an improvement.

"Yes." Edain's eyes glitter as he holds the door open for me. "And apparently you're going to be the one to spring it."

CHAPTER 3

Iskvien

Word comes the following morning.

The meeting will take place at Ruthvien.

"Why Ruthvien?" I ask, as I follow Thiago toward the Hallow in Ceres. The portal is housed in the second-tallest tower of the castle, and of course we have to climb four thousand stairs to get there. Give or take.

Mother could have chosen a thousand places to hold this meeting.

All of them suspect.

But Ruthvien is the heart of the ancient ruined Kingdom of Taranis. A thousand years ago it was a prosperous kingdom blessed with forests and pastureland. Now, the soil lies dry and cracked with a thousand runnels as if even the land itself thirsts.

One of Taranis's northern Hallows was obliterated during the Unseelie wars five hundred years ago, and the blast of energy wiped out half the kingdom and some of neighboring Somnus. Year by year the blight creeps wider, until both kingdoms now lie fallow.

Nobody lives there. The Alliance of Light simply pretends both kingdoms no longer exist.

"Because I wouldn't agree to any Hallow within Asturia and she wouldn't venture into Evernight. She preferred Mistmere, but I refuse to play Adaia's game. Ruthvien was my best alternative."

"Somewhere nice and isolated," Finn mutters under his breath as he falls in behind me. Thiago's tasked the lean warrior with my protection, while Eris looks ready to spill blood as she falls in behind Thiago. "Nobody will find our bodies."

Baylor rests a hand on the hilt of his sword, towering over all of us as he scowls. "Adaia hasn't had time to muster an ambush. Thiago only sent through the location of the meeting two hours ago."

"You underestimate my mother." I can't stop myself from tapping nervous fingers against my thigh. "She only needs a minute's notice for murder."

"You're not helping, Princess," Finn mutters.

"Why are you so on edge?" He's been dueling with me every day in the yard for the past three months. I've never seen him slip the casual mantle he wears. Finn always pretends he'd laugh in the face of a screaming horde.

"Oh, I don't know," he mutters. "One murderous queen who can't be trusted. A peace offering who just happens to be the one person we desperately want back. Did I mention your mother? And peace? Those two concepts together just scream 'trap.'"

"Yes, but I thought you had balls of solid steel."

"He's always like this," Eris snorts. "The second steel is

bared he'll be so cool he'll make a glacier look like it's sweating, but until then…."

"I just hate surprises," Finn grumbles.

I steal a glance at Baylor. Lysander's his twin brother. I've only ever met Lysander…. *Curse it.* I can only *remember* meeting him in bane form, but I saw the flare of desperation in Baylor's eyes when Thiago said that my mother was offering Lysander back as a peace offering.

And I have to say it. "I agree with Finn. This is going to end badly. Why would my mother propose a peace offering? She wants our heads. She *wants* war."

"She's stalling," Thiago murmurs. "This is merely a distraction. I also suspect she'll present Lysander to us, and then have a guard drive a sword through his heart."

Lysander and Baylor can die, but as long as the Grimm is still alive—even if he's trapped in his prison world—the second the moon rises they'll be resurrected.

"He'll rise."

"Still hurts like a bitch. And with every death…." Baylor's face turns to stone. "With every death, it becomes a little more difficult to remember who you are."

"As long as we're near the Hallow we're safe," I mutter, as we enter the Hallow's chamber.

The enormous chamber is round, and thirteen huge standing stones mark the edges of the Hallow. They were built to contain the energy that will rise when we activate the runes carved into their enormous columns.

Everyone takes their place inside the circle, a squad of a dozen guards falling in beside us, and nervousness runs through me.

The ley line calls to me, a soft whisper that stirs over

my skin. I've always felt it, but it wasn't until three months ago that I realized no one else can.

Thiago shoots me a grim look, slicing his finger and pressing it to the rune that marks Ruthvien. A discordant buzzing shivers over my skin as the Hallow begins to draw power from far beneath the surface. "I'm not afraid of your mother. If she has an ambush planned, then we will destroy it."

I wasn't talking about fleeing.

He thinks I used my fae magic to overthrow my mother at the Queensmoot, and I haven't dared tell him the truth.

The Old Ones who ruled Arcaedia before the fae arrived are the ones who consecrated the Hallows and bound the power of the ley lines to the stone henges that litter the countryside. The fae might be able to use them as portals, but the Old Ones could access the power and wield it like a whip.

Until the Seelie locked them away in prison worlds that are tied to the Hallows.

Somehow, I accessed that power.

And when I made a deal with the Mother of Night, she told me I was the *leanabh an dàn*—the child of destiny that is bound to release her and the other Old Ones from their prison world.

Thiago said we couldn't allow the *leanabh an dàn* to live, in case they fall into the wrong hands.

He loves me. I know he loves me.

But at what point do I become too much of a burden? Between my mother and her war, my bargain with the Mother of Night, and now this, how far will he go before he starts to regret marrying me?

"Vi?"

I realize he's holding out a hand toward me as the Hallow starts vibrating.

I reach for him, curling my fingers through his. Thiago's my anchor in any storm. I spent my entire life wishing someone would love me, and even now there's a part of me that thinks he's too good to be true.

"We'll be all right," he murmurs, giving it a squeeze. "We're ready for anything your mother has planned."

I'll tell him the truth one day. I swear I will.

But right now, I force a smile and rest my other hand on the hilt of my sword, prepared for anything.

The Hallow ignites, plunging us into darkness.

Every part of me feels stretched thin. Whirling. Set adrift.

And then we land with a shudder in Ruthvien.

"No ambush," Finn mutters as we spread out from the Hallow.

"Find them," Thiago commands, and the handsome hunter vanishes into the trees that loom around us.

"It won't happen here. My mother likes suspense. She'll want to see your face as her trap encloses us." Even so, my heart races as we scour the ruins of Ruthvien, searching for a hint of danger.

Nothing.

Just a broken city, snarled over with brambles. The forest is slowly reclaiming it, but I catch a glimpse of polished white marble. Ruthvien used to be the Pearl of the West once.

Waves crash against a distant shore. And the jagged remains of a castle perch atop a hill, reaching desperately for the sky as if to escape the forest's clutches. This is no new forest. There's a malevolent feeling to the trees, and little blinking eyes watch us from the shadows. I'm used to demi-fey fluttering through every inch of Ceres with callous disregard for the fae that tramp through their city, but these demi-fey lurk.

And I swear the trees shift, as if to keep us within their field of awareness.

It stands to reason. When the Hallow in the north imploded, the energy transformed everything around it. They say there are packs of deer with sharp teeth that hunt the plains of Taranis, and birds that breathe fire. The fae didn't survive—something about their magic is incompatible with the Hallow magic—but the creatures did.

"Found them," Finn murmurs, appearing out of nowhere. "The Asturian embassy have set up on a grassy knoll overlooking the sea. Three tents. Only twenty guards, from what I could see, which means she obeyed the set terms. The area around them is clear for fifty feet." He nods to me. "Your mother's banners are there. And I caught a glimpse of her within the main tent."

"Then let's do this," Thiago says grimly. He turns to Baylor. "Ready?"

Baylor stares toward the tents with a hard glare. "Ready."

"Keep it reined in until I give the signal."

Baylor turns wolfish eyes on him, filled with blood and vengeance. But he nods.

∽

THE TENTS ARE RED AND GOLD.

Horses shift and whicker at their moorings, and guards stand to attention beside them, gleaming as brightly as the gemstones that linger in my mother's vaults. She's always insisted her personal guard wear armor coated with thin gold scales for appearances sake, though a single blow will leave a dent that requires days of buffing.

My mother's banners snap in the wind, and I catch a glimpse of a golden throne hidden within the main tent, though there's no sign of her.

Every inch of it is planned.

It says: Did you think you had won at the Queensmoot? I let you live, and now I will crush you, as was my intention all along.

"Subtle, Mother."

The silk parts as Thiago strides toward it, and he ducks within, leaving me to suck in one last fortifying breath before I face her. This is no time for nerves, but I can't quite extinguish the breathless feeling inside me. Nor can I fight the urge to rest my hand on the hilt of my sword. I'm dressed for war in a brown leather corset that's hard enough to turn away a glancing blow, and a mulberry-colored cloak over my shoulders, but the skin between my shoulder blades tickles.

The last time we met, I drove her back with the power of the Hallow.

My mother doesn't forget such insults.

And the Ruthvien Hallow is far enough away that I can barely feel the quiver of it. With our recent arrival, it won't be ready to use again until another hour has passed, at least.

"Excellent," I mutter under my breath. I'm practically defenseless, except for the sword.

"Princess?" Finn murmurs.

"Nothing. Just enjoying my last moment of non-judgmental air."

"Relish it. I'm sure she'll manage to suck the wind out of our sails somehow."

Then I'm inside, the lack of light abruptly plunging me into a moment of disorientation. A lantern gleams within the tent, platters of sweetmeats and figs spread across a black and white lacquered table. The scent reminds me of summer days and fields of golden grain whispering in the wind.

Not the musky perfume of a well-lit brazier that my mother prefers.

Curse it. I knew this was a fucking trap.

"Your Highness," Thiago says, recovering from the surprise well. "You appear to have shrunk."

A tall, straight-backed figure reclines before us, her long, lean legs laced over each other and both hands resting negligently on the arms of the throne. Every inch of her is poise, from the braided coronet of hair that settles like a crown on her head, to the slick golden silk of her cloak, pinned at one shoulder with a ruby as big as my palm.

"Hello, Sister," says Andraste, meeting my eyes.

"Andraste." The word trips over my tongue.

The last time I faced my sister, I'd felt alone. The revelation of the truth—that I was Thiago's wife with my memories stolen away from me—had been a recent blow, and I'd been trying to find my feet in this new world.

I'm no longer alone.

A hand comes to rest on my shoulder, Thiago's thumb stroking there with gentle reassurance.

I stare into her face, and I see a little girl lying in the grass of the meadows with me as we slice our palms and press them together.

"I will always protect you," Andraste had whispered. *"You're my little sister. We will always watch each other's backs."*

I don't know where that girl vanished to, or even why.

My stepbrother, Edain, reclines at her feet in silken robes the color of a night sky, that reveal a healthy expanse of his chest. Rings glitter on his fingers and his cheekbones are sharp enough to cut as he reaches for a grape. It's rather like having a leopard at her feet. Edain might be mother's little trinket, but I'm one of the few who knows the truth of what else he is.

My mother's knife.

A blade she wields from the shadows.

In public he's the queen's pet, but they say that if you meet him in the dark of night, then he's the last thing you'll ever see.

"Dearest stepsister," he purrs, "it's lovely to see you again. Married life must be agreeing with you."

"It's all that fresh air," I bite back, "and freedom. You should try it."

Bottling my rage, I turn to Andraste. She's no longer my sister. She made her choice. "Your Highness. The Queen of Asturia's message claimed you had a gift for us."

She waves magnanimously at the laden table before her. "Should we not take repast and discuss—"

"We're not here for your fucking figs and cheese." I smile. "And who knows what drug the wine is laced with. You always were good at providing such sweet poison."

A flash of guilt dances fleetingly through her eyes—so fleetingly it might even be imagined. "Our countries are at war, but that doesn't mean that our negotiations—"

I step toward her. "These are not negotiations. You have something of ours and you will give him back."

"Or?" Edain stretches with a yawn.

Even I feel the coldness in my smile. "Or I will show you what drove my mother back at the Queensmoot."

Thiago remains conspicuously quiet at my side, letting me lead, though his hand comes to rest on the small of my back. A warning. They've got me off-balance, which was precisely what they wanted.

But Edain's no longer entirely at ease either. He wasn't there when I drove my mother back, but no doubt he's aware of it.

"You've grown bolder, dearest stepsister," Edain says, pushing to his knees. "I always wondered how you would flourish once your mother stopped turning your brain to mush every spring."

"Remarkably well, now that those I trusted aren't stealing a year of life from me."

"Don't blame me," he says. "I was merely a spectator."

"Oh, did you think I included you on the list of people I trusted?"

"Edain," Andraste warns.

"What?" He spreads his hands with a boyish smile.

"We're just having fun. Vi and I always were like oil and water."

I ignore him and focus on her. "Well? Why bother with this affair if all we're going to do is insult each other?"

"First strike," she whispers.

What?

Our eyes meet as memory assaults me. My mother sitting across a *fari* board from me as she moves her last piece into place.

"First strike," Mother murmurs with a smile as her knight decapitates my king. Three of her little metallic warriors abruptly turn on my general. "Second strike."

And the third.

The third will always come.

My prince abruptly steps behind my gold queen and drives a knife through her back.

"Third strike," Mother says, satisfaction gleaming in her eyes as she sits back in her chair with her hands folded neatly in her lap. "You failed to see the plays, Daughter. You have lost."

And the *fari* board devolves into a melee as her pieces cut mine down to the last man, until only my little golden prince remains, bowing at the feet of her Red Queen.

Lysander is the first strike.

Andraste's *warning* me.

Thiago slowly removes his gloves as he stalks forward. "You brought us here for a reason. Let us hear it."

"It's easy," Andraste replies with a small shrug. "There doesn't have to be war between our kingdoms."

"I think it's far too late for that, Princess. Your mother murdered a queen and tried to have me executed. She attacked a sacrosanct meeting—"

"And she is prepared to make amends."

"I don't see her here," he snarls, "on her knees, begging for mercy. Or is that why she sent you? Did she think I might be somewhat more lenient if my wife's sister pleaded her cause?"

My eyes narrow. "It's more that Andraste is meant to be the distraction while Mother slips around behind our backs."

"So trusting, little sister." Edain laughs. "We are here because your Mother doesn't trust *him* to contain his daemons if he saw her."

"Of the two of them, Thiago's shown remarkable restraint," I grind out.

"Has he?" Edain offers Thiago a little smile that seems to suggest otherwise. "Indeed, he does seem to have himself well in hand. Far more so than I was warned to expect."

What does that mean?

"Oh." Edain feigns surprise. "He hasn't told you...."

"There's nothing to tell," Thiago replies.

"Mmm." Edain sips his wine with nonchalant grace. "We shall see."

I don't look at my husband.

I can't.

Because I won't give Edain the satisfaction of knowing his arrow hit its target.

Instead, I rest a hand on Thiago's sleeve. "You always did like to hear the sound of your own voice, Edain. Even though your conversational skills are terribly boring."

"We'll see. A gift from our queen," Edain whispers, holding his fist up to his face. He opens it and blows the black dust held there directly toward us.

Within a second we're enveloped in a cloud of shadows. I cough as it hits my lungs, fist clenching around the sword as I shove free of the dust. The bitter taste of it sinks into my tongue, but I breathe a sigh of relief as I realize what it is.

"It's harmless," I say, waving a hand in the air in front of me. "It's merely a binding agent intended to lock a curse to its target."

Too bad mine was broken completely. There's nothing there for it to grab.

Eris locks eyes with Edain as she waves the black cloud from her head. "Permission to kill him?"

Edain merely smiles as his knife slips from his sleeve into his hand. "I would love to dance, sweet Eris. I've heard so much about you."

I grab her arm. "Not now."

Second strike.

There has to be a second strike.

"Nothing to say, Your Highness?" Edain prowls toward Thiago.

And I realize the arm beneath my hand has tensed.

Eris detects danger.

"Only that if you continue coming toward me with a knife in hand, I'll consider our negotiations over." There's a cold, emotionless edge to my husband's voice, but I can sense him trembling with the urge to step forward and repay Edain for his "gift".

Edain pauses, but not with fear, I think. He cocks his head. "I don't think I need the knife. I think the damage is already done. You contain it well, but it's eating away at you, isn't it?"

And then he laughs.

Andraste stares at Edain as if he's suddenly turned into a snake. If this was meant to be mother's strike, then she knew nothing about it.

"State your terms," Thiago says coldly. "Then let us be done with this mockery."

"A gift," Andraste replies, visibly gathering herself, "to beg forgiveness and open negotiations toward peace."

Baylor holds his breath.

"Bring the beast," my sister says, a tiny gesture slicing toward one of her attendants.

A commotion echoes outside. Some kind of snarling, along with the dangerous scrabble of claws in the dirt. Men shout. Steel rings as a sword clears its sheath and then the tent flaps part, and an enormous beast is dragged inside the tent by four fae warriors.

Its arms are bound behind it and gold winks around its throat. The collar is as thick as my forearm, but even with the chains, it looks like it will barely hold the creature.

A bane.

Standing well over seven feet tall, he's a monster of sinew and fur. Half-wolf. Half-lion. All rage and fury. Curse-twisted into a half-animal, half-human shape, he growls as he sees us.

Few have the power to create them, and breaking the curse is near-impossible. Sometimes it requires catching a cockerel's first cry in a bottle, and then drinking it down. Or hunting a phoenix and swallowing its flame. There's an old story that tells of a witch who managed to use her love and magic to keep her bane lover in fae form during the day, though her spell broke the second the moon rose and he would be a beast until the sun cleared the horizon.

Lysander.

"Xander!" Baylor surges toward him and Thiago hauls him to halt. A murderous flash of fury darkens Baylor's face, but the second their gazes meet he visibly restrains himself.

There's no acknowledgement in the creature's eyes.

It merely huffs and snarls as each warrior fans out, hauling on the chains so that it can barely move.

"Asturia keeps its promise," Andraste says, her shoulders suspiciously straight.

She clearly doesn't like having the bane within the tent.

I can't say I blame her.

"Asturia is renowned for keeping its promises," Thiago says, his fist clenching around his gloves. "To the very letter of the law."

His smile could ice over an entire kingdom.

Andraste tenses as if she suddenly senses the predator in the room.

She's always been smart enough to gauge a room with a single glance, and right now, my husband looks like murder dressed in black leather. He knows he unsettles people so he usually reins his powers in hard. He moves slowly. He reclines. He watches but doesn't loom. But right now, the leash is off.

Right now, he's a wolf prowling into enemy territory and though his illusions shield his wings, there's a menacing shadow trailing behind him as if to suggest pure Darkness looms over his shoulder.

"But there's always a twist," Thiago continues. "What does your mother want in return for Lysander?"

"Eidyn and its surrounding lands." Andraste eases into familiar territory. Bartering is second nature to her. "Forswear them now and forever, and she'll allow you to keep the bane."

The border lands have been in dispute for nearly a century. Mother claimed Thornwood and its surrounds, but Eidyn—though it once belonged to Mother—has since stood mockingly out of reach.

Thiago sinks into the chair that is placed opposite my sister. "It's a tempting proposition. It's even believable. Your mother wants Eidyn desperately. She even bartered her daughter away to me for the chance to claim it. And now she's lost both." He unleashes a smile upon her—the deadly kind. "Unfortunately, I don't believe either of you. Adaia thinks herself invulnerable. She has an army poised at my doorstep and Eidyn is within her reach. If she truly wanted it so badly, she would have sent her armies marching across our borders."

"Maybe Mother desires peace." Andraste leans forward. "What happened at the Queensmoot was unsettling for all of us—"

"She murdered a queen," Thiago replies. "The only thing that unsettled her was that Prince Kyrian and I got away before she could slit our throats too."

Andraste continues as if he didn't speak. "And now the Alliance stands in disarray. We must stand strong against the unseelie threat from the north."

"Again, a striking argument. Again, a lie. There is evidence your mother has been in contact with Angharad, and has used the unseelie for her own purposes."

They stare at each other.

Thiago leans forward, resting his forearm along his thigh. Edain doesn't quite shift, but he's no longer at ease.

Every inch of him tenses, and a dark flame flares to life in his blue eyes.

My breath catches.

"Perhaps *I* will make a counter-offer," Thiago purrs. "I will give your mother Eidyn…."

What?

"In exchange for?" Andraste asks boldly.

"Clydain. And everything within it."

Clydain? My gaze snaps toward him. Clydain's an old rotting border keep with a broken waterwheel. Half the lower garrison is flooded. Nobody lives there anymore. The place is supposed to be haunted, and frankly, it holds no strategic value.

But he may as well have thrown a serpent directly into my sister's lap.

"It's a rotting old keep in the far north of Asturia," she says. "And it borders Mistmere. It's miles from your kingdom."

"True," Thiago replies. "But then, I'm not interested in the keep."

And everything within it, he'd said.

My mind races. This has something to do with Lysander. He'd said the reason Lysander was sent to the northern forests of Asturia was to hunt for a weapon my mother was rumored to be keeping.

"Clydain and the surrounding forest is haunted, Your Highness." Andraste loads her voice with scorn. "You may forgive me if *I* think this a trick, for Eidyn is a treasure trove, and Clydain is… a moth-eaten old cloak."

When on the back foot, attack….

"Unless, of course, you want to gain a foothold in Mistmere," she suggests.

47

"It's my final offer," Thiago tells her. "Tell your mother I will trade Eidyn for Clydain and everything currently within it as of this moment. And I will take her gift back home with me, provided there are no further tricks."

"No tricks," Andraste murmurs. "Mother says if you can tame him, then he is yours."

I don't trust this.

They're too polite. And Andraste keeps staring at me.

"If you can tame him."

It has to be that.

Mother thinks Lysander is uncontrollable. It's a gift with a bite, for if we can't control him then…. What? Thiago won't kill him—he can't be killed—and Thiago doesn't turn his back on his loyal subjects.

Baylor pauses an inch from his brother. There's no anguish upon his face, but I feel it within him. "Xander."

He reaches out and touches the beast. Lysander towers above him, thick matted fur clinging to his body.

"How did you recapture him?" I ask.

Andraste tears her gaze from Lysander. "I thought he was dead. The last I saw him he was buried in the woods near Briar Keep, until rumors came of a beast stalking the northern forests—"

"Andraste." Edain places a hand over hers.

Clydain. Lysander was going back to Clydain.

Even broken and curse-twisted, he was trying to fulfill his final quest.

"Xander." Baylor takes another step, his palm soothing his brother's fur.

He's not looking at him.

No, he's looking at me.

The humanity in the beast's eyes vanishes as amber

48

fury rolls across them. A quiver starts in its shoulders. "Prinshess," it whispers, and its hackles rise.

"Get these fucking chains off him," Baylor demands.

Edain tenses. "I wouldn't do that if I were you."

"The problem, whore," Baylor says, as he tears one of the chains from his brother's throat. "Is that you think he will fight us. This is my brother. And he is loyal to Evernight."

"Vi," Andraste warns with a little shake of her head.

Baylor smiles for the first time I think I've ever seen. And his hand grips another chain. "Don't worry, Princess. His teeth aren't that sharp. If you have treated him well, then you have nothing to worry about should we unleash him."

Another chain breaks.

Andraste's gaze flickers to me.

And then I realize her finger is tracing a pattern on the arm of her chair, over and over again. A symbol of a language the pair of us created when we were seven, so we could speak without any of Mother's court chastising us.

I haven't seen that symbol in many years, so it takes a second to realize what she's—

"*Run*," it says.

Grabbing a fistful of his brother's hair, Baylor turns the bane's face toward his, completely unafraid. "Hear the whisper through the trees," he breathes, as his hand curls around the last remaining chain. "Feel the moonlight on your skin. Listen to the thump of her heart." Both of their golden eyes turn to lock upon Andraste. "You can almost taste it, can't you?"

"I don't think we should break his chains," I whisper,

taking a step back as muscles bunch within the beast's form.

"Don't worry about your sister," Baylor assures me with a nasty smile. "It's not as though my brother will hold a grudge. It's not as though she tried to kill him."

And the chain snaps.

But it's not Andraste the beast lunges for.

It's me.

CHAPTER 4

"Traitor!" The bane snarls as it smashes Baylor off his feet.

Thiago is slightly quicker to react, his hand dropping to his sword, but I see a second of conflict on his face—*what is he doing?*—before Lysander crashes into him.

"Vi!" Thiago yells, staggering backward.

Run.

I take Andraste's advice.

Shoving past her guards, I slash a hole in the back of the tent with the knife I carry up my sleeve and then glance behind me.

Lysander swipes at one of her guards, his claws raking off scaled armor. He sees me again and bellows with rage, before her guards go flying.

"*Vi!*"

I dart into the morning light as another enraged snarl echoes behind me. Cloth tears and fae yell as the tent abruptly begins to collapse. Lysander tears his way straight through the silk.

Curse it.

There's nowhere to go except into the forest.

The dark, creepy forest that has eaten its way through the Ruthvien ruins.

Tough decision. Bane behind me. Unknown danger ahead. And no time to think my way through this mess.

"Vi?" It's a whisper in my head, a tickling against my skin as I sprint toward the trees.

"Thiago?"

"Let me in."

I open myself to him and there he is, burning like a supernova in the back of my mind. It's rare that the fae allow others to meld with them mind-to-mind, because it leaves you open and vulnerable, but I know he'd never hurt me.

That doesn't mean we've connected like this on more than a superficial layer.

He won't let me all the way inside, and I've got my own secrets to hide.

Though I can guess at what's he's shielding me from.

Something dangerous lingers beneath the subconscious layers of his mind. Something that looks at me hungrily, trailing dark psychic fingers across my mind as if it wants to devour me. It's an odd sensation. Yearning. Need. Desire. But a threat lurks there too.

The Darkness within him.

I'm panting so fiercely I barely have time to snatch more than a glimpse at it.

"Vi?" He snares my attention, forcing it back on him. *"Head into the forest."*

"Are you trying to get me killed?"

"I'm conjuring an illusion of you. If you can lose him, then I can make it look like you're running into the forest depths."

I chance a glance over my shoulder. *"Losing him might be a problem."*

There's no chance I can outrun Lysander. He's built for speed, slaver dripping from his jaws as he focuses on my heels.

"Use your magic."

Magic. Right.

We've been working on my levels of control ever since the Queensmoot, but I don't like my chance of summoning anything complex. *"Fire it is, then."*

"Don't burn the forest down."

Even from this distance I can sense the wryness of the thought.

"Jester," I mutter out loud.

Fire's my natural gift from my mother's bloodline. Asturians are heat and summer and roaring wildfires that engulf enormous forests.

I lash out behind me with a controlled whip of flame, ignoring the howl of surprised pain. Lysander will heal. I won't if he gets his claws into me.

A branch hangs low. Two strides and I'm up in it, hauling my body behind me.

Teeth clash at my boots, almost catching my heel.

Close. Too close. *"Anytime you want to work your illusions!"*

"Climb higher."

Darkness punches into being, drowning us both in shadow like a squid squirting ink into the water around it. Lysander roars and the branch beneath me shakes as he swipes at it.

Biting down on a squeal I crawl along the branch. The writhing mess of shadow covers the forest floor, but I can just see.

"*Stay still and quiet,*" Thiago orders.

I become one with the forest. One breath eased in and out like I'm balancing a plate on my head. Two.

Something loud crashes through the undergrowth. Lysander stills and then he launches after it, leaving a wake of trembling bushes.

I didn't know he could do that—craft illusions with enough weight to them to disturb the world around them. "*Thank you.*"

Demi-fey hiss at me as I climb higher, unnaturally bold for such small creatures.

"*Stay there. I've sent Baylor and Finn after you.*"

"*What are you doing?*"

There's a silent pause. "*Nothing.*"

"*Thiago.*"

"*Can you see them? Finn will take you back to the Hallow. Baylor's going after his brother.*"

"*No. I want answers.*"

"*Vi—*"

"*Andraste warned me to run. She knows what they did to him. And she knew he was going to attack me.*"

"*Good luck getting answers out of her,*" he growls. "*She's refusing to say a word to me.*"

I freeze, gripping the tree branch as Baylor crashes through the forest below me. "*Just what are you doing right now?*"

A whirl of disorientation and then I'm looking out through his eyes and down into my sister's stubborn face, one hand curled around her throat and the other pressing the tip of a knife to her carotid.

"*Negotiating*," he says.

THE TENT IS A WRITHE OF MAYHEM WHEN WE RETURN.

I sent Baylor after Lysander, and found a pair of Evernight guards awaiting me at the edge of the forest with Finn.

And while Finn wanted to obey Thiago's orders, I told him he could either carry me kicking and screaming toward the Hallow, or he could accompany me back to the tent.

Andraste's voice rings out. "Get your hands off me—"

"Relax, Princess," replies my husband. "None of us *wants* to put their hands on you. Tell me what I want to know and I'll set you free. Or better yet, why don't we ask the pet? He seems to know more about what your mother intends than you do."

Edain laughs. "The queen intends to wait you out. You can't last too much longer, can you? It's already itching through you—"

I try to pause, to listen, but it's too late.

Thiago looks up and sees me standing there in the entrance to the tent. He shoots Finn a murderous look.

Finn holds his hands in the air. "This wasn't my idea."

"No, it was mine," I growl. "What is going on? What is Mother waiting for?"

Edain stands at bay behind the tip of a drawn sword. Eris must have caught him by surprise, because there's no sign of his knife. "Secrets, Princess. All these delicious secrets. There you stand with all your sanctimonious pride, taunting me with freedom, and yet your husband hasn't told you the truth. How much freedom do you truly have, Princess?"

Thiago straightens, lowering the blade from Andraste's throat. "Vi—"

"Did you think the cursebinder was meant for you, Iskvien?" Edain pushes the tip of Eris's sword away from his throat.

The link between us is still there. *What is he talking about?*"

"We'll discuss it later."

"Really? Because it sounds as though you didn't intend to discuss it at all."

Thiago's lips press thinly together. *"He's trying to drive a wedge between us."*

A howl suddenly echoes in the distance.

Curse it. We have larger problems.

"Later," I promise him, and then break the connection. "Let him go," I tell Eris, as I focus on Edain. "I spent thirteen years being betrayed by my own family. If you think I trust you more than I trust my husband, then it's a good thing you're pretty, because you clearly lack intelligence." I rub my temples. "And speaking of lack of intelligence, this was a brilliant plan. We're all stuck here in the ruins with a rabid bane on the loose."

Edain sinks onto the throne, relaxing back in it. "As long as I can run faster than you can, I don't see the problem."

"What did you do to Lysander?"

"I think it's more a question of what did *you* do to him?" Edain replies.

What does *that* mean?

"That's enough," Andraste tells him, wiping the blood from her neck and sidling away from Thiago.

The tent flaps burst open and suddenly everyone has a sword in their hand again. One of our guards points a crossbow at Andraste, and an Asturian guard returns the gesture, only he's not certain whether to focus on Thiago or me.

Just what we need. Nervous guards on both sides with half-cocked weapons.

Baylor stares breathlessly at us, the breeze blowing his pale hair over his shoulders. "I lost him. He was circling back to the tents. He's got your scent, Vi, and he's coming for you."

"Why the obsession with *me*?"

"Ask your sister." Thiago shoots her a hard stare.

"Maybe he's not the only Evernight who lost his head over Vi's smile."

That does it. Three strides and I've got her within arm's reach.

"What did you do to him?" I demand, both fists knotting in her dress.

"He's been in the oubliette," she replies, grabbing my wrists. "You've been taunting him for weeks."

Me.

Or a spell-twisted version of me.

Mother could do it. She has enough of my things, and though I was always careful to burn the hair that collected in my brush or the nails I clipped from my fingers, who knows what she took while I was drugged and unconscious?

It wasn't enough to steal my fucking memories, now

Mother's trying to steal *everything* away from me.

"I think it was more than taunting," Thiago says.

Andraste sighs, the fight leaving her. "Mother had him killed. Every day. And when he would rise, Vi would be standing over him, taunting him with her treachery. Telling him she's been mother's tool since the start, planting the seeds of ruin within your court. And then she would kill him again."

With every death, he'll lose a little part of himself.

But the things he'll hold onto…. His protectiveness. His loyalty. His base nature will tell him to protect my husband at all costs, even as he loses the scraps of himself that remember me.

The sheer cruelty of it is stunning.

Guards scream outside. Lysander won't stop until he finds me, and I know what that means. We either have to kill or contain him, and in this state, containment might be difficult.

"How do we set a trap for him?" I direct the question at Eris and Baylor.

Baylor glances around. "If I can get the chains on him—"

"We need bait." Eris doesn't shy away from my gaze as she says it.

"No," Thiago says coldly. "We're not using her as bait."

"It doesn't have to be me. Can you make me look like her?" I ask, pointing my finger at Andraste. *Think beyond your protective masculine instincts.* "And make her smell like me?"

"Vi!" Andraste stiffens.

"You chose to bind yourself to an evil, self-serving bitch. It's not my problem if her plots bite you on the ass."

I return my attention to Thiago. "It will be the scent that gives us away."

He slowly nods. "I can do it. Maybe."

Resistance comes from an unexpected quarter. Edain grabs me from behind, hauling me against his chest and putting his knife to my throat. "Twitch a single finger, little princeling, and I'll cut her throat."

Ice slithers down my spine. I don't dare breathe. The knife is sharp enough.

A preternatural stillness leeches through Thiago, and his eyes go flat and dark. Dangerous. "I don't have to twitch a finger."

Silence.

Nobody moves.

Outside, an enraged bellow splits the air.

"You're revealing your hand, Edain," I whisper. "What's Mother going to think?"

"Be quiet," he snaps.

"You've been so terribly protective," I taunt. "Mother will know. She'll find out, one way or the other, and then what do you think she'll do?"

Tension slides through him. "I swear I used to like you better when you were memory-wiped."

It all happens in an instant.

Lysander bursts into the tent, throwing a guard into Eris. She staggers back, thrusting him out of the way, but it's too late. Claws lash out, and she has to dive aside or lose half her face.

"Stay still, Vi," Thiago commands.

A warm wave envelops me, sliding over my skin from my head to my toes. An intimate little tingle that leaves me breathless.

"What the—?" Andraste gasps and looks down at herself as her hair darkens and tumbles around her shoulders in a messy tangle, smooth leather encasing her shoulders and chest, and then sweeping down over her legs. Her rings vanish. Her skin darkens. And then I'm staring at myself.

Do I really look like such a mess? Today has not been kind.

Lysander skids to a stop, his furious yellow gaze locking on her.

"Her or me, Edain," I tell my captor. "You'll only get one chance to save her."

And I'm betting all my coin—or my life—on a certain little hunch I've had for a while.

"Fuck." Edain throws me aside and dives in front of Andraste as Lysander launches forward.

He took a raging bane for her. Every suspicion I ever had about my stepbrother's secret fondness for my sister is revealed.

That inky burst of shadow is back, punching into life around the three of them as they collapse in a yelling heap.

"Vi!" Thiago holds out a hand toward me.

I leap onto the overturned throne, but the movement must give me away. Or maybe it's Andraste's voice as she screams curses from within the shadow.

Because Lysander shakes his way free of the shadows, his head whipping around him in a rage. And then he stares at me as though he can see right through the illusion.

"Now!" Eris jumps on top of him, trying to tackle his sheer bulk to the ground.

Finn snaps a golden chain onto the collar he wears.

And it might have worked, if he wasn't so big and strong.

He tows them toward me, shaking Eris free.

Baylor steps forward, driving his sword straight through Lysander's chest as his brother hurls himself at me. The bane collides with him, and while the enormous warrior staggers back several steps, he doesn't yield.

"Forgive me," Baylor whispers, as Lysander roars with pain.

He twists the sword, skewering his brother's heart.

And they both go to their knees as I stagger into the safety of Thiago's arms.

CHAPTER 5

I manage to hold it all inside me on our trip through the Hallow, and it's not until we're standing safely in the tower at Ceres and the guards have filed out that I turn to my husband.

"You can't last too much longer?" My voice is so steady I'm almost proud of it.

Thiago tears off his gloves as the Hallow powers down. "Really? We're going to do this here?"

"Where would you prefer?"

He gives me a look that scorches me all the way from my ears to my toes. "In our chambers."

I remember what he said to me once.

"We kiss. We argue. We fall into bed. We fuck."

But right now, I'm too angry to kiss him. If we go upstairs, then he's probably right. We will end up in bed, but I won't be distracted. Not this time. "Here is fine."

He turns to me, all powerful, dangerous grace. "Vi—"

"I held my tongue while Edain taunted me about all the secrets he knows that I don't. I held my tongue while we were handling Lysander. And I held my tongue in front of my sister and her Asturian guards, because the last thing I want is for my mother to know Edain's little arrow struck home about your little secret." I turn to the others, who are hastily scrambling for the door. "Unless, of course, everyone else knows what Edain was talking about and I'm the last to find out? Is this common knowledge?"

Eris pauses. "Not to me, it's not. I'm as curious as you are, considering that smirking little prick seems to be aware of a threat to our national security, and I'm directly responsible for said security. Baylor?"

He grunts and shakes his head, though his attention is entirely on his brother's lifeless form.

All three of us stare at Finn.

Finn sighs at Thiago, tugging his blood-spattered vest open. "I told you this was going to bite you on the ass."

"*Finn* knows?" It explodes out of me.

"Finn happened to catch his Most Haughtiness at a particularly vulnerable moment," Finn corrects. "And Finn was sworn to secrecy, despite his objections. Thiago made me swear a blood oath to him before he would tell me what was going on."

"It's not a threat to national security," Thiago says.

"She. Cursed. You. Didn't she?" Eris leans toward him, a little hint of fire flickering in her dark irises. "Tell me how this is not a threat to national security?"

"I've got it under control."

"How much stress can your wards handle?" Eris's voice shifts up a level. "Are they still intact? Are those fucking creatures still contained?"

"*Yes.*"

"What creatures?" I demand, though I know she's speaking of his tattoos.

He set them free in order to save me once, and I'll never forget their malicious whispers—or the way they tore a pack of banes into little, bleeding chunks. And he swore he'd tell me what they were, though somehow, we've been so busy dealing with the hunt for the crown and my mother, that it never came up.

I hate not knowing. All of a sudden I'm five months into the past, not certain who the enemy is or what secret everyone is trying to hide from me. I broke Mother's curse, but I don't think I'll ever escape the way it made me feel.

Alone.

"Leave us," Thiago says, cutting them all a sharp glance from beneath his lashes.

Nobody says a word.

Finn helps Baylor lift his brother's breathless body, and Eris offers me a hint of a *kick his ass* smile before she closes the doors behind them with a telling little slam.

Footsteps ring on the marble outside the chamber, slowly growing quieter with distance.

I wait.

And as I wait, the tension in the room builds.

I have no right to be angry. Maia knows I've kept my own secrets from him—and I'm still keeping the most dangerous one of all—but Edain *knew*.

Thiago watches me silently, though I'm reminded of a caged wolf. There's no sign of the charming prince I fell in love with. No sign of his usual charismatic cloak. No, this is the warlord I'm dealing with. One with his guard fully up, as if he knows exactly where I'm going to strike and he's prepared.

"Well?" He throws the gauntlet down the second they're out of hearing distance.

Where to start?

"What was Edain talking about? A curse? Mother cursed you?"

Thiago crosses his arms over his chest. "It's nothing."

"You let me walk into a political nightmare where my stepbrother sneered down his nose about a secret the pair of you were keeping—"

"Don't make it sound as though we were conspiring together," Thiago's voice grows a little harder. "I wasn't aware that he knew. I wasn't aware that anyone knew. Your mother must have told him—"

"Told him *what?*"

For a second I don't think he's going to answer. He paces back and forth like a caged wolf, violence coiled like a lash within him. "I couldn't kill her."

"What?" It's not what I expected.

"When I went after your mother at the Queensmoot, I intended to kill her. I tried, Vi. I threw everything I had at her—everything I could afford to throw—and she managed to brush me aside."

"*Your mother escaped*" is all he said after he returned from the Queensmoot.

"I'm not entirely surprised." When I had a choice between killing myself, killing my mother, or finding someone with the power to break the curse she'd cast on me, there was a reason I chose the latter and sold my soul to the Mother of Night, so to speak.

My mother didn't become Queen of Asturia through chance. And she hasn't held onto that position for over a thousand years out of kindness. Or weakness.

I'm not strong enough to overthrow her, but there was a part of me that hoped *he* was.

"She cursed me," Thiago growls, his voice roughening as he lowers his fingers to his sleeve and starts unbuttoning it. Smooth skin reveals itself. Tugging the linen up his arm, he bears his forearm. "At first I thought nothing of it. I thought she'd *missed*. But this started appearing a week or two after we returned."

Dark ink starts to penetrate through his skin as if it's rising from deep within. Or no, not ink, but a shadow. A curse written deep within his veins. It starts at the pulse point of his inner wrist and curls its way up his forearm, like a twining bramble aiming for his heart.

And he hid it.

Everything within me turns to ice and I grab his shirt, tearing his sleeve open over the heavy bulge of his biceps. "How far does it go?"

There's no emotion in his voice. "Shoulder. It's been working its way slowly up my arm for weeks."

If it hits his heart, I'll lose him.

"And you didn't *tell* me?"

"I didn't want you to worry."

A growl echoes in my throat. "Stop. Trying. To. Protect. Me. Do I look like some poor innocent maid who needs you to make her life all sunshine and roses? I'm not afraid of the truth."

"It had nothing to do with shielding you from the truth." Shadows darken his green eyes. "You need to focus on finding the crown."

"We need to focus on stopping *this*! My mother's spells kill, curse you!"

"It's not meant to kill me."

"Oh no, it's just a nice, friendly little kiss she slapped you with. Maybe you'll start growing daisies in your hair. Or fur. Maybe I'll wake up one day with a bane in my bed."

"I'm not going to grow fur. It will hit my wards. It's meant to fracture them and unleash the Darkness within me."

Dark shapes whirl across the skin that's exposed. Savage, lethal shapes that bite and snarl. I can never see them in their entirety and that's probably a good thing.

Thiago sighs, and then golden runes stamp their way up his skin, glowing from within as if he's stripping his illusions away, inch by inch. "These are my wards. They were inked into my skin with an old magic in order to contain the Darkness within me."

The curse writhes its way between them, and though I can see hints of golden-red where it seems to be eating its way through some of those runes, the rest of them trace stoic patterns over his olive skin. They're like a supernova of light painted over his skin, a tangled web streaming between each point as if to capture something and contain it within him.

I don't recognize any of the markings.

They're nothing like the runes marked into the Hallow stones.

Nor are they anything seelie, and I've spent months searching through books about old lore, so I should know.

"Your mother hit me with the type of curse that was designed to incapacitate me and me alone. It's not meant to weaken me, but to strengthen the daemons inside me. She knows what I am, Vi. And she knew exactly how to try and destroy me from within. If I was weaker, if my wards were simpler, then she might have gotten to me already. They might have broken free."

"They?"

"These," he replies, placing his hand over one of his tattoos. "The souls I carry within me. Thousands of years ago they were an ancient primordial race that hunted the night. If they worked together, they would have consumed every mortal soul on this world, but they don't. They fight among themselves and hunt each other down. The first I knew of them was when I was eighteen and this creature of darkness attacked me. It nearly killed me, but I was drawn to the light within its chest. I... consumed it somehow, and the shadows swarming me evaporated. I could feel it within me though, yearning to be freed. Desperate to feed. It was a constant battle to keep it contained."

"The Darkness," I whisper.

"Yes." His lashes lower, obscuring his eyes as if to hide the flash of hatred I see there. "Others came. I consumed them all. And I began to realize I could sense them out there, because there's a heart of Darkness within me too. It yearns to hunt for those of its own kind. The more you consume, the greater your powers bloom." Anguish touches his face. "I was young. I was foolish. I wanted strength. And I didn't realize that with such power comes temptation. The more you take, the more you want. It's a constant grinding ache. Hunger. Need." A little flame flares to life in his dark irises. "The creature inside me grew stronger. Sometimes I would wake in a strange place with no recollection of how I got there, and I would be covered in blood." He stares at his palms as if seeing something else. "I had to contain it. I had to contain *them*. And so I went to the Morai, and they told me of a blood mage who might be able to ward it all away within me."

Until now. "But Mother's curse is eating away at your wards."

He meets my gaze. "Yes."

"Why didn't you tell me?"

"I had it under control."

"You keep using that word, but I do not think it means what you think it means. That curse has been creeping toward your heart for months and you have it under control?"

"I've spent over five hundred years battling this fucking monster inside me, Vi. I am stronger than it is. I am stronger than the souls that rage within me, desperate for release. And I am stronger than your mother's curse."

"What happens if it hits your heart?"

His jaw hardens. "I'm not concerned with—"

Stubborn, cursed fool. I stab a finger into his chest. "Well, you should be. You're the Prince of Evernight, and your kingdom is at war. Your people can't stand against my mother's army by themselves. If you die, then she will come for them and she will crush them all, because you're the only thing currently holding her at bay. And while my mother might be stronger than you are—"

"I didn't say she was *stronger*. I said I threw everything at her that I could afford to throw."

It momentarily stalls me.

Thiago offers me a savage smile, showing me his forearm again. "I could break through my wards, Vi. I could unleash myself and in so doing, I could crush your mother like an ant beneath my heel, but if I do that then I won't care who gets in my way. Eris. Finn. Thalia...." His voice roughens. "*You*. I will kill you all to get at her. I won't even be myself anymore. I'll be something else. *Someone* else. And you won't like him very much."

I've seen it in him sometimes.

Leashed violence. His eyes darkening until there's no color left in them.

I slip my hands inside his. "I've seen hints of him, Thiago. I'm not afraid of your Darkness. And the truth is… whatever lies inside you is still *you*. And you love me. You would never hurt me. Not even your darker side."

The breath explodes out of him. "Curse it, Vi. You should be scared. You have no fear when it comes to me. I should never have touched you that first time. I should never have—"

I cut him off with a kiss, painting it across his lips.

"You were my salvation," I whisper against his mouth, because I know what my life was like before I met him. "If you hadn't kissed me that first time, then I would be nothing now. I would be trapped within my mother's court, slowly screaming on the inside, dying a little more each day. You set me free. You welcomed me into your arms—into your heart—and I don't regret a single moment of it."

There's no more doubt within his eyes.

Thiago's hand slides around the back of my neck, hauling me toward him. His mouth slams down upon mine, rough and demanding, full of proprietary claim. This kiss is raw fire, burning all my hesitation and doubts away. I could let him claim me. I could let this be the end of it, but….

There's just one thing….

One tiny little thing….

"*Wait*. Wait." I tear my mouth from his and rest my forehead against his chest, breathing hard.

Gentle fingertips trace my cheeks. "What for?"

He's told me everything.

I can't hide the truth from him any longer. Not if there's to be any hope for us.

"Since we're sharing, there's something I need to tell you."

Instant frustration. "Vi, is this really the time?" Roughened hands slide down the curve of my waist. "Because it's been days since I've been inside you."

"Yes. Yes, it is. Because if I don't tell you now, then I don't know if I'll be able to find the courage again."

Thiago draws back, staring down at me.

"Do you remember the night of the Queensmoot when I drove my mother back?" The words blurt out of me.

A new sort of wariness enters Thiago's eyes as if he senses a trap about to spring closed. "Yes."

I press my cheek into his palm, clasping it there. Desperate for it to stay there. "You thought it was part of the bargain I made with the Mother of Night. That she would loan me her power in order to defeat the curse and throw my mother back."

"What are you trying to—"

"She broke the curse and that was all." I press my finger to his lips. Those damning lips that promise to steal my soul. "What if I was to tell you that *I* was the one who threw Mother back? That the power I wielded was… mine."

Silence.

He's not even breathing, and I need him to say something. Anything.

71

"You're not strong enough." Quiet words full of denial, as if he senses a glimpse of the truth.

"Not my fae magic, no."

Shadows sweep across his face, but I stall him again, holding up my left wrist—the one that wears the golden cuff that prevents magic from being able to find me.

"You couldn't work out why the fetch tried to kidnap me," I say quickly, "but you knew Angharad was searching for the *leanabh an dàn*—the child of destiny—in order to sacrifice her to the Horned One."

"Her?" He catches that tiny slip, because nobody ever said it was a female.

I tip my chin up. "Me."

He starts shaking his head, and each step back makes my heart curdle a little. "No. No, you're not—"

"The Morai said it first." I wrap my arms around myself as he retreats. "They said I would break the world apart and bring about the end of Unseelie. That's why they attacked me. And the Mother of Night…. That's why she made a bargain with me. She wants me to set her free. She said my mother slept with one of the Old Ones on Samhain when he was freed for the night, and he spilled his power within her womb. I can feel the Hallows. I can feel the power of the ley lines. I can wield it. I used that power to push my mother back at the Queensmoot."

And a torrent of magic so bright and burning burst from me, driving her to her knees.

"I am the *leanabh an dàn*."

Thiago's jaw drops.

The truth crashes over him like a tidal wave, and every flicker of it paints his face. Horror. Denial. Then anger. It's a storm that bruises his eyes, but he cuts right to the heart of my fear. "You've known for months. Why didn't you tell me?"

My heart feels like a small, helpless thing, crushed by a relentless fist.

"You were going to kill the *leanabh an dàn*," I whisper, "to prevent Angharad from getting what she wants."

Thunder darkens his brow. "And you thought I would... That I would...."

"No, of course not!" He wouldn't hurt me. I know he wouldn't hurt me. "But...."

"But, *what?*" Thiago looms closer, his expression incredulous. "You thought I would turn away from you? You thought I would...." He breaks off with a curse, his lip curling in a snarl. "No. I'm not even going to say it. Because it's such a fucking insult to me. To us. I love you. I've told you a thousand times. I will never stop loving you. But when will you believe it?"

"My mother—"

"Your mother never loved you, Vi," he yells. "That's not love. It's not even a fucking mockery of love. She gave you a crumb and you were pathetically grateful for it. And if she denied you those crumbs, then you would beg for them."

The heat drains out of my skin and I blanch.

And maybe it's true, because that was all I knew.

Every day in my mother's court was a bloodied game. Would she smile at me today? Or would her face be cold and expressionless, her voice chastising? Would she seat me at her side for dinner? Or would she sentence me to the oubliette for some obscure punishment?

Every time she pressed a kiss to my hair, the lump in my throat would threaten to choke me, my heart skittering out of control. Because her love—her favor—was something that always had to be earned, and it could be torn away from me with a single wrong word.

I told myself I stopped caring.

I wouldn't wear the gowns she insisted upon. I refused to perform her little tests. I hammered armor into shape around my battered heart and gave her a merciless little smile whenever she turned scathing words upon me, but the mortal blow she struck was etched upon my heart as a little girl.

And no armor can defend against a wound which is already taken.

"I know," I whisper. "I know it wasn't love."

The only hint of love I've ever known before I met him was what I felt for Andraste, but even that was torn away from me.

Thiago swears under his breath. "I knew something was wrong with you. I *knew* it. I could feel you holding me at bay—"

"I wasn't trying to—"

"What?" He spins back to me. "Lie to me?"

Oh, *really?* "I didn't lie. I just didn't tell you. Rather like a certain curse you may have forgotten to mention."

His jaw turns to granite. "I'm sorry. I shouldn't have said that. I just want to understand…. I was trying to protect you. But you… You don't trust me to stand by you?"

"I didn't know what to do!" It all bursts out of me. "I'd just found out you were my husband of thirteen *years*. But you kept me locked away in Valerian, away from everyone you thought might betray my little secret to me. So yes, I know exactly what this feels like. To know that there's something going on, but you're not part of it; to know that everyone around you is conspiring against you…. Yes! I *know*!

"And then the truth about us was revealed, but I couldn't remember a fucking thing about our past. You said you loved me. I was starting to trust that it was true, and then the Morai said I was this… this monster." I stare at him helplessly. "You were the only anchor I could hold onto. When I was in your arms, it was the *only* time I felt safe. Or… Even myself. I didn't want to lose that. I just wanted to pretend it was all a horrible dream and it would all go away—"

"I could have protected you."

"I didn't… know." My hands shake. Something wilts inside me. A dawning hope that I wasn't aware was so fucking fragile still. "I didn't know what to do. I didn't know if you would…."

Stop loving me.

His face darkens. "I am not your mother."

"Everything I have ever loved has been taken away from me." The knot of emotion suddenly chokes me. "I didn't want to lose you too."

"Vi. Mother of Night." Thiago captures my face and breathes the curse across my temples, holding my face between his trembling hands. "Never. I would never forsake you. No matter what happens. You are my breath, my heart, my soul. I'm sorry if I ever gave you reason to doubt that. I'm sorry if you didn't feel as though you could… trust me."

It hurts him to say that, I think.

"I should have told you," I whisper.

A sigh escapes him. "I should have told you about your mother's curse. Can you forgive me?"

"If you'll forgive me," I whisper.

He kisses me fiercely.

And then it's no longer enough to merely kiss. I throw myself into the embrace, hands sliding desperately up his chest. He's still wearing his leather vest, but I can feel every hard inch of his body beneath it.

Mine. He's mine. Forever. No matter what. Relief and desperation form a firestorm of passion within me.

A tremor runs through him, and then teeth sink into my lower lip. My back hits one of the stones that guard the Hallow. Thiago hauls me up into his arms, my thighs locking around his hips.

There's a part of me that didn't think he'd accept this.

But there's possession in his touch and no mercy in his eyes.

"No more secrets." He punctuates the words with a punishing kiss. "No more lies. I spent thirteen fucking years trapped in a web of deceit. I won't do it anymore. I won't. And I promise you I won't hide things from you anymore."

I don't want that either.

His tongue drives into my mouth, fingers digging into my ass. Every hard inch of him shoves me back into the granite, until I rock against him, hips begging for more.

Our eyes meet, and for once we're in perfect harmony.

Then my hands steal between us, tearing his shirt loose from his trousers and tugging at the buttons on his vest. Teeth rake across my shoulder, a flashpoint of heat igniting within me. It steals a gasp from my lips, but then his mouth covers mine again, and I can't breathe, except for him.

I don't think I ever need to breathe again, if this is what I can exist upon.

A growl echoes in his throat as I find him, hot and hard. He thrusts into my palm, consuming me. I can barely feel his cock through the leather. He's just one enormous, demanding force that fills my palm. Slick heat wets my inner thighs. I know what that cock feels like, filling me up.

I tear my mouth from his just long enough to say. "I want you inside me."

"Then it's a shame that you don't make the orders around here." My feet hit the ground and he spins me around, one hand sweeping my hair into a knot at the back of my head. "Would you say please, Vi? Would you beg me?"

If this is a means to make amends, then I'm all for it.

Thiago's other hand slides over my breasts and continues its way down, tracing lazy circles over my abdomen. He kicks my feet apart, leaving me vulnerable and aching.

"Do you *want* me to beg, my prince?" I bite my lip, trying to contain the shiver that works through me. "Do you want me on my knees? Do you want me at your mercy?"

Mother of Blessed Night. Hard fingers drive between my thighs, molding the leather of my trousers to my skin. It's just a hint he's not as in control as he'd like. The friction is delicious, and my nipples ache as they rasp against the stone. Goose bumps shiver over my skin as his other fist knots in my hair.

"I should make you wait, after that," Thiago whispers, with a wicked chuckle. "And no. I want you right here, just like this. Besides" —his breath caresses the bare slope of the back of my neck— "what makes you think you're not already at my mercy?"

He knows exactly where to touch me, his fingers dancing over that ecstatic bundle of nerves that will ignite me. The hand in my hair fists, earning a gasp from me. I can't move. I can't touch him. All I can do is feel as he tugs the laces on my trousers open and then slides them down my quivering thighs. He slips his fingers inside my drawers.

Instant. Bliss.

I moan and press my forehead to the wall in surrender. Thiago's fingertips find me wet and swollen, and then he's tracing teasing little circles around where I need him most. I grind into his touch, trying to bite back the desperate little sound that growls in my throat.

"Give in," he breathes.

Two fingers drive inside me so suddenly I cry out. "*Never.*"

There's another dark laugh behind me. "You're so fucking stubborn, Vi. Let's see who breaks first?"

It's me. I know it's going to be me.

But I let my hand steal between us, plucking at the ties that close the flap of his trousers. The heated weight of his erection spills into my eager fingers.

"Behave." He slaps me between the thighs—a shock of sensation that makes me forget to breathe.

He's never done that before.

Always, always, he is gentle and dedicated and controlled. But this…. I like it.

I squeeze his cock in response, letting my wrist glide up and down. "What are you going to do if I don't?"

A hiss through his teeth, and he grinds against me. "Don't say I didn't warn you."

Sensation spears through me as he thrusts those fingers inside me. He curls them slightly, and I feel myself clenching around him. I'm so close to the edge. His hips drive into me, forcing me against his hand. Then his thumb is tracing pure lightning over my clit.

I sink my teeth into my lower lip, desperate not to betray myself. A mouth closes over the side of my throat and he suckles hard as he drives me toward the edge. I don't know where I end and he begins. My palms slap against the wall, his erection digging into my backside. I lost the battle before it even began.

Thrusting slowly, he lets his cock glide between my slick folds. "Would you promise me forever if I was to let you come?"

That's not fair, I want to cry, *because I'll promise you anything.*

The words die on my lips, because his cock threatens to enter me, and suddenly I need him inside me so desperately I ache.

"Promise me," he demands, his fingers ruining me. "Promise me, Vi. Give me everything. Every inch of you."

The coil tightens within me.

"Forever," I cry.

It hits me with all the force of a lightning bolt. I shudder and gasp, every inch of me clenching around his penetrating touch. He doesn't let up his excruciating onslaught. Instead, he replaces his fingers with his cock, just the tip of his shaft entering me.

My nails dig into his hand. "More!"

There is no mercy.

Only him.

My knees hit the floor, and then he shoves me onto my forearms, tearing my trousers down my legs until they're knotted around one ankle. My drawers are gone. Torn from me with a single snarl.

I arch my back for him, fingertips curling into the stone as I brace for his thrust. The world comes alight for me, light emanating from underneath my nails.

Yes.

It's a tremble of power, a whisper stealing through my veins. My gaze suddenly focuses. Dust and gravel shivers across the slate floors. One by one, the brass runes carved into the floor begin to glow—

And I sense an awareness turning toward me from far, far away.

Thiago rocks against me, his fingers leaving little bruises in my hips as he prepares to—

"Stop." I gasp as I realize what's happening. What we're doing.

There's no sheath. It's a terrible time. And I can feel that bitch focusing her attention on us.

"Stop!" I scramble away from Thiago, hauling my trousers back up my legs.

The ley line falls into stillness.

The runes fade.

But I can't hide my shuddering breath. That was so close. We nearly forgot, and I could almost sense the Mother of Night smiling.

Pleasure evaporates.

"Fuck." Thiago scrapes a trembling hand over his

mouth. "*Fuck.*"

"Not here." I manage to catch his arm. "And not…. You can't come inside me. Not today."

The truth of everything my bargain might cost us flashes through his eyes. "You felt her?"

I don't know what I felt. Maybe that was me? Or whatever part of me calls to the ley lines? Just…. "We have to be careful."

We can't risk a child.

I will *not* let some poor innocent suffer for my actions.

Thiago rests on his knuckles on the floor, his cock at half-mast as he considers me. "Not inside you."

It's as if a decision has been made.

Stuffing himself back inside his trousers, he gathers me up into his arms and strides for the door. "Fine. I can work with that. Now, let's finish this discussion in our rooms."

"What did you think?"

Thiago rolls onto his side in bed, his head propped on his palm. Muscle bulges in his shoulder, but though my eyes linger, I need at least an hour's recovery. He carried me up here and spent hours wrecking me with his mouth and hands, and has been thoroughly focused upon 'earning his apology' as he puts it.

He won it long ago, though I didn't have the heart to tell him that.

Or maybe I did and I was just being selfish, because I swear Thiago was put on this world by Maia herself to please females. In every way.

"About?"

"Clydain."

"You don't want to talk about what I said upstairs—"

"*No*. I do not. I need to think about what to do," he growls out, "and unless we're in a fully warded, impenetrable room, we're not even going to *think* about your revelation."

Not where others can pluck the words or even our thoughts from the air. That's sobering.

Fine.

I trace my fingers over his biceps. These are my favorite moments. He likes to talk after sex. It's almost as though he wears his 'Prince of Evernight' mantle outside our bedchamber doors, but the second we're through them, he lets down his guard.

I've never been a part of something like this. I was always kept on the edges of my mother's court, watching, listening, bursting with ideas that could help our kingdom, but to speak up would only ever earn a chastening look and an arched eyebrow.

"Do you think yourself queen, Iskvien?" Mother would mock. "Do you yearn to rule?"

And her courtiers would laugh, even as I buried my hopes and dreams.

But Thiago wants it all.

"You know your sister best," he says.

"Andraste was surprised when you mentioned Clydain," I reply, "though I'll concede that so was I. Considering I wasn't aware you were going to present such an offer."

His mouth twists. "I wasn't. It was a spur-of-the-moment thought when she brought up Eidyn. I wasn't expecting the trade and I wanted to see what she'd do if I suggested Clydain."

"Why did you send Lysander toward Clydain in the first place?"

"One of your mother's border lords retains his allegiance with me, and sent word years ago that he'd seen Adaia riding from the Vervain Hallow to Clydain during the full moon."

"It can't have been her. My mother worships Selena and the full moon every month. She plies the court with wine and mead, and takes Edain to her chambers for several nights."

Asturia is known for the bounty of its harvests and forests, and my mother is bound to the land as queen. Fertility rites are as important to my people as breathing, and if the queen is blessed by the goddess, then so the lands shall be.

"The things I do not need to know. I almost pity that poor bastard," Thiago replies with a grimace. "But my spy swears he's seen her riding through the forests there several times over the years. I think your mother locks her pretty little whore away in her chambers with food and wine, while she slips away in the middle of the night."

That's interesting. She never misses a full moon. But if she's not truly within her chambers…. My gut starts churning. It would be the perfect means for Mother to do whatever she wanted, without a thousand watchful eyes upon her.

What is she up to?

I sit up. "But why?"

"I don't know why. My informant can't get close to Clydain. There's a mist there that encircles the place and whenever he enters it, he wakes up miles away from where he entered with no recollection of what happened within the mist."

Rumors of the place being haunted. A magical mist that wipes away memories.

"Fuck," I whisper. "She *is* hiding something."

"Wagons go into the mist according to my spy. He's seen enormous piles of metal in the back of them. And caught a glimpse of strange lights flashing in the skies over the keep, from a distance. At first I didn't think anything of it, but his reports kept coming and any secret conspiracy your mother is involved in needs to be investigated. And so I sent Lysander. It was the last time we saw him until today. He vanished, and the first we heard of him was when you said you'd seen him curse-twisted into bane form."

"Lysander got through the mist." The only one in Asturia with the power to lay such a powerful curse is my mother. "And she cursed him so he wouldn't be able to report. But how did he escape her? Why would she not simply lock him away?"

Or kill him.

No, that one's easy to guess. If she killed him, then she could no longer use him as a weapon against us.

If she killed him, it only hurts once.

"Bane's are unpredictable and Lysander is... was one of my best." There's a roughness to his voice that tells me he feels his friend's loss too.

I catch his fingers and squeeze them. "We'll get him back."

"Vi." Dark lashes flutter over his eyes, but he squeezes my hand. "You saw what he was like today. Lysander loved you. I would never have thought anyone could turn him against you, and yet he was going to kill you."

I press a finger to his lips. "We'll get him back. We are *not* going to let her win this game."

A sense of implacability sweeps over his face. "I won't put you at risk. He could kill you."

"Then he can stay locked away until we work out how we're going to break his curse." Rolling toward him, I press a gentle kiss to his lips. "If I can break one curse—"

Thiago captures my face between his hands, holding me there. "You are *not* going to ask the Mother of Night to return him to his fae form."

The thought hadn't occurred to me.

I nip at his thumb. "I was desperate to save your life. This is different. We have time. We have opportunities. Surely someone knows how to break a bane's curse. Unless you just happen to have his true love locked away in a tower somewhere, ready to bestow her kiss upon his lips? That might work."

Thiago breathes out a laugh. "I forget how much you've forgotten."

"Why?"

"Lysander has no true love. And certainly not one wearing skirts."

"Ah." Something tickles my memories just then. It's just a flash of a sinfully devastating face swimming into view, a wicked smile sent from a man who looks disarmingly like Baylor—if Baylor ever met a smile he didn't drag into a back alley and stab.

Singing in the background. Something ribald about a sailor named Thom, who had the prettiest lips a sailor ever did have.

And then it's gone.

"Memory?" Thiago murmurs.

It vanishes like the ghostly flutter of butterfly wings against my skin.

"I think so." I can never predict them. But I do know one thing. "Lysander gets along well with Finn, doesn't he?"

There'd been too much mischief in his smile.

"Terribly well. I try to keep them apart as much as possible."

I sigh as I push away from him. "We'll get him back."

"And then we'll discover what your mother is hiding at Clydain."

I FIND BAYLOR SITTING OUTSIDE LYSANDER'S CELL, HIS knuckles clasped together and his head bowed. My feet are silent on the stairs—an old habit—but he looks up as I approach, his golden eyes flaring amber for a second before they return to normal.

"Princess." He shifts to stand, but I wave at him to stay where he is.

"Are you all right?" I murmur, slipping onto the stone bench beside him.

Baylor leans back against the bars. Inside the cell, his brother's body lies still beneath a white sheet. "He will rise with the moon."

That's not what I asked.

A shrug slips through him but I insist upon squeezing his shoulder. Baylor's the quietest member of my husband's loyal court—still waters running over stone—but that doesn't mean he can't be hurt.

And it hurt him today to drive a sword through his brother's chest.

"Thank you," I whisper. "For saving me."

Despite everything that has come between Andraste and me, I know exactly how that would feel. She's my sister and we loved each other once, before my mother turned us against each other. There's a part of me that will always love her, and I have to hope that her warning today meant something.

"He would never have forgiven himself if he hurt you," Baylor finally says. "I know you barely remember him, but the two of you…. You were close friends." A muscle tightens in his jaw. "To see him like this, so twisted by hate and rage…. It's the worst thing the queen could have done to him, for my brother is love and laughter. We were born from the same womb, but he was always the one that others loved more."

It's an arrow straight through the heart, because I feel that too.

My mother's people adore Andraste. She inspires confidence wherever she rides, because she's the perfect princess. She's better than I am with a sword. She's dared to argue against my mother in court for the rights of some minor lord, whereas I never had that lenience. She proffers wise counsel, and she makes the court laugh.

She is the sun and I am the moon, and somehow, I never truly fit into the Asturian court.

"Some are easy to love," I tell him quietly, "because they shine so brightly it's difficult to look away. But others…. We don't love them any less, Baylor. Because they are steadfast and true. They are solid rock beside quicksilver, but they will not break when quicksilver is too soft. It is a different kind of love. Steadier, perhaps."

Thiago taught me the truth of that. And I'm learning to love myself—or trying to love myself as much as he does.

"Do you think he'll remember himself when he rises?"

I won't pretend I'm not a little nervous about meeting Lysander again.

"Dying hurts," Baylor replies. "Sometimes it takes time to remember who you are and where you are." He looks toward his brother. "I don't know what he's been through this past year."

"Thiago told me about Clydain."

What sort of weapon would my mother be keeping in the far north of Asturia?

Could it turn the tide of war?

"Do you think he found something?" I whisper.

Baylor stares blankly at the wall in front of him, running his knuckles back and forth over his knee. "I think he found something," he finally rumbles, "though whether he'll remember it is another matter."

CHAPTER 6

"I need to go into the city," Thiago murmurs the next morning. "Do you want to come?"

"I thought you'd be holed up with Eris and Baylor, plotting a counterattack against my mother?"

There's a touch of leashed violence about my husband this morning. "An attack is what your mother expects. It's what she wants. As someone pointed out, the border lords aren't entirely in her favor. They will be if I strike now. No." A thoughtful look comes into his eyes. "I won't play into her hands. When I strike back, she won't be expecting it."

"And Lysander?"

Lysander woke with the first rays of moonlight, but Baylor is locked down there with him alone, trying to find some hint of his brother within Lysander's monstrous form.

Mother did her job well. One of Thiago's most dangerous warriors has been removed from the game board, and Baylor, as implacable as he is, has taken a blow.

"Thalia heard a whisper that the Prince of Shadows *might* have someone in his employ who is a hexbreaker. Hence my interest in venturing into the city."

"Prince of Shadows?"

Thiago rolls his eyes. "Technically, I'm not supposed to know about him. He rules the catacombs under the city, and it's rumored that—if such a person existed—he might be in charge of the assassin's guild in the city."

"Does such a person exist?"

"Such a person might once have sent me a warning about a threat. I told him if anyone ever tried to hire him to have me killed, if he came to me with word of it I would double his fee. In return, as long as his assassins don't cross certain boundaries, I won't make it my life's duty to ferret them out of my city and destroy them. In general, we pretend the other doesn't exist."

I close the book I've been reading. It's an old collection of fairy tales about magical relics, though there's no mention of any crowns. It seems there's no mention of them anywhere to be found, which is starting to irritate me. "I'll come."

"Just like that?" he drawls. "Was it the mention of assassins? Shadowy princes? Blood bounties?"

"You've been reading too many of my books. No." I throw the blankets off my lap, where I've made a nest for the day's research. "I'll come, because I think it's highly unusual that my overprotective husband wants to take me on his excursion to visit an assassin's guild."

Thiago crosses his arms over his chest. "You're not coming with me to visit Theron. You're going to a book-shop to see if you can find what you're looking for."

"If I can't find any books about the crown in the enormous castle library which is run by thirteen highly inquisitive scholars, then I doubt I'm going to find it in an old bookstore tucked away down in the city. It's almost as though you're using me to cover your tracks, which would suggest you're trying to keep your movements quiet from your advisors. Thalia was the one who brought you the news. Baylor is currently occupied. I saw Finn heading to the courtyard to spar…. Which leaves Eris. And knowing Eris as I do, she wouldn't approve."

"Eris is the only one of my people who has met the Prince of Shadows in any sort of capacity. She threatened to hang him from the tower walls by his heels if she ever saw him again. The prince retaliated by leaving a Sorrow's Tear on her pillow. Every now and then she finds a fresh rose in her bedchambers as if he's taunting her. The last time it happened, she took a practice sword to a dummy in the yard and there were only slivers of it left by the time she'd finished. If she knew where I was going, she'd start sharpening her knives and your mother's war wouldn't be the only one we're facing."

"If Eris discovers your ruse, she's going to throw *you* off the tower," I point out.

Thiago laughs, leaning on his knuckles on the bed, his eyes sparking with mischief as he steals a kiss. "Yes, but I can fly."

The wind blows sea mist in off the harbor. Ceres is built around a natural bay, with two enormous outcroppings of stone guarding the entrance to the harbor.

An enormous statue as tall as the castle walls stands on

each of the outcroppings, staring fiercely out to sea. The first one wears loose fae robes draped around her lean form like scalloped marble. One hand rests on the hilt of the sword sheathed at her side and a sunburst crown sits atop her head, but it's the lantern in her hand that gives away her identity. Maia, guarding the mouth of the harbor, lifting her lantern as if to defy any ships that enter to pass by her with any darkness in their hearts.

Maia is the sun, the shining beacon of hope we pray to.

The other statue represents Selena, the goddess of Night.

Her crown bears seven stars, though a thin gold circlet hovers over it, representing their radiance, and while her face is serene, the implacable way she stares into the bay is a warning. Night is a time for mystery and seduction, but it is also a time of secrets and assassinations. Selena, once the patron goddess of Evernight, is the goddess that thieves, whores, and assassins have claimed. To pray to her means to ask for her protection, no matter the cost, and I've been here long enough to hear petitions from the powerful guild councils that rule the old town, asking for her statue to be removed.

They do not wish to pray to a goddess who offers a whore or a thief solace.

Thiago refused. She was the goddess chosen by Evernight when a curse struck the northern part of the country and cast a veil of constant darkness over it. Only by her grace was the curse turned back before it blighted Ceres too, though some say the queen that was bound to the land at the time fought the curse by herself.

It's only now, with no queen in Evernight, that the

shadow of constant night has been creeping south mile by mile each year.

Thalia found pamphlets that were circulating in the city suggesting the reason for the blight's advance is the prince who overthrew the rightful rulers of the kingdom. Thiago ignored it, but I saw the look Thalia exchanged with the others. It bothers her.

It bothers me a little, because the etched figure on the pamphlets was of a monstrous creature ruling over all from on high, with vicious horns and flaring bat wings.

It looked like something my mother might have conjured if she was asked to describe my husband, and while Thalia doesn't know where the pamphlets came from, they seem to be everywhere these past two months.

My mother has a finger in it. I know she does.

Because an army can be beaten back, but vicious rumors are the hardest battle to win.

If we go after the printing presses, the secret gatherings clearly going on, and the leaders of this whispered rebellion, then we'll only confirm the rumors. *See*, they'll say. *The Prince of Evernight is vicious and dangerous. He promises us he'll be a benevolent ruler, but only if we fall in line. Only if we dare not have a voice. He is a tyrant.*

But if we don't do something, then the rumors will only spread.

Any fae in the city who suffers hardship will start looking upward—to the castle looming over them—as the cause of their suffering. And the leaders of this rebellion— the one stoking anger in the guild halls and rumors in the streets—will find flames that only need fanning.

"This way," Thiago says, lacing his fingers through

mine. He's wearing an illusion so well-crafted I almost wouldn't recognize him if not for his smile.

A constant little tingle encases my own skin. I'd jokingly asked if I could be a redhead for the day, and he'd complied, though it feels strange to catch glimpses of myself—pale-skinned and blue-eyed—in the shop windows as we pass.

I squeeze his hand. I won't let my mother or her efforts hurt him, and while he might be focused on the war—the direct thrust, so to speak—I will be waiting for my mother in the shadows, and all her gossip and innuendo too.

The older part of the city was born when the fae first arrived in Arcaedia.

It was built close to the cliffs guarding Ceres's back, where it has prime view of the harbor. It's marked on the map as Oldgate.

We walk beneath an arch that's guarded by two stone drakon sentinels and slip across the Bridge of Bones. Water thunders through a sluice gate set high in the walls, plummeting past us into the gorge far below. I've studied the maps; there's a walled dam far above the city, melded into the stone of the mountains. Once this section of Ceres was heralded as the City of Waterfalls, but the building of the dam means they're mostly dry, except for this one which is named Phoenix Falls, though the locals call it Maia's Tears. During the winter months, for a week or two the sunset will catch it at just the right angle so that it looks like a spill of pure fire.

Once we're across the bridge into the old quarters of the city, something inside me relaxes. Hawkers call out their wares in the bustling marketplaces, and there are fluttering demi-fey in cages at one stall, and an assortment of potions promising all manner of glamors at another.

I can be no one here.

Not my enemy's wife or my mother's daughter. Just another female in a sea of fae going about their daily business.

"If you venture through there" —Thiago points to a long, narrow alleyway— "you'll find yourself in the catacombs that weave through the mountain under this half of the city. The people here call it the Bone Church, and rumor insists that the fae lord who calls himself the Prince of Shadows rules down there."

He says it carefully, just in case anyone overhears it.

"I thought the wicked prince who rules this city would squash all upstarts who seek to claim power within his walls?"

"Perhaps he's not as wicked as they claim."

"Oh, he's definitely wicked," I purr in his ear, enjoying the chance to melt against him. "You should see what he does with his mouth."

"Behave." Thiago drags me onward, shooting me a possessive look. "The Prince of Shadows and his followers worship the god of Death, and make offerings to him. You'll recognize Theron's assassins because they have a blood moon tattooed on their face—though the only time you ever see them coming is when they're sent to deliver you into Kato's arms."

"Does that not make it easier to differentiate them from the general populace?"

"Theron's glamors are powerful enough to rival the Prince of Evernight's. Call it a double-edged sword. To become one of his people, you must wear the tattoo. In response, the only way to remain anonymous is to wear his veil of magic."

"Sounds like an easy way to ensure loyalty. Betray him and you'll never walk the streets again without everyone knowing exactly who and what you are."

Thiago's lips quirk. "I think you underestimate our good Prince of Shadows. Betray Theron, and they'll find pieces of your body floating in the river. Or not at all."

"Will they let you into the Bone Church?"

"If I pay the entry fee," he replies.

"One tenth of your fortune?"

Another dangerous smile as he plucks a red-black Sorrow's Tear rose from within his cloak. "I have something Theron might consider more enticing."

Brushing it against my lips, he winks.

It's gorgeous. The scent of it is dark and heady, and hints at magic. They grow only where the blood of a Sorrow has fallen, and the thorns are tipped with a poison that's lethal to the unseelie, and toxic to the seelie. To get them to bloom requires a Sorrow's tears. They're impossibly rare.

"If Eris finds out you're using her to catch this Theron's attention—"

"Oh, he'll know it's not from Eris." Thiago chuckles. "Eris wouldn't send him flowers. But he'll be curious enough to wonder what I want."

"And I'm to wander through the bookstore? Alone?"

Thiago gives me a long, slow, heated glance. "You won't be alone. Finn's been trailing us since we left the castle." He captures my chin as I unconsciously turn to look. "Don't. You won't recognize him, and I don't want any watchers marking him."

I bite his thumb. "I knew this was unusual. You can't help yourself, can you?"

Fingertips trace little circles on my cheeks. His voice roughens. "I spent thirteen years hoping that one day I would be able to hold you in my arms. Forever. And every morning since the Queensmoot, when I wake it feels as though I'm still dreaming, because you're right beside me. I don't have to send you back to your mother. I don't have to beg you to remember me. I don't have to feel that knife to the heart every time she gives you back, when you look at me as if I'm a stranger. You're mine, Vi. Finally mine." He places a punishing kiss on my mouth, tension shivering through him before he finally lets me up for air. But the beautiful green of his irises is gone, leaving nothing but chips of polished obsidian in their place. "But sometimes it feels like it's too good to be true. Am I still dreaming? Is the dream going to shatter if I wake? And I won't let it. Nothing will take you away from me again. Not your mother. Not Angharad's fetch. Not the Mother of Fucking Night. I will drown this world in Darkness before I ever let you go again."

I clasp his wrists, trying to catch my breath.

Around us, shadow dapples over the cobbles as clouds gather above the city.

Fae cry out, pointing to the skies.

"Thiago. *Thiago.*" I dig my nails into his wrists so he's forced to look at me. All his attention locks on me, and suddenly we're the only two souls in the world. "I love this world. And this world needs light." Heat flares in his eyes, but I press my finger to his lips. "Nothing is going to take me away, but if it does, then I will fight my way back to you. No matter what it takes. No matter who has me.

And if the worst should happen, not even death could part us. I would wait for you on the edge of the Bright Lands."

The god of Death rules over all, eventually. According to ancient myth we were once immortal, but when we fled the origin world and arrived here in Arcaedia, we were cursed by the Old Ones and fall prey to Kato's judgement in the afterlife. He dictates whether we ascend to the Bright Lands or are doomed to suffer eternally in the Underworld.

His breath exhales with a rush. "And I would wait for you in the Darkness."

In the Darkness...? I frown, but he captures my hand, brushing my knuckles against his lips. Inch by inch he swallows down the daemons inside him, until his eyes blaze with emerald fire.

"Thank you," he whispers, as the clouds above the city thin.

I swallow down the hard lump in my throat. All this time he's been wearing the mantle of charming prince, but I didn't realize how close to the surface his daemons lurk. Or maybe it's the curse, sinking its hooks in him. "I'll go to the bookstore. I won't look for Finn. And I promise I'll come back to you."

"This way," he says, offering me his arm and vanishing the rose.

There's no sign of the hint of violence I just caught a glimpse of. He absorbs it all and simply suppresses it.

But now I desperately need to talk to Eris. Or Thalia.

Because my husband lives and breathes control, and if I hadn't stayed his hand, then he might have let it over-whelm him.

Later.

An enormous oak tree leans against the cliff face ahead of us. Its roots are so thick that doorways and windows have been carved among them, and I'm not sure where the cliff ends and the oak begins. A jaunty little sign with a pair of books on it hangs directly above one of the openings. Another sign features a wine barrel.

"The Wayfarer's Oak." Thiago points to the hundreds of fey lanterns that drip from its branches. "Each night the lanterns help guide its people through the old quarter. Nobody knows who lights them—or whether it's simply an old magic long forgotten—but it's said that the day the oak falls is the day the city is doomed."

Image intrudes; A brief flash of laughter and dancing as we dine in a little restaurant not far from the oak. It's a memory of the pair of us, and I can almost smell the wine and taste his kiss on my mouth.

My head turns, and there it is.

The Wayfarer.

The restaurant is hewn directly into the cliff walls, and wisteria chokes the brass frame of the awning outside the restaurant. A half dozen tables sit scattered beneath it, wearing skirts of white linen tablecloths. Little demi-fey flutter here and there among the wisteria, breathing fire into glass orbs that nestle within its vines. At night it would be breathtaking.

"We've been here." I want to chase down the memory, but it vanishes like a dream upon waking.

"Yes. We've dined there sometimes. There were years when the curse broke early and you would remember me and we had more time to enjoy the city."

"What else did we do?" There's no point dwelling on

all the memories that slip through my fingers. I may as well explore my city again.

"You spent hours in Binder's," he says, dragging me through the crowd, toward the little door with the book sign hanging above it.

And now I know another reason why he brought me.

He thinks the more I immerse myself in things I've done with him, the more I'll remember.

A bell tinkles as we enter. A tired little face looks up from the counter, a smile flashing as the hob recognizes rich customers—judging from our clothes, no doubt—and then Thiago offers a polite greeting to one of the customers who stands by the counter.

Books. Books everywhere. The castle may be ours, but this feels like home in a way I've not experienced for… however long it has been.

I brush my fingers over the spines of several books. They're old and weathered. Not new books, kept pristine in a castle library, but well-loved, well-used, promising to lure me into mythical worlds.

It takes me a moment to realize there are eyes resting on me.

I look up through the stacks, and see my husband smiling as if he knew a part of me vanished the second we arrived here.

"You have an account," Thiago muses, his eyes sparklingly wickedly. "Get whatever you like. I'll have them sent up to the castle and after I've finished my errand, we'll dine at Wayfarer's."

Hesitation steals through me. He shrugged off that moment in the square, but I can feel it still, lingering in every look he grants me.

"Dinner," I promise.

AN HOUR PASSES.

Thiago slipped back inside not long ago, saying he'd left his message and was waiting for the Prince of Shadows to contact him. He muttered something about ordering food for us, and I promised I'd meet him shortly as I stole into the darker recesses of the bookshop.

There are little nooks and crannies everywhere, filled with bookcases that seem carved out of the roots of the mighty oak. But it's the trail of breadcrumbs I'm following that steal my attention.

The hob promised this section contains all the old lore to be found.

So far I have nothing.

Every royal crown on this section of the continent has a bland background. Thiago knew a little about the unseelie crowns, but nothing of interest.

What I do know is this: The Crown of Shadows was named as one of the powerful relics that drove the Old Ones back during the wars against the alliance the Unseelie and Old Ones formed. Thiago thought it could be used as a conduit for the fae to access the Old Ones' power, but it was lost during the wars, and there's been no word of it since.

The only entity I could ask who might possibly know the truth about it is the Mother of Night, but I don't trust her to tell me the truth.

It has to be here somewhere.

There has to be some myth, some old tale… *something*.

Relics of power.

Blaedwyn, one of the queens of Unseelie, wielded the Sword of Mourning against the Erlking. They say her heart turned to stone the moment she set hands to it.

I should know. I used it. It was never meant for another hand, but as I struggled to lift it, the Mother of Night appeared and somehow, she absorbed its weight so I could wield it.

If I clench my fist I can still feel the sword out there, driven deep into the heart of the Hallow that trapped the Erlking.

How did the Mother of Night touch it?

She wants the crown and she can touch the sword.

I start thumbing through books. Maybe it's not the crown I need to find. Maybe it's the sword. Who forged the sword? Something like that isn't easily crafted. They'd have to be an expert, highly practiced in magic.

And powerful.

I'm not alone—the murmur of quiet voices rumbles in the background—but one word strikes me out of my absorption.

"...finally let that slut out of the castle," whispers a harsh voice. "Does he think we're going to bow and kiss her feet the way we're forced to kiss his?"

"For now," rumbles a second voice.

My hands still, the pulse kicking in my throat.

"Patience, friends." A third man cuts through the undertone, his voice like a knife through velvet. "The Gray Guild is meeting on Elms Day. That bastard may present himself as prince all he likes, but he doesn't rule beneath the city. And there are means to counteract his magic."

Heart quickening, I slip closer, reaching up to ease the

book I hold back onto a shelf. As I do, I catch a glimpse of three cloaked figures hiding within the next row of shelves.

One of them is tall and cloaked in dark gray, the others of middling height. The leaner one of those two wears black, and the other a dark green.

"They say he's going to bind her to the lands and offer her up as queen," hisses the one in green.

It's me.

They're talking about me.

I squat down, toying with several books as if I'm completely focused upon them, but every inch of me stiffens.

"If the bastard does that," says the second man, "then the city will rise. She's not one of us. She's not—"

"Neither is he," the green cloak points out.

But it's the taller man who cuts them short. "These are the types of words...." He pauses, and then waves his hand in the air. Gold sparks form out of nowhere, widening into a circle around them, and then, even though I can see their mouths moving, I can't hear what they're saying.

A ward.

But if there's one I learned in my mother's court, it's how to slip through one.

Splaying my palm against the floor, I let my conscious crawl across the floor and slip beneath the edges of the ward. If I stay as small and quiet as a mouse, they won't even notice me. It's not the sort of thing I'd try with someone of Thiago's power—he'd sense me for sure—but the throb of power around these three doesn't push at the skin, the way Thiago's does.

The sudden crack of words is almost startling

"...doesn't have the power to bind the lands," murmurs the tall man. "My contacts in Asturia tell me she's pathetically underwhelming. Can barely light a hearth. Be patient. This game is not over yet."

"And if she does manage it?" says a cold, hard voice that I think belongs to the black cloak.

"There are pieces in play. Keep your mouths quiet until Elms Day. We have a plan that shall remove this blight from the throne forever."

Silence falls as they both stare at him.

"He's protected," one of them says slowly.

"Not for long," says the taller man. "The bastard may rule the dark, but he's not the only dangerous fae in the city. And I have... friends who would very much like to pay him back for past endeavors. We can't counter his magic, but maybe we don't need to?"

They start toward me and I realize I'm not very well-hidden down here.

I turn and slam into a tall, hard body.

Before I can suck in a sharp breath, a tattooed finger presses against my lips, and a hooded stranger pushes me against the shelf.

Where did he come from?

A hand claps over mine as I reach for the knife at my hip, and the pressure of his finger intensifies. The shiver of magic slipping over my skin feels like cool water, rather than the molten glide of honey that reminds me of Thiago's magic, but he's clearly laying a veil over me.

Fine. I fall into stillness. I can be quiet. Besides, this is not the place for a sudden struggle, and I suspect he's not involved with the trio of conspirators.

The man in the green cloak sweeps past, tossing his hood back as he slips out the door of the bookshop. Blond, handsome in a foppish way. He doesn't even glance at us. The others have vanished, but that doesn't mean they're not still here. Glamor and illusions are gifts that many fae wield, though few of them are quite as skilled as Thiago.

The stranger is skilled.

The fae in the green cloak should have noticed us. We're right *there*.

My breath catches. Thiago's only mentioned one other male who might be able to veil like this. I take a closer look at him as he slips his hood back.

Long, silky-black hair gathers into a half-knot at the back of his head, and intense eyes as black as the heart of night itself return my stare. There's a hint of the Danesh Su about his face—those eyes and cheekbones that could cut like a knife—but it's the tattoos that crawl up his throat that capture my attention.

A blood moon, glowing red for a second, before it fades into whorls of black ink.

Erlking's hairy cock....

"The Prince of Shadows sends his regards," the stranger purrs, lifting his finger from my lips.

CHAPTER 7

I try for the knife again, and the bastard simply takes it off me.

"Ah, ah, ah," he chides, balancing the tip of it on his finger before he flips it, and then presents the handle to me. "If I wanted you dead, Princess, then you wouldn't have seen me at all."

True. It stills a few of my nerves. Not all of them, though.

"How did you know who I was?" I can still see my fake red hair tangling over my shoulders.

The Prince of Shadows twists his hands together in front of his forehead, then slowly parts them. A golden eye appears. A tattoo of pure magic, not ink. "Long ago, I traded my soul for the ability to see through magic itself."

Very mysterious. Also, very hospitable of him to answer. "I'd swoon, but my husband has inured me against charming strangers. He also lies through his teeth when I try to corner him on a topic. "Theron himself, I presume?"

"Such a name might exist." He produces the Sorrow's

Tear, brushing the red-black petals against his lips. "I received your husband's calling card."

"My husband is waiting for me at the Wayfarer, and you're probably lucky he's unaware you've cornered me here."

Where in the Darkness is Finn?

Theron smiles, as if I'm blundering down the path he wants me to take. *Oh, look at me, a mysterious charming scoundrel who wouldn't dream of sticking a knife in someone's heart.*

"Ah, Princess." He brushes the rose against *my* lips. "I'm not afraid of your husband. You're in my territory now."

I bat the rose aside. "Touch me again with that rose and I'll shove it up your ass, stalk first."

"Strange. You seemed to enjoy it earlier."

So he's been watching us. "My husband has the right to touch me. You don't."

He holds the rose up in surrender, a smile on his lips.

"As enjoyable as this is," I continue, "you're not here to try and charm me."

"You're right. I'm not. What does he want?" Despite the earlier smile, there's a dangerous look in his eyes.

"Why don't you ask him?"

"Because he's being watched."

I run the tip of my tongue over my teeth. "By whom?"

"Friends," he replies. "Not friends."

"This… Gray Guild."

Silence. Theron stares at me for a long moment. And I realize there's no reason to suspect he's not involved in this.

The guilds rule the city. They rose to power during

Queen Araya's reign and Thiago allows them to remain, for it gives the people of the city a voice. It also saves him from having to negotiate petty little treaties and grievances.

As long as the guilds remain in their place, there's no reason to strike them down.

But Theron is the head of his own guild.

"Trouble comes," he murmurs. "But which side of the blade will it come from?"

"If trouble comes, then Eris is going to tear this city apart to snuff it out," I point out. "And she will remember who stood at my husband's side. And who did not."

"Then consider this a gift, freely offered. The guilds meet once a month in public, but there are... certain members who meet privately too. Two months ago, a fae lord appeared in the midst of their gathering offering them assistance in their cause."

"To overthrow my husband." Two months ago.... Right about the time those pamphlets started circulating. I knew Mother was somehow involved in this. But who would she send? "What did he offer?"

"Gold," Theron replies bluntly. "Information. And warriors."

"And how much did he offer you?"

Theron arches a brow. "Enough gold to drown myself and all the souls of this city."

"I believe my husband said he'd match it if you came to him."

He glances at the rings on his fingers. "I'm not merely interested in gold. This city is my home. And every time I glance into the waters, I see darkness coming. A storm is on the horizon, Princess. Do I care who rules the kingdom?

Not particularly. But the storm? I wake from dreams where bodies flood the streets on a tide of water, and I see my own men and women there, pale and bloated. I see a city in swampy ruins. I see children crying for their parents as they wade through receding waters, and parents crying for their children."

There's always a price for gaining the ability to See through secrets and lies, because sometimes you start to see the future too.

Water. And a storm. My mother has fae who can channel water, but a storm itself? They're aggressive and unruly and even the best Stormchaser can only direct a storm for a mile or two before it spins out of control.

"And after the water breaks the city, night falls. But this time, it doesn't lift."

Our eyes meet.

The curse that gnaws at the north of Evernight has been gaining ground inch by inch for centuries, but it's still contained to the north.

Evernight. Or *ever* night.

How is my mother involved in this?

"But every dream I have," he continues, "circles back to one moment. You. You walk through water as high as your waist and it parts. The water recedes. The city repairs itself. Corpses jerk to their feet and vomit water from their lungs, returning to life. Night falls and there you are, glowing like a beacon in the darkness. Glowing so bright that you become the sun. Dawn breaks over you."

A shiver runs through me. "I don't have the power to do any of that."

"As I said, I don't care who rules the city. But I care *for* the city. And there's a chance you can save the city."

Drawing his hood up over his face, he nods to me. "The Gray Guild will meet on Elms Day to carry out their attack. I don't know where they meet, but I will know. And I will send word."

"Wait!" I grab his arm as he turns to go. "There is something else I must ask."

One of his brow's arches.

I consider how best to word it. "Thiago's friend has been cursed, and it's reputed that you have a hexbreaker among your... crew."

Instant suspicion. "I have no hexbreaker."

As expected. Curses and hexes originated in Unseelie. To suggest the possibility of one means there are unseelie in this city who shouldn't be here.

"If you had a hexbreaker who could break his curse, then we would be *very* grateful," I stress.

"Grateful doesn't fill my coffers."

I pluck the Sorrow flower from his fingers. "Roses won't earn you a moment of her time. But this might."

"What makes you think I wish for a moment of her time?"

The fact that I don't even need to say Eris's name.

"You want her attention," I point out, "or you wouldn't keep stealing into her rooms."

His eyes narrow. "I'll... consider it. Tell her I don't have a hundred horses, but... maybe I won't need them." He tugs the book from the shelf behind me—the one I was looking at—and examines the cover. "You have an interest in old myth."

"I like history."

"Crowns too, by the sound of it."

Clearly, he's been watching and listening ever since I

entered the shop. "Unfortunately for my interests, they don't seem to have what I want here—"

"Nobody will have what you're looking for." An enigmatic smile crosses his face. "After the wars, the Seelie queens decided the information you're searching for is too dangerous to be allowed to fall into the wrong hands. They tore through their kingdoms and burned every book that might hold details of the Old Ones, and the relics used against them."

He really *has* been watching me.

My heart sinks.

Why would they do such a thing?

"All except one queen." His voice drops as he realizes he's caught my attention. "Lucidia of Ravenal collected books as though they were weapons. She gathered every treatise on myth that could be found within her kingdom and claimed to have burned them, but rumor suggests the old bitch kept them for herself. Her library at Ravenspire is closed to all but the royal family, and some say the reason for that is because she didn't want the other kingdoms to know what she held."

"Some say?"

"There's not a single locked door on this entire continent that is able to hold me out." He replaces the book on the shelf beside my head. "They won't let you in, but let me assure you…. There's only one place where you may find what you're looking for, and that's within the library at Ravenspire." He winks. "And now I think I've been more than generous with my information."

The shop door slams open, and I jerk my head in that direction, but it's only a scowling hob, carrying too many parcels in his arms.

"Thank—"

When I glance back, the assassin prince is gone.

"You," I say softly.

I PLACE THE SORROW ROSE ON THE MIDDLE OF THE COUNCIL table.

Eris was leaning back in repose, but now she slams forward, all four feet of her chair hitting the ground. "That motherfucker." Her dark eyes narrow on me. "Where did you get that from?"

Thiago prowls around the table. "I needed to talk to the Prince of Shadows—"

"You, *what?*" Eris stabs her knife through the rose. "You went to see him? When? How many guards did you take?"

"Just one," Finn says, raising his hand.

A demonic light comes to life in her eyes. "What did he say?"

I tell them everything.

The Gray Guild. The storm coming. Ravenal. My mother's plot.

But it's the comment about one hundred horses that draws the most interest.

"My, my," Thalia says, trying to hide her smile. "Someone's confident."

"I'm going to tear that sneaky little bastard apart with my bare hands," Eris growls. She wrenches her knife out of the table, and shoves to her feet.

"That sneaky little bastard might be the only way we're

going to break Lysander's curse," Thiago calls as she's halfway to the door.

Eris freezes. "Argh!"

She throws another knife at the door and it lands with a thunk.

"Fine." Swinging around, she hauls her chair back out and drops into it. "I'll murder him after his hexbreaker unwinds Lysander's curse. And only because it would break Baylor's heart."

I hold my hands out. "Does someone want to tell me what one hundred horses have to do with all of this?"

Thalia's still smiling. "Eris—"

"Not another word," Eris growls out.

"You can only blame yourself." Thalia can't hide her amusement. "How many horses do you own by now?"

"Close to fifteen hundred," Finn says in a cool voice. "She sold several herds."

"Didn't realize you were counting." There's something in Thiago's voice that draws my attention.

I glance between him, Finn and Eris.

"Eris breeds horses?"

Thalia glides around the table, capturing Eris's shoulders in her hands as she leans down and gives her a kiss on the cheek. "Permission, E?"

Eris groans, but there's a nod there too.

"Two centuries ago, a certain visiting fae prince set his sights on Eris," Thalia says. "No matter how much she rebuffed him, it only stirred his interest. He set out to woo her and he was incredibly persistent."

"Thiago wouldn't let me kill him," Eris growls.

"He was here to sign a political alliance," Thiago points

out. "I thought sending his head home in a box would send the wrong kind of message."

"To end the matter, she set him a challenge...." Thalia continues. "If he met her over the edge of a blade and defeated her, then she would become his wife. If she beat him, then she would take one hundred of his finest horses. She said she could only ever submit to a male who was powerful enough to beat her."

"Oh." I'm starting to see how this went wrong.

There's no doubt in my mind that she destroyed him. But that's the kind of tale that grows in the telling. And there are thousands of arrogant male warriors out there who must now see her as the ultimate challenge.

"That was only the start," Baylor breaks his silence. "How many males have come?"

"Seeking the hand of our fair Eris?" Thalia muses. "Dozens. It's been a while since the last one though. Thirty years, maybe? I think she broke every bone in his arm, and that's put a few of them off."

Eris slides her hand over her face. "I shouldn't have said it. I was desperate. How was I to know every fae male in the southern alliance would see it as a personal fucking challenge?"

"There, there," Thalia says, massaging her shoulders. "It weeds out those who know they can't beat you. And if you're lucky, one day a prince will stride through those doors and hold his own. You never know."

"No one is going to hold their own against her," Finn's voice sounds like gravel, "because that implies that someone has to beat her in order to capture her interest. Males like that aren't interested in Eris. All they see is the glory and the pride involved in crushing her spirit. That's what they're interested in, and frankly, if there *is* someone out there who's good enough to take her sword off her, then I'm going to pick it up and drive it straight through his fucking throat."

Eris stares at him incredulously.

"What?" he demands.

"This is the one time I actually agree with you." She frowns. "It feels wrong to even say that."

Finn shrugs. "Not that you need me to pick up your sword." He cracks his knuckles. "Let me know when Lysander's hex is broken. I might help you throw that prick off the tower."

Eris considers it, then reaches over and bumps her fist against his. "It's a deal."

"No," Thiago says, pointing at her. Then he turns to Finn. "No. I don't want to start a bloody vendetta against an assassin's guild. Besides, we might need him on our side come Elms Day."

"I'll talk to Vi," Thalia promises. "Once I have a description of the fae she saw, I might be able to work out who they are. I'll send my little birds out into the street and see if they can hear something interesting."

She means that literally, for there are numerous birds up in the aerie that belong to her. She's spent centuries cultivating the demi-fey of the city, and now she has hundreds of them that will ride one of her sparrows into the city and report back to her, in exchange for milk and honey.

The fae ignore the demi-fey, because they're capricious and so difficult to keep focused that they make it seem easier to corral cats. But if there's one thing the demi-fey are good at, it's remembering something word for word, and if you actually *can* get them to communicate with you, they're surprisingly effective.

Thoughts brew in Thiago's eyes. "We need to get you inside the library at Ravenal."

"I think concentrating on this plot is more important."

"And Thalia will have information for us as soon as she can," Thiago counters, "but I'm not merely trying to assist your search. Ravenal lost its queen. I've sent missives to the crown princess, but she's been putting me off, and to be honest, I haven't turned my attention to our allies enough." He gives me a dangerous smile. "Your mother is waiting for a counterattack? Well, why not give it to her? Ravenal sits at her flanks, and she murdered their queen. If I can give the crown princess a reason to march her armies north, then we might be able to crush Asturia between us. I think it's time we sent word to Kyrian and Lucere and see if they want to crush a queen."

CHAPTER 8

The towers of Ravenspire loom ahead of us as we ride from the Hallow we arrived at mere minutes ago.

Nervous energy runs through me.

Queen Lucidia ruled over Ravenal with a miserly hand for centuries, and I see the effects of that in the countryside as I ride past. The fae we pass wear tattered homespun, and everything is much-mended—though there are smiles on the faces of the children, and they run alongside our horses for miles, waving brightly colored ribbons.

Now that she's dead, her eldest great-granddaughter, Lucere, has made a claim for the throne, and she's well-backed by her brother, the Prince of Ravens.

Not every member of the Ravenal royal family agrees with that choice, but the Prince of Ravens holds the military and if he backs Lucere, there's little the others can do about it.

"Do you think Princess Lucere will hold me accountable for her great-grandmother's death?" I murmur as I ride beside Thiago.

Ravenspire looms over the forest, and a single watchfire in the main garrison looks like an eye watching us as we approach.

He reaches out and squeezes my hand. "She knows you have nothing to do with your mother. Adaia killed Queen Lucere, and it is Asturia who will bear the malice for that act. Not you, Vi. You cannot take on your mother's sins."

The Prince of Ravens waits at the balcony as we ride into the courtyard, fae light glittering over the obsidian scales carved into his tunic. Glossy black feathers rain from his shoulders, though I can't quite see whether they're wings or a cloak.

"Has to be a cloak," I mutter.

None of the seelie would ever align himself with an unseelie trait.

"It is a cloak," Thalia says. There was some argument over whether she should stay in Ceres or not, but they left Baylor in charge. By the time we return, her little spies should have enough information for us. "Though there's rumor Corvin bears Lucidia's gift in his blood. They say he owns the ability to both see through the eyes of his ravens and shift shapes. Eris always threatens to put an arrow through any ravens she sees."

Beside him stands his sister, Princess Lucere, who is angling to replace the title with Queen. My breath catches when I see her gown. It's pure white, carved of tiny white scales that blink in the night. Gold netting is woven through her blond hair, and the way she's standing makes the light fall on her just so....

Beside Corvin's pure black, she's a glowing moon.

"Ah," mutters Eris. "There's the bitch herself."

"White." Thalia *tsks* under her breath. "Always wearing white. Who does she think she is? A maiden of Maia?"

"You're wearing white."

"That's because I look good in white," Thalia replies.

I gather my mare's reins. "We don't like the princess of Ravenal?"

Eris's eyes thin. "Shall we just say that ravens aren't the only creatures in the vicinity I've threatened to put an arrow through."

I share a glance with Thalia, but though she goes to speak, she clearly thinks better of it.

"Later," she promises with a nod toward our audience.

"Welcome to our friends from Evernight," Lucere calls. She gestures to her retainers, who leap forward to take our horses. "Please come. We have refreshments prepared. And Prince Kyrian is already arrived. He will be joining us shortly."

Thiago makes a great show of moving to lift me down.

"I can do it myself, you know?"

His hands come to rest upon my waist, and there's a twinkle in his eyes. "Maybe I just enjoy touching you?"

He lifts me down easily, and as the toes of my slippers touch the ground, I rest my hands on his shoulders.

"I think you're going out of your way to play the gallant."

He tucks my hand through the curve of his arm as he turns to face the prince and princess of Ravenal. "Maybe I'm merely enjoying the fact I no longer have to hide my affection for you when we're in public."

119

Nobody's fooling anybody.

He'd said Ravenal would be a snake pit, so I let him play the surly, protective overlord. "Would you like me to simper at you?"

He laughs under his breath. "What's that going to cost me?"

"Everything."

"You already have everything I own. My lands. My heart. My soul."

Very smooth.

"Prince Thiago," Prince Corvin greets, though he waits for us the climb the stairs—like supplicants. "I see you've made good time through the Hallow. They're so unpredictable these days."

"Corvin," Thiago replies with the tilt of his head. "My condolences on the loss of your great-grandmother."

The Prince of Ravens's smile thins. "She is with Kato now. His judgement shall allow her to pass onto the Bright Lands. Or not."

"And the Princess of Asturia," Corvin says, his dark eyes glittering as he takes my hand from Thiago's arm and lifts it to his lips. "Beautiful enough to bring two countries to war and an entire Alliance to the brink of shattering."

I tug my fingers from his hand with the faintest arch of my brow. "If you knew my mother at all, you would understand I was merely the pawn she used to give herself an excuse to march."

"And she is the Princess of Evernight now," Thiago corrects with a dangerous edge to his voice as he replaces my hand on his forearm. "You would do well to remember that."

"Either way, my beloved great-grandmother is dead, and Ravenal stands without its queen. We *do* remember that, Prince Thiago."

His sister, Lucere, claps her hands as if she wishes to draw attention to herself. "Ah, but Corvin.... Great-grandmother would have chided your manners. These are our guests, and we have given them poor welcome."

Stepping forward, she rests her hands on Thiago's shoulders and reaches up to brush a kiss to his cheek that manages to completely pretend I don't exist. "It's been too long, Thiago. You are most welcome here. And you always will be."

I look at Eris.

Did she just—?

Eris rubs her mouth and then turns the gesture into a finger drawn sharply across her throat. She, at least, agrees.

"Thank you," he says, lifting my hand. "Iskvien and I are most thrilled to partake of your hospitality."

He turns to me, and now I have to pretend the bitch didn't just practically invite him into her chambers.

"Princess Lucere." I smile and nod, but I don't bow.

She's not a queen yet.

"Princess Iskvien," she replies. "As lovely as you were the first time I laid eyes upon you."

"Thank you," I manage to say, though I cannot recall her. At all.

I hate these moments.

She snaps her fingers to the servants. "Bring wine and set the feast. We have to celebrate the first appearance of the mighty Prince of Evernight to humble Ravenal." She graces Thiago with another smile that promises wicked delights. "If you would follow me."

I exchange a glance with Thiago as we follow them inside the Great Hall.

We'd hoped for allies here, but it's clear tension exists.

Ravenal's always been the poorest of the kingdoms, though some say Lucidia had more of a hand in that than any other. There's gold enough in the treasury, and from the decadence of the jewels that glitter on Lucere's and Corvin's fingers, they've managed to unlock the mighty vault.

But the castle stands in stark repair, and though the great hall has been swept, with bunches of feathers and flowers strewn in every corner, a close look reveals the threadbare quality of the tapestries on the wall.

"Let us talk," Thiago says as they offer us wine.

Corvin raises a goblet of wine to his lips with a vapid smile. "Later. Tonight is a night for dancing."

"Your Highness." Lucere sets her wineglass on the stand and shoots Thiago a coy look as she holds out her hand. "I would be most honored if you would assist me in opening the celebrations."

Bitch.

The muscle beneath my hand tenses as if Thiago agrees with me.

And while the insult is clear, I've been playing these games for far too long.

"Go and dance with her," I say, shooting him a light smile. "I plan on stealing you all for myself for the rest of the night, so it will do the court good to see two monarchs playing nicely."

There's a light in his eyes that tells me he understands perfectly. "As you wish."

And then he stands and slips through the crowd toward her with a dangerous grace, and I enjoy the view for several seconds before I realize I'm not the only one doing so.

Princess Lucere watches him with hungry eyes, her hand outstretched toward him.

I turn to Eris with a bright smile. "More wine? Please, more wine?"

She leans over my shoulder and fills my glass. "I can make sure nobody ever finds the body."

When we first met, I was certain Eris hated me, but I've started to understand who she is. And I earned her loyalty. If I say the word, Eris will head out into the forest with a shovel.

"Not yet." My cheeks ache from smiling. "We're running out of allies."

Eris snorts as she watches Thiago take Lucere in his arms. "We can find more."

We're not the only ones here to celebrate.

Prince Kyrian of the Kingdom of Stormlight is Thiago's closest ally, though the last time we met, he thought I'd betrayed my husband. He was the only ruler to walk away from the Queensmoot unscathed, considering he refused to watch my mother attempt to execute Thiago.

I'm a little nervous as the prince saunters down the stairs into the throne room, surrounded by several female warriors dressed in red. A leather thong binds half his hair back off his face, though his green eyes lock on me with an intensity that threatens to set my undergarments on fire.

Or no, not on me.

Behind me.

I suddenly feel like I'm standing between a cat and its prey. A glance over my shoulder reveals Thalia, glaring back at him mutinously.

"Thiago," Kyrian calls, greeting him with clasped hands. "You survived."

"You doubted." There's a hint of reproof in my husband's voice, though he returns the swift embrace.

Kyrian turns that dangerous stare upon me. "It's not so much your wife I doubted, so much as the nature of true love."

I snort. "Perhaps if you'd stayed to watch, you might have learned a thing or two about love."

A slight narrowing of his eyes reveals that this is a point to me.

"You should have stayed," Thiago muses, "if only to see the look on Adaia's face when Vi defied her."

"What's that noise?" I ask.

We all fall silent.

The ticking continues and Kyrian looks down in surprise, before tugging a golden compass from his pocket. When he flips the lid open, the arrow is flickering between east and west, quivering as if some magnetic force draws it.

It finally comes to a halt.

And it's pointing directly at Thalia.

Kyrian slowly looks up, his other hand falling to the hilt of his sword. "You're one of the saltkissed?"

"So lovely to see you again, Prince Kyrian," Thalia

says, with a faint curve to her lips. "I can still hear the sweet ringing compliments you threw my way the last time we dined. And yes, my father was of the sea."

"I knew there was a reason I disliked you."

"What's wrong?" Thalia demands, setting her hands on her hips. "Are you worried I'm going to ensorcel your heart? I've heard it's too late for that. You gave it away, didn't you? And you no longer have one."

Kyrian takes a step toward her, his nostrils flaring, but Thiago stops him with one firm hand in the center of his chest.

"That's my cousin," he reminds the prince.

Kyrian looks like he doesn't give a damn. He looks like he wants to shove Thiago out of his way and then physically cast Thalia out of the window. Their eyes meet, and I can see both of them battling their monumental pride.

It's Kyrian who gives way first, his lips thinning as he turns to the ballroom. "I think I need a drink."

"That's right," Thalia declares, with a vicious smile. "Run. The way you did last time."

Kyrian stiffens, clearly thinks about answering, and then keeps walking.

"You said you argued," Thiago growls at his cousin. "This doesn't look like a mere argument to me."

Thalia's smile slips, and then she shrugs her shoulder. "You don't need to know everything. Suffice it to say, Prince Kyrian and I have been at odds from the moment we met." She straightens the lapel on Thiago's coat and gives him a wink. "It doesn't mean he doesn't want to fuck me."

"Mother of Night. *Thalia*."

"What?" She gives him big, innocent eyes.

Thiago shakes his head and turns to follow Kyrian. "I need something to drink too."

Thalia simply laughs.

THERE'S DRINKING AND DANCING, OF COURSE, AND LUCERE can barely hide her thrill at having a new dance partner. Kyrian sweeps her around the clearing in vigorous circles, though his smile remains cool.

He dances well though. There's an athletic sort of grace to him that begs you to imagine him aboard a pirate ship, and while Lucere might beam in his arms, it's quite clear he's controlling every move of the dance.

A soft sigh echoes beside me. "It's such a shame that such a delicious body houses such an unruly spirit." Thalia throws back her glass of wine, before she catches me watching her and rolls her eyes.

"Hmm." I hadn't missed the hot glare the pair of them had shared. "There's a story there. And not merely an argument."

"No story."

I poke her in the ribs. "Oh, no. You're not going to get away so lightly. You know all my secrets, and yet I've never heard you mention Kyrian's name."

"Because there's no reason to mention it."

"Liar. There's a reason he watches you like a scalded cat lashing its tail. And you were baiting him."

"Fine." Thalia sighs. "Kyrian and I have met. Numerous times, though Thiago tends to keep us apart as often as he can these days. Suffice it to say that one of the saltkissed ensorcelled him. He was so enamored, he was poised to marry the girl before he woke to find her above him with a knife, intent on carving his heart out of his chest. They fought and she escaped to the seas, but not before he learned that she'd never truly loved him.

"She'd been sent by her father to seduce him and then assassinate him, and, fool that he is, he tripped over his own feet the second he heard her sing." Thalia rolls her eyes. "So now he despises the saltkissed, and spends the storm season hunting the seas for Meriana. That compass he has? It's a magical device he stole that can find anything in the world. The bearer just has to wish for it, and the compass needle will point directly toward it."

"It was pointing at you."

Thalia pokes me back. "That's because he uses it to hunt the saltkissed, and there's enough salt in my blood to make me flare like a beacon whenever it's around me. I had to hide what I was every time we met. But I'm done hiding."

"That still doesn't explain why you're so determined to bait him," I tease.

"That's because he's an arrogant, insufferable fool. One saltkissed woman does him wrong, and now he's determined to hunt the entire race? That's sheer idiocy speaking."

"And it has absolutely nothing to do with the fact he's as handsome as the Horned One."

"Princess or no princess, I will plunge you into the wine barrel head first," she threatens, "if you keep making such inane comments."

Someone's touchy.

"Besides," she sniffs, gesturing an hourglass shape in

the air, "as pretty as he is, he doesn't deserve to get his hands on *this*."

Every inch of her is perfection, and she knows it.

The fae are physically inclined to be tall and lean as a race, but Thalia owns an abundance of curves she clearly inherited from her saltkissed brethren. She crosses the line between curvy and voluptuous, and *every* male in the entire gathering has noticed.

That might have something to do with the gown she's wearing. It's virginal white, though there's nothing virginal about the plunging neckline that sits just off her collarbone. Billowing fabric flares from her shoulders, gathering again around her wrists, and leaving her upper arms bare. I don't know what her dressmaker has done to her skirts, but they drape in the center where a silver band bedecked in pretty diamonds emphasizes the curve of her waist.

Lucere sparkles like the moon in her white gown, but she pales in comparison to Thalia. I don't know if my friend knew Lucere would be in white, but I suspect she did.

When it comes to wardrobe decisions, nothing Thalia wears is left to choice.

Nothing I wear is either, since she's been in charge of my wardrobe the second she saw me wearing "some kind of loose Asturian handkerchief that does nothing for my shape". She'd spent fifteen minutes lecturing me about how I'm the Princess of Evernight now, and I represent their kingdom.

I gave up, told her she could do what she liked to my wardrobe, and the very next day I walked into my dressing chambers and discovered rows of silk and velvet she must have already had prepared for me.

I might have fought more for my own sense of style, if Thiago hadn't taken one look at me the second I walked downstairs and dropped his spoon in his porridge, sending a wave of mushy oats directly into Finn's face.

"Fine," I agree. "Kyrian doesn't deserve to touch so much as the hem of your skirt, but that doesn't explain why you're still staring at him...."

Thalia's smile holds a hint of the wolf in it, and it's all Thiago. "Just because he doesn't deserve to touch me, doesn't mean he doesn't want to," she purrs, handing me her empty wineglass. "Excuse me, I'm going to go dance."

"He's not going to dance with you."

"And he's not going to. You." She points at a nearby blond who snaps to attention so swiftly, he spills wine all over his friend. "Dance with me."

"WHAT ARE WE DOING?" THIAGO PURRS, DRAPING HIS ARMS around me from behind.

I'm still watching the dance floor, though I sensed him swimming through the tide of courtiers toward me like a hungry shark. "Admiring your cousin." I can't help laughing. "She's absolutely merciless."

Thalia's also danced with every handsome fae male in the vicinity, leaving a trail of lovesick swains behind her.

So far she's pointedly ignored Kyrian, but he noticed her the second she graced the dance floor. At first it was just a scowl. And then it devolved to red-hot glares. And now I swear he's grinding his teeth through the fake smile he wears.

Neither of them will concede the dance floor, though Kyrian's effortless grace seems to be a little less effortless, and he's practically ignoring the woman in his arms.

Because Thalia can *dance*.

And if she had every male glancing at her earlier, now she has them tripping over their own feet.

"I knew I shouldn't have brought her."

I lean back into his embrace. "No, no, I'm enjoying it."

"You would." He smacks my bottom.

"Anything to see my nemesis humbled."

"He's an ally," Thiago points out.

"He's arrogant. And he hates me."

Stillness leeches through my husband. "It's not as simple as that. Come on, let's dance."

I turn and slip my arms around me as he sends us whirling into the dancers. I love these moments. Having my arms around him, body to body and knowing it will lead elsewhere if I play my cards right. "You were saying?"

Thiago must have inherited some of Thalia's grace, because he moves lightly for such a tall man. Clasping my left wrist, he spins me under his arm. "Kyrian doesn't hate you. But there are similarities between us. He was with me the night I met you, and the second I saw you I knew you were the one Maia had made me for. But you were my enemy's daughter. In his eyes, I might as well have been ensorcelled."

"Well, you weren't."

"What Meriana did to him was cruel," Thiago says,

sweeping me in circles. "Ensorcellment isn't an easy spell to break. Every day he woke, he could feel it gnawing at him. He could barely eat or drink, and couldn't sleep. He spent years trying to break her hold over him." Thiago gives me a long look. "I saw what it did to him, Vi. I've seen torture before, and none of them looked as desperate as he did. I was there to help him pull through it and he's never forgotten it. He doesn't want the same thing to happen to me. Give him some grace. Let him come to terms with the fact your love is true."

I sigh. "You're making me feel sorry for him."

"I will always defend you, if he doesn't watch his tongue," he says, shooting a glance across the room. "But I understand where it's coming from."

Tension suddenly sweeps through him. I follow his gaze to see what's caught his attention and realize the dance is changing.

The music becomes a sweeping reel, and one glimpse toward the musicians shows Lucere there. No doubt she wants to force me and Thiago apart, but she didn't count on who else was dancing.

Thiago and I are forced to change partners. I arrive in the arms of a redhead, and then several beats later, I'm spinning toward a blond.

Thalia and Kyrian whirl toward each other with the inevitability of a ship facing an iceberg.

There's a second where the two of them spin toward the next partner and realize they're facing each other.

Both of them freeze.

Without another word, Kyrian stalks away, leaving her standing there behind him.

It could have been rejection, but Thalia throws back her

head and gives a sultry laugh, before she summons a redhead with a crook of her finger.

She claims it as victory instead.

I try to roll my eyes at Thiago, but find him dancing with the crown princess of Ravenal, and suddenly the music is changing again, becoming smooth and gentle. No more changing of partners.

Well played, Lucere.

"Your Highness?" asks the blond, offering to continue.

"Thank you." I don't bother with a smile. "But I think I'm going to get some wine."

CHAPTER 9

"They make a stunning couple," says a voice from behind me. "A ray of light gleaming beneath the stars, and a dark lord garbed in strict black. One can almost imagine a painting done thusly."

I almost slosh my wine over my hand. *Curse it.* "Prince Corvin, do you dabble with paints?"

Corvin settles at my side, his eyes upon his sister and my husband. "No. Though I have an appreciation for beauty."

Eris appears out of nowhere. "That's just you looking in the mirror, Corvin."

"Ah, the sweet Eris." Corvin leans his shoulder against the arch we're standing beneath. "As diplomatic as ever."

"You want to fight? Then I'll go get my blade," she says. "You want to fuck? Then just say it plainly. I need a good laugh. And I don't pretend to be anything other than what I am."

Their eyes meet.

And Corvin smiles. "I forget how refreshing you are. It's like a glass of icy water dashed into one's face."

"And you're as smooth as Finn's ass. You lie through your teeth, flirt with one woman even while your eyes are watching another, and can't be trusted an inch."

"And yet, I'm not the one who betrayed his oath." Corvin surveys the dance floor as he sips his wine. "It's rather bold of Thiago to stroll back in here with a wife on one arm as if nothing ever happened."

I straighten. "Excuse me?"

"She speaks," he taunts.

But it's Eris he should be watching, because she's glaring murder at him. "Don't listen to a word he says."

Corvin holds his hands up in innocence. "It's not as though I'm lying, am I?"

Eris shuts her mouth.

What, by the Erlking's cock, is he talking about? "Perhaps you *should* explain."

"Didn't you know there was once talk my sister would marry your husband?" He smiles pleasantly and tips the wine to his lips as he gestures to the dance floor. "Negotiations had begun, and it had been arranged for the two of them to meet at the Queensmoot almost... oh, thirteen years ago, wasn't it? Except when my sweet sister Lucere arrived at the Queensmoot, he was already dancing with another and he couldn't tear his eyes from the woman in his arms."

Me.

"Lucere shouldn't have presumed the deal was done," Eris growls. "They were only to meet. Thiago never agreed to anything more."

It's real?

"She's hated you ever since, did you know?" Corvin says quite pleasantly. "She thinks you stole him from her." Leaning closer, he whispers in my ear, "So I wouldn't drink anything Lucere gives you tonight, my sweet. Just in case."

I don't drink anything that isn't poured in front of me, courtesy of the drugged wine my mother would give me before she cursed me. "I wasn't planning to."

His smile seems a little satisfied. Eris is right. This bastard likes to play games.

But we need his alliance. "I'm sorry for your great-grandmother's death. My mother betrayed us all."

"Oh, I'm not." He tosses a coin in one hand, and I have no idea where he got it from. "Nor is anyone else here in Ravenal. The old bitch starved us for years, and now we can finally feast. She deserved to die."

I can see the look on Lucidia's face as the bane sprang upon her from behind, his jaws clamping over the back of her head as he crushed her skull. "Not like that, she didn't."

Corvin's smile holds a wealth of meaning. "Surely the daughter of Queen Adaia isn't showing her enemy mercy?"

"Perhaps she's a changeling stolen from her cradle?" I tense as a voice purrs over my skin from behind. "For a true daughter of Adaia would slaver for even the tiniest hint of blood in the water."

Lucere slinks toward me as though she's hunting me. I guess the dance is over.

"If you've ever been hunted by a bane, then you would know that I would wish such a fate upon no one."

"Are you having fun with my brother, Princess?" Innuendo drips from her voice.

"More fun, perhaps, than you." I glance to where my husband is muttering in Finn's ear.

Her smile shows teeth. "Thiago's just as... sophisticated as I recall."

My eyes narrow.

Thiago is many things, but sophisticated? Only when he's trying to hide who he truly is.

"If you knew him at all, then you would know the sophistication is merely a thin mantle he wears when in public. I prefer him in his darker aspect. Raw. Demanding. No longer playing at... sophistication."

Lucere's eyes narrow, but Corvin seems to choke on his wine, as if he's trying not to laugh.

"And as to my condolences," I turn back to Corvin, "I wasn't aware we were enemies. Thiago tells me Evernight has enjoyed a strong alliance with Ravenal for years."

The siblings exchange a glance.

"The Alliance of Light was created five hundred years ago," Lucere says, stealing a glass of wine from a passing servant's tray as if to prove *she's* not afraid to drink it. "Five hundred years is a long time, Princess. Ravenal is hungry. For too long we've been choked with a gilded leash, but now it's time to prove the kingdom deserves more than the scraps she's been fed."

"And now the Alliance is shattered," I reply, because this is the entire reason Thiago needed to come here tonight. "My mother betrayed us all, and now we find ourselves little islands in the night, forced to deal with threats from both within and without."

"Ravenal's borders are strong," Lucere counters. "And

Adaia's attention is north."

"Did you think my mother distracted with vengeance? Did you think her focus narrowed upon Evernight?" I step closer, capturing her hand as if we're friends. "Evernight is merely the key to the lock. It's the pretense she needed to shirk the mantle of the Alliance." I stroke my thumb across her wrist, my voice dropping. "My mother isn't interested in merely conquering one kingdom. In her dreams she sees herself ruling the southern half of the continent. The *entire* south. First she strikes at Evernight. If we fall, then she is free to turn her attention south. And although she despises the Prince of Tides, Stormhaven is a difficult beast to swallow. It's well-fortified out there in the Innesmuch Seas. To strike at Stormhaven and the Kingdom of Stormlight, she needs southern ports and a clear path to the sea.

"We all saw the Queen of Aska strike a deal with my mother. Queen Maren will abstain from interfering, and in return, my mother will leave Aska alone. Which leaves one kingdom between her and Stormhaven. If I were Ravenal, I would start to wonder how it would feel to have the Queen of Aska to the west and my mother to the north, without the knife of Evernight at her back to distract her." I let go of her hand. "If we fall, then Ravenal is next."

Lucere clutches her fist to her chest. "How strange then that Queen Adaia promises us peace if we abstain from interfering. We received a letter from her but days before you arrived. It's almost as if she knew you would come to beg for an alliance."

Of course, she did. My mother's no fool. Every move she makes is well-plotted. "If you trust your great-grandmother's murderer to stick to her word, then you're a fool."

Lucere sets her empty goblet of wine down with a clank. "Be careful who you call a fool, Princess. You are talking to a future queen. One who has much to thank the Queen of Asturia for."

And then she's gone in a whirl of skirts.

Prince Corvin smiles at me faintly. "There are some who say my dearest sister didn't even shed a single tear when we received news of great-grandmother's death. In fact, it's almost as if she... expected it."

Fair warning.

"I hope she enjoys her reign then. Because if Lucere expects my mother to concede to any of the demands she makes, then I think she'll find it... brief. If you'll excuse me?" I don't give him the chance to answer.

I'm the fool. I should have foreseen this. My mother knows we need allies, and while the night of the Queensmoot may not have all gone her way, she always has a second plan up her sleeve.

I stalk across the gathering, though I'm only halfway when I realize someone is swimming against the tide of fae in my path. A dark head appears, and then a set of familiar broad shoulders.

My husband's hot green eyes lock on my face. "A dance, my love?"

"Another one?" I tease as I accept his hand.

Music swirls around us as if the orchestra realizes the mood of the crowd and wants to stir more mischief.

"What did Corvin say?" he murmurs. "You looked like you were going to choke him on his own wine."

We can't speak of anything important here, with ears listening in on every side.

I smile sweetly. "He was just informing me about your

almost-betrothal to Lucere. You'll forgive me my shock, as I thought you would have mentioned such a thing before we arrived."

You promised there would be no more secrets.

Thiago's gaze cuts to Corvin. "I ought to pluck that bastard." His attention returns to me. "I didn't mention it because nothing came of it. And it wasn't a betrothal. Ravenal opened negotiations. I said I would discuss it with them at the next Queensmoot. Except I never got a chance, because the second I arrived, there you were, gowned in pure starlight. I couldn't look away from you then, and nothing has changed since that moment."

It eases something inside of me. "You should have warned me."

"I should have. But as far as I was concerned, there was nothing to warn you of. I honestly didn't think of it."

I stare at him. *Men.*

His grip tightens. "Don't tell me you're jealous?"

Maybe.

It's difficult to shake off years of neglect when you spent your entire childhood competing with your sister for a scrap of your mother's attention.

I don't want to be jealous, but the tight, burning feeling in my chest betrays me.

"You have no reason to be." His hand sweeps down my hip, his fingers becoming a little possessive. "You are mine, Vi. Now. Forever. Always. And I don't care who I have to fight to keep you in my arms."

I hate this. I hate the fact that no matter how many times he pledges his love to me, there's a little piece of my heart that feels as though I don't deserve to be loved. "I love you," I whisper.

Thiago blinks, and then he draws me closer, the look in his eyes growing heated. "Do you?" His breath stirs the silken strands of hair that are tucked behind my ear. "I can count the number of times I've heard those words from your lips on both hands."

"Really?" Surely, I've told him before.

"You used those words to say goodbye to me," he tells me starkly, and his fingers dig into my skin unconsciously. "You would say it before I had to return you to your mother, and then the next time I saw you, your eyes wouldn't even recognize me."

And he would have to earn my heart all over again.

The cage of my gown constricts me. "I hate her so much."

"As do I."

"They didn't believe me. I tried to convince them my mother will see us all to the Underworld, and they laughed. My mother has offered them peace."

He stills for a second before he sweeps me in another circle. I spin under his arm, and as I twirl our eyes meet, every single time.

Finally, the music slows. And so does he.

I float to a halt as Thiago takes me in his arms and then leans down and kisses me.

"Then we'll see what we can offer them in return," he purrs in my mind as we link.

"Come." He draws me through the doors, into the gardens beyond.

"Where are we going?"

But all he gives me is a dangerous smile as he lures me into the darkness.

CHAPTER 10

"Thiago!" I gasp as he pushes me against the garden wall. I steal a swift glance toward the bonfires in the center of the gardens. "Someone might see us."

Hot kisses score my throat, and then his hands are sliding through my hair. "I don't care if they do. You're my *wife*. I want all the world to know it."

Gods, the way he says things like this….

There's a part of me that still yearns to hide all the feelings that tremble within me. I love him. I will never stop loving him. But when you've spent years hiding your every emotion, it's instinct to keep such thoughts close to your heart, where no one can ever, ever know.

It takes conscious effort to shed the mantle I use to guard my heart.

Each and every fucking time.

Maybe one day it will be easier.

So I kiss him instead, yielding to his touch. Let them see. Let them all see. I have no further need to hide.

My fingers tangle in his shirt, and I tilt my head to give him better access to my throat.

"You are mine," he whispers, palms skimming beneath the silk and up my back. "And I am yours, and I want the whole cursed world to know it."

The flush of his power tingles all over my skin, his oath sliding over his tongue like honeyed mead and sinking into my flesh like a barb. His kiss *burns*, both with power and with promise. It whispers dirty little nothings in my ear, lets me imagine just how good this would feel if there was no material between us. Nothing but naked skin, nothing but the power of his muscled body pinning mine beneath him, burying me in silken sheets while he took and ravaged and....

He slips the gown from my shoulders, baring my breasts to the moonlight. Teeth graze my nipple, and then he's suckling it into his mouth.

I want him inside me.

I want what he promises.

Capturing a fistful of his hair, I draw his mouth to mine and bite his lower lip. "Then do it," I whisper. "Take me. Right here. Right now."

Fingers skate beneath my skirts, and he finds the golden chains that are woven around my thigh.

His eyes darken as he realizes I'm not wearing a thing beneath the silk, and a rough laugh escapes him. "Were you planning to seduce me?"

"Maybe." I throw my head back against the stones and bite my lip as his fingertips graze the slick skin between my thighs. Oh gods. Thirteen years of stealing my heart means he knows exactly what I like—while I'm still trying to work out his own little secrets.

My dark prince likes to be in control, though he'll cede it to me if I demand it. But sometimes I like the way he captures my wrists and presses me against the bed—or a wall. And I love the feel of his teeth in my skin, as if he wants to mark me.

"Maybe I just like knowing I have a little secret from the world," I whisper in his ear. "Maybe I like feeling that slickness between my thighs whenever you look at me, knowing I can have you whenever I want. Maybe I just want you to lift my skirts and fuck your way into me." I curl his hand around a fistful of fabric. "Just. Like. This."

"Mmm." His gaze darkens. "Are you wet, Vi? Have you been dreaming of what I'd do to you once I finally got you alone?"

I bite his lip. "All night."

Especially when I saw Lucere smiling at him.

It's one thing to know he'll never look her way, but the very idea she might try makes me want to stake my claim upon him. I'm feeling not at all myself tonight.

"Enough talking," I tell him.

His smile holds all manner of sins. "I like it when you're a little bit possessive."

Thiago shoves my skirts up, this thumb stroking between us. A delicious shiver works its way through me, but it's not what I want. If I give him a chance, he'll spend hours torturing me.

I just want him inside me.

The timing's better, and I've been drinking bitter nettle tea every day.

Capturing his face in both hands, I kiss him desperately, and I think he gets the idea, because his hand dips between us, but it's not me he's touching.

And then he steps forward, his hips wedging themselves between my thighs. One hand hooks under the curve of my ass as he lifts me and impales me with one smooth thrust, driving my back against the wall.

My fingers dig into his shoulders as my body is forced to welcome him. I'm dripping wet, and yet he's large enough that my body needs to accustom itself to him, and some part of me loves that fierce ache.

Mine.

He's mine, and no one will ever take him from me. I want to feel his possession. I want to wake tomorrow with my body aching and know that my first thought will be a memory of tonight.

Firelight flickers in the distance.

A myriad of shapes dance around it as the people of Ravenal seek to celebrate our arrival.

Anyone could see us.

But when I look up, Thiago's not watching them. He watches me, as if he wants to own every thought that races through my mind.

"Have I told you how beautiful you look tonight?" he breathes as he thrusts with ruthless intent within me. "You look like all the stars woven into one." His gaze dips to my breasts. "You look like you were made for me, and me alone."

"I was," I whisper.

His gaze jerks to mine.

"As you were made for me. Did Maia not show you my face? Did She not promise that we were meant for each other?"

A shudder runs through him.

I can sense the Darkness within him wanting to break free. He's always fought it, trying to cage his own nature.

"Harder," I whisper as the stones bruise my backs and hips. "Show me that we were made for each other."

And he does.

It's not sweet or gentle. This is need. This is a claim. *Mine,* says his body, and I surrender everything that I am, drinking at his mouth as he fucks his way in and out of me.

It's a battle to see who will break first.

I laugh as I squeeze my inner muscles, watching feral need ignite in his eyes. But then his teeth graze my nipple, and his hands grip my hips, and everything feels wickedly good.

I let him ride me beneath the moon, head thrown back and spine arched unabashedly. Firm fingers dig into my thighs, the corded muscle in his throat clenching as if he's getting close, before he throws his head back with a hiss.

I want him to lose it.

I want to have him wild and uncontrolled. I want his gasp. I want the little tremor that shivers through his abdomen when he comes. I want to see his white teeth sinking into his lower lip.

I want him undone.

Clenching my inner muscles around him, I work him until the point where I know he's about to lose it. And then I capture his face and kiss him.

It's sloppy and messy, and somehow, he sees it as his turn. Slipping from my body, he flips me onto my front on the grass, and then he's back, driving into me from behind.

"It was my turn!" I protest.

"I'll make it up to you," he promises, and then he

thrusts into me hard, fucking me from behind with my legs curled up beneath me.

Blessed Maia. I clutch the grass and his hand curls over mine, our fingers lacing together.

Each thrust slows, until he's grinding over something deep inside me.

"Vi." A hot gust of breath whispers against my cheek, and then his other hand wraps around my throat.

"Don't stop! Don't—"

I come with a soft cry as he gives one last thrust, and he shivers over me, grinding with slow intent before he pulls free at the last minute. Hot seed gushes on my leg, and the second I feel it, my heart stutters a bit.

This was the deal we both made.

The price of my bargain with the Mother of Night.

Bitter nettle tea notwithstanding, we cannot risk allowing his seed to take root.

We both collapse on the grass, breathing hard.

Thiago curls over me, his teeth skimming up my throat. "No one else, Vi. There will never be anyone else for me. You and I were born to fall in love. And we will chase the stars together, or we will drown in darkness. Together. There is no other option."

I trail my fingers down his sweat-slicked chest, fussing with one of his missing buttons. He was right. Everyone is going to know. It's written all over our skin and faces.

And I want to laugh with joy, because he's finally mine and now I get to share that with the world. No more hiding.

"Together," I whisper. "Forever."

Thiago kisses the tips of my fingers, and then he sets about cleaning me up, grumbling under his breath at the fact I'm not wearing any underwear and he has to use the hem of his cloak.

"Poor little princeling," I tease, my gaze dipping over the generous vee of his chest that his shirt reveals. "All mussed and torn. You'll have to find a new shirt."

And I watch his face as he props himself on his knuckles, giving me a satisfied little smile. "Fuck the shirt. We'll just say I fell into a thicket of thorns. Repeatedly."

CHAPTER 11

Ravenal's library is what I'm here for, and the following morning I slip away to find it.

The lock is easy to pick and I slip inside, summoning a tiny faelight to brighten the gloom. Heavy drapes spill to the floor, but the tower that houses the library is silent. Cold.

Empty.

Perfect.

Thiago rode out with Lucere, Corvin and Kyrian while I pleaded a light headache.

He gets to enjoy the company of the Ravenal siblings and the Prince of Stormlight, while I can go play in the library. I don't envy him.

If I were an ancient book about dangerous crowns, where would I hide?

I spend the first half hour investigating the shelves to the south of the room, but there's nothing of interest.

I tug *Age of Immortals* by Galen the Great down from a shelf.

Hmm.

I flip through the gilt-lined pages. When the Mother of Night tasked me with finding the Crown of Shadows, she told me it was lost to mortal memory. But words mean a thousand things in the fae courts.

And there are still a handful of true immortals remaining in Arcaedia.

"What are you doing in here?" a voice demands.

I nearly drop the book on my foot. The faelight winks out with a thought, but there's nowhere to run. A trio of faelights bob toward me, one hovering right in my face so I can barely see the woman stalking toward me.

"Reading?" I suggest.

The light lowers, and then a slim young woman comes into view, scowling at me. "This is a private library that belongs to the royal family of Ravenal. And it was locked, because I was the one who locked it."

"One of the maids directed me this way. I was looking for something to read."

"And did they unlock the door for you too?"

I shrug. "Don't tell me you've never slipped through a locked door when there was an entire treasure trove of books on the other side."

"That is beside the point."

Ah. A fellow book thief. "I didn't think the crown princess would mind. She told me to enjoy the hospitality Ravenspire offered. I took that as invitation."

"Well, the library doesn't belong the crown princess. The library is mine," the young woman snaps.

A royal library…. There were other princes and princesses introduced to me last night—Lucidia's line was particularly fecund—but I don't think I saw her face in the crowd.

"What's your name?"

The young woman replaces the book on the shelf. "Imerys."

"Princess Imerys? You weren't at the ball last night."

She steps forward and I catch a better look at her as the faelights back away.

I'm a little envious, to be honest. Her hair falls down her spine in a silken waterfall so black it almost gleams like a raven's feathers, although some strands of it are dyed blue on the ends.

My hair is neither straight nor curly, and the second there's any humidity in the air, it's a mess.

Imerys has cheekbones that can cut, and there's a touch of the Danesh Su about her features. Their empire lies to the west of the Far Isles where the fae male I once thought was my father still lives, though merchants from the empire make up a large majority of the Far Isles' population.

"I have more important things to do than drink and dance all night."

"I'm Iskvien."

"I know who you are. And I know what you want." She turns to walk away. "You need an alliance so you can take my kingdom to war. But you're not going to find it in the library. And I'm not going to kiss your feet and offer you welcome, like my sister has, when you're going to get my people killed."

Your kingdom is already at war. But there's no point saying it. "I think you and I share different ideas on the type of welcome your sister has granted me."

It startles her.

"And what I want is a list of the Arcaedian immortals that survived the wars," I call. "That's all. And I hear the library here at Ravenspire is the best in the south."

"A list of immortals?" Her footsteps stop, and she stands within a halo of light that streams down through the central core of the tower. "Why?"

"Curiosity."

Imerys turns around.

I know her type. I *am* her type. Books filled the void within my life that my sister's loss left. Books were sometimes my only companions when my mother exiled me from the main chambers of her court.

When my favorite nanny vanished when I was eleven —or was probably *made* to vanish—I found the library at Hawthorne Castle and with it, peace. A world outside my own. Families who loved each other. Friends who existed within the pages when no fae dared extend a smile in my direction.

An escape.

Imerys can no more ignore my question than I could have, because it's a chance to prove her knowledge and a lingering itch to share her world with me.

"There are no true immortals anymore," she says. "The Old Ones cursed the fae to lose their immortality. Some say it was the true reason we hunted them to the edge of extinction."

"Artemius says there were other immortals," I reply and notice her expression warm. "I've read some of his work, though he never states precisely who or what cursed the fae, he mentions that Arcaedia had its share of immortals before the fae arrived through their portals."

"You've read Artemius's scrolls?"

"Only the first three. My mother had the last two burned."

Her eyes widen in horror.

"I know." All that history, lost. And for what reason?

Maybe she didn't like what Artemius wrote. Or maybe my mother wanted to rewrite history herself.

I push past Imerys, running my fingers over a sexy grimoire that wants me to read it. "I was studying the Hallow in Ceres and realized some of the runes carved into the sentinel stones are symbols that represent the Old Ones. But there are only thirteen Old Ones locked away in their prison worlds, and nearly sixty-one different runes. Do the runes merely represent the names and locations of Hallows? It would be easy to think so, but the runes themselves give some hint of the Old Ones those Hallows are tied to. So I began to wonder if there were more Old Ones who haven't been recorded and then…."

Down the rabbit hole I went, says my rueful smile.

Imerys closes the grimoire I'm stroking with a pointed look. "I've only ever heard of the thirteen."

"That doesn't mean they didn't exist."

Oh, now I've got her.

She looks at the shelves that rise into the darkness. The library at Ravenspire fills one of the circular towers, and this level alone seems to house more books than I've ever seen in my lifetime.

"I was reading a grimoire from Prince Kyrian's library and saw mention of the Morai. They existed on Arcaedia before the fae arrived, but they're not classed as Old Ones. And I was wondering what the difference was, because the Morai are certainly powerful in their own right."

Also, horrifically terrifying.

"He allowed you in his library?"

"Allowed is a strong word. I thought I'd ask permission afterwards."

Imerys snaps her fingers, and her trio of faelights appear again. "You steal one of my books, and I'll break your fingers."

"I wasn't planning on stealing anything. Just knowledge."

"Hmm." Imerys takes off through the shelves, her faelights chasing after her like playful kittens. "Down here, I think."

Chains bind the heaviest of the books to their lecterns. Demi-fey flutter through the air in this section, and a phoenix feather burns within a warded glass dome.

"Halt, foolish intruders," hisses a little demi-fey guard, lunging forward with a tiny spear. The flutter of her wings is so fast they're transparent, and she wears a smock made of nettle thorns and thistledown.

I've never heard one of the demi-fey talk. They're mischievous sprites and sylphs who tend to congregate around the fae, but most of them lack the intelligence to follow basic orders, unless they're well-trained like Thalia's little squad.

"It's just me, Gossamer." Imerys clicks her fingers, and one by one, faelights spring to glowing life throughout the stacks. "I have a friend with me, though if you see her here alone when I'm not around, you have to let me know. She steals books."

"I don't steal books—"

Imerys shoots me a long look.

"I borrowed it. And Prince Kyrian was more than aware of that fact."

Gossamer starts to glow. Golden at first, before she turns a blushing pink. "Steal books?"

Great. Now a fluttering moth is chiding me like I'm three. "I. Do. Not. Steal. Books. I borrowed it and then he said I could have it."

The pair of them exchange a look.

"Old Ones. And runes." Imerys slides the ladder along the shelf, thoroughly caught up in the quest now. "Here. This is Anduluvian's *Myths of Arcaedia.* It's old. And hungry."

She tugs on her mesh gloves and then takes the fat book from its shelf, where it rustles a little as if it can sense her. A thick chain rattles over the shelf, but Imerys unlocks it with the key around her neck.

"Some of the books bite," she admits, flipping the pages. "And you don't want to get blood on any of the spellwork contained within, or you might find yourself with some company you'd prefer not to keep."

"Lucere?" I say jokingly, because I've read the mood of the court. "I'm fairly certain she's hunting in the woods with my husband, so I'd say we're safe."

Imerys's eyes go wide. And then she chokes on a laugh. "I was talking about daemons, though they might be preferable to my sister at times."

"You don't back her claim?"

"I back her claim." Imerys places the book on one of the lecterns. She blows a lock of hair out of her eyes. "Don't mistake me, Your Highness. I am loyal to my family. And I think my sister will make a powerful queen. But she and I do not always see eye to eye. Lucere is bold and wishes to prove herself a threat to be watched by the other queens. And princes," she adds belatedly.

"She has to," I admit, thinking of the state of the Alliance. "She's found herself the bystander in a war that will sweep her up and use her, no matter which way she chooses to cast her allegiance."

"She could abstain from war."

"I wish we all could if I'm being honest, but I know my mother. I know her ambitions." I see it all laid out in front of me. "If Lucere doesn't bare her claws now, my mother will sweep her off the board. She's wanted war for a long time, and I..." Regret sours my tongue. "I'm the reason she will use to provoke it."

Imerys watches me. "If you could make your choice again, would you side with your mother?"

"No." It's not even a choice. "I love Thiago. And it doesn't matter if I did not—Mother would have found some reason to cast off the shackles of the Alliance."

Imerys stares at me for a long time.

And then she clicks her fingers, and a book floats toward her from the top shelf. "This one too, I think." She places it next to *Myths of Arcaedia*. "As I said, they're hungry. Will you do the honors?"

There are certain rules among the fae.

To give another your blood, hair, or fingernails grants them the ability to link a spell to you. If you're powerful, then you needn't worry, but that's why we rarely cut our hair, and nails are tended in the privacy of your rooms where you dispose of them yourself.

It's a rare curseworker who can wield the magic in your blood, but I've had more than enough experience with curses in my life.

And yet... to deny her is to tell her I don't trust her.

I need the information in that book.

And more, I need to find some sort of alliance within Ravenal.

"Move aside," I murmur, tugging the dagger from my belt and pricking my finger. I press the bloody smear on the cover of the book, where the leather—or what I hope is leather—absorbs it.

Golden light flares over the lock, and Imerys's face brightens as she unlocks it and opens the book with slow reverence. Every page is yellow with age, and dark ink blots across the page like little spider scrawl. I can barely understand a word of it.

"Anduluvian was one of the first refugees from the home world," Imerys murmurs. "She speaks the Old Tongue, so some of it is difficult to decipher." Flipping through the pages, she pauses when she comes to a familiar rune.

A crescent moon, full moon, and waning moon super-imposed over each other.

"The Mother of Night." I swallow the lump in my throat. Just thinking of the creature I made a deal with sends a shiver down my spine, as if the mere thought is enough to summon her.

Another page. Another symbol. A triangle with a set of horns. "The Horned One," Imerys murmurs.

The Old One that Angharad wants to use my blood to raise.

I shiver.

Each page reveals new symbols, some of which I've seen on the corresponding Hallows. The Dream Thief. Red Mag. Bloody Mara. The Frost Giant. The Green Man. All of them Old Ones that have been locked away in their prison worlds.

But then the pages keep turning, and there are other symbols.

A pair of half-circles joined together, like a child's equivalent of a bird. Behind it is a full circle, which could be a full moon. I've seen it on the stones in Valerian, though I don't know what it means or which Hallow it aligns with.

"You were right. There were more Old Ones." Imerys's fingers continue turning the smooth pages. "But only thirteen were ever captured. Only thirteen went to war against us."

And we couldn't even truly kill one of them.

Imagine if all of them had picked up their weapons and fought the fae?

"The Old Ones were worshipped by the creatures who ruled these lands before the fae arrived." Imerys pauses, running her finger down the page as if she's trying to translate. "This is the Daughter of the Three Moons. She was once worshipped as a huntress of the night, before the Mother of Night took over her aspect. I wonder if her worshippers forgot about her and turned to the Mother?"

Which would mean the Mother grew in strength while the Daughter of the Three Moons faded in power. Prayer and belief give the Old Ones their strength, and at their height of power, there were entire cults dedicated to them. Every sacrifice that was given to the Hallows they used as nexus points would have directly strengthened them.

More pages flutter by.

"You were right," Imerys breaths. "There *were* more of

them. The Prince of Thorns. The Silent Lady. The Fire Whisperer. Jack of Frost. Brother Tooth."

Brother Tooth? "I've heard of him. My nurse, Nanny Redwyne, used to tell us stories about how Brother Tooth would steal our teeth during the night if we didn't leave a coin out for him on Samhain."

"Did you?"

"Of course I did. I didn't want any creepy nightcrawler stealing my teeth while I slept. The coin was always missing by morning."

We share a smile.

"Though now that you mention it, I do recall Nanny Redwyne showing off her lovely red velvet cape one week after Samhain, when I was six or seven."

A breeze stirs across my skin, and I lift my head. I shut the door when I came in, but there's no sign of anyone else. "Did you feel that?"

But Imerys rifles through the pages with quick grace. "There's another section in the back of the book, detailing the creatures who lived in this world before the fae arrived."

Every single candle snuffs out, leaving only the light that spills through the circular window in the ceiling far above.

Both of us freeze.

I'm quicker to move than she is.

Drawing the dagger sheathed at my hip, I spin around. Imerys snaps her fingers, and light blooms throughout the library, stinging my eyes.

"What's wrong?" Imerys cranes her neck. "What's going on?"

I don't know.

Gossamer peers over a pile of books, no longer threatening to halt any intruders.

Nothing moves. But the bracelet around my wrist gives a twitch.

It's not until I notice my breath is coming in a cloud of fog that I realize how cold it is in here suddenly.

Something moves down one of the long rows of bookcases.

"What was that?" The pulse still kicks in Imerys's throat.

I cross the floor, knife held low. There's no sign of anything shifting in the shadows. No stir of breeze.

But my heart's racing, and the coppery taste of blood magic dances over my tongue.

Something was watching us.

The fetch?

Angharad, one of the queens of Unseelie, set one hunting me four months ago. The bracelet around my wrist keeps it from finding me, but I know it's still out there. Once one of the Heartless are given an order to hunt, they don't stop until they capture their prey.

But if it was watching me, then why didn't it attack?

"Do you mind if I take the books back to my room?"

For a second, I think she's going to deny me. But fear wins out over her sense of protectiveness. "One night," she says, "and then you return them."

"You have my word."

Imerys snorts as she shuts the book. "I have more than that, Princess. I know where you sleep, and if they're not back by noon tomorrow, I'll send Gossamer to fetch them."

❧

I find Thiago in the stables, examining a handsome golden colt with the crown princess. "Vi."

"Your Highness." Lucere moves away from his side with a furtive smile, as if she's trying to suggest there's something more happening here.

"How was your ride?" I paste a smile on my lips, even if I don't feel it in my heart.

"Wonderful." Lucere glides out of the stall, still putting distance between them, though her eyes linger on my husband. "Thiago brought down a stag, and he will be the main course at our banquet tonight. He was glorious."

Thiago's lashes lower. "The poor bastard broke his leg in the chase. It was mercy, Lucere. Not any particular interest of mine in hunting."

He'll hunt for food, but I've never known him to partake in it for sport like some of the southern kingdoms do.

"What do you think of him?" Thiago asks, turning my attention to the colt in the stall.

I pat that velvety nose. The color of his coat shines like a newly minted coin, though his mane and tail are as silver as moonlight. The arch of his face hints at elfin blood, and as I run my hands down his legs, I admire the quality of his structure. "He's gorgeous. Absolutely breathtaking."

"A gift," Lucere purrs, "for Evernight."

Thiago's gaze cuts toward her, and he strokes that glossy coat. "A gift worthy of a royal fortune. I fear my offering last night was a mere trinket in comparison."

The rubies are already around her neck, though she'll choke on them if she knows Thalia was the one who chose them.

Lucere strokes the gems as she demurs. "Of course not.

I shall be the envy of the Alliance. I fear this small exchange is barely worth a single ruby."

Thiago smiles at me. "He's yours, Vi."

Lucere's eyes flare, and her smile freezes.

"A worthy mount for my beloved." Thiago nods gracefully to her. "Thank you. Wherever the Princess of Evernight rides, all folk shall know of the generosity of Ravenal."

"*You're evil,*" I tell him as we link thoughts. "*I think she's going to bite through her tongue.*"

There's a touch of wickedness about his mouth, but he offers me his arm. "I fear I've abandoned you too much this morning. Shall we take a walk around the gardens? Lucere was telling me that there's a lovely little grotto with a waterfall."

Oh, I'll bet she was.

"That would be lovely." And then, because she's been eyeing my husband like a piece of steak, I smile at her. "Thank you for the gift. I will always cherish him."

"What's wrong?" Thiago demands the second we're in the gardens where no one can hear us.

"Besides that bitch salivating all over you?"

His eyes hood. "She's going to be the future queen of Ravenal. We have to play nicely."

I sigh. "I know. That doesn't mean I like her."

"I'm not particularly fond of her either."

Really?

His expression darkens. "I have a wife, and she knows

it, and yet she's constantly trying to touch me in places she shouldn't."

"Should I know about these places?" I tease.

"I nearly shoved her off a cliff this morning," he says with a sigh, raking a hand through his hair, "when she put her hand on my thigh."

This time *my* eyebrows arch.

"Don't look at me like that. Lucere reminds me of your mother. Because she knows she has something I want, she pushes me. I'm not her fucking pet, but she's trying to treat me like one."

I didn't think of what it would be like to deal with that from the other end.

"If you push her off a cliff, who's next in line for the throne?"

He looks at me. "Corvin. Though it will probably go to Imerys. They're very matrilineal here, and he'll back his sisters."

"I like Imerys."

"I'm not murdering a crown princess," he says dryly. "Even if she has grabby hands."

"I'm fairly certain Eris would volunteer if you gave her the eyebrow."

"The eyebrow?"

I mimic one of his favorite expressions; cool, calculating, off-with-her-head…. "I jest. We need Ravenal—ruling princess aside. And I don't like to think that I'm starting to sound like my mother, so no pushing anyone from the battlements. But if she touches you again, I can't promise I'm not going to draw my dagger and challenge her to a duel."

"Mmm." His voice drops. "Now tell me what's wrong. The guards are gone."

"I think there was a fetch in the library."

He goes so still, I wonder if he heard me. "They shouldn't be able to find you while you're wearing that bracelet."

"I know," I whisper, stroking his arm. Just two lovers stealing a kiss in the gardens. No one from Ravenal needs to know that one of the Heartless might be stalking the shadows of Ravenspire.

"Are you certain it was a fetch?"

"The bracelet felt cold, and it was almost tugging me toward whatever was in the shadows. Imerys thought she saw something too."

"Did you see it?"

I shake my head. "Just a shadow."

Thiago's thumb rubs over the back of my hand. "You don't go anywhere without either myself or Eris from now on."

"It might not have been the fetch."

His eyes narrow, and he leans down, close enough to kiss me. "I don't care. Nowhere, Vi. Not alone. I didn't spend thirteen years winning your heart only to lose you now. Promise me."

With a sigh, I wrap my arms around his neck. "It shall be a great hardship, but I shall glue myself to your side until we leave Ravenal. All day. All night...."

"Mmmm." His gaze drops to my lips. "Why don't you tell me about these nights?"

CHAPTER 12

I can't sleep.

Every time I close my eyes, I find myself falling into a deep, dark hole I can't get out of. A baby cries on the other side of the wall and I scratch at the rock, desperate to rescue the child. But the water that lines the bottom of the hole starts rising, and soon it's sweeping over my head, and I choke and cough and splutter and then it's too late....

I wake with a gasp, the scream trapped in my throat.

Just a nightmare. Just another nightmare.... But the sound of a baby crying seems to echo almost on the verge of hearing.

I turn my thoughts toward the Mother of Night. *Stop it! If these dreams are yours, then I hope you choke on them!*

But there's no response.

There never is, and I'm not sure whether it's because she doesn't hear me—or because she's silently laughing to herself.

Thiago stirs, but I stroke a hand over his bare shoulder

and then ease from the bed. It's not the first time this has happened, and while he'll usually wrap me in his arms until the nightmare fades, tonight I want to be alone. Dressing swiftly, I slip onto the balcony and bow my head, trying to stop my heart from racing.

It felt so real.

It always does, but tonight I can practically feel the grit under my fingernails.

A shadow moves out of the corner of my eye, and I nearly leap out of my skin until I realize who it is.

"Bad dreams?" Eris asks, leaning against the watchtower at the end of the balcony.

I rest my hands on the battlements and sigh. "Every night it's the same nightmare. I need to find the crown."

"You have nine months," she says.

Nine months. I wish she knew what kind of precognitive tremor those words send down my spine. I'm not pregnant, and we've been so careful, but still....

"We've had three," I point out, walking toward her so the sound of our voices won't wake Thiago, "and we're no closer to getting our hands on it. Walk the battlements with me?"

She follows as I head for the stairs that lead down onto the ramparts.

Eris slowly rubs her thumb over the sharp blade of her knife, almost unconsciously. "I could return to the Morai. I've never been. They'll have to answer my questions."

What? "You hauled me out of their cave after we set fire to it. I'm fairly certain answering your questions isn't going to be their first priority if they see you. Besides, their cave is too close to Blaedwyn's territories, and I'm not entirely certain who's in charge there with the Erlking on the loose."

"He owes you two favors."

And I promised I would never call them in. "Thiago doesn't want me to capture any more of his attention."

The Erlking is one of the most dangerous Old Ones. He leads the Wild Hunt, and whilst I've heard no mention of it howling free since I set him loose, the golden antler tattoos on my hand aren't there of my own volition.

"I could… subdue the Morai," she finally says. "I could make them tell me where the crown is."

Devourer, they'd called her as they flinched away from her.

But I saw the look in her eyes, and as much as Eris walls herself away from the world with an uncaring shrug and the curl of a lip, it hurt her in some way to see them shudder before her.

How would it feel to be the one thing the monsters are afraid of?

"We have nine months," I say instead. "If we can't find any trace of the crown before then, then we may have to look at such alternatives. Making any headway with the Prince of Ravens?"

"*Corvin?*"

"I saw the way he looked at you. *And* he asked you to dance."

"I declined."

"He's handsome."

"Trust me. He's not interested in me." A winter's night holds more warmth than her voice right now. "None of them are truly interested in me."

"Do I want to know?"

She looks down her nose at me. "Do I want to ask what sort of power you were channeling at the Queensmoot?"

I freeze.

Eris looks out over the castle. "I'm not a fool, Vi. The others were distracted by your mother's assault, but I'm the weapon at Thiago's right hand. I'm supposed to be his shield. I've spent centuries training to recognize threats. And the only time I've ever felt the hairs rise on my arms the way they did at the Queensmoot was when we went to Mistmere and you made that bargain with the Mother of Night. Are you going to tell the others?"

"I...."

All of a sudden, I can't breathe.

"I won't tell them," she says curtly. "It's your secret, not mine. Because I don't think that was the Mother of Night's power. You were channeling the ley lines, and there's only one creature I know who is supposed to have the power to do that."

The *leanabh an dàn*.

Somehow, I start breathing again. In my mother's court, a secret such as this could be catastrophic. But... "If word of this got out...."

"As I said, it's your secret."

"Just like that?"

"Just like that." Eris takes a deep breath, looking troubled. "None of us will turn away from you, Vi. I know you find it hard to trust, but we're family."

"That's a word that holds a different meaning for me."

She looks at me for a long moment. "They were going to kill me."

"Who?"

"When I was younger," she says, resting her hands on

167

the parapet and looking over the bailey, "I was not... wholly in control of myself. I would try to contain the creature inside me, but sometimes I'd scent blood or hear an injured animal calling out, and it was enough to force me to the killing edge." Her face locks down. "I'll spare you the details, but by the time the hunters finally caught me, the entire Seelie Alliance sat in judgement over me. They wanted my head. It was safer. Kinder, they said. The only difficulty lay in *how* to execute me safely, and I'll never forget that feeling—listening to them debate just how they were going to do it without rousing the creature inside me. There was only one ruler who stayed silent. Only one of them who watched me, his eyes slowly narrowing. And he asked me what I would do if I was offered a chance of absolution. And I said *anything*."

I see it in her face, what that hope did to her.

And I know who that ruler was.

"Thiago said he would help me learn to bind away the creature inside me and control it. He would take me into his kingdom, take me under his wing, and if I broke again —if I lost control—then he would bear the burden of my execution." Eris releases a shaky breath. "It cost him the border lands. Your mother was the only one who refused to consent until he offered her the one thing she desired most, just to save me."

I've always wondered how Eris came to be the shadow over his shoulder, the threat that cows the world.

My mother used to say that Thiago leashed "that bitch," and it was the worst mistake she'd ever made— allowing it.

But it's not a leash.

And I love him all over again for being the kind of

ruler who can inspire his people with such hope. They will all die for him and give their lives gladly, and my mother doesn't understand that.

"He gave me a reason to fight," she continues. "If I lost control again, then it was no longer merely my own head on the executioner's block, but his too, and through him, an entire kingdom. But more than that, he gave me the greatest gift anyone has ever offered me in my fight. I'd given in to despair, and the monster feeds upon despair. It choked me with loneliness until there was no reason not to give in. But when he believed in me…, I was no longer alone. I was no longer lost in the dark. There was a hand reaching through the darkness for me, pulling me to my feet, offering me strength.

"Finn, Baylor, Lysander, even Thalia…." Eris turns her ancient eyes upon me. "They're my family now. We are all broken in some way. We are all considered monsters or outcasts. There's no other place for any of us to go, but he gives us a home. He gives us hope. And all it costs us is loyalty. There's a reason he was drawn to you, Vi. It's the same reason he was drawn to all of us—because he sees a piece of himself in us. He sees the boy that he was, and the choices he was offered, and the things he was forced to do to survive—and he sees that same desperation within us."

I think I understand what she's telling me.

"You're not alone, Vi. We are your family—no matter what happens. And he's your husband. Don't let your inner monster win."

I rest both hands on the parapet and say dryly, "My inner monster sounds a lot like my mother."

Eris gives a rough laugh. "Mine sounds like my father."

I look at her at that, but from the expression on her face, she's done sharing.

Indeed, her attention shifts to the wind. "Can you smell smoke?"

I'm about to shake my head when I catch a whiff of it. Far too strong to belong to a hearth fire. "Yes."

There's no sign of flames in the bailey. No hint of light flickering out in the night.

"Stay there," she urges, tossing me her knife, and then she turns and strides along the battlements.

I pace for long minutes, breathing in the acrid scent. It's getting stronger, and there's no sign of Eris.

"Eris?" I call softly.

The fae might flee from her in fear, but that doesn't mean she's invulnerable.

And the smell of smoke is getting stronger. Something's wrong.

Don't get involved. She told you to stay here.

But a soft grunt echoes through the night, and then something clatters as if a sheet of metal hits the cobbles.

Or a sword.

What was that?

"Eris?"

I can almost imagine the tongue-lashing I'm going to receive if I disobey her and she's fine, but there's a tingle along my arms that doesn't feel right. It feels like magic. It feels like a cool breath blowing over the back of my neck.

Rounding the tower, I stop in my tracks.

The library's on fire.

"Fire!" I call, scurrying down the stairs toward the library tower. Ravenal's guards have been following me and Eris around like flies buzzing over a corpse ever since we got here, and now is the one time they decide to go searching for the water closet? "Is there anyone there? Fire!"

Silence.

Where are the guards?

"Eris?" I yell.

There's no sign of her.

A tiny figure darts across the courtyard, flapping her hands at the flames. "No, no, no, no, no!"

We both skid to a halt, but I can tell Imerys barely sees me. The wall of heat makes me lift a hand to protect my face. I can't believe how quickly it's going up. When I first saw it, flames were licking at the door and through the windows, but glass shatters as I watch, and a fireball blooms through the window.

"Fire!" she screams. "Halvor! Endarryon! Where are you?"

Imerys takes a step inside the building, and I grab her around the waist, hauling her back from the flames and the smoke.

A cough tears from my throat. "You'll burn!"

"The books!"

"Books can be replaced." She's strong for such a lean woman. I slam her against the staircase, forcing her to look at me. "If you go in there, you'll die!"

"You don't understand!" Horror stretches her face. "My great-grandmother's collection is the best in the world. All the remaining history from before the wars is shelved in that tower. It's irreplaceable!"

"Think about it! There are no guards," I hiss. "There are usually guards in this section of the bailey, aren't there?"

After all, I'd spent enough time working out their rotations before I made my previous mission into the library.

Imerys's nails dig into my forearms, but she's looking at me now.

"Eris went to see what was happening. And I can't find her. She wouldn't disappear like this. And now the library's on fire." It's not just the flames we need to worry about.

Imerys's eyes sharpen. "You think whoever did this happened upon her?"

I've seen Eris with a sword in hand. If they did, then they're regretting it right now. "Where's the nearest water tower? Where are your magic-wielders? Surely someone can wield water?"

Imerys suddenly gasps. "Gossamer!"

And before I can grab her, she bolts into the burning tower.

"Imerys!" There's no answer. "*Imerys!*"

Gone to rescue her demi-fey.

I look around desperately, but despite our yells, no one has come.

And I can't just let her burn.

Fire is the gift of my fae heritage after all.

It has to be enough.

Yanking my cloak over my face I leap through the doorway, warding the flames away from me. They part like the sea, but there's so much of it. Too much smoke. Too much heat.

A gust of hot air sweeps around me, and I wield it away. "Imerys!"

"Gossamer!" I hear someone scream.

There. To the right. She's trying to battle through a wall of flames. Focusing on them, I clench my hand and they die down. Imerys shoots me a grateful look and then leaps toward the desk where the little demi-fey guard flutters helplessly.

"This way!" I yell, sweat dripping down my temples as I try to contain the fire. A chained grimoire makes a leap off its shelf, the chain yanking it back. It slaps against the bookcase, and a spurt of flame catches in the black-edged pages. With a hiss, the flames turn green, and then an amorphous shape howls free, screaming as if it was somehow trapped within the book.

Sparks of white catapult past my nose, and another book screams loudly enough to shatter glass.

Maia's blessing. There are so many spells contained within these pages that I wouldn't be surprised if the entire tower explodes.

"Imerys!"

She tucks the little demi-fey under her coat and sprints toward me, ducking a belch of flame. I wave it out of her way, and then she's slamming into me, shoving me back toward the door.

"Watch out!" she yells.

A burning strut crashes down, knocking the shelves into Imerys. They jam her between them, and I fall free at the last second. It's easier to breath down here, but I cough out smoke, my eyes stinging.

"*Vi?* Vi!"

A voice.

"Over here!" Tremors run through my arms as magic backlash starts to fry my nerves. This is the most I've ever used my magic, and I can feel it starting to drive a knife right through my brain. Too long disused.

I just have to hold the flames away long enough for our rescuers to reach us.

An enormous shape appears in the smoke and for a second my heart lifts, thinking it's Thiago, but then the smoke clears enough to see more of him, and I recognize Finn.

"Finn!"

By the look of it, he's come straight from bed, and my eyes nearly bug out of my head when I realize he's dragged on a pair of leather trousers and little else. "Hardly the place to be languishing, Princess."

"What? Burning to death in a library isn't your favorite way to make the shift into the Bright Lands?" I push to my feet, a gush of flame wafting closer. "The princess is trapped."

He follows my glance and curses under his breath. "Get out. I'll bring the girl."

"You just want to play the hero." I shake my head. "I have to stay. Someone has to ward the flames away from you."

The markings on Finn's arms start to glow. "Are you certain you're up to it?"

It's the hardest thing I've ever had to do.

But I grit my teeth. "The longer we wait, the less likely I can contain it."

He gives me a clipped nod and then vanishes.

I feel like I'm trying to pry stone from a wall with my bare fingers or part a river with only my mind. Flame curls away from Finn as he wades toward Imerys, and only my desperation manages to keep them from swallowing him whole.

Sweat drips down my temples. I grind my teeth together and silently scream.

Finn squats and hauls the burning bookcase off Imerys and then throws her unconscious form over his shoulder. The little demi-fey guard scrambles up his body and clings to his shoulder as Finn starts back toward us.

"Hurry!" I yell.

I can't hold it much longer.

He shoves past me and I back away, trying to ward off the flames as we escape. And then we're through the door, collapsing on the cool cobbles with a gasp.

"Vi?"

I think I'm going to throw up. Every inch of me trembles, and I lost the ward just before we escaped, which leaves me coughing out the sudden lungful of smoke I just swallowed.

A dark form materializes next to me, fingers finding my own. I catch a glimpse of black tattoos, swirling more hungrily than usual, and the light of a fae lantern catches on the fierce glint of Thiago's eyes.

Relief burns there. Along with a dozen I'm-going-to-kick-your-ass later questions.

I'm fine. I wave Thiago away with a hand. "If the pair of you don't put some clothes on, you're going to start a riot. Imerys?"

"Alive," he says curtly. "Do I need to ask why you were in there?"

I roll onto my back and stare at the night sky, feeling like a house just collapsed on me. "Someone has to rescue... foolish princesses who run into burning libraries."

"Does that count princesses who run into burning libraries to save them?"

"I'll owe Finn a debt of gratitude." But later. Much later.

"We'll discuss it when we're in private," he growls, then turns to the library. "I'll see if I can do something about this, now you're all out."

"Vi!" A cloud of perfume envelopes me and then Thalia drags me into a hug. "Maia's blessing, what were you doing!"

I try to explain as Finn sits beside me, resting on his hands and sucking in fresh air. Imerys guzzles water from a flask beside him, her face dark with soot.

"You saved us," Gossamer says, patting Finn on the arm. "I owe you a debt."

I might be imagining it, but I'm pretty sure she caresses the muscle in his biceps for a second longer than necessary.

Maybe Finn senses it too. "No debt, my lady," he says, lifting his fingers for her to settle onto. He lowers her to the ground. "It was my pleasure. And now I am one up on Eris."

I look around. "She's not here?"

"What do you mean?"

I tell him what happened.

Finn pushes to his feet, cursing under his breath. "Eris doesn't simply vanish. If she was on watch tonight, then she'd be stuck to your ass like a burr." He doesn't say that something's wrong, but I read it on the grim line of his face. "I'll find her."

And then he's gone.

A huge dome of shadowy clouds envelops the library and collapses in upon it. Thiago stands in the yard, holding his palms outstretched.

"What's he doing?" I whisper.

"Everything needs oxygen to breathe," Thalia says. "Even fire."

The clouds of smoke roil and thrash, but it looks like they're being contained within an invisible glass dome. Flame licks at the edge of the ward, but they're slowly being choked out.

Another figure steps from the shadows.

Prince Kyrian, his face grim as he wields his own magic. Twirling his finger, he sweeps Thiago's darkness into tight coils that seem to crush the building. Flames writhe, but they're slowly dwindling as if his smoke-coils choke the life from them.

The fire burns low… and dies.

Finally, it's done.

The air reeks of smoke. Blackened marks scorch the library tower, and every window in the place is merely an eyeless gaping hole.

But some of the library remains untouched.

And nobody died.

Though, as I see Princess Lucere bearing down upon me, I don't think we've escaped entirely unscathed.

"What in Maia's name did you do?"

CHAPTER 13

"**M**e?"

"Your natural gift is Fire, isn't it?" Lucere snarls. "I think if we need to find the culprit, then we need look no further than right here."

Thiago steps forward. "Vi had nothing to do with this."

"Were you with her?" Lucere demands, turning on him in a rage. "Was she in bed with you when this happened? Can you vouch for her whereabouts?"

And he pauses.

"I was on the battlements," I reply softly, "with Eris. I couldn't sleep."

Thiago cuts me a look telling me not to say any more. "Vi has no reason to attack you and your court—"

"Doesn't she?" Lucere demands coldly. "Perhaps she didn't like the way you danced with me. Perhaps she—"

"If you think me foolish enough to attack a foreign kingdom over something so *petty* as jealousy," I snap, "then you know me not at all. I am not my mother. And I know who Thiago chose all those years ago. He spent thirteen years winning my heart, over and over again, and you think I'd believe that his head is turned by another woman?"

The color fades from Lucere's cheeks, but I see a faint smile on Thiago's sultry mouth.

I step closer. "From the moment I have arrived in this court, you have greeted me not as a fellow royal but as an enemy to be held with contempt. You have insulted me. And you have sneered at my relationship, but let me assure you, I do not see you as a threat. I pity you instead."

"How *dare* you?" she demands.

"I dare because I have held my tongue until this moment," I reply, "because at least one of us remembers their manners."

"Princesses," Kyrian chides. "Let's not accuse anyone of any wrongdoing unless we have proof."

She makes a move toward me, her face absolutely furious, but Corvin snatches her arm, and when she turns on him in a rage, he stares her down.

"No," he says softly. "Whether she was involved in this fire or not, we will not offer anything less than courtesy, nor will we—"

"She wasn't involved," a soft voice says.

All of us turn our heads.

Imerys stands with her arms wrapped around herself, her eyes soft and aching. "She saved my life, Luce. All I could think of was Gossamer, but the princess came in after me. She warded the flames away so we could get out."

Lucere's color mottles. I think she'd probably set *me* on fire right now if she could.

"Your Highness!" someone calls.

We all turn, which is the problem when four of you have spent your life listening to that title.

Finn staggers around the corner of the main tower, carrying someone in his arms. There's a guard beside him, hauling another guard.

"They're all asleep," Finn says. "Just lying there. Like this."

And I finally see what's in his arms.

It's Eris.

Her dark lashes remain soft as they shield her eyes, and her arm hangs laxly so that her fingers almost brush the ground. Nearly six feet of solid muscle and contained rage, and at that moment she's so still I don't know if she's even breathing.

I shove past Lucere, my blood running cold. Finn carries Eris with ease, but I can't help reaching for her.

Eris of Silvernaught doesn't do vulnerability. To see her sprawled bonelessly in Finn's arms feels like the last shock I can take for the night.

"Is she all right?" I demand.

Healing is a gift in my bloodlines, though I've never spent time studying the art and I'm too tired to even access my gifts right now, but the pulse in her throat remains steady beneath my fingers.

"Asleep." Finn frowns as he lays her on the cloak Thiago spreads on the ground. "Wake up, Eris." He taps her cheek.

Her head lolls to the side, and in that moment—if she wasn't wearing the firm leather body armor she lives in—she'd almost look like the sleeping fae princess of the tale.

"E?" There's an odd tremor in Finn's voice.

"Let me." Thiago kneels and lays his hands flat on her

chest, closing his eyes. Wind swirls around him, rifling through his thick dark hair, and a faint white glow hums around his hands as he tries to heal her.

He opens his eyes as the glow around his hands fade. "I can't rouse her, though there's nothing wrong with her. There's a… silence within her. An emptiness."

Thiago never reveals his vulnerability in company, but the muscle in his jaw tightens.

"There are more," says the guard, who lowers his friend to the ground. "They're all like this. Just… asleep."

Lucere's expression tightens, but I meet her eyes.

"Not one of my fae gifts," I point out.

"What could have done this?" Kyrian demands.

Corvin kneels beside their guard. "Our guards are warded against mental attacks." He tugs a leather thong from within the guard's tunic. "They all carry a crystal that should protect them."

There's nothing on the end of the strip of leather. Just a shard of fractured obsidian.

I straighten slowly. A fire could be a coincidence. An untended candle. The phoenix feather finally igniting.

But this….

"This was an attack."

A flash of cold fury crosses the Prince of Ravens's face.

"If you don't wake up, then I'll kiss you, Eris," Finn whispers in her ear. "I swear I will."

I keep waiting for her to shove him out of the way with a grimace, but there's… nothing.

"I don't think I've ever wanted her to punch me so badly in my life," Finn growls, sitting back on his heels. Cupping his hands behind his head, he lifts his eyes.

"She's not harmed. She's not suffering. She's simply been sent to sleep."

"There's only one fae who could have done this." I hear the cold tremor in Thiago's voice as he brushes Eris's hair out of her face.

Lucere and I both look at each other, and for a second, all I see is a crown princess who's struggling to hold on to her country in the midst of a brewing war.

"Queen Maren of Aska," I whisper. "My mother's ally and the Queen of Nightmares."

CHAPTER 14

"I cannot help thinking it seems awfully convenient," Lucere growls, pacing the floor before the fireplace in her rooms. "You come here demanding an alliance with Ravenal, citing that the queen of Asturia will ruin us all, and when I tell you she's offered us peace, *this* happens. Half my library is burned, a full company of guards falls into a dreamless slumber, and now you're trying to tell me this is an attack by Queen Maren."

"She's the only one who has the power to do this," I point out. Eris still hasn't woken, though Finn's chosen to sit by her bed. "I served at her court for two years. I know what she can do. Queen Maren is the nightmare we all pretend we can't see, and Eris's wards were—"

"Impenetrable," Thiago says, and the quiet menace in his voice alarms me.

We both look at him.

He's shaking his head at me. "Even if Queen Maren did attack us here, she couldn't have gotten through Eris's wards by herself. They were laid by thirteen of the finest of our sorcerers after the Battle of Nevernight."

Lucere's lip curls. "To contain that vicious creat—"

"If you dare finish that sentence," Thiago tells her, his voice growing rough-edged with fury, "then you will not merely be a morsel caught between the jaws of Asturia and Aska, you will face me, here and now. Eris is my finest general. She has served the Alliance faithfully for nearly five hundred years. And she is one of *mine*."

"Manners, Luce," the Prince of Ravens purrs, though he's barely deigned to join the conversation thus far. Lying on the daybed near the window, he strokes a white cat that wears a black leather collar. "As exciting as it would be to see the two of you shred pieces off each other, Ravenal's already bled enough, hasn't it? Great-grandmother is dead, war is brewing, and now someone set half the castle on fucking fire. We don't have time to play games." He arches a brow at Thiago. "We all know what your general can do. And we all know where Maren's gifts lie. The only possible way Maren managed to do this is if she was wielding the Dreamthief's Mirror."

"That's a myth," Lucere snaps.

"No, it's not," says a quiet voice near the fireplace.

Imerys hasn't said a word since we all retreated to Lucere's private chambers, but despite the paleness of her skin and the streaks of ash that dull her blue-black hair, she drags the cold compress from her face and stares at her sister. "The Mirror exists. It was one of the great relics, created to trap the Dreamthief himself."

"The great relics?" I can't help myself. "You know of the great relics?"

"With it, you can access the Dreamthief's powers,"

Imerys replies. "You can control him, even as he lies bound within the Hallow."

Prince Corvin straightens, looking dangerous in black leather with a cloak of pure raven feathers. "If Maren has the mirror, then she's more dangerous than any of us can predict. She can steal into our dreams, she can trap us in endless nightmares, and even if we were to somehow fight off sleep, she can send us into the dream world in an instant." He looks at Thiago. "And nobody knows how long it will take for them to wake. Or *if* they will wake."

"What do we do?" Lucere asks.

"I told you what you needed to do last night," Thiago replies. "The only way to defeat Adaia and Maren is for the three of us—Kyrian, you, and myself—to join—"

"Join what?" she demands. "Your war? Ravenal is finally free of my great-grandmother's clutches! We have *years* of rebuilding to do. There's barely anything left of the kingdom as it is, and—"

"There won't be anything of it left if you allow Adaia to march in and burn it."

"You and your fucking wife will drag us all into ruin!" she suddenly hisses. "Did you ever think of that when you first claimed Iskvien as your wife? Did you even give a thought for anyone else when you told the world that you would burn it to ashes if any of us dared intercede with the marriage?"

"Anyone else? Or just you?"

"You will ruin us," she says bitterly. "You will ruin us all, and for what? *Her?*"

Shadows lengthen as Thiago's eyes darken. I recognize the set of his shoulders and the press of his mouth. There's no sign of the charming suitor who won my heart for all those months, no sign of the careful prince who tries to rule his country with a fair and even hand. No, this is the predator. The dark prince they all whisper about.

Even my breath catches, because I've never seen the warlord who earned that reputation long ago fully unleashed. It's like a glimpse of the male beneath the mask, and I don't *know* him.

Not completely.

"Is it ruin to seek salvation in the only hope you have ever seen?" he asks in a gentle voice that holds an edge of malice.

The two of them stare at each other.

"You should thank her, you know." Thiago takes a step toward her, eyes glittering darkly. "Because you know nothing of what I am capable of. You know nothing of the depths that call at me. There is only one thing that reminds me of who I am and what I wish to remain, and she's standing right in fucking front of you."

Kyrian steps between them, not as a threat, but as a warning that we need to keep a cool head here. "We're playing directly into Adaia's hands."

I catch Thiago's arm.

And our eyes meet.

"I can fight my own battles, thank you very much."

"I'm aware of that," he growls in my head.

"Then stop acting like—"

"Like what? Like I just saw my wife being dragged out of a fucking burning building? You said you would go nowhere without me."

My eyes narrow. *"Or Eris. Who was with me."*

His thin in return.

"Later," I tell him. *"You can chide me later. Right now, you're threatening our allies."*

"What I have in mind has nothing to do with 'chiding,'" he promises. But he turns to the prince and princess. "My apologies. I spoke out of turn. It's not every day you see your wife nearly die."

"She wasn't the only one," says Imerys, suddenly coughing. "And that's enough, Luce. We're only talking ourselves in circles."

"Immy?" Corvin kneels next to his youngest sister as she continues coughing. "How are you feeling?"

"Like someone just burned half my fucking library." There are tears in the corners of her eyes.

I keep seeing the library in my mind, going up in flames. Lucere and Thiago doused the worst of the fire, but so many of the books were burned.

Especially those on the level where Imerys and I were searching the other day.

Where something was watching us.

"Go home," Lucere says through clenched teeth. "I think you've done enough here. I don't know what the truth is. I don't know who attacked us. Or why. But as I told Adaia the other day, Ravenal intends to stand by itself. It will uphold the terms of the original Alliance. We do not side with either of you. We stand by ourselves, and will remain neutral in this coming conflict."

Thiago doesn't move. "Remember this moment when Ravenal's borders are being overrun with red and gold banners. This was the moment where you could have saved your people and your country."

And then he turns to shoot us a dark look.

"Let's go home."

Kyrian catches his arm before he turns to go. "Keep me apprised. If you need help, I will do what I can."

<small>FAILURE TASTES AS BITTER AS I THOUGHT IT WOULD.</small>

"You did your best," I murmur as we're about to mount and head for the Hallow. "Her eyes and ears were already closed before we even arrived."

Thiago stares moodily ahead. "Your mother won this skirmish. I could see it on Lucere's face—she's afraid of what Queen Maren can do to her. If she bows her head before your mother, then maybe, just maybe, she won't be crushed. She can ride their coattails to victory, clap enthusiastically when they deliver my head on a plate, and smile hollowly as her cities are slowly overrun. She'll be the first knee to bend before your mother."

"She'll also be the last," I remind him. "Kyrian despises my mother, and Queen Maren doesn't know the meaning of the word 'yield.' Maren's the one unpredictable factor my mother can't control. It wouldn't entirely surprise me if Maren thinks to use my mother to draw fire from their enemies before she knifes Adaia in the back and sets her crown on her own head."

"Do you think this was truly her doing?" He meets my gaze.

I swallow. "I'm starting to think it wasn't the fetch in the library the other day. If Maren has the Mirror, then she might be able to watch us through the World of Dreams."

But why burn the library?

"Either she thinks I found something in there," I whisper. "Or this was a threat to stop Lucere from allying herself with us."

But which one?

Hope dies in his eyes. "I nearly had her. I thought I nearly had her—"

"This game isn't over yet. Lucere has yielded. For now. That doesn't mean she won't come to her senses. Or maybe we can return to my original idea."

"I don't think Lucere's going to be standing near any open windows in the near future. And I thought you frowned upon that kind of behavior."

"I do." I would never plot another queen's death. "She hasn't made her pledge to the lands yet. She hasn't bound herself, and until she does, she is only heir apparent. Not queen. Perhaps someone else will grow a sudden ambition."

"Hmm." He turns back to his horse, but I know he's thinking. "Remind me not to play *fari* with you."

I can't help seeing the moves on the board the way my mother taught me. It doesn't mean I have to make those moves, but if there is one thing my mother is very adept at, it's predicting the path people will take.

And being unpredictable herself.

The thought bothers me. Because until this moment, she's been making all the right moves; her armies at the borders, an offer of peace with Ravenal....

But it's what Lucere would do. It's what an untried queen would do.

Somewhere out there, my mother is moving pieces.

It has to be the vision that the Prince of Shadows saw.

"Are you coming?" Thiago calls, mounting his horse.

I told him I wasn't some precious princess who needed

help getting up and down from her mount, and clearly he's taken me at my word. I gather the reins of the mare that was lent to me and prepare the stirrup—

Feet slap on the cobbles behind me.

Imerys captures my wrist just as I set my foot in the stirrup. "You're going?"

"It seems to be the best option for all of us. I don't think your sister is interested in extending the invitation."

Over her shoulder, I see Lucere pace to the edge of the balcony, looking down on us with a cool expression. Her gaze locks on Imerys.

"Thank you. For saving my life and Gossamer's."

"I'm sorry about the books."

Imerys squeezes my hand. "And speaking of books, I was thinking about what you were asking before. About the relics. Is that what you were truly searching for?"

"Searching for?"

"Oh, please…. I'm not an idiot. You broke into my library and you were searching for something. It wasn't about the Old Ones, though I think you're interested in them too."

The urge to ask dies on the tip of my tongue. I left her books on my bed, for I didn't feel right about taking them, after everything.

"I owe you my life," she points out. "If I can help in any way…. I swear I will not tell another soul."

I have to trust someone. And while my husband and the others would slay any monsters we came across, when it comes to finding information, this is what I need. Someone with knowledge. Someone who has access to information.

"I need to find the Crown of Shadows."

Suspicion dawns in her eyes. "Why?"

I don't want to lie to her. "Because I'm tired of living under the yoke of another, and this is the only way I can free myself."

Imerys nibbles on her lip. "I've heard of it, though I don't know where. Or what. Just…. The name sounds familiar somehow."

Curse it. It couldn't be this easy.

"If I find anything, then I'll send it your way," she promises.

"Thank you."

CHAPTER 15

Thiago sentences me to our chambers for several days, because although there's no outward sign of damage, my throat remains raw and I have a pressing headache that stabs harder every time I use my magic.

I don't know if he's pleased I made such progress— he's been training me to access my powers for the past three months with little response—but he does insist I rest.

"Maybe I've been going about this the wrong way?" he muses. "Maybe you don't need solitude and meditation to access your magic, but something more pressing."

I pause, halfway through a bowl of soup. "You're going to send me into a burning building next training session?"

"No." There's a certain sort of wickedness in his eyes. "But I'm sure I can conjure... motivation."

"Just remember: I can set your britches on fire."

He snorts as he pushes away from the bed. "Or our sheets."

"That only happened once!"

"Once is enough," he says with a wink, as I'm about to

throw my buttered roll at him. "Unless you mean that metaphorically, in which case I'm quite happy to volunteer. Get some rest."

"Did you hear anything about Lysander?"

His face sobers. "The Prince of Shadows sent his hexbreaker. She worked her magic, and Baylor said there's a little difference, but Lysander's still trapped in animal form."

I sigh. More unfortunate news.

"Rest," Thiago presses. "Curses are twisted things. It will take time to undo, much like your own memories. I'll see you at the end of the week. I need to check in at the border. With Eris and Baylor out of action, the others sometimes need a little more watching."

I spend the afternoon lolling in bed, and wake the next day with the need to *do* something.

With strict instructions that I'm not allowed to light so much as a candle, I head to the drilling yard, where Finn will put me through my paces in Thiago's absence.

Every woman in the castle lets their eyes linger on Finn. He's six-and-a-half feet of lithe strength and pure arrogance, with cheekbones that could cut like a knife, eyes the color of an alpine lake, and the kind of smile that makes even my heart skip a beat—even though I'm promised to another. He's just *that* pretty. Long dark hair is bound back from his face in braids, and there's a faint golden tattoo just above the center of his brows in the shape of a flame.

"Can't rest?" he calls, stringing a bow.

I shake my head ruefully. "Please tell me that's for me."

He hands it over, then kicks the quiver up into his hands with some kind of graceful hopping motion that would probably see me flat on my face if I tried to emulate it. "For my lady fair," he says, handing over an arrow. "It's been a while since we've trained together."

It's frustrating to be told you used to do something with someone, only to have no memories of it. "Did we?"

He clucks under his tongue. "How could you forget a male like me?"

"Well, considering I had no idea I was married to Thiago, surely I can be forgiven for not remembering *you*?"

He sighs. "Unremarkable. Unkissable. Unmemorable. I swear the three of you ladies are trying to give my pride a mortal blow."

I nock the arrow and face the target set up at the far end of the bailey. "If I thought your sense of pride was in any danger, I'd beg forgiveness, but you seem to be doing an immeasurable job of supporting it."

"I can't help that I'm dangerously good-looking, ridiculously intelligent, and can steal a laugh from even the coldest of hearts. Are you going to shoot the target? Or merely glare at it?"

I stare along the arrow and send it flying. It feels good to be doing something physical, even though my shot's slightly off center.

"Have you heard from Thiago?" I ask as he takes the bow.

Finn puts an arrow through the center of the target with ease. "All is well on the western front. There's a line of red and gold as far as the eye can see, but your mother's forces seem to be digging in deep. They're not pushing forward, but there's every sign they don't intend to lose ground."

Finn fills me in on the situation at the border as we

pass the bow back and forth. He manages to hit the dead of center ten out of ten times, until I finally concede.

"Do you ever miss?"

Taking one last arrow, he looks me in the eyes and shoots blind.

Dead center.

"With a bow? No. With a blade?" A faint shrug. "The only time anyone beats me, it's Eris. Baylor keeps me on my toes too, but I can defeat him."

"And Thiago?"

This time his smile is bright. "Once. I got the drop on him once, and I've never let him forget it. He's the only one who can match Eris, but I've never beaten her. Not yet."

"You're good," I say, examining the target again.

"You should see me when I have a blindfold on. Or on the back of a horse."

"Let me guess…," I drawl as we head toward the target to fetch our arrows. "You spend almost as much time practicing with a bow as you do staring in the mirror?"

He claps a hand to his chest as I wrench an arrow from the target. "Straight through the heart, Princess. And while I spend the same time in the training yard as anyone else, I don't live for it the way Eris does." He pauses. "It's my Sylvaren blood that gives me the advantage."

"You're Sylvaren?" I'd thought his ears were slightly tapered at the top.

More so than most of the fae.

"I don't speak about it very often," he says, glancing at the castle walls as if to check who's listening. "It's not the sort of thing one advertises, though the fae here are aware. I tend to keep to myself."

The Sylvaren were once fae, like us. They were refugees from the mother world who arrived with their queen, Sylvian, nearly two thousand years ago.

Of the five fae kings and queens who led their people to the safety of the new world of Arcaedia, Sylvian was the only one who sought to conquer the creatures that lived here already. The other kings and queens pushed their cities into the forests and burned the monsters out of their caves, but were content to stake out small territories and rule them. She was ruthless and bold, and claimed the lands far to the north, where Unseelie now lies, and she wanted to spread her empire from coast to coast.

Maia, her sister-queen from the home world, was the one to confront her when their peaceful treaties with the monsters of this world threatened to be destroyed. Maia slew Sylvian's lover, Gethred, and broke her crown. They say Sylvian cried a sea of tears when she buried Gethred deep in his earthen barrow, but when she had finished grieving, she swore that none of her people would ever have peace with the other fae courts.

And so she took her people—her fae—and she warped them with her magic.

She made them faster and taller and more muscular. She gave them the reflexes of a cat and the viciousness of a hunting hound. Hearts grew in darkness and rage, and they pledged, one and all, to serve her. She turned them into the ultimate warriors, until they were so fierce, they could barely keep peace among themselves.

Warsworn. Warriors who were bred for violence.

A tide that broke over the southern part of the continent like a dam bursting.

The four other kings and queens who had fled the

home world with Sylvian were forced to join together to fight her people.

And I don't entirely know what happened—Maia showed her godhood when she defeated Sylvian at Charun, in Unseelie, but in doing so, she gave her life.

The skies wept for her loss, and the remaining three kings and queens bent knee to worship Maia's sacrifice.

We remember.

Most of the Sylvaren died during that encounter, but those that were left were slaughtered by the thousand, and the rest put in chains. Others fled and went into hiding, though there's rumor that warbands of Sylvaren still haunt the far north of Unseelie.

Finn sighs. "Don't look at me that way, Princess. I'm no Warsworn. I'm not even a Follower of the Way. I have enough Sylvaren blood to make it wise to stay out of barfights and tavern brawls and anything that might tempt me to violence. That's why I'm here and not at the front. Thiago doesn't want me getting a taste for war."

"Is it really that hard to abstain?" They say the Sylvaren are born with a thirst for blood.

"Every day. That's why I prefer to take month-long walks in the snow during winter and swim the bay during summer. That's why I spend ten hours a day drilling here in the yard if I haven't found a friend to help me burn off some of the excess energy."

Is he referring to…?

"Fighting—in a controlled environment—helps me burn off the urge to kill. So does fucking."

He is. "Right at the top of my list of things I didn't need to know, thanks, Finn."

"You're awfully prudish for Adaia's daughter."

If there's one thing I can grant my mother credit for, it's keeping her private life well away from me. "When you're Adaia's daughter, you become very good at pretending you didn't see—or hear—anything. And I kept to myself mostly. Andraste was better at dealing with court life. She had her coterie of friends and I—"

I had the library. I had my horse, Anavel, and an entire forest to ride through.

"I... was friends with some of the border lords' daughters," I admit. "Those my mother kept as hostages, who strained at the shackles of being bound to the castle. We'd ride. We'd hunt. Anything to get out of Hawthorne Castle."

"Sounds lonely."

"So does heading into the wilderness for a month-long 'walk in the snow.'"

We share a look.

"Is it loneliness to enjoy your own company? Or is it lonelier to be among enemies who spend their entire days plotting to tear you down or whispering behind their hands at you?" I sigh. "I like it better here." A glance up at the castle turrets reveals the familiar sandstone towers. "I think that was the hardest part of not knowing who Thiago was to me or why my mother had sent me to him as tribute. My first few months in Evernight felt like my life in Hawthorne Castle all over again. I knew there was something you were all keeping from me, I just didn't know what."

"He had to keep you away from the castle, Princess. Her spell threatened to melt your brains out of your ears if it broke before you were ready to face the truth, and too many people knew your secret."

"I know. I don't blame him for that." I look down at the arrow in my hands. "I'm just grateful that I don't have to play that game anymore. I've never truly had a home before. Evernight is everything I've ever wanted, and yet, with my mother marching her armies north, it feels like she can take everything away from me."

Finn looks away. "Stop it. Or you're going to make me shed a tear, and that isn't very manly, Princess."

"One thing that I'm learning is that it isn't weak to admit to uncertainty. And if you keep calling me Princess, I'm going to come up with some terrible nickname for you and then I'm going to tell everyone in the castle about it."

"Too late," he says as he heads toward the target to fetch our arrows.

"What was it?"

"Oh no," he calls. "I'm not going to *remind* you."

THREE DAYS LATER, ERIS IS STILL TRAPPED IN DREAMS.

Thalia spends most of her time trying to ferret out the guild plot, what with Elms Day fast approaching. Otherwise she's at Eris's side, trying to break the curse that binds her to sleep. Every day her eyelashes will flutter, or her fingers will twitch, but it feels like some net keeps dragging her back.

The only laughter the day brings is when Finn arrives to take over the night watch. He doesn't want to leave Eris in the dark, and I'm glad someone is due to sit with her. Though he threatens to kiss her a half dozen times if she doesn't wake, until both Thalia and I are exchanging glances across the bed.

"It's meant to be true love's kiss," Thalia tells him sweetly, "and I think—unless there's something you haven't been telling us, Finn—that you're not on the shortlist."

"Hardly," he says with a careless smile. "Eris might desire my heart in a box if I irritate her enough, but at her feet? I don't think so. Besides, I don't have a hundred horses to spare, and I know who wins that battle if we both draw swords."

"That's so sweet of you," Thalia tells him. "You're acting quite the gallant this past week, Finn. It almost makes me wonder—"

"Gallant?" The smile on his face dies, and his eyes are practically glacial as he glares at her. "Me?"

"All this joking about kissing her," she continues in a completely innocent tone, "and protecting her honor. Next thing we know, you'll be composing sonnets."

"I swear to the gods...." He pushes to his feet, grumbling under his breath. "Just for that, you can have the night watch as well as this afternoon."

"I was only joking," she calls as he strides toward the door.

"I wasn't!"

After that afternoon, he doesn't threaten to kiss her again.

"I think I struck a nerve," Thalia muses the next morning while we watch him sparring in the yard through Eris's chamber window.

I think she struck more than that.

But our smiles last only a few seconds.

"Wake up, E," Thalia says, squeezing Eris's hand. "Please wake up."

It's beginning to wear on all of us, I think.

To see her like this—struck down and motionless, with only her fingers twitching occasionally—makes me feel sick.

"Get some rest," I tell Thalia. "You've been hovering by her side day and night since we returned. I'll watch over her for the night."

Thalia sighs. "I can't afford to rest. You heard what the Prince of Shadows said about Elms Day. So far none of my little spies have heard anything. And without Eris we're severely undermanned. Elms Day is only five days away and I have nothing."

"Can you get in contact with the Prince of Shadows?"

Thalia arches a brow. "We don't hire assassins, Vi. Tolerating them when there's no proof of actual murder isn't the same thing as hiring them."

"Then tell Theron that we want these conspirators alive. And offer to pay him double if he can get them to talk."

"EVERYTHING'S TURNING TO SHIT," I TELL ERIS LATER THAT night as I sit at her bedside. "I wasn't foolish enough to think my mother would merely accede to this marriage once we broke the curse. She lives and breathes vengeance, after all, but I was so focused on Thiago—on saving him— that I didn't think about the true cost of what I was doing."

Eris remains still.

There's a woven web hanging above her bed—a six-pointed star threaded with iron beads—in order to keep

Queen Maren out of the room should she attempt to reach for Eris again, but so far, not a single bead has broken.

"I keep waiting for my mother's next strike. Elms Day means something, and I don't like not knowing who is involved." Pushing to my feet I pace to the window. "And as if that isn't enough, we don't even know what Angharad is doing in the north."

She's the true threat, though my mother cannot see it.

Or no, not cannot.

Will not.

Five hundred years of peace. And I am the catalyst for breaking it. I rub the bracelet that locks around my wrist. The fetch can't see me while I wear this, though the bone-white imprint of its hand is still scarred into a manacle around my wrist from where it grabbed me.

"I need you back," I tell Eris. "I even asked Thalia to use Theron and his assassins to help us. That's how desperate I am."

Nothing.

I know Thiago's tried. I know Thalia's tried. Even Finn, in his own manner.

But I've never tried.

My gifts from my fae heritage are negligible. Thiago thinks they'll grow stronger with practice—my mother's curse didn't just take my memories of him, but everything I've ever learned about magic too.

But I'm not talking about my fae gifts.

It's far too easy to reach out and pluck at the power of the ley line. Ceres was built right over the top of a nexus point, where several ley lines cross. Perfect for inter-Hallow travel, but also... the power of the lands is stronger here. It doesn't just vibrate through me. It sings. It feels like a pair of warm hands curling around me, finally welcoming me home.

"Wake up," I whisper, setting my hands on her chest. "Come back, Eris. Wake up."

In my mind I see a glimmer of light deep within her, like a seed. Darkness surrounds it. The light remains trapped like it's in a dark maze, with nowhere to go, no way out, except to twist and run through the shadowy hedges of her own mind.

There's also something else there.

Something deep and dark and hungry. It doesn't feel like an enemy. No. It feels like part of Eris herself. It turns into my touch, drawing in a breath as if it can scent me.

"Who are you?" it asks, turning its full attention to me.

Something about it feels wrong. It's too hungry, and it captures my mind, nibbling at a delicate thread of my power. Instantly, the storm of darkness doubles in size, until the seed of light is lost even further. Sharpened hooks latch on to me, siphoning away my strength, and through them, the power of the ley lines.

"Free me," it suggests. *"Free me and she will wake."*

But the words are merely meant to stall.

I try to pull away, but it's as if my resistance only encourages it. Its teeth sink into me, and it's lapping at my power, drinking it down in hot, greedy gulps—

I lash out, cleaving straight through the darkness with my power, and it parts like smoke. And then I'm free, staggering back from the bed even as Eris cries out softly.

What in the Underworld was *that*?

"Eris?"

Her head writhes as if she's suffering a bad dream, but

then she slowly, slowly subsides. Silent once more. Still once more.

And I'm left trembling, feeling as though half of my soul has been gouged out.

A shaking fills me. I need to sit. Badly.

But even as I think it, I eye the chair and how close it is to the bed.

If that thing reaches out for me again—

Sweat presses a clammy hand down my spine. I know what they say about her. The Morai called her the Devourer, and even they—as monstrous as they were —feared her.

But this is *Eris*.

And she's alone and helpless right now, and as much as I don't want to go near the bed, she's my friend.

I've been alone before. Ever since I turned twelve, if I'm being honest.

So I force myself to haul the chair next to her bed, and I sit there and, while I don't dare touch her, I tell her that I'm here.

And that I'm staying.

It's nearly dawn when I slowly lean forward on the bed and rest my head on my arms. Every inch of me aches as if something big and gnarly has taken bloody, invisible bites of me, but the wounds no longer feel raw.

I'm healing.

Just tired.

"*So tired,*" someone says.

And as something tinkles and falls to the coverlet, I

swear I sense a man's hand caress the back of my neck before he pushes me down into sleep.

I dream of spiders crawling all over my skin.

And a forest where I'm running, always running....

And somewhere ahead of me, a baby cries.

"*Not that way,*" whispers a voice.

We explode into a different forest, but this one is green and verdant and somehow *alive*. It's like no other forest I've ever seen, for there are ferns and soft fronds of barely formed plants that thicken the undergrowth. There's a hint of the untouched about this forest, as if we're so far from the nearest civilization that it's forgotten what a city looks like.

Sunset falls, bringing with it a thousand shining stars as we creep through the trees. Plants part before me, as if to welcome me.

Ahead of us, voices chant in unison.

There's laughter. Smoke from a fire. And children squealing as they chase each other through the ferns.

We walk among the camp, unseen and unknown, and though there's a hand in mine, leading me, I find it impossible to turn and look at my companion.

The creatures wear ragged deer pelts and simple homespun smocks. Stubby horns peek through their hair, and I catch a glimpse of hooves and tails on some of them. One even wears a set of bat-like wings. Some of them have swept gold dust along the angle of their cheekbones and painted thin black lines along the bridge of their noses, sweeping it across their foreheads.

All of them have black eyes.

No pupil. No iris.

Just bottomless depths.

I don't know if there are different clans depending on their animalistic features, though I notice the ones with horns seem to linger together, and the little children leaping through the forest on hooves seem all of a kind.

And through it all, the creatures I know as demi-fey weave like little drunk glistening fireflies.

The otherkin.

I feel breathless. They no longer exist now except in stories or in the features I sometimes see bred into unseelie faces. When my kind fled through the stars and arrived in this land, these were the beings that lived in what we now call Arcaedia.

Monsters, all the history books say.

But there are no monsters here.

"This way," says the voice. *"Let me show you what we are."*

Rune stones appear. A Hallow. But the rocks remain mere sandstone, unblemished by any mark or rune. They simply exist, surrounding a smooth plane of rock that looks like it's been polished for centuries.

Otherkin kneel there, singing and weaving back and forth in some sort of... prayer?

The Mother of Night appears, walking among them in a gown of shimmering black that look like she's stolen a piece of the night sky and woven it into some sort of material. Little black horns poke through the glistening strands of her dark hair. She's always looked ageless to me, but something about her tells me she's younger in this moment.

As she passes the otherkin, she ruffles her hand through their hair and smiles at the children, and perhaps it's the smile that undoes me.

This is wrong. This is all wrong.

"Why am I here?" I demand, tugging my hand from the one that curls around mine.

Instantly the forest disappears.

I'm standing on the icy-cold island in the middle of the Mother of Night's prison world.

"Because we wished to show you the truth," says the male voice at my side.

The truth?

"I want to go back! What have you done to me? What have you done to Eris?"

"She is but sleeping," says the voice.

"You could end her sleep." The Mother of Night appears, walking up the rocky shore. *"You could wake her with but a single word."*

"And does that word have anything to do with 'yes'?" I demand. "Yes, I will free you from your prison world. Yes, I will free you all. Because if that is to be the price of… of Eris's waking, then you do not know me. And you do not know her. Because if Eris were here to tell me what to do, I know what she'd say. No price is worth the risk of seeing you and your kind free."

There's a long moment of silence. *"We are not monsters, Iskvien."*

But I've had enough.

"You pulled me into this dream, didn't you? And you did something to Eris. It was you who plunged all those guards into sleep. It wasn't Maren, after all."

All of this, just to push me into a place I don't want to be.

The Mother exchanges a glance with the creature beside me. *"Maren wielded the Dreamthief's Mirror, and with it his power. It took your friend. But she did not realize that the second she wielded the Mirror, the Dreamthief was granted access to you. We can help you and your friend, Princess."*

I've played this game before. "You're lying."

"We're not lying."

I glare at the Mother of Night. "I will find your crown and I will give it to you by the end of the year. And then you will rot in this prison world, because I will not be your pawn. I will not be your *leanabh an dàn*! You can all rot!"

I turn and lunge for the forest I first found myself in. The one with bare branches that hook toward the sky and snow underfoot. The baby is screaming now, the sound cutting right through me.

I've been trapped in these dreams for months.

"You're just trying to scare me!" I shout.

And I turn and run the other way as the baby's cries echo louder.

And then Thiago is there, his eyes flashing with green fire as he grabs me by the upper arms. "Why didn't you tell me you were the *leanabh an dàn*? Why didn't you trust me to love you?"

"Because you said the child of destiny needed to die!" I gasp.

"But that's not the truth, Vi," he snarls. "I would have loved you. I would have trusted you. I would have given you everything. And you have ruined it."

The protest dies on my lips, because there's something quivering around his hand, an enormous twist of shadow writhing into a nest of shadowy snakes.

He hurls them at my face, and I try to scream, but they evaporate the second they hit my skin, leaving me to inhale the smoky residue of their being.

It tastes like death.

At that I wake, gasping in a suppressed scream, every inch of me hammering with alertness. My hands shake. My pulse thunders. And I swear I can still taste the kiss of the grave.

But I'm in the room beside Eris's bed, and though the candle has burned low, it's the same candle I lit hours ago. I wave a hand through the flame, just to feel the bite of its heat.

"It's just a dream. Just a fucking dream." I reach for Eris's hand to squeeze it, but she doesn't squeeze back.

She's still asleep.

Still shockingly vulnerable.

Every bead in the web of dreams lies crushed into dust on the pillow around Eris's dark hair.

I want to run. I want to hide. Even my nights are no longer safe. But I reach out for the power of the Ceres Hallow, feeling it tremble awake somewhere close by.

"Prove you're not monsters. Let her go."

It's a foolish thought, thrown out into the night in the hopes that the Mother of Night will hear it.

I don't dare hope for anything more.

But nor do I lay hands on Eris again, because that hungry, slavering darkness within her knows I'm there.

And I think it knows that I'm the key to freeing itself.

Even though, Maia help me, I'm the one in chains.

CHAPTER 16

The next day, I'm slumped in my bath, trying to wash away the residue of oily smoke that still somehow clings to me, when I receive a note from Thalia saying the impossible has happened.

Eris is awake.

Slipping into my training leathers, I hurry through the hallways of the castle, though the sound of someone yelling makes my footsteps slow as I reach Eris's apartments.

And then Finn bursts out of Eris's room.

A boot follows him, and Finn snarls as he turns and catches it. "I missed you too," he yells through the doorway. "Next time you swoon, I'm going to leave you in the dirt!"

"Swoon?" comes an enraged hiss from within. "I didn't swoon, you ass. That bastard hauled me under with his magic."

"Who?"

"If I knew that, then I would have slit the prick's throat and broken free!"

And then Eris appears in the doorway, her eyes widening when she sees me.

We stare at each other, and my foot shifts before I remember that endless slick of darkness within her.

"Vi?" She sees the hesitation and tips her chin up.

Eris has known a lifetime of fear. I won't add to it.

Though it takes everything I have in me, I step forward and hug her. Startled arms come up around me, though she stiffens a little, as though the act is unnatural.

"You're awake."

Is this a gift from the Dreamthief?

Eris eases out of the embrace, and I see hints she's not as sanguine as she acts. Her dark skin is paler than usual, and there's a hint of unease in the gleam of her eyes.

I don't think I've ever seen Eris display anything other than a stoic *fuck you* attitude to the world.

"What happened?" I ask. "Did you see anyone?"

"Did you feel Queen Maren?" Finn demands.

"Maren?" She looks startled.

"Tall. Evil. Possibly the most beautiful woman in the world, but with a heart made of ice," Finn muses. "She used the Mirror against you."

Eris turns back into her bedchambers, and I follow as she gathers a robe and drapes it around her shoulders. The scarlet silk looks like nothing she'd ever wear, though I suspect Thalia's been in her wardrobe. "You. Out."

Finn crosses his arms over his chest. "I have seen you in your nightclothes before, E."

Her eyes narrow.

"And I'm pretty sure you've seen me naked," he muses.

"I can't recall. It must have been an underwhelming experience," she growls.

Finn takes a step toward her.

She points at the door. "Out. And I don't care what you think of my nightclothes. Just get out."

Finn shoots me a filthy glare. "There's a tray on the table. Perhaps you can get Her Royal Pain-in-the-Ass to eat. I wash my hands of it."

And then he's gone.

A faint flicker of relief crosses Eris's face, and while I definitely think there's a reason Finn's been wearing a rut in the floor for the past four days, I'm uncertain whether Eris feels the same way.

I set the tray by the bed. "Let me guess? He threatened to kiss you?"

Halfway through the process of slipping back beneath her blankets, Eris nearly loses her balance. *"What?"*

I tell her about how Finn's been calling her the Sleeping Princess of Somnus all week, promising her every night that if she isn't awake by morning, then he'll bestow a kiss on her lips.

"He would." She sinks into the enormous feather mattress and sighs. "The last thing I remember is hurrying down the stairs to see where the smoke was coming from. The second I entered the courtyard, I saw six guards lying flat on their backs." She shrugs. "I drew my sword and checked to see if the closest guard was still breathing and realized he was merely snoring. And that's when I felt it."

I sink onto the bed beside her.

"There was a man walking across the courtyard in long

black robes that left his chest bare. Tattoos marked his chest, and they were swirling. It looked like Thiago, which is why I didn't react at first. It even smelled like him. But when he smiled at me, I knew something was wrong. There was a look about his eyes, a hint of... something glowing. I went for my sword, and he reached out and touched my forehead.... And the next thing I know, this enormous lummox"—she gestures at the door where Finn's ghost still lingers—"is leaning over me and asking me if I know where I am. What did he mean about a mirror?"

I tell her that Maren used the Dreamthief's Mirror to ensnare her.

"And that bitch Lucere tucked tail. I shouldn't be surprised."

"She's the crown heir of a kingdom that's been ravaged both by its own queen and by outside forces. She has few allies. All her cousins want her throne. And somehow she's caught between the jaws of two powerful enemies." I shrug. As much as I don't like Lucere, I have to start thinking like a ruling princess. Not a jealous wife meeting the once-betrothed of her husband. "She's trying her best to protect her kingdom. I have to respect that. None of us wants war."

"Without her—" Eris bites off a curse.

"We will have to find someone else to help us."

"There *is* no one else."

"There are *always* opportunities."

"Ugh. You're starting to sound like Thalia."

I grin.

She pushes herself further upright. "What did you do last night? I felt you. I heard you calling to me in the dark.

213

And it...." She shakes her head, bleakness flashing through her eyes. "*It* knows you were there too."

"What is it?"

"Oblivion," she says with a whisper. "Something that is best kept locked inside me. Forever." And then she's angry again. "And I had it locked away. I had it buried down deep inside me until you woke it!"

"I'm sorry. I was just trying to help you."

Eris throws the bedspread back, slinging her legs over the edge. I reach to help her, but she waves me away sharply. "Don't *touch* me." And then a little quieter, when I rear back. "Don't touch me. It can sense your presence. It wants to drain you dry."

"Will you be able to... handle it?"

Tension tightens her jaw. "I have to."

There's strain on her face as she dresses swiftly. And I wonder if this is what every day of her life feels like.

"I'll hold myself together," she growls, "until Thiago gets back, and then he can ward me seven ways until Sunday."

SOMETIME DURING THE NIGHT, WARM ARMS CURL AROUND ME in bed, a gentle kiss pressing against the back of my neck.

"Did you miss me?" comes a familiar rumble.

It draws me out of sleep—nice dreams for a change— and as I blink in the light of a lantern that's been newly lit, I realize my husband is home.

"You're back." I turn into his arms, pressing my face against his shirt and the hollow of his throat. I don't quite cling to him. "How was the front?"

"Busy." He steals a kiss, and I melt into it.

Every hard inch of him drives me into the mattress, and I run my hands through his hair as I drink at his mouth.

Finally, I can breathe again.

"What are we doing today?" I murmur.

He gives me a rather pointed nudge.

"That's only an hour's worth of distraction," I tell him. "After that?"

Thiago smacks my hip. "And after that we do it again." He kisses my chin. "And again." A kiss to my throat. "And again."

And then he's working his way down, his fingers brushing against the silk nightdress I no longer need to be wearing.

CHAPTER 17

Elms Day brings with it the sound of bells.

They ring through the streets below the castle as Thiago stares down at the note that appeared on Eris's pillow this morning. He sniffs the Sorrow rose. "The Prince of Shadows sends word. He's found the conspirators behind this little plot and he has them in chains." Thiago looks up at me. "Something about a triple fee for producing them alive."

"Double," I tell him. "It was double. Who are they?"

Thiago flips the note over. "I don't know. He doesn't say. He says he has them contained in holding cells in the Bone Church, and will expect payment upon delivery."

This is what I get for using an assassin.

Untrusting soul.

"You are not going into the city," Eris says flatly. "Not today."

Thiago runs the letter over his lips. "They're going to attack my city. And we don't know if any of them work in the castle. They could be among the guards, the servants, or even the kitchen staff. What makes you think we're safer up here?"

"What makes you think the Prince of Shadows isn't involved?"

"Just a… feeling," he muses.

"Finn," she says, turning her attention to the handsome rogue.

Finn leans back in his chair. "I'm just here for my good looks and charm. Besides, I know better than to argue with him when he's in this mood. Look at him."

We all look at Thiago.

His eyes narrow. "What?"

"He has his brooding face on," Finn continues. "That face says 'someone threatened my wife and now they're going to die.' That face says 'Adaia turned one of my closest friends into a bane.' It says 'I really, really want to punch someone.'"

I sip my tea. "It also says, 'For fucks sake, Finn. Shut up or I'll hang you out the window by your heels.'"

Thiago holds his hands out. "She's not entirely wrong."

Eris snatches the letter from Thiago's hand and scrunches it into a ball with a passion that makes both men wince. "Fine. Let's walk into a potential trap. Let's march into an assassin's quarters and offer our heads for the chopping block. We'll take Baylor. He can unleash a little of his pent-up aggression on people who want to kill us. It will be fun."

"This is what I like about you, Eris," Finn says, rubbing her shoulders. "You're always so optimistic."

"THERE'S NO STORM," I POINT OUT AS WE MARCH INTO THE Old Quarter, because Theron said there would be a storm. "Not even a cloud in the sky. Maybe he misread the situation?"

"Does anyone else wonder if we can trust Theron?" Finn asks. "I'm not saying I agree with Eris, but I am merely pointing out that he is head of the Assassin's Guild, and he happened to walk into a bookstore where our princess was listening to what appears to be a conspiracy to overthrow our precious prince. Who's to say he wasn't there for that meeting and didn't panic when he saw Vi?"

"Trust me," I drawl. "I don't think Theron knows what panic means."

"You didn't think of this earlier?" Eris asks, her hard gaze darting into every alley we pass. She hasn't taken her hand off the hilt of her sword. "When I was trying to convince everyone this was a bad idea?"

"This is a good idea," Baylor says, cracking his knuckles.

Everyone looks at him.

Even Thiago.

"Alive," Thiago reminds him, as we cross the bridge into the Old Quarter. "We need information and—"

There's a tremor deep underground.

I freeze, looking down. "Can you feel that?"

Thiago takes a step toward me, and the sharpness of his features assures me he knows exactly what I'm talking about. Every inch of him becomes alert. "Eris?"

"Fan out," Eris snaps, and she takes the point as Finn and Baylor both draw their swords.

"What is that?" Finn mutters.

There's no immediate threat. No sign of impending doom.

But I can feel it spiraling out beneath me as though magic is being breathed to life in the world nearby. An *immense*, dangerous sort of magic.

Somewhere nearby, the earth is screaming.

A frown furrows between Thiago's brows. "Baylor, take Vi back to the castle. I need to—"

"Not without you." Our eyes meet, and then he gives a curt nod as if he recognizes I'm not merely going to tuck tail and run.

"Then take these." He flips a pair of daggers into his fingers and offers me the hilts.

"Why do *you* get the sword?" I joke, trying to swallow my sudden nerves. My skin *itches*.

"Didn't you know? Size matters to all males."

"Yes, but as all females know, you can still feel a little prick."

An incredulous laugh escapes him, before he starts to scan the skies. "Later. You'll pay for that later."

"I'm trying to concentrate here," Finn says, making a gagging sound.

A horrible rumbling sound ruptures the world, but there's a distance to it that makes me uncertain. So deep I can't quite pinpoint where it's coming from. It feels like a leviathan is crawling up from the world's magma core, and slowly, slowly bring the force of its propulsion with it.

Up. It's coming from— "The dam," I whisper.

Pebbles rain down the cliff face.

Fae stagger out of their shops, all of them looking about.

"What in Maia's name?" My whisper dies as the beast finally emerges.

An explosion of stone detonates far above us.

I scream as rock bursts into shards, flinging my arms over my head. And then Thiago is there, sweeping me under the overhang of a shop as enormous chunks of stone slam into the streets.

Seconds later a ward forms above us, quietening some of the noise.

"Vi!"

"I'm all right! I'm fine!"

"Where are the others?"

I catch a glimpse of Eris and Finn ducking under an overhang across the street. Baylor simply stands in the middle of the street and slowly looks up.

There's a rushing noise, like the sound of—

"Water," I breath.

It was never a storm.

Thiago scans the cliff as that rushing noise begins to grow louder. And then his face suddenly whitens as a sluice of water pours toward us, trickling through a crack in the dam walls. "The dam. They've set charges on the dam."

BOOM.

Another one.

Fae scream.

Thiago takes a step in that direction and as if his illusions are a veil, I catch a hint of wings spreading. "Go with Baylor. He'll keep you safe."

Safe?

Grabbing his arm, I haul him toward me. "You're not going up there?"

A third explosion echoes, this time weaker than the others and further along. Bells begin ringing throughout the Old Quarter—the same bells that had rung for Elms Day—though these ones sing the song of alarm. Panic echoes through the quarter, and the bells are the symphony.

"The dam walls haven't broken yet—they're solid stone. If I can stop those charges...."

The world will see what he is.

They will know the truth.

I can't fly, but he can.

I see it in his eyes, and then he gives me a crisp nod. If those dam walls break, this part of the city will be washed away. Thousands will die. And if he can stop it from happening, then it's worth the cost of his unseelie secret.

"Let me go." An implacable sort of violence crosses Thiago's face as he turns to face the threat. "Finn! You're with me. Eris, get to the Bone Church and find out what Theron knows." He takes two steps, then turns back to her. "Don't kill him."

She makes an innocent gesture to her chest as if to say, *would I do that?*

"Baylor and I will help these people to evacuate," I tell him. "They'll die if they stay here."

"And so will you."

"Not if you stop the dam from breaking."

"Vi!"

"You want me to be your queen?" I push away from him, staring up at the water gushing down the cliff. "Then you need to let me be your queen. If I survived my mother's court, then this should be a laugh. Panic will only inspire death. Someone needs to take control."

Thiago's jaw clenches. "Promise me you'll get out before it's too late."

"I don't intend to die here." I dart toward him and kiss his startled mouth. "I have an appointment with my mother, and she's not going to escape my vengeance this time. Now get up there and stop those explosions."

He grabs my face in both hands, kisses me hard and furious, and then steps away. "I'll veil as best I can."

Ripples of invisible force stir through the air as he spreads his wings wide, and then he launches himself into the sky, vanishing in an instant. Finn curses under his breath, sheathes his sword, and then hauls himself up the side of a shop and onto the roof. He takes a running jump and leaps onto the side of the cliff face, finding handholds where none appear to exist.

A veil is all good and well, but I catch glimpses of Thiago as he flies. Even the best veil is prone to wind shifts and body movements. "They'll see his wings," I tell Baylor.

"He knows what he's doing. Come on."

Time to follow through on my own promises.

I consider the topography of the city. The old quarter has excellent views of the harbour below it, but if that dam breaks then it will be under water.

The highest point of the city is where the castle looms. I'd like to think it was mere happenstance that saw it built in a defensible position, but my familiarity with queens makes me suspect some long-ago royal liked looking down on her subjects.

"To the castle!" I yell.

My voice is lost within the cacophony of screams and fae scrambling for cover.

Curse it. I need to be heard.

There's a spell my mother uses when she's speaking before the court. Few know what she's doing, but she can modify her tone so it either cuts like a sibilant whisper, or is loud enough to send her border lords to their knees.

It's not something I've practiced.

My childhood taught me to amplify voices so I could hear what was being said several rooms over, but not how to amplify my own voice.

Maybe I can twist that spell somehow?

I scramble up on top of a shoe shop and quieten all my senses. Instead of reaching out, I reach within and feel my magic brewing.

"Evacuate to the castle!"

The words tear from my throat and vibrate through the air. Bells shatter. Birds squawk. Baylor winces, clapping his hands over his ears. The spell shreds my throat and nearly sends me to my knees, but I know everyone in the Old Quarter heard me. Possibly everyone in the city. Coughing blood, I try to croak something else, but my voice is gone.

Curse it. That will have to do.

Fae flee in all directions, but I see heads turning, looking for the castle.

"Go!" I mouth silently.

Above me, a shuddering groan of rock indicates another fracture of the dam walls. A black shape forms, elegant wings flaring wide. Fae stop and point and my heart is in my throat as I watch Thiago strain to contain another explosion.

Fire blooms, but he vanishes it in a whirl of darkened shadow.

It's like what he did with the library. The explosion is

223

somehow contained, its damage swallowed by those clouds of darkness.

"The prince!" someone points.

"He has wings," another cries.

Thorns erupt through the cobblestones of the street like some sort of monstrous bramble-creature that's clawing its way up from the underground.

One of them lashes out and snatches up a butcher. He vanishes with a scream, swallowed whole by the chasm. And suddenly fae are moving again, fleeing in terror.

What sort of attack is this?

Baylor meets the next blow, but a thorn lashes out and wraps around his waist. It hauls him inside the crevice.

"Baylor!" I whisper hoarsely, leaping into the street with my daggers in hand. The brambles whip and writhe, snatching an older female off her feet and dragging her toward the gaping chasm.

Lunging forward I drive both daggers through the thicker, fleshier part of the bramble and a hissing screech echoes.

"Take—" *my hands*. My voice dies in a croak, but the female clutches at me and I haul her to her feet. A shove in the back sends her limping into the flurry.

And then a fae warrior is thrown up through the crevice, as though the bramble-creature tossed him.

He lands lightly on his feet in the middle of the street, and before his red cape has even finished swirling, his sword clears its sheath and slices a man's head from his shoulders.

Gold-plated armor. Red cloak. The crown of thorns emblem on the pommel of his sword.

An Asturian warrior.

Mother.

And not just one of her guards, but one of her elite, hand-picked Deathguard, judging by the blank gold mask that covers his features.

A two-pronged attack—one group no doubt sent after the walls of the dam, and the second sent into the city to create as much havoc as possible.

Second strike.

My mind flashes back to that encounter in the book-shop. This 'Gray Guild' that wants to overthrow my husband is working with my mother.

With her? Or for her?

Do they even know what they've begun?

"Baylor?" I try to yell, but the sound is a muted whisper.

He'll have to take care of himself. I have my hands full.

The warrior whirls, cutting down an enormous merchant who charges at him. He moves like lightning, barely pausing to shove the man off his blade before he spins and guts a woman who tries to brain him with a meat cleaver.

Another Asturian warrior is launched through the crevice. A female, this time.

Then a third. And a fourth.

There will be five in this pack; they always hunt in groups of five.

But the fifth is no warrior clad in gold.

Instead it's a bane, wearing a thick golden collar the size of my forearm.

It lands on all four legs, its slavering jowls quivering as it roars, and then it bounds after a pair of women that scream and flee toward a restaurant.

I have to get these people out of here.

Or create a target they might focus on, to give the merchants time to escape.

Summoning a bow of raw aether, I forge an arrow out of flame and nock it swiftly. Heat sizzles near my cheek. It was a trick Thiago taught me; he can't wield Fire, but he knew it would teach me to control every inch of flame. I lock on the bane and sent the shaft blazing through the air.

The bane screams as my arrow strikes between its shoulder blades. Its fur catches fire instantly, until it's a howling inferno of rage and pain.

I don't have time to focus on it. My fingers are blistered —I'm still perfecting my fire arrows—and now I have the attention of the remaining four Deathguard.

And no voice.

My bow vanishes into nothing.

"What's wrong, little girl?" The warrior sneers, wiping his fingers along the edge of his blade and flicking blood onto the cobbles. "Scared?"

Voiceless. Impotent rage simmers within me, but there's more than one way to communicate.

He grabs for me and I punch him in the face, driving the force of my blow through my knuckles.

His head snaps back and he staggers, but he's twice my size and recovers quickly.

"You'll pay for that," promises the female.

I spin low, beneath the sweep of her sword, swiping her feet out from under her. The second she crashes to the ground, I scramble for her fallen sword.

Four-on-one aren't great odds and my daggers are barely half a foot long. Jokes about little pricks notwithstanding.

The one I punched sneers and takes a step toward me. But the blond grabs his arm and removes his mask. "Wait."

"Let me go!"

"Don't you know who she is?" The blond's eyes lock on me and I realize I've seen his face before. One of my mother's guards. Halvor, perhaps? "That's the princess."

All four of them focus on me.

"Worth her weight in gold," adds the last guard, "if we bring her back to her mother. Alive."

I take a step back as they all advance. I'd rather die than be returned to my mother. I won't be the bargaining chip she uses to destroy my husband and our people.

Placing my palm flat on the ground I summon fire. Flames circle me with a hiss; a warning.

And Halvor smiles. "She's weak. Fire's her natural gift, but the rest of her arsenal is limited. Attack."

A rather accurate assessment of the princess who'd been sent to Evernight as a tribute.

But Thiago—for all that he loves me—hasn't been letting me rest easy. I'd said that I wanted to relearn my magic, and so he's spent the last three months pushing me to the brink in order to force it to flourish.

I've cursed him every day for that decision, but right now, I could kiss his feet in gratitude.

Without a voice, I merely place my palm out flat and gesture toward Halvor.

Come on, then. Let's dance.

He launches himself over the ring of flames and I step into the movement, driving my sword up to meet his. There's an instant of shock on his face, and then he lands with a jarring rattle of armor, the force of his blow emanating through my shoulder.

The armor gives him the advantage. It may slow him down eventually, but my blows will only glance off the shining metal.

But if they want me alive, then they can't hurt me too badly. It's armor of its own.

I attack with a daring he's clearly not expecting. Beating him back, I push him almost into the ring of flames, before he looks up with a murderous glare.

A foot hammers toward me, driving into my chest. The breath slams out of me. I hit the ground hard and roll back over my shoulder.

A net shoots through the air, fanning out over me. No time to think. I simply burn it with a thought and little cinders fall to the cobbles.

Ash floats through the air like snowflakes, tangling in my hair.

"You're better than I expected," Halvor tells me, straightening as he prowls in a half circle around me.

And he's done exactly what he needed to do.

Distract me, so that his friends can surround me.

They pace outside my ring of flames, blocking off all my exits.

I can't beat them.

My mother's Deathguard are stolen from their mothers at birth, and a knife is put in their hands before they can even walk.

The sword is a living extension of my hand, but it's not going to help me out of here. And I can't look for Thiago. He's busy.

There's one thing left to try.

"Not good enough," I somehow rasp.

Halvor laughs. "No. You were never good enough."

Words I've heard a thousand times before, but this time they ignite something within me that's no longer desperate and lonely and fearful.

They will not take me alive.

I will *not* return to my mother.

Unless it's with a knife in hand.

Sweeping my hand wide, I send flames licking toward the warrior on my right. He leaps out the way, but a cinder catches his cloak and I slam my fist shut, igniting it with a thought.

A shape drives toward me—an armored fist hammering toward my face. It's like being hit with a sledgehammer. I spin off guard and as my vision blurs, a gauntleted hand locks around my throat, hauling me back into an armored chest.

Halvor.

"You should have had the decency to die at the Queensmoot," he hisses in my ear, one hand clamping on the top of my head, his other arm cutting across my windpipe until my eyes bulge. "You're a problem to be dealt with and I'd slit your throat here and now if you weren't the weapon that can cripple that filthy prick."

Erlking's cock.... I can hardly breathe.

Grabbing his armored wrist, I grit my teeth and force myself to draw my energy inward. "Burn you—" *wretch.*

Heat ignites through my skin.

My hair whips around us and Halvor gives a shout as I erupt into flame.

His armor is cooking him from the inside out, broiling him within. I catch a glimpse of his reddened face as he falls away, before I turn and run, leaving dripping pools of fire behind me.

Everything hurts.

Everything.

My skin is blistered and peeling, and the ends of my hair have sizzled. The flames were crafted from my magic, which means I should be mostly impervious to them, but clearly my control slipped for one crucial second.

My lungs rasp for breath, and my throat is bruised from his crushing grip.

I stagger through the old quarter in a mindless dash, and even though I've barely had the chance to learn this part of the city, some part of my memory must be trickling through, because my body knows the way better than I do.

"She's down here!" A voice cries out.

Fire rages unchecked through this part of the city. Not thanks to me. Someone else perhaps. Or maybe the Death-guard on my ass aren't the only ones who were sent.

BOOM.

Another explosion.

The sky is falling. Little white flakes drift through the air now. Burning. The world is burning. Gravel rains down. I throw my hands over my head as I dart beneath an arch, and it's so fucking hard to breathe right now, bruised throat notwithstanding.

"*Thiago?*"

Where in the Underworld is he?

My heart skips a beat. This was clearly an assault designed by my mother. Even though he's one of the most powerful males in the alliances, she'd have accounted for him.

And he should have stopped those explosions by now.

Maia's mercy. I need to get out of here. I need to get moving.

Shoving off the wall, I take two steps just as something moves in the square ahead of me. I skid into a narrow space behind a barrel, heart hammering as I crouch there.

It's just a wisp of a red cloak, but I know the hunters are closing in.

A shadow ripples over me, and I glance up as Halvor leaps from rooftop to rooftop above me. He pauses on the lip of the gutter, his hair a ragged, smoking mess and the left side of his face blistered.

If he looks down, he'll see me.

I press my spine into the stone, trying to make myself as small as I can.

"Come out, come out, little rabbit," he calls softly, his gaze scanning the courtyard. Every inch of him trembles with suppressed violence, and violent clouds of smoke whirl around him.

Fuck. What am I going to do?

It's a sound on the edge of consciousness at first. I'm so attuned to the crunch of armored feet on gravel debris that I barely hear it at first.

A rushing, gushing sound.

Halvor stills, as if he senses it at the exact same moment I do. He turns and his eyes go wide.

"Run!" he screams to his men, before he vanishes.

What the—?

And then I realize there are no more detonations. Only an eerie silence filled with the rush of water. A *lot* of water.

231

I take his advice.

Sprinting into the courtyard, I snatch a glance to my left.

Water gushes and roars as it races through the streets. *The dam.* The dam's blown part of its walls.

And for a second I can't breathe, before my mind catches up with me.

If I stay here I'll die.

Fear gives my feet wings. There's only one path forward. I sprint through streets, waving my arms as I see a group of fae scrambling on top of a roof.

"Go!" I croak. "Run!"

The house won't be tall enough.

But there are more merchants here, as if they paused in their mad rush. There's a bucket chain and one old lady holds a bucket in hand, gaping behind me as if she's just seen the end of her existence glaring down upon her.

These people will die.

They'll all die.

And I can't stop it and I can't run fast enough, and then I skid around a corner coming face-to-face with mayhem.

The Wayfarer's Oak looms over us, but the streets are a warren here, and they're a death trap for the hundreds of fae trying to escape.

A little girl stands in the street, crying for her mother as fae trample past her. Screams filter through the air. Incoherent cries. Some people try to reach for others in the swimming mess of fae bodies, but others merely shove them apart as they try to escape.

It's the little girl that catches my eye.

Alone. Terrified. A blonde plait hanging down her back.

And pounding through my memories is every nightmare I've ever had of a baby crying.

Thiago said to get them out. There's no time for this. No—

I shove through the crowd, darting a look at the shining curtain of water that thunders down the cliffs. It hits the streets, gushing toward us in an ever-churning wave.

It churns into shops, smashing glass, and sweeping tables and chairs along with it. Almost upon us.

One little girl. If I can save one little girl....

"Ayelet!" someone screams, and I catch sight of a woman reaching for us with horror written all over her face as she's pushed into the crowd.

"Hold still," I whisper hoarsely. "I've got you."

Dragging the little girl into my arms, I close my eyes and try to will us away from there. I can feel the Hallow in the castle, plugged directly into the ley line. It's a drumbeat that calls to me.

And maybe if I wish hard enough I can somehow get us out of here.

Nobody's ever been able to travel without a Hallow portal.

But I have the blood of the Old Ones in my veins and maybe....

Maybe nothing. There's no link to connect with. The Hallow's too distant.

Water roars down the streets toward me. I can't outrun it. I can't channel it. I can't evaporate it.

My magic is useless, and—

A little whisper of memory stops me.

The Gray Guild whispering about how Thiago wants to bind me to the kingdom.

A bound queen rules the lands. She gives herself over to them and they rise and fall with her blood. My mother bound herself to Asturia a thousand years ago, and she can wield the land's hungry power like a whip.

"You want a queen, Mother?" I rasp. Dragging the knife across my palm, I slam my hand against the cobblestones, marking it. "Then let me give you a queen."

This is not the way it's supposed to happen. To bind a queen to the land is a cause for joy and celebration. Not one of desperation.

Nothing happens.

There is no great spiraling rage of power. There is no surge. The stone feels cold beneath my bare palm, and I withdraw my fist, clenching it against my chest.

It didn't work.

I've never felt more unworthy in my life.

But then my eye falls on the Wayfarer's Oak.

If the oak falls, the city will fall, they say.

It's the type of prophecy my mother would like.

Even if the city stands, even if most people escape, if the oak falls then it will crush the heart and soul of these people. Symbols stand for a reason, and I grab Ayelet and fight my way toward it, determined not to let Thiago wear the burden of this loss.

I won't let her win.

Not this way.

I've spent years polishing my anger until it's a shining blade of retribution.

I want her to lose.

I want to destroy every plan she's ever set in place.

I will *not* let her have this victory. I will not let her take my city—my kingdom, my husband—from me. Ceres is mine. Evernight is mine.

And Thiago is mine.

Water sweeps the woman and her friends away.

My bloodied palm slaps against the tree just as the first gush of water slams into my feet. Ayelet screams and throws her arms around my waist.

Maybe it's a combination of fury and the desire to protect what I've come to cherish, but the second my blood marks the tree, it sets off an alchemical explosion within me. Something suddenly unlocks within my soul. I reach out and thousands of roots spear out from the tree, sinking my mind down, down, until the earth beneath my feet answers, the lands suddenly singing through my veins.

I can feel it all.

I am the city.

I am the lands.

I am Evernight.

"*Vi!*" Thiago screams in my mind.

Nothing can touch me right now.

Water parts around me, thundering past as I splay my fingers wide. The spray of it stings my face, whipping my hair behind me, but I can't focus on the physical.

Hear me!

The earth groans beneath my feet. And then cracks begin forming in the cobbles as I clench my fist together. Water plunges between the cracks, gushing down into the sewers and caverns beneath it. I feel them snaking through the earth. Catacombs. Underground rivers. Hollows and nooks where the rats lurk. I send the water down, letting it pour through those hidden tunnels.

I am a woman standing before a flood.

I am a queen with the power of the lands shivering in my veins until I can barely see the world around me.

I am every inch of earth beneath my feet, every little earthworm creeping through the dark unknown, every bone in the ground, every stone that forms the numerous catacombs beneath me. I am water gushing through newly opened channels, plunging into the sewers and tunnels that form an underground town beneath me.

I can't keep forcing all of this water down into the underground caverns, and there are millions of cubic meters of it in the dam above.

The dam.

Pain screams through me as I turn all my focus upon its stone walls. Rock turns molten, hissing with steam as I force it to fuse, until there are no more cracks, no more mortar. Simply an enormous expanse of solid rock forged together.

And then it's slipping through my grasp as a spearing slash of pain drives through my right eye. Behind it.

I stagger away from the tree, and suddenly Ayelet's the only thing holding me up.

"You're safe," I whisper, running my hand through the fringing of hair that shields her face.

She starts crying, but she only squeezes me harder.

And it finally hits me.

We're alive.

We're all alive.

The street lies in ruins, and I'm ankle deep in water, but nobody was swept away. The Wayfarer's Oak still stands.

Indeed, it seems to be growing as I watch, new buds unfurling from the ends of its branches, and bright green leaves bursting into life.

Did I do that? I can feel it still, its roots anchoring deeper and deeper, almost.... Almost as if it reaches for the ley line.

A shadow falls over me.

I'm so weak I can barely keep my feet, but as I sway a dark figure lands in front of me, strong hands capturing my arms.

Thiago.

"I think I broke your city," I rasp and try to smile.

I lean against him and one of his wings tucks protectively around me.

"Vi." There's a look upon his face that I've never seen before. "You were supposed to get out."

"You were supposed to fix the dam situation."

Curse it, my throat feels like I've swallowed pure fire.

"I thought you were—" He bites off the words, his jaw locking as he turns to the side. "I didn't think I would reach you in time."

And my bleary eyes take in the crowd of people gaping at us.

Distrust fills their eyes and the way they look at him—and his wings—hurts my heart. They slosh through the draining water toward us, barely daring to let go of each other.

He is the monster they all fear.

Even in losing this hand, my mother wins.

Until a single woman breaks the spell, daring to step toward us.

"Ayelet," she whispers, and then she's no longer

tremulous. She runs toward us and snatches the little girl up into her arms. "Ayelet." Drawing back, she runs both hands over the child's face as though she can scarce believe she's still alive. She looks at me over the top of the child's head, tears sliding down her face. "Thank you. Thank you. You saved us all."

And as I look around I realize they're no longer looking at Thiago's wings, they're looking at our feet, where the water has finally cleared.

Flowers bloom around us, little blades of grass pushing through the crevices in the cobble stones. A thin vine curls its way up my leg, caressing my calf.

What in Maia's name?

"I've heard them say that when your mother bound herself to the land, the earth blossomed at her feet for her," Thiago says. "There is summer in your veins. The city blooms for you."

It starts with one man.

He goes to one knee, bowing his head. "My queen."

And then the handsome fae youth at his side lands harshly on his knee. "My queen."

One after another they fall to their knees, and it's no longer a whisper, but a rising chant that pulses in time to my heartbeat.

"My queen."

"My queen."

"*My queen.*"

It echoes through the streets until there are hundreds gathered, all of them bowing toward me.

Thiago looks around. Something raw touches his expression; a mix of awe and love and admiration. And then he too is going to one knee, capturing my hand and squeezing it between his. "My queen."

Every inch of me aches.

Burned fingers. Bruised ribs.

But more than that, the heavy cloak of fatigue that hovers over me like a pile of boulders about to collapse.

"Get me out of here." I know too well the power of symbols. *"Before I fall flat on my face."*

And my dark prince sweeps me up in his arms, cradling me close. "As you wish."

Then he launches into the sky, not bothering to hide the sweep of his wings.

Because nobody's looking at them anymore.

CHAPTER 18

"What in Maia's name just happened?" Finn groans, sinking into a seat at the council table. "I stopped to sit on the dam wall for a second and now I have thorns embedded in my ass."

Thiago woke me an hour ago and I'd crawled out of bed for the meeting. He'd been wearing muddied leathers, and his dark hair was grimed with blood and dirt the last I saw him.

And now he's late.

Finn and Thalia are the only ones pacing the council chambers.

I couldn't be bothered dressing, so I simply drew a dressing gown over my nightrobe and ventured down here with bare feet.

"Maybe if you ask nicely, Eris might remove them," Thalia tells Finn with a sweet smile.

Finn cuts her a look. "If I asked her to remove them, she'd pour salt in the wounds."

"Few rewards are won without enduring great hardship."

The pair of them bicker back and forth, while I lean forward and steal a handful of dried figs off the plate in the middle of the table. It groans with soft cheeses, hard-baked biscuits and dried fruits. Thalia's doing, no doubt. She seems to take it upon herself to feed us at any and all opportunities.

"Speaking of Eris, where is she?" I stretch and yawn, tucking my feet up beneath me on my chair.

"Ransacking the city," Finn says absently, staring at the map on the table.

"Cleaning the blood from her sword," Thalia replies.

The double doors to the room slam open and Thiago strides in.

"Torturing our enemies," Thiago says curtly.

Baylor follows at his heels, his green cloak swirling around his boots. I didn't see him after Thiago rescued me, but he looks none the worse for wear.

"Princess," he says, going to his knee in front of me. "Forgive me. I failed."

"You didn't fail," I point out. "An enormous thorny rosebush attacked you and I had to run. I shouldn't have left you." I glance at Thiago. Bruises darken the side of his face and I'd been so exhausted when he put me in the bath, that I can't even remember getting out of it. "What happened to your face?"

He gently touches the darkest bruise along his cheekbone. "What do you remember of your mother's attack?"

Water gushing. Explosions. People screaming in the streets. A shiver runs through me. "That we drove her back."

He bends to press a kiss to the top of my head. "You drove her back. I was too busy trying to defeat an enormous bramblethine that someone had dropped in the dam. It was punching holes straight through the stone walls."

Not explosions then. But a bramblethine's knotted power.

"Someone must have dropped a seed in the dam." That's why Mother's Deathguard had been sent. Not just to attack the city and draw resources away from the dam, but to allow the bramblethine time enough to grow to full size.

I know I shouldn't be shocked by now at the depths my mother will stoop too, but a hex like that? Bramblethine's are twisted semi-animate creatures with no will of their own. They're hexes brought to life. Take a wolf's heart, knot a twisted string of brambles around it and bind it all together with a rabbit or squirrel's entrails, until they form a kind of 'seed'. Curse it and whisper enough hate to it over the years, and the hexes grow in power until you can practically feel the rage emanating off the seed.

Then all you need to do is add water.

They'll grow several feet in a day, until they're a monstrous creature that will lash out and kill or destroy anything that comes into close contact with it. They're difficult to stop, and have ruined entire cities before.

They say there's a castle in Somnus that is wholly swallowed up by a bramblethine. Originally it was in order to protect a princess cursed to sleep inside, but some stories say that when she woke from her enchanted sleep, the monster wouldn't let her escape and so she lies there still, only now her sleep is eternal.

"How did you kill it?" Anger brews. There are innocent fae in this city. I blink and water is gushing toward me again, Ayelet's arms wrapping tight around my waist as she screams—

"Finn found me just as I was trying to burn it alive. He sang it into submission, and then I drove a knife through its rotted heart. Vi. *Vi.*"

Thiago captures my wrist and I realize thorns are curling up my calf again. They've burst through the ancient flagstones of the floor, until I'm standing in an angry thicket of brambles.

"Sorry." There's a look in his eye I can't read. I try to will them to shrink, but they seem to react to my mood, and not my conscious directive.

"We might have to hold future meetings in the Queen's garden," Thalia says. "Any chance you can grow roses? Araya used to have the most beautiful garden, but it has fallen into disrepair over the years."

"I could try, but I don't think I'm controlling it. They just... sprout."

"The land reacts when you're angry," Thiago muses. He nudges one with his foot, and it strokes his boot. "Thorns, hmm."

I am not my mother, though it doesn't escape my attention that she sits on a throne melded of thorns. "Don't ask me. None of this was planned."

"Not by you," he murmurs, then turns his attention back to the others. "Report."

"The Old Quarter's a mess," Thalia replies, hooking one knee over the other, so her slit skirts part and she flashes a healthy sliver of thigh. "I paid the Prince of

Shadows a visit, and while he is pleased to see the city above him standing, he's wondering where he's supposed to house his people now that the catacombs are flooded. I said I'd assist him with the clean-up efforts." She shrugs. "I might not be able to sing the sea into a storm anymore, but I can help channel the water to drain away."

"Hmm." Thiago's gaze fades away. "Tell him that if he brings me the heads of the conspirators who let the Queen of Asturia's assassins into my city, then he may have the Palace of Many Moons."

The room falls silent.

"I thought you wanted them alive?" I blurt.

"Thi...." Thalia gapes. "That was Araya's favorite summer residence."

"And it's been locked away since she died," he replies sharply. "It's not as though I can use it. And Theron's made quite pointed reference to how he'd like to move up in the world. If he wants the palace then he can have it. All he has to do is bring me those fae, bend the knee and accept the mantle of legitimacy. He proved himself true today."

I arch a brow. "He did?"

"He saved Eris from the water," Thiago says. "She doesn't swim very well."

"She still hasn't forgiven him," Thalia mutters. "Apparently he liked the way her shirt molded to her figure when it was all wet."

"You're going to take his assassins under your banner?" Finn blurts. "A *legitimate* guild?"

"He warned us this was coming. I'd rather have him at my side, than at my back. And he and his people need accommodation."

"Sorry," I say.

"Don't be sorry." Thiago squeezes my hand briefly. "You saved the lives of everyone in the Old Quarter."

"And drowned who knows how many beneath the city?"

It's a thought that's been bothering me since I woke.

"Your mother drowned those people," he points out. "You did your best. Continue."

I drift away as Thalia reports on healing tents set up in the city, and food refuges. But it's her hesitation that captures my attention.

"And the rumors?" Thiago says, his voice laced with a soft sort of malice.

Thunder rumbles in the distance.

Thalia bites her lip. "There are stories that the prince is unseelie. That his wings were stained black with blood as he landed in the city. That he serves Angharad. That he stole the throne from the rightful heirs." She sighs. "My little birds haven't heard too many mentions of that last one, but again, I don't think right now is the time to be giving away Araya's summer residence—her summer palace—to an assassin."

Thiago rakes his hand over his face. "We knew it was coming."

Thalia pushes to her feet. "Then we need to be proactive. No more hiding away in the castle up here. We need to twist the narrative. The people of Ceres are frightened. Their city was attacked, and their prince revealed himself. But there is one shining ray of light."

Every head turns toward me.

"Give Iskvien the Palace of Many Moons," Thalia says, "and then she can make the gardens bloom. The people want a bound queen? Then let's give them a bound queen."

Whoa. "I'm not the... queen. Thiago rules the kingdom. I don't want this."

"You're my wife," he says, taking my hand in his. "You rule at my side. I wanted this, Vi." His eyes darken. "If anything ever happens to me, then my kingdom is safe in your hands."

He's talking about the curse.

"Nothing is going to happen to you—"

"Thorns, Vi!" Finn calls, brandishing a chair against a particularly virulent bramble.

"Stop doing that!" I tell the brambles in exasperation and they all slink against the floor like whipped puppies.

The doors bang open and Eris strides in, clad in leather boots up to her knees and wearing the happiest smile I've ever seen.

"You found them?" Thiago demands.

She tosses a golden sword on the table in front of us. The circle of thorns in the pommel winks at me.

"Queen Adaia's Deathguard have been dealt with. I left two of them alive," she says with a shrug. "They're down in the dungeons and I promised I'd pay them a visit later, once they've had a chance to think about what they've done. One of them wanted to know if our little bitch-princess drowned, so I spent a good half hour showing him what it might have felt like, before I let him know our *queen* was alive." She sinks into her seat, her fingers curling over the arms of her chair as she shivers with delight. "Let's just say, he was delighted to tell me everything. I have their names. I have all their names. Theron missed a few."

Her smile is terrible.

Clearly she's recovered from her near-drowning.

Thiago nods curtly. "Then give their names to Theron. Tell him I want their heads as well. In return, he can have all of *their* palaces and guild halls."

And then he heads for the doors, leaving them swinging shut behind him.

I FIND THIAGO ON THE PARAPETS OUTSIDE OUR BEDCHAMBERS, staring down at the city. Enormous wings flare behind him, thick with glossy feathers. He's no longer hiding himself.

I don't know what that means.

Rain trickles down, the skies turning gray. In the distance, lighting flashes.

I thought at first it was his favorite place, where he can peacefully watch the bustle and flow of the city he loves, but I've come to realize over the months that he comes here because it's safe here. He loves this city, this kingdom, but there's a part of him that will always watch from a distance, uncertain of his welcome.

He's still a young fae prince who was left alone on an altar in the woods, and no matter whether he wears a crown now, or surrounds himself with people who love him, there's a part of him that doesn't believe he deserves any of it.

It makes my heart break a little.

Wrapping my arms around his waist, I rest against his chest and close my eyes, listening to his heart beat.

I don't know what yesterday meant.

Queen, they chanted.

And he called me his queen too, as he knelt to me in the streets.

Only a queen can truly rule the lands, my mother always says.

But I don't want him to think that. I don't want him to believe he is somehow unworthy of ruling this city, or that I tried to supplant him in some way.

"I love you," I whisper. It's getting easier every time. "I don't want to rule."

I did once. I was desperate to be named my mother's heir, before I realized it was all a cruel trick she played on me. But after months here, I've slowly realized I never truly yearned to be Queen of Asturia. I wanted her approval. I wanted her love. And in some sick way, I equated love with the position of crown heir.

But then, I knew nothing of love.

He curls his hand over mine, half turning his head. "You don't? What do you think I've been hoping for all these years?"

"But you're...."

"A prince who has spent *years* hoping for a queen to rule by his side," he says fiercely, turning and capturing my face in both hands. "A prince who has seen five hundred years go by while he stands alone. I've spent centuries dreaming you into being, hoping that you would be half the woman you are, and yet, my wishes couldn't even come close to being true." His thumbs stroke my cheeks. "When I took the crown, I knew I broke several traditions. I wanted.... I wanted to make my mother proud. I wanted to be a son that she would have loved. And I loved this kingdom, this city, even if they didn't love me. I want my people to love you too, Vi. I want them to be proud of you. The way I am. I have never wished to rule over everything. Alone. All I have ever wanted is to share it with someone special."

"Your mother?" I ask, for he's never mentioned her before.

"Vi…. Don't." He goes to his knees, one fist clenched as he rests it on the cobbles.

I barely dare touch him. "Thiago?"

Reaching out slowly, I stroke the curve of his bare shoulder before my touch turns molten. Despite the coolness of the night, the heat beneath his skin is like a banked furnace.

He shivers into my touch, turning his face into my hand.

"What's wrong?" I go to my knees, cupping the back of his neck. "Look at me, curse you. Have you slept?"

He slowly lifts his head, though his eyes remain shut. "I don't think you want to see me right now. I can't hold it in. I thought I could, but the look on their faces—"

I brush featherlight touches across his eyelids. "*I* want to see every inch of you. I want to see through all your secrets." Leaning forward, I brush my mouth to his. "I fell in love with every piece of you, even the Darkness. And I'm not afraid of it."

Still quivering, he opens his eyes. "You should be."

Black eyes, tattoos painted starkly up his throat….

In that moment, he's not the prince I love, but a stranger.

There is no kindness in his eyes. No hint of the husband I know.

Hunger. Rage. Fury.

It glints within him like the honed edge of obsidian.

But I promised that I would love every part of him.

I kiss him as lightning flashes in the sky, highlighting the shadows of our bedchambers behind us. The storm is finally here. Thick, fat raindrops spatter on my skin.

"Inside," I whisper, and he sweeps me up into his arms and carries me inside.

The second our lips touch, his mouth turns ravenous. Hands slide through my hair, tangling there as he sets me on the bed. He's always been gentle. Always exquisitely careful of me. But that was when he was trying to woo a reluctant princess who didn't remember how much she loved him.

It's like he's finally shaken free of his traces. Nothing restrains him anymore, and as his tongue slides against mine, I bite his lip, reminding him that he's not the only one who's angry.

We need this.

I need this.

I want to wipe the memory of the past two days from my mind.

He kisses my throat, beneath the jaw and the sides of my neck. And then he's claiming my mouth again. Raw, openmouthed kisses that bruise my flesh and taste of salt and heat. I go to my knees on the bed before him, stroking the glossy black of his wings as I kiss his chest through his damp shirt.

"Off," I tell him, because I have no idea how the shirt works with his wings.

He tears it loose, throwing the remnants of it aside with a wet slap.

Thiago pauses, shuddering as he kneels on the bed and rests his forehead against mine. "Last chance, Vi. If you stay here tonight, then you won't be dealing with your husband. You'll be dealing with the darker side of me."

"Good," I whisper against his lips. "I want to know every inch of you."

His fingers dig into my ass. It's not quite enough to be painful, but the edge is there. A promise that although he won't hurt me, he won't be my usual patient, gentle lover.

"Vi...."

"Every. Inch."

Lifting me, he wraps my thighs around his hips, and then he's tumbling me back on the bed, and hasn't allowed my mouth a moment's respite.

We crash down on the mattress, lost in a tangle of arms and legs and heated breaths. I catch a glimpse of his black eyes as lightning flashes once more. The shock of his body is painted against the back of my eyelids as we're plunged back into darkness. Taut jaw, aquiline nose, dangerous mouth....

And it's that mouth that ruins me as he claims me again, and again, and again.

He taunts me, soft little brushes of his fingers against my inner thigh, stirring the fabric of my nightgown higher. My robe's fallen open, and he tears the wet silk with claws that spring from nowhere.

I meet his mouth hungrily, the fury in me turning to lust. A gasp steals loose, and I tug my hands free and drag his mouth down, trapping it against mine. His body is so hot against mine, his skin feverish. It takes away some of the chill that kisses my skin. I want to rub myself against that heat, to pretend, just for a moment, that nothing will ever take it from me.

Thiago puts a hand to my hips and tugs me close. Every inch of his firm body presses against mine, and I rub myself against him, moaning deep in my throat. Through the window, thunder rolls in the night sky, and I gasp, head thrown back in pleasure as his teeth skate down my throat. His lips are on my skin, his hands on my nightgown. He tears it open, the wet silk shredding in his hands.

"Yes!" I arch my spine, grinding against the firm press of his cock.

Then his hands are on my wet skin, cupping my breasts, his mouth like a burning brand on my throat. I drag his head lower, feeling the white-hot flare of his lips closing over my pebbled nipple through the silk. I want more, I want to be naked beneath him, skin slick against skin.

I dig my nails into his shoulders. Thiago hisses between his teeth and then his hips rock against mine. He bites my nipple and I cry out, my body driving into his. My thighs are milky wet, my sex throbbing. Each hard little thrust of his hips takes me one step closer to the edge.

As if he senses it, his hand is suddenly between us, exactly where I want it. I drag my hands up his back, drowning in feathers. We kiss angrily, desperately, bordering on violence... I can feel pleasure building like the coming storm, feel my body cresting as his fingers thrust inside me. Lightning flashes, too close this time, and I explode.

I scream, digging my nails in. Thiago fucks me with his fingers, pushing me into a furnace of desire. Again and again, his thumb riding over the swollen bud of my clit. It feels as though he hurls me into the teeth of the storm, anchored by the heat of his body, his teeth against my throat. Aftershocks quiver through me, leaving me shattered and boneless beneath him.

Slowly he withdraws his fingers and braces himself over me, leaning down to place a kiss on my stomach through the silk. He dips his tongue into my navel, our eyes meeting.

My breath catches.

This is the part where he ruins me. I've had his mouth on me in every single way I can imagine, and if there's one thing I'm certain of: I think I married him for that mouth.

And while it's promising me hours and hours of bliss, right now I don't want to be shattered.

I want to be claimed.

"No," I crunch up, capturing his face. "I want you inside me. Now."

There's a dangerous glint in his eyes. "What makes you think you're giving the orders, Vi?"

I bite my lip. "Please."

"Beg me," he whispers, and the low rasp shivers over my skin.

And so I do.

I promise him the world. I promise him every inch of me.

And just as his mouth is skimming down over my hips, I promise him my heart.

Thiago pauses, his teeth grazing my lower abdomen. And then he smiles. "Oh, Vi. I've had your heart from the start. You just didn't know it yet."

"Fuck me." I writhe beneath him. *"Please."*

And surrender is finally here.

"As you wish."

His hands drop to his leather trousers, and he eases each button open slowly, then lets his cock spring free. I swallow as my eyes drop to it. He's enormous, thick and proud, the veins distended all along his marble length. He strips the leather down his legs and then flings it behind him.

He kneels on the bed in front of me, and I can't help looking my fill. The prince is completely unashamed, and with good reason. Years of bladework have honed his physique until there's nothing of softness about his body. From his callused hands to his broad shoulders and rippled abdomen, there's not an ounce of fat on him. His chest is carved of heavy musculature and painted with those dangerous tattoos, although it's the vee of his hips that captures my attention. I follow the trail of hair down, arrowing south from his navel toward the thick thatch at the base of his shaft.

"Sometimes I think the gods molded you into mortal flesh and set you in this world just for me," he croons as he captures my jaw and forces me to meet his gaze. A shudder runs through him. "Especially when you look at me like that, with no fear in your eyes, only desire."

"I'm not afraid," I gasp. "I'll never be afraid. Not of you."

He shoves me onto my hands and knees, one hand sliding along the length of my spine until he's caught a fistful of my silky hair. Yanking me upright, he finds my shoulder with his teeth as he curls the other arm around me.

"You should be afraid," he whispers, and there's a

roughness to his voice I've never heard before. "Sometimes, I want to consume every inch of you."

I laugh. "That doesn't sound like something to be afraid of."

"Mmm. I think I've been too gentle with you."

Hands slide up my abdomen, and then he's cupping my breasts and rolling my nipples between his fingers. He pinches me sharply, and I gasp again, but it's not with pain.

Thrusting forward, he sheathes himself in my willing flesh, and both of us suck in a sharp breath.

"Fuck, Vi. You're so wet." Harsh hands dig into my hips, and I know there will be bruises by morning.

He thrusts again, slowly, slowly. And one hand knots my hair around it, drawing me back until my spine arches. It forces his cock to rasp over something deep inside me, something that makes every inch of me knot with tension.

"You're so beautiful. You're my promise…. You're my dream." His teeth sink into my earlobe. "I begged Maia for one single sign of hope, and there you were. And now you're here in my arms, and I'm never letting you go, Vi. *Never.*"

And then he's slamming into me.

Each thrust drives me forward until I can barely hold on. My fingers claw in the sheets, and only the fist in my hair stops me from ramming into the headboard. His other hand slides between my legs, and I'm begging him again.

Fuck me.

Fuck me harder.

Make me scream.

And by the time he finally lets me come again, he's fulfilled every single one of those promises, until my voice is hoarse, and my body deliciously bruised, and every inch of me has been claimed.

∾

MOONLIGHT SPILLS OVER US AS I LIE IN HIS ARMS AND TRACE small circles across his chest.

The wings are gone. His eyes are green again.

But as my fingertips graze his skin, I can see swirls of inky dark tattoos forming there, as if his illusions can no longer quite keep them contained. They stir at my touch, like contented cats being stroked, and every now and then I swear I see a set of eyes watching me back.

It's a little unnerving.

They may stir at my touch, but they're still dangerous.

"I didn't hurt you?" Thiago murmurs, tracing his finger between my brows and along the ridge of my nose.

I bite his fingertip before suckling it into my mouth. "I don't think you ever could."

"I was—"

"Rough." I nip him again. "But I liked it."

There's something primitive in the way he claimed me. Emotion too raw-edged for words. Need. Hunger. But more than that, fear. He nearly lost me yesterday, and tonight is his answer to that.

There are shadows in his eyes, and he captures my face and kisses me again, leaving both of us breathless and flushed.

"The moment I saw your face in Maia's vision, I knew hope for the first time," he whispers. "And every time the Darkness closed over me and threatened to drag me under, I would think of your face and know that somewhere out there—someday—you would be waiting for me. I just had to hold on a little longer. I just had to fight a little harder. And you would be my reward."

My heart gives a little clench. "I bet you didn't count on the psychopathic mother."

A rough laugh escapes him. "Evil mother notwithstanding, you're the best thing that has ever happened to me. When all you've ever known is darkness, you don't regret a single ray of light, Vi. And you'll fight to keep it in your life, no matter what comes your way."

"I think you've been talking with Finn too much," I joke. "That's the sort of epic poetry he comes up with."

Thiago looks at me. Simply looks.

And I know I tend to shy away whenever he speaks of love, because a little piece of me feels uncomfortable—perhaps even unworthy still—when he says words like that.

He clasps my hand on his chest, forcing me to still. I don't know why, but my heart is racing.

"I love you," I blurt.

It's hardly poetic. I don't think I'm getting better with practice.

"You believed in me, even when I didn't," I whisper. "And you make *me* believe that there's something worth loving in me."

Thiago's eyes darken. But he kisses me again, and the hunger of his mouth tells me everything he doesn't put into words.

Something pushes against my hand, and a swirl of intense blackness ripples across his chest, as if the Darkness doesn't like being ignored.

"Were you born with it?" I whisper.

Thiago sits up, raking a hand through his hair, his spine bowed. "I'll tell you the truth...." Reluctance bleeds through every inch of him. "But not here. Come."

He slips from the bed, tattoos rippling down his spine as if they're delighted to have their story told.

CHAPTER 19

The temple is ancient—carved alabaster glowing beneath the moon. The storm rolled over the city and now everything is wet. Every step I take leaves a trail of grass and flowers peeking through the cobbles.

Maia's sigil—a golden sun rippling between a pair of mountains—is carved over the lintel. Even though it's the middle of the night, the doors remain open because Maia always has time for her worshippers.

An inner courtyard gleams beneath the light of the moon, but I'm told the temple is best viewed by sunlight, for there are hidden arches that correspond with where the sun sits in the sky, and depending on whether it's solstice or not, they light up little secret glyphs carved into the cobblestones.

Acolytes move about the temple, gowned in pure white. They're fae maidens that have given their life to Maia, though there'll be fae youths somewhere about the temple too. Maia was renowned for welcoming virile young men to her bed, and several of her rites tend to get... a little hedonistic.

"Is there a reason we're here?" I ask Thiago as he gestures me over the lintel.

Maia's Flame can ward away the darkest of spirits, but surely he's not afraid of what he's about to say.

"I think it's easier if I show you," he murmurs, leading me deeper into the temple.

We slip past one of the fountains. Golden coins wink within. Toss a coin to Maia, and she may just answer your prayers. Judging from the glimmer of golden light within the waters, a great many practitioners have knelt by this fountain. One of the cobblestones in front of it even looks a little more worn than the others.

And then we're through the outer courtyards and facing the enormous golden doors that guard the heart of the temple.

All the past queens of Evernight are entombed within these walls as an honor for those who ruled with a fair and benevolent hand. Portraits hang in the Queen's Gallery that reveal the identity of those within, and it's there that Thiago leads me.

The tombs have been walled away, but I catch a glimpse of the first of Evernight's queens staring down at me, with three moons in the sky behind her. A golden halo of light gilds her raven-dark hair. Queen Laerah was the third of Maia's daughters and granted the lands that make up Evernight, though it was called by a different name when she ruled it.

Evernight only came into use once the north was cursed to an ever-present twilight.

I've seen the same painting in Hawthorne Castle,

though the painting there is of her sister Rosia, the original Queen of Thorns, and instead of a halo of light, she wears a glowing crown of thorns.

Next to Laerah is her daughter, and then her granddaughter, and so on....

I can't help searching the faces hungrily.

In my mother's court, we rarely spoke of the Kingdom of Evernight, unless it was with hate. I barely know any of my new kingdom's history, and I can't help mouthing the names of those ancient queens: Bardh, Aleyna, Grenweih....

We reach the end of the walkway, where Queen Araya's tomb is enshrined, and Thiago's footsteps slow.

This is the queen he served.

And the queen it's alleged that he murdered—though he explained the truth of that moment to me. He was the first to find her, but believes one of her sons struck the mortal blow.

There's a plaque on the wall, but unlike the other queens, a red velvet curtain covers her portrait.

"I ordered her portrait hidden away from the world," he whispers, staring at the velvet drapes. "They say it's further proof of my guilt but...." Shaking his head, he reaches up to reverently brush his fingers against the velvet curtain hiding the alcove. Little runes flare to life on either side of the curtains, chiseled into the stone themselves, but they fade when they recognize him. "I couldn't destroy it, but I was tired of maintaining the illusion that shielded my face. Once the first generation of fae folk passed into the Bright Lands, I knew the chances of someone seeing the truth were slimmer. I let the illusion slip, inch by inch, century by century, until I could finally wear my true face, but there's a part of me that wonders if someone will see her and know."

"Your true face?"

He gathers the curtains in both hands and takes a deep breath. "It's easier if I show you."

Hauling the curtains open, he steps back.

Gilt lines the edges of the enormous portrait. A serene woman stands there, her hands resting on the battlements I recognize from the palace, and her blonde hair blowing back in the wind. A banner with the Rising Sun of Ceres snaps in the wind behind her, and golden rays of sunshine highlight every inch of her face.

I gasp.

She's beautiful. Possibly the most beautiful woman I've ever seen.

Or perhaps I'm biased, because I recognize those green eyes and full mouth. The same finely cut cheekbones adorn Thiago's face, and they share the same brows, though hers are plucked thinner than his.

What does this...?

"Queen Araya." His fingers find mine. "The last ruling queen of Evernight. When she died, the wards shielding Valerian from the snow and the dark finally shattered, and now the city dwells in almost eternal darkness, for her light no longer warms the world."

"She's your mother," I blurt, because there can be no other answer for the similarity between them.

His lashes shield his eyes. "Yes. Though my birth was a matter of secrecy and I was never formally recognized. The only one who ever knew the truth was her son, Arawn."

His brother.

Who had gone to war with him over the throne when Araya died.

It all makes so much sense now.

He'd spoken of the two princes—Arawn and Emyr—but never with any kindness. They had blamed him for the queen's murder, and he'd been forced to kill Emyr in his escape.

"How…. Why? Why was your birth a secret?"

"You know the answer to that, Vi," he says, looking at me with his smoky eyes.

He's bastard-born, but marriage lines are not vital when it comes to the fae. The Seelie kingdoms are matrilineal, which means mothers are always given first rights when it comes to any children they birth. Even if the father remains unknown, there is never any shame….

Unless….

I've seen his wings, his horns, and his eyes when the Darkness rises within him. My mother always called him "Unseelie" and spat when she said his name. And though he uses his illusions to hide the wings and horns, there's always a hint of the otherworld about him.

"Your father?"

Thiago's face shutters. "Is unimportant."

"If he was unimportant," I point out, "then there would be no reason to hide the truth." I squeeze his hand. "I know this is hard for you. If you don't wish to speak of it, then I won't ask again."

Thiago turns toward me. "The creature who sired me was one of Queen Angharad's bannermen, and I don't believe my mother was granted the… the choice to submit to him. She was captured in the north by his warband and imprisoned in Falkirk for a month. I don't know the details, because once my mother escaped, she never spoke of the ordeal again. She locked herself away in Valerian and ruled for the next year from the north with only her most trusted by her side, and it's said that when she returned to Ceres, she would not speak of the past year."

A year.

A year in which to hide a pregnancy and—

"And you?" I whisper.

"I told you once that Old Mother Hibbert accepts all lost and abandoned children and raises them herself." His thumb rasps down my cheek. "I never knew my mother when I was a child. All I remember is a little cottage in the wilds and dozens and dozens of children." He glances up at the painting, the stiff line of his shoulder betraying him. "They say she was strong and ferocious in her youth—a battle hungry queen—but by the time I arrived in Ceres, hoping to win her attention, she'd become a shade of her former self. She preferred to pretend her court was gaiety and light and ignore the shadows around its edges. She would not hear of trouble in her lands and often retired to her chambers of a night with her wine."

"And so your brothers had free rein," I guess.

"I don't know if I can even blame them for looking for power. They lacked in attention, and so they sought it elsewhere."

"Why hide her painting? She should have been honored to have you as her son, and perhaps the towns-people won't... won't think you an outsider."

Or her murderer.

Thiago presses his fingertips to the oils of her robes before he turns away with a sigh. "I don't know. Habit, perhaps. Or perhaps.... All I've ever known are the shadows. It's safer there. If others knew of our link, then there are ways that information can be used against me." He looks up at the portrait one more time before he draws the curtains closed and seals the wards with his blood so none may peek. "Besides, if I announce our kinship to the world, there will be questions asked about the other side of my heritage, and I want her to remain untainted."

He shouldn't be forced to bear this burden. "You're not tainted."

Thiago smiles bitterly, holding out his hands. "You've barely seen a glimpse of the truth, Vi."

I take them and stretch up onto my toes to kiss his lips. "If you were tainted then you wouldn't have spent thirteen years patiently trying to win my love, only to have me forget you the next time we met. And I'm more than a match for your darkness." I smile at him. "Evil mother, remember? Possibly an evil father too."

It steals a half smile from him.

"Oh, Vi. Everything is so easy when it comes to you. Come." He drags me toward the fountain in the center of the courtyard, where the moon hovers, fat and bloated, on the silvery waters. We walk hand in hand until Thiago gestures for me to sit on the edge of the fountain.

He seats himself beside me, our knees touching, and then he dips his fingers into the fountain. "Do you remember Cian? The unseelie prince I met in the wyldwoods near Valerian last winter?"

I have more recall of my most recent stint as his prisoner in the north—before we broke the curse—than of earlier years. "How can I forget? I thought you were working with Angharad and he was her spy."

"He's my foster brother," he says, "and he's my spy, not hers."

"Your foster brother?"

Thiago looks down at the waters. "We were both raised by Old Mother Hibbert. Cian was shunned by the other children, and I made them uncomfortable, so we bonded together. When it came time to leave—when I was forced out—he came with me."

"Why were you...?"

His smile twists. "My father came looking for me. My kind live alone, but they can sense another from miles away. We were never born to interact; we were born to kill each other and claim their souls. It gives us power and strength, but it also increases the... the killing urge. And my father sensed me.

"Old Mother Hibbert kept us on the move for months, and we were always one step ahead of him, but I knew he was out there. I knew he would kill all the younger children, simply because he could. If I stayed, I was sentencing them to death, and when she looked at me one day, I knew she knew it too.

"She does her best, Vi. But she was no match for my father, and so it wasn't a choice. She gave me an old sword she had wrapped in the bottom of a trunk, a warm cloak, and as much bread and cheese as she could spare. And when I left, Cian came with me.

"We were on the run for years. I could always sense my father over my shoulder, but if I kept moving, sometimes he would lose me for a few months. And that's when I went to the Morai for the first time. I needed to know if I could shield myself from him. I needed to know how to escape him. I needed to know how to control the creatures inside me."

And they'd cast him out, prophesizing ruin if he ever returned.

"The Morai live in the south of Unseelie. Further south than I'd ever been. And for the first time, I felt another sort of pull." Our eyes meet. "I thought it was you at first. Or the woman who would one day be my wife. It was always an itch I couldn't escape, but it meant crossing the borders into Seelie, and my kind are hunted down and killed the second they pass the northern wall. But one summer, the itch grew too strong, and I left Cian behind and rode south." He shrugs, but his face darkens. "I knew I couldn't ride into Seelie wearing my Unseelie visage, so I vanished my wings and claws. I locked the darker half of myself away, and then I followed the call on the wind.

"The first time I saw her...." He closes his eyes. "I was walking through the markets of Ceres when the royal family rode past. My mother rode at the head of the party on a white palfrey, and the second I laid eyes upon her, I knew she was the one I was drawn to. Perhaps she felt it too, for our eyes met and.... The next thing I knew, her guards had me surrounded. I was going to fight my way free, but she insisted upon an audience."

"And?"

He glances down, trailing those fingers through the water again. "She cried once she realized who I was. And I...." His hand stills. "I was angry with her for abandoning me. I stormed out of the castle and got blind roaring drunk. But she came for me the next morning, wanting to explain. She knew what I was. She knew the dark urges that rode through my veins, and she'd hoped to spare me from my father's attentions. If he learned I'd been born, then he would have either killed me or chained me, she said."

My heart aches for his mother. "And so she gave you away."

"And so she gave me away."

A shadow lashes against his throat. I've always wondered what they mean—what they are.

"Look at them," he whispers, and so I slowly unbutton his shirt.

I place a hand against his chest, watching as those tattoos swirl and writhe across his skin. Sometimes they look like hungry wolves. Sometimes they look like monsters hidden in a dark forest. And sometimes they're simply faces, watching me as I lie in his arms at night.

"The word you're looking for is *darkyn*," he says softly.

"What?"

Our gazes meet, and I feel the kick of his heart beneath my palm.

"In the ancient tongue, it meant *dark kind*. Over the centuries, that was shortened to darkyn."

"What are they?" I whisper.

He holds his arm out, and as I watch, those tattoos crawl beneath his skin, little eyes forming and a hungry mouth gaping—

I jerk my hand back as teeth clash shut.

It was instinct, and even though the tattoo creature is contained within his skin, I see the look Thiago gives me.

"Darkness," he whispers before tugging his shirt closed again. "Pure, utter darkness, and let me assure you, Vi. You don't want me to lose control of them. Not even for a moment." And then he leans forward and presses a kiss to my temples. "Is that enough for the night?"

It's enough.

But I capture his face in my hands and steal a proper kiss from his mouth. "Thank you for sharing your truth with me."

Thiago lowers his forehead to mine, our fingertips touching. "Thank you, for loving me, despite the shadows on my soul."

CHAPTER 20

Abound queen can make the lands yield to her whims. A bound queen can heal her people. A bound queen can shatter an invading army with a single click of her fingers.

I stare at the cell in front of me.

This was Thalia's suggestion.

The hexbreaker managed to shatter Lysander's curse long enough for him to regain his fae form, though every night he shifts again as the moon overrides his instincts.

Baylor steps forward, lifting his torch. "Brother?"

A shadow separates from the wall, a man prowling out of the darkness. He's completely nude, and even though he's been provided with every amenity Baylor can offer, Lysander clearly hasn't bothered to wash in days. His silvery-blond hair is bound back in a ragged knot at the back of his head, his jaw lined with several days' worth of scruff.

His eyes are a brilliant, flaring gold.

A wolf's eyes.

"I can smell her," Lysander whispers, his gaze raking the shadows for me. "Are you here to torment me again, you bitch?"

"That's enough," Baylor growls. "She is your queen and you will offer her your respect."

A hard knot forms in my stomach.

"You don't have to do this," Thiago murmurs, at my side.

I have to try. For Baylor's sake. For Lysander's sake.

And for Thiago's sake.

Taking a deep breath, I push the hood of my cloak back and step into the light. "Hello, Lysander."

He bares his teeth at me, his nails elongating into claws. "I won't betray my prince." He shoots us all a glare. "You're a lie. You're all a lie."

"Use your fucking nose," Baylor growls. "If you'd bothered to take a wash, you'd be able to smell the truth."

Lysander snaps his teeth at him.

"Vi," Thiago murmurs. "Make it quick."

I close my eyes and try to reach for the link I share with the land. The scent of flowers fill the air. Lilies. I can feel them spearing through cracks in the floor and trying to bloom.

"What is this?" Lysander growls. "What sorcery is this?"

"Vi is your bound queen," Baylor says. "It's no lie. She's real. She's here to help you."

I reach out but there's nothing to grasp. I can sense Baylor and Thiago's presences, and if I wanted to, I could probably link with them.

But Lysander is a burning ball of rage that rejects my touch.

"You witch!" he hisses, throwing himself at the bars. "You won't fool me again. I won't—"

"Vi?" Thiago grabs my arm.

"He won't let me in," I cry. "There's nothing to grab. No link between us."

"I will kill you," Lysander whispers, rattling the bars of the cell. His jaw starts to twist, his eyes burning hotly amber. "You murderous bitch. You traitorous bitch. This is all a lie. Your lie."

Baylor steps between us, anguish on his face. "Go," he says to me.

"I'm sorry."

There's no emotion on his face. And maybe that's harder to take. "This isn't your fault. This was never your fault," he says.

A howl tears through the room.

Something slams against the bars.

"Come on," Thiago says, hauling me up the stairs and out of the cells.

I can still hear Lysander raging after the door is shut. Leaning my back against the wall, I unleash a harsh breath, every inch of me quivering.

Thiago drags me into his arms, kissing my forehead. "You tried, Vi. You tried."

"When you go up against my mother and her little games you have to do more than try," I gasp, clinging to his wrists. "She's won this battle. What are we going to do?"

Thiago strokes my face. "Wait. We're going to wait and give this hex a chance to vanish completely. Lysander's taken over by the beast right now, but he was always disciplined. I know he will fight his way back."

"You're going to leave him there? In the cells?"

Thiago hesitates. "I have no other choice."

I CAN'T SLEEP. AGAIN.

I see Ayelet screaming as that wall of water washes toward us. I see Lysander's eyes fusing to gold as he loses all his hard-won gains. And I see Thiago on his knees, his head bowed against the weight of what this revelation has cost him.

What my mother has cost him.

I slip from the bed and steal away from our chambers as soft moonlight gilds Ceres. There are few guards within the heart of the castle, and I manage to evade all of them as I make my way to the second-tallest tower within the keep.

I can't defeat my mother.

Not with a sword, not with my fae magic…. I can't even make the land rises against her, because I have no power beyond Evernight's borders.

The Hallow lies still and dormant as I enter, but I can almost sense someone watching me.

Slowly, I light the torches that surround the room before turning back to the center of the Hallow. It hums like a contented cat, the vibration of that power shivering over my skin. Ever since I made the bargain with the Mother of Night, I've felt it whispering to me in the night and singing to me during the day.

I close my eyes. *"Are you there?"*

Power rushes through me, snatching me up in its gaping maw, and then the trap snaps shut around me. It feels like an enormous hand closes around me and then it's tugging me through the floor....

I fall a thousand miles, lungs screaming for breath.

And when I hit the water, it's almost a relief to stop falling.

Splashing desperately, I kick for the surface. Little glowing balls of light stir through the water around me, and as I break the surface, I realize more of them stream toward me as though the ripples of my entrance draw them like a fly twisting in a spider's web.

Curse it.

The shore—

I reach for the power that envelops me here, and then it's turning me inside out, twisting me through *nothing*. I land on my hands and knees in the shallows, cursing under my breath. I hate this place.

But as I lift my head, I know the worst is yet to come....

The Mother of Night walks down the slopes of her island prison, her black silk robes swishing around her ankles and a satisfied smile on her lips. "Of course I'm here, Iskvien. I am always here, watching over you. And I always will be."

Scrambling to my feet, I splash out of the water, but there's no escape. She drew me here. How in the Underworld did she do that? She's supposed to be trapped in the Mistmere Hallow, so how did she reach through the Hallow in Ceres—?

"I didn't," she says calmly. "You called *me*, Iskvien. And you opened the link between us. Since I cannot leave my prison...." She gives a sinister little smile and a shrug.

"Send me *back*."

She tilts her head. "I thought you wished to talk?"

Every muscle in my body freezes. "The last time we *talked*, you trapped me into this fucking quest for a crown that doesn't seem to exist."

Dark, merciless eyes. "It exists," she says and then turns and walks away.

I stare at her back.

"Then why is there no trace of it? Someone has to know where it lies. Or maybe it was destroyed—"

"It cannot be destroyed."

She has to be lying. For every Spell of Making, there is a Spell of Unmaking.

"The crown is the key to everything. Come, Iskvien. If you wish to know how to defeat your mother, come…."

And so I follow her.

CHAPTER 21

The Mother smiles as she sinks onto her throne. Carved of ebony basalt, it would seem almost menacing if not for the filigreed pattern of stars and moons woven into the stone. Someone has painstakingly carved moonstone and used it to fill the chiseled moons.

"You could defeat her, yes," the Mother finally says. "Power sings through your veins, Iskvien. You have the promise of the best of my kind as well as your mother's ancestry. If you learned to harness your gifts, you could force your mother to crawl at your feet. You could make her regret every little betrayal she's ever given you. You could tear apart mountains with a thought and cause forests to grow in a night. You could sing the stars from the sky if you wished it."

She's lying. She has to be lying.

"You want me to free you. You'd say anything to make me free you."

"Of course I wish to be freed. I never said that you *will* defeat her," the Mother replies. "Merely that the promise is there. Do you think you are the first to be born of such a powerful coupling? Do you think you will be the last?" She leans forward. "I am patient, little princess. If not you, then another will come. If not you, then I will turn my attentions elsewhere. You're not the only one who makes the earth tremble with their footfall. You could even hear them walking the lands if you learned to listen."

My fingers slide to the golden filigreed bracelet trapped around my wrist. "There's another *leanabh an dàn*?"

She merely smiles. "That is your question to answer."

In the silence, all I can hear is my heart beating.

If there's another one out there, then perhaps Angharad will turn her attentions upon them if she finds me too difficult to rein in. All I have to do is keep away from her hunters.

Find the crown.

And kill my mother.

"Why did you come to me?" the Mother murmurs. "For questions you could answer if you continue to search your books?"

I don't know why....

Or do I?

I swallow. "Why did you help me? Why did you let Eris wake?"

"You wanted proof," she says. "It's difficult for the Dreamthief to escape the command of the Mirror, but he can do it, if the cause is strong enough. We have never been your enemy, Iskvien. But you know that, don't you? That's why you're here."

"You weren't always the enemy of my people. The last

queen who ruled Mistmere was fae, and she also worshipped you."

The Mother of Night glances down. "Abalonia was a special case. She was wise and powerful and… she could be reasoned with. Mistmere is the border between two peoples—the seelie and the unseelie—and Abalonia knew it. She created a haven for her seelie, and yet she also welcomed the unseelie and the sylvaren within her territories. Hers was the only kingdom that knew true peace."

I hesitate.

"What do you want to know, Iskvien?" Her depthless eyes seem to see right through me.

I rub my hands up my arms. "You said I was the *leanabh an dàn*."

"Yes."

"Who is my father?"

She cocks her head. "And what will you give me if I answer?"

No. "I'm not making any more bargains with you."

"Then I have no reason to answer."

This time it's my turn to smile as I stalk up the hillside toward her. "Something just occurred to me—you were waiting for me to reach out for you, weren't you? You've been sitting here like a spider in the dark, waiting for me to turn toward the Hallow so you have a chance to reach me." I pause at the foot of the throne. "You cannot force me to free you and your kind. But you can persuade me to consider your argument. Well, this is your chance. Persuade me. Convince me you're not a monster."

"Oh, but I am, sweet child." Curling her fingers over the arms of her throne, she leans forward, and it feels as though she grows. The shadow of her throne lengthens, sweeping across the island behind her. A vicious chill seems to settle. "I am the monster in the dark that my people prayed to. I am the cold, merciless vengeance they needed when their enemies stalked them. I am the beast that protected them when the bright and shining fae came with their wars and their armor. I am the Queen of the Whispering Dark, and I am the reason the fae feared the night."

A little pit of terror curdles in my veins as she catches my gaze.

And then she leans back, and she's merely a hooded woman with dangerously red lips and a smile that knows the fate of the world.

"We are all capable of becoming monsters for the ones we love, little queen. Even you."

"I am no monster."

"If you want to destroy your mother, then you must become the thing she fears," she says in a merciless voice.

I rub my hands over my arms. "My mother fears nothing."

"Your mother fears many things. Think, Iskvien."

I open my mouth to say my husband's name, but it's not fear she feels for him so much as hatred.

So I think of everything my mother has ever done. The books she has burned, the border lords she has crushed, the way she stole the children of all those who opposed her and "raised" them safely within her court.

"She fears the power of men," I whisper. "She fears the past."

A slight nod.

But it's not enough.

I am not my mother's past, I am....

It strikes me then, what my mother is most afraid of.

Her future.

Her downfall.

Her ruin.

"She fears... herself," I whisper. "A young, ambitious princess with the power to overthrow her." The shock of it lances through me. The way my mother loved me once. The way her heart grew colder with every passing year, until she was favoring my sister over me and pitting us against each other....

She loved me and then she didn't anymore, and I never knew why.

I never knew what I had done to displease her so.

And it all began in my eleventh year, when my magic first came in.

"Your mother fears a younger, more powerful queen," the Mother of Night says with knowing eyes.

"But I wasn't powerful! My fae magic is weak, and—"

"You made yourself weak," she says coldly, "to appease a woman who would never love you. And while she may not have known what sort of changeling was placed in her womb, she knew enough to fear you. Power stirs within you, little queen. The kind of power that can make the ground tremble beneath your feet and the oceans writhe. And every time your mother looks at you, she sees a hint of it, although she doesn't quite know why you make her uneasy or why she should fear you."

It's one revelation after another.

And it feels like she stabbed me through the heart and my body is only just starting to realize the injury it took.

"If you wish to destroy your mother," the Mother continues, "then you must become the future she fears.

You must become a dark queen full of ambition and power. You must rise. And you must crush the little girl inside you who still calls for her mother."

I press the heels of my hands to my brow. It's too much to consider. I breathe a wretched laugh. "I came here to find answers, and you leave me with *this?*"

"You came here because you know the answers, but you don't want to face them."

I lower my hands. "I wish I'd never made that bargain with you."

"Do you?" She arches a brow. "Never regret, Iskvien. Regret is the weakness that chokes the mighty. Your husband was fated to die three months ago. Your mother would be settling his crown on her head as we speak, as her armies sweep through the southern kingdoms. One thing averted fate. You. Your choice. Your bargain. You are the child of destiny, Iskvien. No fate can ever be set in stone with you walking through the world."

"I will not free you and your kind!"

"Come," she says, pushing to her feet. "I think you need to see something."

I stare at her back as she walks away from me. Did she even hear me? Or does she simply not care what I said?

The island reaches a precipice, and it's there at the top that we find an enormous well, filled with fog and glistening lights. It's even colder up here, and I swear some of those lights pause in their slow circling of the misty waters as if they sense they've caught my attention.

I remember everything my childhood nurse, Nanny Redwyne, told me.

Don't look to the lights.

Don't let them know you can see them.

Don't listen to their whispers.

"Let me show you who the monsters truly are," the Mother of Night says, holding out her hand.

I eye it like she's gifting me with a snake. "No. A thousand times no. I'm not entering that water."

"You want to know the truth about me and my kind? These are the waters of the past. And they will show you what you wish to see. You want to know me and my kind, Iskvien? Then *open your eyes.*"

I steel myself.

On one hand: *Don't look to the lights.* On the other: *Know thy enemy.*

I stare at her hand for a long time.

"Promise me thrice that no harm will befall me and that you will lead me out of those waters safely within the hour. And then you will release me back into my own world."

The Mother smiles.

And then she promises.

Thrice.

The second the fog closes over our heads, the darkness of the cave vanishes. Every step makes that chill water creep higher, until my lungs clench in shock and I can't quite get my breath.

A hand closes over my head, and then the Mother shoves me under, and just before I open my mouth to scream, I stagger into a new world.

A figure sits by the fire, wearing a crown woven of iron thorns and little daggers. He's playing a woodland flute, and in front of him, dozens of dancers leap and twirl. I see the little horns in their hair and the cloven feet on some of them. Otherkin. Worshipping in a Hallow somewhere.

"When the fae arrived in Arcaedia, they named us monsters," the Mother of Night muses as she stares at her kind, "and our words and customs were twisted until we became monsters who deserved to be slaughtered. But these were my children, little queen. They knew love. They knew kindness. They knew peace and happiness. Until your forebears arrived."

I swallow hard. "There were blood sacrifices—"

"There were." Her eyes darken. "The land requires blood to power the Hallows. Have you not felt them weakening?"

A queasy feeling fills me. "That is wrong."

"Is it? Some were chosen by their people," she continues. "And some volunteered, seeking a better life for their loved ones."

"Volunteered?" It sounds like a cleaner way of saying "were manipulated."

"Tell me," she says coldly, "is it any cleaner a death when your mother sends prisoners to the Abyss? Can you vouch for all of her victims? Are they all evil? Are they all guilty? Are none of them mere victims of happenstance— or worse, your mother's whim?" She leans forward. "Innocents die, Iskvien, and they die at your mother's hand. Is that any better than a sacrifice made to still the lands? You know not of what you speak.

"The seelie cut down our forests. They murdered my children and took their sacred Hallows from them. They bred them and forced them into mines to work, and still it wasn't enough." The Mother towers over me. "Was it wrong of me to demand vengeance? Was it wrong of me to risk everything I had—all my power, all my lands—to go to war against your filthy brethren?"

She shakes her head and laughs, a hollow, echoing sound. "History belongs to the victor, and what is truth when lies serve your purpose so much better? Have you ever read a book that was written before the wars? I can answer that for you—no. Because your mother's ancestors burned everything they could get their hands on that countered the lies they told, and then your mother finished the job. Do you know why they call me the Mother of Night?"

I can't speak.

"Who do you think my children turned to when their babies lay weakened and barely breathing in their arms? Who do you think midwives and mothers begged for mercy when their children struggled to be born? Who do you think breathed a single precious mouthful of power into weakened lungs so their children would survive?" She bows her head and stares at her hands. "When I was mortal, I was the one they turned to when children struggled to be born. I was life incarnate. I was the spark of light in the darkness of the night."

"When you were *mortal*?"

There's another dangerous smile. "I was born into this world as you were, little queen. My heart beat and I felt blood rush through my veins, just as you do. But there was Old Blood in my veins, and my father's seed bled power. For every whispered thanks, I grew in strength. For every prayer that begged for mercy, I could feel the earth starting to stir beneath my feet. You speak of sacrifice? When I made that long, slow walk down to the Hallow in what you now call Mistmere, I could feel the cold stone beneath my feet and my people's eyes upon me as they begged the old gods to accept my sacrifice and restore the lands. I can still feel the kiss of the knife across my throat." Her fingertips brush the hollow of her collarbone as if she senses it now. "The Hallow took my mortality, but it gave me something so much more. My blood and my life bound me to the lands, and I finally realized what I was destined to be. I was no longer *leanabh an dàn*, I was immortal and the champion of my people."

She lifts her head proudly. "You and I are not so different. All we want to do is protect our own. That's all I want. And I cannot protect them from here."

"You're lying."

She would say anything to get me to free her kind.

"Free me," she says, "and I will protect those of my people who are scattered across the continent. Free me, and I will stand at your side when you go to war against your mother. Free me, and I will not falter. I will be the ally you need to stand against the darkness that is coming."

"Free you and start a war? There has been peace for five hundred years!"

"Peace for whom?" she demands. "Your kind? Or mine?"

I swallow.

There are otherkin out there still, hidden in the forests. We rarely see them—they stick to the north, to unseelie, where they are safe—but I know they still exist.

Sometimes my mother displays their heads on pikes along the castle walls, though it's rare to see one in Asturia.

And my stomach twists, because the only otherkin I have ever seen were murdered by my mother.

"We are as much a part of you as the fae are," she says

285

coldly. "You disappoint me, Iskvien. Your people need you, and yet you turn your back."

"I'm not—"

"You *are*."

I shake my head. I can't trust her. I *can't*. She would say anything to be free of this prison world.

But what if she's telling the truth?

What do I do?

If I free her, then everything that the Seelie Alliance fought so hard for five hundred years ago will be undone. I need to talk to Thiago. He was there. He faced their armies. He faced the Old Ones and the otherkin and the unseelie.

"Take me back," I tell her.

"Not yet."

I turn to go. I can feel the power of the Hallow. This isn't her prison world, though she can clearly access the Hallow. She has no power over me here.

"You wanted to know who your father was?" she calls, and despite myself, my steps slow. "Then I will give you a gift. He was once called Arion, many a moon ago, when he was still mortal. And he too yearns to be freed for more than two nights a year. You could know him, Iskvien. Your mother may have turned from you, but she's not the only line you come from."

I can't let her keep speaking.

This is only manipulation.

She's been in my head; she knows what lies in my heart.

"Wake up," I whisper, closing my eyes and drawing on my power. "Wake up."

And then the shock of feeling like my head is being

forced underwater makes me gasp. I see a Hallow emblazoned with torches. I feel a hand pressing me to my knees as the crowd writhes and chants. And I see the priest come forward with a knife in his hand and a bowl of polished stone to catch my blood.

I barely have time to realize I'm not in my head—I'm in hers—and then I lift my chin and stare proudly at the priest.

"Make it swift," I whisper. "Let me see my family again."

And the priest nods behind his feathered mask and steps behind me.

I don't see the knife.

But I feel it as it slashes across my throat and spills my lifeblood to the ground of the Hallow.

I SIT UP WITH A GASP, PALMS SLAPPING AGAINST THE COLD stone floor of the Hallow in Ceres, even as the Mother of Night's laughter echoes in my ears.

You could know him, Iskvien….

A line of fire burns across my throat, but when I clamp my hand there, there's no blood. Merely the ghostly sensation of a knife being drawn across my skin, and a part of me realizes she gave me one last gift: The gift of her final mortal memory.

Every inch of me shakes, and I can't hide the tremble in my hands.

My mother, the otherkin, my father….

I don't even know what to believe anymore.

Except that I am dripping wet and my clammy nightgown clings to my skin. "Definitely not imagining it," I whisper to myself.

"Not imagining what?"

Soft footsteps echo up the last few stairs of the stairwell as I shove to my feet, and then Thiago slinks into the light, his eyes watchful and a frown on his brow as he watches the last of the Hallow's glyphs fade.

"Vi?" There's a wealth of questions in that one word. "What are you doing down here? Why are you wet?" The muscle in his jaw throbs. "Where have you been?"

"I was trying to find answers."

"Answers to what?" he snaps, gesturing me to step free of the Hallow, as if he's afraid to step over the lines marked in the floor. "You went to her, didn't you?"

"I need to know how to defeat my mother," I whisper. "And I thought... the crown—"

"Forget the fucking crown," he explodes. "What in the Underworld were you thinking? The Mother of Night has trapped you once. You don't have the power in her world. If she locks you away down there...."

I push past him, my bare feet slapping on the cold stone and my heart racing in my ears. "Something is happening to me and I don't understand it. You can't explain it to me. But she can. And maybe, just maybe, if I learn to control these new gifts, I might be able to save Lysander."

Thundering down the stairs I head toward our rooms, hearing his feet behind me.

"I said Lysander will wait," he calls. "Hexes take time to unravel."

I spin on him. "Do you not think I know that? Me? I feel like I fight for every memory I unearth. It's been months and I'm still unravelling myself, Thiago. What if he never recovers?"

He pauses in front of me. "He will recover. It took him years to break free of the Grimm's hold over him. He can break through your mother's twisted little games."

I lean my back against the wall. "I hate seeing Baylor like this."

"Promise me you will be patient," he says. "Promise me you won't go to see her again."

Our eyes meet.

"I can't make that promise."

"Vi, she can trap you there forever."

I press the heels of my palms to my eyes. "She doesn't want to trap me. She wants to be free. She said—"

"She's a monster!"

We are all capable of becoming monsters for the ones we love....

"And so am I." I wrap my arms around myself.

Heat flares in his eyes. "Is that what this is about? You're not a monster. You're—"

"Half Old One," I point out. "If you think her a monster, then what does that make me?"

The muscle in his jaw flexes. "It makes you my wife. And it's not her power and heritage that makes her dangerous. You're nothing like her, Vi."

He doesn't understand. Not truly.

"Promise me you will tell me before you contact her again. So I can get you out, if she won't let go of you."

It's a reasonable deal, and if I wasn't so tired I wouldn't have pushed him so far. "I promise," I whisper, reaching up to kiss his cheek.

CHAPTER 22

"Come," Thiago says, three days later, lifting his hand to mine.

I glance up from the candle flame I've been making dance over the tabletop. He insists I learn to control my newfound powers. "Where are we going?"

"I want to show you something," he says.

"What?"

He rolls his eyes. "Can I not have one surprise?"

Lights suddenly shatter in the night sky, painting the world through the window in a kaleidoscope of color. My heart kicks faster, but there's no alarm on his face, only a smile.

"What's going on?" I rush to the window, leaning closer to the glass.

Another night-blooming flower blossoms in the sky above us, hissing sparks crackling down over Ceres's harbor. The city below us is fall of people. All the squares writhe with banners and colored ribbons. Market stalls seem to have flourished from nowhere.

I'm not aware of any major holidays. Imbolc is behind us, and the next equinox is weeks away.

A warm presence encircles me from behind, Thiago's lips brushing against the back of my neck. "They're celebrating their queen."

My head turns to his, but there's a quiet sort of joy in his eyes.

"Want to join them?"

I've been locked away for days. "Please."

He tugs a mask from within his shirt. "Then you'll need to wear this."

Masked dancers fill the streets.

I've never seen anything like it. The people of Hawthorne Castle don't celebrate like this, as though they're sharing our joy.

"Come on!" Thalia cries, dragging me through the gates of the castle and into the throng. The entire court was gathered in the keep's bailey, and Eris even threw a handful of mistletoe over the top of me.

Silver paint highlights Thalia's cheeks, and her silver gown is cut low enough that men glance past her, glance back, and then stagger into buildings or market stalls. The sleek fabric clings to every curve, and cut-out panels reveal her narrow waist. There's a tiny diadem on her brow.

"You look amazing," I say.

She rakes her gaze down my gown with a critical eye. "What in Maia's name are *you* wearing?"

"You were the one who's had a hand in every aspect of

my wardrobe, so you can only blame yourself." I finger the lilac silk. "And I like it."

"That's not the point!" she says in exasperation. "Thiago didn't show you *the* dress. I had it made just for tonight! It's black and gold, and the cape is so amazing I might stop breathing! You were supposed to look like a queen!"

"I don't care, Thalia." I squeeze her hands. "These boots are perfect for dancing in. And tonight's not about me. Tonight is about the future. About Evernight."

She sniffs. "Tonight *is* about you. Evernight hasn't had a queen in over five hundred years."

"Thalia." I growl. "I'll be fine."

"I even managed to get Eris into a dress."

"You did?" All I'd glimpsed as Eris decorated me was an enormous velvet cloak that covered her from head to toe.

As if summoned, Eris stalks forward. "She did."

"E!" Thalia grabs Eris's hands, and the black cloak that Eris wear slips from her shoulders. "Show her!"

Finn catches it just before it hits the ground, and then Eris whirls in circles with Thalia, rolling her eyes with a roughened laugh.

She's not wearing leathers.

Nor is she wearing the type of dress she wore at Ravenal for court appearances—polished silver chainmail. No, this is a *dress*, and yet it suits Eris perfectly; a mix of femininity and dangerous smoky allure. A dress fit for a warrior queen.

It's like a corset comprised of black lace, though the panels that circle her waist are sheer. Little gold stars are embroidered all over it, and a golden rope knots around her waist and loops up around her throat. From midthigh down, her skirts are sheer, with a thousand more little stars, and they wisp around her ankles like the froth of the sea.

Gold-hilted knives are sheathed on her forearms, and a gold mask hides her eyes.

But there's no hiding the look on Finn's face as he stares at her as if she just punched him in the throat. Or lower.

Gold tattoos highlight Eris's dark skin, and they cover her entire décolletage and shoulders. Whimsical, featherlight designs that speak of an ancient culture I don't recognize. She's such utter perfection that I know Thalia's had her hand all over this.

I reach up and close Finn's mouth with a finger to his jaw.

He shoots me a dark look, then his hand crushes her velvet cloak into a wad and he shoves it at my chest. "I need a drink."

Then he's gone, stalking into the crowd.

"Dance with us, Baylor!" Thalia snags his arm.

Baylor scrubs at his mouth, his long silver hair tangling down his back. "I need a drink too," he growls under his breath, and then he vanishes in Finn's direction.

I shoot Thiago a helpless smile. "Vanquished by the threat of dancing. Surely you're made of sterner stuff than that?"

He takes my hand and presses a kiss to the back of it. "Go and enjoy yourself. I'll dance with you later. If I don't let Thalia have you for an hour or so, then I'll never hear the end of it."

"I intend to hold you to that!" I warn as Thalia grabs my other hand.

She drags me into the dancing, the laughter on her face so infectious that I can't help laughing back. But it's Eris who shocks me. Eris who whirls and leaps with such grace that fae pause to watch her for a second. She's always been so elegant with a blade, but I didn't know she could move like this.

And I lose myself in the music, in the laughter, in the sway and bump and grind. There are cobblestones beneath our feet, and every so often someone staggers into us. It's such a far cry from the formal balls my mother held. Such different dancing. A riot in the streets as fireworks crash and shatter in the air above us.

This. This is what it feels like to rule a kingdom with love and not fear.

A pair of handsome fae males push into our group, one of them slinging an arm around Eris's waist. He'd probably faint if he knew who she was. "I like the way you dance," he yells over the music.

"Think you can keep up with me?" she demands.

"Oh, I know it."

With a wink in our direction, she whirls him into the flurry of bodies.

"This way!" Thalia yells, grabbing my wrist and hauling me onto the ruins of an old city wall that looks like it's been gobbled up by little houses and turrets. People have built onto it, underneath it, over it.... But I catch a glimpse of ivy-choked walls and an ancient city arch that bridges a street.

The view from the top of the arch is glorious. The city square is packed with fae, and I catch a glimpse of Thiago drinking with Baylor and laughing at something Finn says. Our eyes meet across the crowded square—he's known exactly where I was the entire time.

"*Enjoying yourself?*" he murmurs.

"*Immensely. You should join us.*"

He glances at Finn, who's scowling into his drink as he rests both elbows on the bar in front of him, his back turned resolutely to the crowd.

And I remember what Finn said about violence and the anger he fights each and every day.

"*Stay with him,*" I tell my husband. And then I dare....

"*Does she know?*"

"*I don't think he even knows. I'll find you later, once he's got a rein on it.*"

And then he's gone, with one last caress against my mind.

It's quieter up here, and sweat slicks my skin, so I'm glad of the respite. Eris has vanished. Thalia leans against the wall, a glass of wine she's stolen from someone in the crowd in her hand. "Want some?"

I take a sip. Sweet, fruity. And then I hand it back.

The music has died in the courtyard below. It seems a lone harpist struck a few chords, and everyone turns toward him. The dancing stills. The loud singing vanishes.

It's merely the harp.

And a song so bittersweet that my heart squeezes, even though I don't know why.

"The Lament of the Golden Dawn," Thalis says, closing her eyes and leaning into the music. "The last dance of Araya of Evantine."

Thiago's mother.

It's so beautiful. So heartfelt. Faelights flicker to life as the fae in the streets below lift their hands and conjure them. A sea of flickering lights fills the night. These people loved her.

I reach for him, just a psychic brush against his mind, full of warmth and love.

His touch is a mental squeeze—a silent thanks.

A soft hum echoes in Thalia's throat, and the sound.... Sweet Maia, it almost seems as though she's hitting two different pitches at the one time. There's something slightly mournful about the music, and the next wave that strikes the sea wall crashes up the beach, further than it's ever been, foam chasing toward us as if it can hear her call.

She breaks off with a sigh and smiles a little sadly at me. "Once I could have sung the waves into the city itself if I wished."

I know she bartered the magic of her voice to a sea witch, but beyond that, my memories of Thalia are still vague. "Why did you give it away?"

Turning her gaze towards the sea, she unconsciously pets the stone wall. "Because it was both my gift and my curse. The saltkissed are creatures of the sea, formed of foam and water and cold, marble flesh. And the fae are bound to the land. Every year I aged, I could feel the choice splitting me in two. The sea called to me, but I was frightened to answer it." She tilts her face into the spray of mist as another wave hits the sea wall. "My grandmother spent too many years beating that fear into me."

I squeeze her hand.

"The was a fae prince from the Far Isles who wished to make an alliance with Thiago over a century ago." She hesitates. "The second he heard me sing, he insisted upon marriage. I was young, and it was the first time a male had looked at me and seen something of worth." She falls quiet. "I wanted to believe him when he said he loved me. Thiago warned me against it—he said I barely knew the prince—but I accepted the marriage proposal."

I wait for her to continue.

"Prince Riu invited me to his palace in the Far Isles for our courtship." Thalia sighs. "There were little things that began to make me uncomfortable. He used to talk of his 'collection' all the time. He had the finest collection of musical instruments I've ever seen. The finest paintings. An entire menagerie of nightingales. 'Sing for me,' he would say, and at first I obliged willingly, for I loved to sing. But over time, my throat grew sore and tired. I begged to take the night off, but he would grow angry. He struck me once, and that was when I knew I had made a foolish mistake.

"But he wasn't the only one listening. There was a sea witch who lived in the nearby waters, and she warned me that I wasn't the first bride Riu had taken—and nor would I be the last. His gift was the ability to absorb another's magic, but it was a hungry gift. If he did not utilize it, then his flesh would begin to age. Every time I sang, he would feed off the power in my voice, and it didn't matter if my vocal cords were bleeding, he would demand more. He'd captured the witch's sister a hundred years before and stolen her life before he dumped her withered body in the seas.

"Give me your voice, she told me, and I will go to Riu in your guise and break his hold over you." Thalia falls silent. "And I was desperate and thought myself alone— and so I gave her my voice."

"And did she free you?"

"She went to him," Thalia says coldly. "And she tore the heart from his chest and ate it, for she too had a hungry power. And now she sits on his throne and rules his lands and sings with my voice. And she keeps the offspring of his nightingales in golden cages to remind herself of where she came from."

I don't ask whether she tried to get her voice back. Of course she did. It's a part of her, and I know that yearning for your magic. It's like an amputated limb.

"I'm so sorry. Maybe once my mother is defeated, we can sail to her lands and get it back for you—"

"Thank you." Thalia looks down at where our hands are linked. "Thiago has already tried, Vi. The sea witch could not take my magic from me—it had to be given freely. And thus, if I were to hope for its return, then the terms must be the same. She must give it of her own volition."

"Everyone wants something," I point out. "We just have to find out what she wants in return for it."

Thalia gives me a tremulous smile—but there's none of her usual light in it. "Thank you. For the thought."

It's more than a thought, but I don't say that. If I can break my mother's hold over me, then I can do anything.

And if there's any means to return Thalia's gift, then I will find it.

Hours later, I finally stumble into Thiago's arms, begging for mercy.

"No more!" I tell Thalia when she tries to lure me back into the streets again. "No more!"

She pouts, but then turns and throws her arms around Finn.

"Here's trouble," Finn says, but he grins and swings Thalia into the air. She's insatiable. And though the laughter and dancing are beginning to die down, apparently her stamina hasn't. They whirl away in a riot of silver and white.

"Having fun?" Thiago teases, kissing my hair.

"How did you manage it so swiftly?" There must be thousands of masks on fae faces, and the wine barrels and fireworks....

Thiago slips behind me, his arms locked loosely around my waist. "I've been planning it for weeks," he whispers in my ear. "Or more importantly, Thalia planned it. I was just waiting for you to be ready to bind yourself to the lands."

A lump in my throat threatens to choke me.

"Evernight has been too long without a queen, my love." He looks serious. "This is something I've never been able to give my kingdom or its people. When your mother sneers at Kyrian and me, there's a little bit of truth to her words. I am not a female descendant of Maia. But you are. Her blood runs through your veins, her power calls to the land beneath it—through you. You are the land's link to the people." He captures my face in his hands, thumbs stroking my lips. "You ask me why I love you, and while I have a thousand reasons, what you're really questioning is your worth. I know it troubles you to think of everything it has cost me to love you, but have you ever thought of what you've given me in return? What you can give my people? Hope, Vi. With you at my side, we can make this kingdom blossom to the type of power and might it hasn't known since my mother was bound to the land."

I curl my fingers around his wrists and close my eyes. He's everything I've ever wanted, and he speaks of a world I've never been able to imagine. A world where we will rule side by side.

It's more than I have ever hoped for.

"I love you." The roughened words trip over my tongue as I kiss his thumbs and slowly open my eyes.

A set of night-blooming flowers blossoms in the sky behind him, and in that moment, the shock of hope and joy on his face overwhelm me.

"You rarely say it," he whispers, leaning down with a smile. "But I cherish each and every time you do."

And then his mouth brushes against mine, his lips stirring heat through my veins. He kisses as if he wants to consume me, as if he wants to drown in every breath I make.

Gentle fingers stroke down my right breast, tracing eloquent circles around my nipple.

"Home," I whisper, taking him by the fingers and leading him back into the crowded square.

"Not yet. Tonight is a night to celebrate." His voice dips to a growl. "And as much as I want to take you up on your offer, I haven't danced with you yet."

"My poor wretched feet."

"I'll kiss them better later." There's hunger in his eyes and ruin in his smile. "I like the dress, even if Thalia doesn't approve."

"I'm sure you'd prefer me without it."

"Mmmm." His gaze grows hot. "You're not going to

tempt me. Not yet, Vi. I want you desperate before I take you home."

I slide my hand down his side. "I bet I could make you break your promise."

He captures my hand and kisses the slope of my shoulder. "But my willpower is stronger than yours."

"Do you want to test that theory?"

He laughs. "First one to break."

I feel breathless as I undulate against him, our gazes lost in each other. I've never felt so alive, so in tune with another person. And then there's a fiddle cutting through the night, as if someone's noticed that his dancers are flagging.

I know this song.

"Lord of Summer."

It's played in Asturia on May Day.

Bang. Bang. Drums kick in to accompany the fiddle. And then the sound of it soars through the air, stirring my blood in my veins, a flute trilling high in accompaniment. Despite my sore feet and tight calves, I feel my toes tapping.

"I hope you're saving your energy," he whispers as he swings me in his arms. "Because you're getting no sleep. I'm going to make you scream until dawn."

"That's a little cruel."

"Trust me, you'll love every minute of it."

And then we're dancing, one of his arms flung around my waist as he swings me in circles. Our gazes meet, and we share a secret smile as Thiago's fingers tighten against me. *Later*, his eyes say.

Nobody knows us here.

We splash through fountains until my dress is soaked

and slick against my body. I can tell from the look in his eyes how much he appreciates this fact, and he captures me at odd corners, stealing hot, breathless kisses that threaten to turn into more, before he always breaks away.

"Are you trying to drive me to the edge of frustration?" I growl, capturing a fistful of his shirt. "Kiss me."

He does, shoving me against the bricks of a house and stealing the very breath from my lungs. And then once again he's gone, vanishing through the crowd with a lingering glance over his shoulder as if to say, "*Come and get me.*"

Fine.

I'll play his game.

I push after him, shoving my way through laughing fae. Another explosion of fireworks echoes above us, and I glance up, an oily sensation slithering down my throat.

A hand captures mine, and I'm just about to push away when another cascade of white flowers light the sky. There's a hooded figure in front of me, and the fireworks highlight a pale, eyeless face that steals my happiness in an instant.

The fetch.

It's not supposed to be here.

I was supposed to be safe in my city, with the power of the lands throbbing through me.

It wasn't supposed to be able to find me, with the bracelet on.

But the icy burn of the fetch's touch is a shock.

I scream, but another hand locks around my other wrist and then shadows overwhelm us. The world starts to fade until all I see is Thiago, shoving toward me.

"Vi!" he yells, just as the shadows swallow us whole.

CHAPTER 23

Between one breath and the other, I am plunged from laughter and music into a world of silence and cold. To travel along the Shadow Ways feels like the world turns me inside out and then it's twisting me in knots again.

The cloud of darkness vanishes, and I hit the ground, palms slapping onto cold stone as every inch of my body rebels. My gods. What just happened? Even my eyeballs hurt. The loss of Ceres leaves my mind raw and bleeding; in binding myself to the lands, I gained a massive amount of power, but the loss of that connection, the shock of it....

I didn't realize that in a handful of days I'd grown so used to the feeling that now the forest around me is dead and gray and dull. There is no life here. Not for me. This is not my land. It does not welcome me.

The fetch stalks toward me.

My arm throbs, the white imprint of its hand burning to life in my olive skin. I scramble to my feet, feeling the urge to retch, but I don't even know where I am.

Alone.

In an old and silent forest where little demi-fey bob through the branches. I trip over a pile of rocks—perhaps an old stone wall smothered in moss and ivy—but there's nowhere to escape.

Except....

A pulse beats through my skin. There's a Hallow nearby. And maybe, if I can get to it, then I can escape.

The creature straightens as if the journey took something out of it too. "You cannot run, little faeling. I've been hunting you for months. And you were invisible to my eyes, until you lit the world on fire. Now you are back. Now you cannot escape me."

There's a tiny dagger in my boot, but that's the only weapon I have, and when I draw it, the fetch laughs.

"Cold iron won't kill me, little faeling."

"No?"

Only sunlight or the blood of the purest....

Time to test a theory.

I draw the knife across the back of my hand, and blood wells. I fling droplets of blood across its face.

Instantly it screams, clutching at its face, and I don't waste my chance.

Darting past, I sprint into the forest ruins, scrambling over rock and raw slate. Vines tangle over stones, but I can sense the Hallow drawing me toward it like a lodestone.

Where did the fetch bring me?

I don't recognize the ruins, but that doesn't mean anything. There are dozens of Hallows in Unseelie.

Hallows are means of transportation, but they don't open to just any other Hallow. You have to follow the ley lines, unless they're located at a nexus point—like Ceres—with ley lines crossing to numerous other Hallows.

Slipping and sliding down the slope, I skid across the smooth slate floors of the Hallow.

Curse it.

Each rune has been chiseled from the guardian stones, until all that remains is a hint of copper. I don't know which Hallow they align with, and several of the Hallows were destroyed during the wars—if I pick the wrong rune, then I might will myself out of existence.

Slamming my palms against them in frustration, I turn to face the fetch as it stalks through the ruins toward me.

"Nowhere to run," it whispers, and a knife gleams in its hand.

"Who said anything about running?"

There's one last option remaining.

I reach for the Mother of Night, using all of my power to call to her. "*Help me. Please.*"

Something dark and alien slips beneath my skin, and when I open my eyes, I could swear I'm seeing through hers. A heartbeat passes. The fetch glides toward me with insolent slowness, as if it knows there's nothing I can do.

"*What do you want, child?*"

"*I need to get out of here.*"

There's a hesitation. "*I don't grant gifts, Princess.*"

"*No? Well, if you want to prove to me that you're a benevolent being, then it starts here! If I'm locked in a cell or dead, then you'll never get your precious freedom.*"

Silence.

"*Think,*" she whispers. "*What weakness does one of the Heartless have?*"

My blood and sunlight. But the moon hangs bloated in the sky and dawn is hours away.

"*You have the power to move the tides themselves,*" she

continues callously. *"You don't need the sun to rise, Iskvien. You just need the light."*

I press both palms against the Hallow stones and close my eyes. I don't know what I'm doing. I don't know if this will even work.

"Open yourself to the earth beneath your feet," she says. *"Open your mind. Open your heart."*

For a second, it sounds like some sort of rhythmic drumming echoes through the world, but maybe that's just the echo of my heart.

"You are not just fae, you are also one of us. We walked these lands when the sun was young and the earth green with new growth. We bled into these soils and bound our lives to the land. We heard the first birds chirp and saw bright scales flicker through our streams. We are everything that makes up the whole of Arcaedia."

Light flares beneath my hands. It's working.

"Use your power," the Mother demands. *"Control the Hallow."*

It feels a little like preparing to translocate. Energy wells beneath my feet, and I can feel it shivering through the Hallow stones into my palms. Heat and exhilaration rush through me, like the best kind of orgasm.

I lift my face, light shining through my skin.

I am power.

I am the land.

I am light.

And I catch a glimpse of the fetch's shocked face as it sees what's happening.

"Burn," I whisper, and light explodes out from the Hallow.

Even through closed eyes, it sears my eyeballs, until

afterimage blinds me. Heat gushes through me. My hair whips back. I could move continents with this power. I could stop the tides and haul the moon from the sky.

I could ruin my mother.

The power skitters, jarring through me as though it wants to be unleashed.

But then the edge of power twists within me, and I realize it's burning me out, burning me hollow. I'm too close to the edge. Too new at this.

I panic, and the light dies, the heat fading until my knees threaten to dump me on my ass.

Vines have burned away, leaving the center of the Hallow free of debris. Little copper runes glow in the sentinel stones, slowly fading as the power leaves me.

The fetch is gone.

"Foolish child." I sense a gentle hand stroking through my hair. *"You sip the merest taste of true power and you want to gobble it all down like a glutton. Everything has a price."*

My knees give out, and I hit the stone. What's happening to me?

"Sleep," she whispers. *"Recover. I will watch over you until the dawn rises."*

There is no choice. My eyes close even as the last glowing rune dies out like an extinguished firefly.

And then there's nothing but silence.

SOMETHING WARM RESTS ON MY CHEST, AND A VIBRATION trembles through me. I dream of sunshine and clover—the scent of my sister's hair—and for a second we're lying in her bed, tucked away from the world and the dangerous whispers of the court.

"Nothing can tear us apart," Andraste tells me solemnly, pulling a little dagger from its sheath. She holds out her palm and slices the knife down it.

"Forever sisters," I reply, taking the knife from her and mimicking her actions.

We clasp palms, and a shiver of bells tinkle in the background as though Maia herself hears our pledge.

But Andraste betrayed me. *This isn't real*, I want to scream at myself. And the weight on my chest is heavier.

I blink, and a pair of lambent yellow eyes stare directly into mine.

Mother of—

A yell escapes me and as I scramble to sit up, a set of razor-sharp claws dig into my chest. I slam a hand into it, and a hiss escapes the mound of dark gray fur as it lands in the leaf mulch beside me.

Blessed Maia. I shove to my feet, trying to work out where I am and what happened and where the cursed cat came from.

"Shit." Everything comes rushing back in upon me.

The fetch. The Mother of Night. The way I used the Hallow.

Dawn light silvers the sky far to the east, but nothing's changed. I'm alone, and I have no idea where I am or how to get home. I swear I could sleep for a week too, but there's no peace to be found here. I have to keep moving.

"I don't suppose you know where we are?" I ask the cat.

"Meow," it says, sitting and licking its paw.

"That's precisely what I thought." I give a sigh, and then start down the slope toward the Hallow.

The second I step through the lintel stones onto the slate circle, my heart falls.

There's no buzz.

No whiplash of energy.

Nothing.

It feels like the Hallow's been sucked dry.

Curse it. Hallows need at least an hour to recharge after they're used as a portal, but whatever I did last night seems to have drained it.

I stare at the spine of mountains in the distance, an icy wind stirring the silk of my skirt. Thiago will be frantic, but there's no help for it.

"I guess I'm just going to have to wait," I tell the cat.

NIGHT FALLS, AND WITH IT COMES SHADOWS MOVING UP THE mountainside.

I slip through the trees, shivering despite the summer blood that warms my veins. I didn't want to leave the Hallow, but clearly the ray of light I shot into the air last night served as some sort of beacon.

I'm being hunted.

One knife. Limited magic. No Hallow to draw upon.

And no idea of what's out there.

I slit my skirts apart, tying the ends around my calves so they form a simile of trousers, and pin my hair into a tight knot. And then I head into the trees.

There's a stream burbling nearby, and I've spent enough time in the mountains to know that if I follow it downhill, I should come upon *some* sign of civilization. If there's a Hallow here, then there are fae.

Or there were fae, says the cold, practical part of my mind I can't deny. *You saw those glyphs. Something chipped them out of the stone. A long time ago.*

The cat meows plaintively at me.

It's following me.

Curse the night, but this little bastard is going to get us both killed. Shooting it a glare, I try to silently shoo it away.

It blinks those lambent yellow eyes at me, then licks its paw, which I take to mean is its version of *eat nightshade.*

There's nothing I can do. Perhaps it will grow weary of tracking me if I continue past the boundary of its home territory.

Wishful thinking.

Meow.

The high-pitched call echoes through the woods.

Meow. Meow. Meow.

My hand clenches around the hilt of my knife. *Mother of—*

But no, we're not thinking of her.

I slowly turn around.

The cat levels that unblinking stare upon me.

"Listen, you furry little asshole," I whisper. "I don't know why you're following me, but this is a stupid idea. We're deep in a forest crawling with trolls or something worse." It doesn't even blink at me. I snap my teeth together. "Trolls will eat you. Go back to where you came from."

Nothing.

I give up. "Fine. Follow me to your doom. Perhaps they'll floss their teeth with your tail."

"*Perhaps you should listen, you feckless idiot,*" it says, the words skipping past my ears and imprinting themselves directly in my brain. "*I've been trying to tell you that you're going the wrong way for the past mile.*"

My mouth falls open, and I clear an inch of steel from my sheath before I catch the mocking gleam in its eyes.

"What did you just say?"

It spoke. I swear it spoke.

The cat scrapes that long pink tongue across its paw.

I'm in Unseelie. Of course it's not just a cat.

"What are you?"

It ripples through the shadows, and I can barely make out where it begins and they end.

"*I came to find you,*" it says cryptically. "*And I am not a what. I am a who.*"

Curse the night.

It's a grimalkin.

CHAPTER 24

We make camp near the Hallow, though I'm still not entirely certain how "I" became a "we." I also seem to be doing all of the work, though the grimalkin assures me he supervises.

"*Make a fire. I'm cold,*" he says.

"If I make a fire, then every predator in the vicinity is going to smell it."

The grimalkin gives me an unblinking look. "*Do you insult me?*"

"How is that an insult?"

"*I am the Lord of Shadows.*" He pushes to his feet and stalks toward me. "*I am the Merciless Night. I am the Teeth That Tear At An Unprotected Throat and the Claws That Slash Like Knives. There are no predators in these parts, for they fled the second they heard me moving through the woods.*"

Someone thinks highly of himself.

"There were shadows on the mountainside," I grind out.

"They will scent me and know to avoid me. I am the Terror With No Mercy."

"If you're such a terrifying creature, then why are you following *me*?" A thought occurs. "Did she send you to me?"

The last thing I remember is the Mother of Night's touch across my forehead.

"I have no master or mistress. I came because I Saw you. And I need you." He sniffs and settles himself near my feet.

"Need me to do what?"

"Do I look like I have hands? Make yourself useful for once and fetch some wood. And then do the thing that makes the fire. We have hours before the Hallow is recharged enough to use, and I intend to spend them in comfort."

I grit my teeth. "I am not taking orders from an overgrown cat."

It continues licking its paw, but this time, little scythes cut through the furry pad, and it looks at me as if to say, Claws That Slash Like Knives.

"Make the fire, and I will tell you where you are and which rune aligns with your home."

"You furry little son of a—"

"Careful."

"You know which rune I need?" I push to my feet.

And the grimalkin stares back at me, unblinking.

Of course it knows.

And of course it's not going to tell me unless I do what it wants.

A minute later, I'm slipping through the underbrush, gathering dry timber as I curse under my breath. Somehow, I've gone from being the ruling Queen of Evernight

313

to cat lackey within the space of a few hours, and I don't know how it happened.

I dig a hole into the dirt in order to hide the flames and then set the fire.

"There doesn't appear to be enough wood," the grimalkin tells me from his perch on a nearby rock.

"We're not laying the Samhain bonfires," I reply through gritted teeth. "And I intend to use the Hallow to get out of here the second it's recharged."

Snapping my fingers, I set the pile of tinder on fire.

The grimalkin's eyes thin to pleased slits, and it basks in the heat. *"You are useful, after all. I may keep you."*

"And you owe me answers. Where are we?"

"The ruins of Charun."

I rub my arms and look around. Not so far north of Valerian and Evernight, but too far for comfort. And deep in the lands of the goblin horde. "Why would the fetch have brought me here?"

"I know not what fills its filthy mind," the grimalkin assures me, *"though perhaps it sought to meet someone here."*

"Thank you for planting that thought in my mind," I mutter, suddenly wondering if the shadow to my left is a tree or a monster.

"There is also a direct ley line to the Black Keep from here. There are very few Hallows that lead to the keep."

"Also not helping."

The Black Keep is where the Horned One finally fell and was locked away in a prison world. Though it's not the seat of Angharad's power, if she wants to resurrect him, that's where she will do it.

And she needs my blood to resurrect him.

I need to get safely home, but he's right. The low-level

buzzing through the Hallow tells me we're still hours away from it replenishing itself.

Pushing myself to my feet, I wince at my aching bones and cross to the edge of the circle of firelight. The Hallow stones form slowly as my eyes grow accustomed to the lack of light out here.

This is where Maia revealed her godhood and overthrew Sylvian. This is where they both fell, and where Maia ascended to rule over us all. Charun's been a holy site for centuries, and the fae used to make pilgrimages here until the lands were ceded to the goblin horde during the Wars of Light and Shadow as payment for siding with the seelie.

I press my palm against the nearest Hallow stone.

Little pockets scar the surface where the glyphs were once laid, and I frown as I lean closer. I'd thought they were chiseled free, but the stone beneath my fingers is roughhewn and pitted, as if the stone itself exploded.

And then I blink.

There are three moons in front of me. One in the night sky; one reflected in the water of the lake; and the last shimmering in the distance, just above the lake's surface.

I don't know whether it's a trick of the light or—

"*It's what remains of the crystal keep,*" the grimalkin muses.

"The what?"

"*It was built by the otherkin who worshipped the Daughter of the Three Moons. It stood here for centuries until the fae arrived and destroyed it, as they destroyed everything.*"

I shoot him a look.

"*What?*" He tilts his head. "*Do your history books not speak of the invasion? The fae came and conquered all who*

315

walked these lands. They chained them, and broke them, and shattered their Hallows. Your great goddess herself is responsible for the one you stand beside."

There's a dirty taste in my mouth. "Maia was trying to overthrow Queen Sylvian. She'd gone mad."

"Ah, yes," the grimalkin purrs. "But have you ever wondered precisely how Maia conquered her fellow queen? They were much of a muchness, were they not? And little Queen Sylvian had her own personal army of fused warriors. An army that could not be defeated, they said, and yet your precious Maia broke them with her power alone."

I'm not imagining it.

The bastard's staring at me with beady little eyes as it slowly licks its paw.

"What is the answer going to cost me?"

I swear it laughs. "You're learning, little fae queen." And then it blinks at me. "The time is not yet right for you to know. Ask me again when the moon is full, your heart is torn in two, and you have no more hope remaining."

I roll my eyes. "It's not as though we have anything else to do to pass the time. Unless the Mother of Night instructed you to keep such secrets?"

"You think the Mother of Night sent me to you?"

I still. "You were sitting on my chest when I woke, and she'd promised to protect me."

"Yes. You were warm. My feet were cold."

A strange thought occurs. "What brought you to these woods?"

"I was waiting for you to arrive."

My hand curls around my dagger. "How did you know I was coming here?"

The creature rolls its eyes. "I'm a grimalkin. I walk the

shadows—the same way the Heartless do—but sometimes, in walking that world, I can catch a glimpse of a future unmapped. I needed help, and when I requested such from the world, your face kept appearing, as uninspiring as it is. And so I am here."

My feet feel weighted to the ground.

"Put the knife away," the grimalkin continues. *"You're only going to embarrass yourself."*

I glare at it, but suddenly it's no longer there.

I spin around.

Nothing.

And then there's a mocking purr in the tree above me, and something swipes at my hair.

Lambent yellow eyes appear, and then the fucking cat lolls on its back in the branches above me as a piece of my hair sifts to the ground.

"I could have gone for the tendon in your right heel," it points out. *"And you would never have seen me coming."*

Fuck.

I dwell on the creature. It could have killed me while I was unconscious near the Hallow. It wants something from me. I just need to work out what. "Do you have a name, o Lord of Shadows?"

It's eyes thin, as if it's not entirely certain whether I'm being sarcastic. *"You may call me… Grimm."*

No fae creature gives out its real name. But…. "That's terribly original."

"It will suffice. And your own?"

"Vi." I resheathe the dagger. "You said you needed my help."

The grimalkin disappears, and I nearly fall over as it suddenly wends its way between my legs. *"Excellent.*

You're starting to listen. Yes, I need your help. I have lost my child."

Oh. "I'm so sorry, I—"

"Not my kit," it says with some dissatisfaction. *"As if I would lose my kit. My fae child. I am its owner, and I have been charged with protecting it from the world. It is foolish—though allowances may be made for its age—and small, and it frequently smells because it has a tendency to fall into bogs and all manner of... messes. But it is mine, and no grimalkin loses its child."*

My mind's trying to work out the logistics. "You're a familiar."

"I am not *a familiar. It is* my *child. My fae is impossibly sweet. I keep telling her that she needs to grow thorns, but she's nothing but a rose itself."* He sniffs to himself, as if it's a despicable thing to be so gentle. *"And now she's in trouble, and I need to protect her."*

"Well, if she's in trouble, then why are you here?" Grimalkin are curious creatures. They're not pets—indeed, I'm rapidly learning they consider us to be *their* pets—but when they bond with a creature, it's for life. "How can I help?"

The grimalkin stares into the flames for a long moment. *"Because the future tells me I need to be at your side. You're going to help me rescue my fae."*

"I would help you if I could, but I need to find a crown and slay an evil queen." A rough laugh escapes me. "And that's only if I can manage to return to my husband. You're better off finding someone else to help you. The Heartless are trying to capture me."

The shadow-cat's head turns eerily toward me without any corresponding movement of its body. Its eyes remain unblinking. *"No. No, I think I shall remain by your side."*

A little shiver tiptoes down my spine—almost like little pawprints. "What do you see?"

The grimalkin's attention returns to the flames. *"A child crying. A princess screaming. And a dark goddess laughing."* It licks its paw. *"And don't ask me to explain any of that, because the future is too broad and nebulous for your puny fae mind to grasp."*

Grimalkin.

"Well this puny fae mind is the—"

"More wood is required."

I glare murder at it, and then dump another armful of branches on the fire. "I'm sorry that you've lost your child, but I'm returning to Ceres as soon as that Hallow recharges."

"And I will accompany you." I open my mouth to argue, but it gives me a narrow-eyed look. *"Oh, did you think you had any choice in the matter? I can walk through shadows, little fae. You cannot hide from me, not matter where you go. I will find you."*

I swear the fucking thing is smiling at me.

"I protected you while you slept. You owe me a boon, and so my demand is this: You will take me with you until I choose to depart your side."

"How does that help you find your child?"

"The future is a strange and nebulous thing. Try not to think about it too much. You'll strain a muscle."

There's only one good thing about this entire situation: Grimm is going to drive Thiago and Eris to the edge of frustration.

I can hardly wait.

I'M ALMOST NODDING OFF WHEN SOMETHING SUDDENLY YOWLS in my ear.

Clapping a hand to my chest, I sit up sharply, but the grimalkin merely bumps its head against me. *"Wake up, pudding brain."*

"What's wrong?" I gasp. "Are we under attack?"

"If we were under attack, then you would see the ground littered with the corpses of mine enemies." I swear it rolls its eyes. *"The Hallow is nearing completion. You should be able to use it shortly."*

I blink.

And he's right. I can feel the Hallow's echo starting to ripple out through the lands, like some sort of sonar frequency.

A heavy weight forms on my shoulders, and suddenly I have a fur cloak.

"Well, what are you waiting for?" Grimm demands. *"We haven't got all day."*

CHAPTER 25

The second we arrive in Ceres, I stagger out of the Hallow's copper ring, feeling utterly drained.

The Hallow stands in the second-tallest tower in the castle, and for a second, I simply close my eyes and breathe it all in. Home. I'm home. Bells ring in the distance, seagulls squawk through the open arches that lead to the sky, and I swear I can smell bread baking.

And I can feel the land welcoming me back—a big, deep breath of air that relaxes every tense muscle within me.

"Are you always so slow?" Grimm demands, already sauntering down the stairs of the tower. *"Did your mother drop you on your head as a baby? Come on."*

Thiago and Eris.

Their faces when they see my new companion.

I grind my teeth as I stomp down the stairs after it, my skirt still in ruins, and bruises and dirt covering my skin. No queen now, but an untidy vagabond who desperately needs a bath. "My mother would have had to cradle me in

321

her arms in order to drop me, and I'm sure the second she birthed me, she handed me over to the nursemaids. I was merely appreciating the fact that I'm...."

Alive.

I hadn't let myself dwell on what had happened too much. It's easy to push such thoughts aside. I've been doing it all my life. *Just focus on what's in front of you and keep moving forward.*

But this is the first time the fetch has made a deliberate attempt to kidnap me since it lost me the first time.

Angharad wants to cut my heart out on the stone floor of the Hallow in the middle of the Black Keep, and she came very close to doing it.

"I see the future, not read minds," Grimm tells me.

"You wouldn't understand."

"I assure you, my faculties are quite adept."

"An Unseelie queen wants to sacrifice me to the Horned One in order to resurrect him," I snap. "Forgive me if the thought makes me a little uneasy. I'm grateful to be home."

Grimm stops on the stairs, and for once there's no snide remark.

"We cannot allow that to happen." He continues padding down the stairs.

"Thank you."

"Not until you've found my child."

"Is it possible she ran away from you?" I growl under my breath.

"Impossible. I am a grimalkin. I am her shadow. There's no place she could go that I couldn't follow."

"Then how did you lose her?"

For once, he's silent.

I'm almost tempted to apologize.

"I don't want to talk about that right now."

We circle around the final curve, and as light spills through the archway ahead, I realize there's an enormous shadow hovering in the arch.

Thiago stands frozen, one hand resting on the rail, his foot on the first stair, staring up at me. He looks like he's seen a ghost.

My heart skips a beat.

"Vi?" Thiago's voice comes out with a quiver, and the look on his face—I don't think I've ever seen him wear that expression before. As if he doesn't dare hope, doesn't quite believe his eyes and ears.

"It's me," I whisper.

And then he's rushing up the stairs and I'm in his arms, and suddenly everything is going to be okay.

I'm home.

I'm safe.

And the rib-crushing hug he gives me makes me want to simply lose myself in his arms and never lift my head again.

"Where were you?" he rasps. "What happened? I've had Thalia's spies and sparrows searching everywhere. We've been to every Hallow we could find, and turned to every fae with the gift of foretelling. None could even catch a glimpse of you."

"I'm fine." I squeeze his biceps. "The fetch took me to Charun, and I managed to escape it, and—"

"Escape it?" There's an edge of the predator in his eyes, and I know he's battling the instincts that demand he heads north and tear apart everything that had a hand in my kidnapping.

323

"I used the power of the Hallow to make enough light to rival the sun. I burned it, but I don't know if it managed to blink into the shadows, or if it... died. But doing so drained the Hallow dry. We had to wait for it to recharge before I could return."

There's a weight on his brows. And then he kisses my hand. "Sunlight."

"The only way to slay a fetch." I give him a light smile, but we're both aware of what I'm not saying.

I did something that no fae could manage.

"Good." Thiago lets out a slow breath. His hand slides through my hair, and he leans down and captures my—

"No!" I squeak. "I'm filthy! And I smell. And I haven't scrubbed my teeth."

He kisses me anyway, his hands sliding up and down my waist as if he can't resist touching me. "I don't care."

I do. "Bath," I growl, pushing at the hard planes of his chest.

Thiago backs away, but the glint in his eyes promises me ruination the second I'm clean—or deemed to be so. He lifts my hand to his mouth and kisses my palm. "As you wish, my love."

"Maybe you can help wash my back."

"Hello? Have you forgotten something?"

A furry weight bumps against my legs, and Thiago looks down with a scowl. "What... is this?"

There's so much to say. So much to explain. But perhaps the easiest thing to start with is this. "I have a cat."

His eyebrows arch. "Vi, that's not a—"

"Pfft. Semantics." I press my finger to his lips. "I know what he is. The bastard's only too delighted to point it out every chance he gets. But for now, he's my cat." My voice roughens. "He guarded me while I slept. And he's lost and alone. He told me he can't find his last owner."

"He probably murdered them," Thiago mutters.

"I owe him a boon. I told him I'd help him find his child."

And the fae must pay their debts or suffer the consequences.

Thiago's eyes turn into thin slits. "It's not sleeping in our bed."

"I'll sleep wherever I please, little princeling."

From Thiago's icy glare, it's clear he heard it too. "If I see a hint of your beady little eyes in my bedchamber, I'll throw you through the nearest Hallow straight into a troll's cave."

Grimm launches into my arms, and I'm forced to contend with twenty-five pounds of pure arrogance that butts its head against my chin.

"Just try it, you big bat," Grimm purrs, and his claws sink into my arm. *"The queen is bound to help me find my owner, and until then, I'm staying with her."*

Thiago shoots me another look, one that clearly says *stop making deals with Unseelie creatures.*

I bare my teeth in a half smile, half wince. "He's cute. And he's nice and warm at night. And he won't shit in the bed."

Grimm does this kind of snigger-purr that I take to mean, *unless the prince really annoys me.*

Thiago stabs a finger toward Grimm. "Don't eat the demi-fey. Don't let me find you in our bedchambers. And don't get too comfortable. As soon as we get a chance, we're going to find your owner and then you're gone, do you understand?"

"Aw. Is the wittle pwince afraid she likes me better?"

I swear I see steam shoot from Thiago's ears as he stomps away.

CHAPTER 26

The next morning, I groan as I roll out of bed.

"Breakfast?" Thiago purrs, proving himself the best husband in the world as he snaps his fingers and a tray appears, laden with all my favorites.

I glance at the towel wrapped around his hips even as I reach for a piece of bread. "That depends."

"On?"

"Whether you intend to be breakfast."

He crosses the room, resting both hands on the sides of my chair as he leans down to give me a kiss. "Don't think I'm not tempted, Vi. Last night was fun." But his thumb strokes across my cheek. "But you look like you need more sleep."

I feel like it too.

"I guess the Hallow wasn't the only thing that was drained," I grumble, sipping at my cup of peppermint tea. *Bliss.* "You could do all the work?"

He smiles, but there's a glint of worry in his eyes.

"Patience holds its own rewards. I'll wait until you're more rested."

I roll my eyes. "What are we doing today?"

He walks away from me, tugging the towel loose. "Discussing our next move. If that bracelet doesn't hide you from the fetch, then we need to figure out how to protect you."

I tilt my head sideways. Oh, now that's really unfair.

His bare ass practically begs for my teeth.

"Vi?" It's clear from the twinkle in his eyes that he's said my name a few times.

I warm my hands on my cup. "Yes?"

"Later," he mouths, and then he winks.

Fine. Grumbling under my breath, I reach for the second teapot on the tray. Peppermint to start the day, and then bitter nettle to prevent any unwanted side effects from last night.

But my fingers freeze on the teapot lid.

I didn't drink any tea yesterday. Or the day before.

There's a hollow ringing in my ears. It should be fine. Thiago withdrew last night. And I'm almost due for my monthly bleeding, in fact….

When am I due?

I'd jokingly said to Thalia that maybe it was best if I didn't wear white the other night—just in case. But I haven't thought about it since. Everything's been so hectic.

But the thought ringing through my head is: *I should be bleeding by now.*

I can't stop myself from counting, but there's a breathless feeling in my chest that sends my thoughts scattering the second I get to five weeks.

Nearly five weeks since I had my last monthly.

Five. Weeks.

"Vi?" Thiago's voice roughens. "What's wrong? You've gone pale."

"I'm late," I whisper, my hands starting to shake.

"We've got time—"

"*Late.*"

This time Thiago looks at me, and I see a myriad of expressions in his eyes. Confusion. Understanding. Then horror. "No."

Pressing my hands to my midriff, I can't stop my nails from digging in. We were so careful. He always withdrew or used a sheathe, and I've been drinking bitter nettle tea every cursed morning.

"How late?"

"I don't know! Three, maybe four days." It's enough to make worry worm like a hole in my gut. My bleedings have always been regular.

This should be a moment of joy, but all I can taste is a mouthful of ash.

I want this child so badly, but I cannot risk it. Not now.

"Are you sure?" he asks.

"No, I'm not sure!" I shove to my feet, my nightgown swishing around my legs. "I don't feel any different." Should I not be feeling queasy by now? I don't *know*. This is not an area I've ever given much thought to before. "Just tired."

But that can be explained.

Lack of sleep.

Attacks every time I turn around.

Endless nightmares.

I squeeze my eyes shut and I *see* her, running through a

field of wild poppies, tracing her fingers over their petals as she laughs and looks back at me—

Right before the shadows swallow her whole.

I think I'm going to be sick.

I bolt for the wash chambers, sliding to my knees in front of the bath. My stomach rebels, but even as I gag, nothing comes up, and I don't know if this is shock or something more.

A hand rubs my back, soft words rumbling through him.

"It's alright, Vi. It's alright."

It's the first time he's ever lied to me since we made our promise.

Finally, I managed to swallow down the urge to vomit. A cool rag is draped over my neck, and Thiago squats on the cool tiles beside me as I drag my knees to my chest and cradle them.

"We will find the crown," he assures me, squeezing my knee. "No matter what I have to do. She won't have our child, Vi. She won't."

I want to cry, but I just feel so wretchedly hollow.

"I might not be with child," I whisper.

Our eyes meet.

"I won't know for sure until…." I can't say the rest.

But there's a certain bleakness in his eyes as we nod. We both know it's inevitable.

The Mother of Night always gets what she wants.

Thiago's circle meets in the usual set of chambers.

Thalia and Eris were there to greet me last night, but

not the others. I bend to press a kiss to Finn's cheek as he welcomes me and nod at Baylor. The gruff giant keeps to himself, and I respect that.

"You look terrible," Finn says, leaning forward in his chair to peer at me. He turns an accusing glare on Thiago. "Have you not been letting her sleep?"

Usually it's a joke, but it falls flat this morning.

"I'm fine," I mutter.

I am not fine. Not at all.

"News from the borders, my prince," Baylor says, flipping open his set of notes as per usual. "We've—"

"Later." Thiago takes his seat with curt grace. "The borders can wait. Adaia can wait. We need to make the Crown of Shadows our priority, and we need to come up with some means of keeping Vi safe from the fetch."

They all share a glance.

"I'll guard her," Eris says. "Day and night."

"Well, you didn't do much of a job of it last time," says an irritatingly annoying voice from somewhere to my left.

Finn has a knife in hand as he leaps to his feet, "What in Kato's name is *that*?"

Eris hurls her dagger, but Grimm merely vanishes, and two seconds later Baylor yelps as a shadow forms on his lap before leaping onto the table.

"You couldn't kill me if you tried," Grimm sneers, managing to walk across all Baylor's papers and simultaneously kick them to the floor.

"Stop!" I yell as Eris flips another knife into her hand. I glare at the grimalkin. "The doors to this chamber are locked and warded. How did you get in?"

His tail lashes. *"Please. There's not a ward in this world that can stop me from getting into a place I desire to be. And if*

331

all else fails, I simply stand outside and meow loudly until someone rectifies their mistake."

"You *know* this creature?" Finn demands.

"Careful, pudding brain." Grimm's head swivels toward him. *"I am not a creature. I am a grimalkin. I am He Who Walks the Shadows. I am —"*

"Yes," I say abruptly, and then hastily explain Grimm's appearance before we learn about the Merciless Night and the Claws That Slash Like Knives.

Eris sinks into her chair.

Baylor mutters under his breath as he picks up his notes, a growl escaping him when he sees the paw prints that smudged his ink.

Finn crosses his arms over his chest. "Pudding brain?"

"Pea soup?" Grimm purrs.

Finn's eyes narrow. "It's one thing to be insulted by Eris. Quite another to have a walking carpetbag try and abuse my intelligence."

"Try? I'd have to find evidence of it in order to insult it."

"Well, I think he's adorable," Thalia coos.

Grimm examines her, and then he jaunts across the table toward her and nudges her hand for a pat. *"This one is my favorite."*

"He's not staying," Thiago warns.

Thalia gives him her best impression of wide eyes.

"That hasn't yet been decided," Grimm tells him, eyeing my husband with disdain. *"I quite like this castle. I may decide to rule it if the cooks keep leaving warm milk out."*

Thiago closes his eyes, and I swear there's going to be a royal order demanding all milk supplies to the demi-fey who litter the castle cease immediately.

"That's not your milk," I growl under my breath to the grimalkin.

He looks affronted, as if to say, *who else does it belong to?*

"Can we focus?" Thiago snarls. "On matters belonging to the security of the realm?"

Thalia picks at the bacon on her plate, breaking it into bite-sized pieces and offering it to Grimm. "I intercepted an interesting letter to Vi from Princess Imerys. About the crown."

Thiago shoots her a look. "Why do I feel like I'm not going to enjoy this?"

"Because you're not. It involves sending Vi into Unseelie again. Without you."

His shoulders square. "No."

Thalia points the fork at him. "You can't go. We don't know where your father is or if he's still looking for you—"

"He's still looking for me," Thiago growls. "He will always be looking for me. The answer's still no."

I glance between them. As his cousin, she knows more of his history than I do. But this is the first time his father's been mentioned in anything more than a "I don't want to talk about it" kind of way.

"Why Unseelie?" Eris asks.

"Because that's where the saithe oracle is," Thalia replies. "Imerys writes to say that she finally remembered where she'd heard the name of the crown. It was in a written treatise on prophecies that the saithe oracle has made."

My stomach bottoms out.

I don't know why I didn't think of it before.

Or maybe I do.

The oracle will show you a glimpse of the future or the past, but it comes at a cost.

"No," Thiago says sharply. "Vi's lost more than enough of her memories. She doesn't need to lose any more."

"I'm merely presenting it as an option," Thalia says, spreading her hands. "The oracle isn't technically immortal—she passes from body to body—but she's a repository for all the memories of all the oracles that have come before her. And those memories she's taken in payment from those who journey to see her."

Silence rings throughout the room.

Thiago's still shaking his head, but he's not the one who makes this decision.

"How do I get there?" I ask quietly.

Every head in the room turns toward me. Thiago's nostrils flare, but I hold up my palm.

"We need to find the crown," I tell him, and our eyes meet as I try to remind him why this is suddenly urgent. "No matter what we must do."

CHAPTER 27

The saithe oracle lives alone in a swamp deep in the heart of Unseelie.

My stomach keeps tying itself in knots, and I don't know if it's purely worry or because I actually am carrying Thiago's child.

"Relax," Eris says, hauling back on the oars of the little boat we rented from a hob. "You're knotted tighter than my bow. The local fae are going to start looking at us closely if they notice how nervous you are."

"Sorry." I stare across the waters, trying to fight the urge to tap my fingers. "I'm just tired. Every time I think we get closer to the crown, my leads shrivel up and die."

"You have over eight months to find it," she says.

I think I'm going to be sick.

"Vi?"

Sometimes I forget how perceptive she is, but then she was born on a battlefield, and she's spent her entire life reading the room.

"I'm late."

Unlike Thiago, she understands immediately.

"Well, fuck," she says, tugging out the flask she carries and taking a swig from it.

"We were always careful. But somehow…."

"Fate," Eris says roughly. "Sometimes it doesn't matter how much you try to prevent such a thing, it still happens. How certain are you?"

"I don't *know*. Five days late, maybe. Tired. Hungry. But I don't know if my mind is conjuring symptoms simply because I fear they're there, or if I just need a week in bed."

Eris hauls back on the oars. "Then we find the crown, pay your debt, and kill the Mother of Night."

The breath explodes out of me. "Do you have any idea how difficult that would be?"

"Everything can be killed. Even a goddess."

I slump back in the boat with a weak laugh. "Sometimes I wish I had your assurance. And if the entire alliance couldn't kill her—could only lock her away—then what makes you think *I* can manage to do it?"

"*We*," she corrects. "The darkyn prince of Evernight and his queen, the *leanabh an dan*; his cousin, one of the salt-kissed; a general who once belonged to the Grimm; a dangerous sylvaren warrior; and me."

"The scariest fae in the world."

Eris gives me a look.

"You think I'm talking about that Devourer bullshit?" I snort. "You're terrifying enough on your own."

She looks away. But she smiles a little. "Here we are."

I don't comment about how neatly she managed to distract me as she rows the boat toward a floating island in the middle of the swamp. I'm no longer worried about the Mother of Night.

No, now I have to deal with the saithe oracle.

Eris flips me a small vial. "For the oracle," she says. "It's one of my memories."

I curl my fingers around the vial.

The oracle is one of the few free immortals who remain in the world, and they say she exists now on the taste of mortal memories. Nobody knows what she does with them—whether she simply swallows them whole and gluts herself on them—but the more painful or joyful the memory, the more it sustains her.

"Eris, I can't—"

"You've given enough memories for him," she tells me. "And you are my queen. Let me spare you this. I don't need this memory. Trust me on that, if nothing else, Vi."

I look at the small glimmer of swirling white trapped in the vial.

A memory is part of your identity. It's part of your whole. And I'd been worried about providing one, considering I have so few left.

"She will take it," Eris growls, as if she senses my hesitation. "Painful memories are the ones that bring the most sustenance, and this one is full of blood and tears."

"I'm very tempted to hug your right now, E." The words thicken in my throat. "But then I'm going to embarrass us both, and I know you hate displays of emotion."

She shies away from me. "Please. Don't. I'd hate to have to dump your undignified ass in the swamp."

The pair of us smile, both of us playing up to the extremes of our character.

And then Eris scowls at me. "Well, go on. Go and find our crown. I don't just give away memories for nothing."

She shoos me toward the ruins on the island.

I tuck her memory away. "You're not just a friend, Eris. You're mine now, you realize? You're part of my new family."

The words strike her like a blow, but she merely tips her chin up. "I expect to be named godmother."

I laugh as I turn toward the ruins. "I think you'll have to fight Thalia for that honor."

THE SAITHE ORACLE RECLINES UPON AN ANCIENT STONE throne, those all-black eyes focused on me so intently it seems as though she can see right through me. Every last little hope. Every dream. Every nightmare I ever owned.

But it's the look in her eyes that makes me swallow.

She's otherkin. Born of the same peoples as the Mother of Night, and I can see the resemblance there in their pointed chins and the little horns that curl in their hair.

Not an Old One—Thalia's sources tell me the oracle was never worshipped, nor sought out others of her kind —but she is bound to an ancient power that guards the swamp, and can never leave its waters.

"Little queen," she says, her brightly painted nails scratching over mossy stone. "You have finally come to me."

I hate the way oracles and seers always act as if they've been waiting for you.

"I have brought a memory." I tug the vial out of my leather coat. "And in return I have questions."

Her dark gaze locks on the vial. "This is skirting the rules," she chides. "The memory is due to be one of your own."

"This belongs to Eris of Silvernaught. It is full of blood and tears, she assures me. A worthy meal."

There's hunger there in her dark gaze. But fear too. "The Devourer."

"No. My friend."

She slinks from her throne, barely able to hide her eagerness. "You're a little fool if you think her your friend. Eris of Silvernaught is prophesied to swallow the moon whole. If that thing inside her gets loose, then she will drink in the souls of all that walk these lands."

I want to ask.

I want to know what Eris hides.

But it's not my place to demand answers of another. Eris will tell me if she chooses to do so.

"Do we have a deal?"

The oracle snatches the vial from my hands. "We do."

"Promise thrice," I insist, relaxing only once she says the words.

Slipping the cork from the vial, the oracle dips her fingers inside, coating them in the shiny, silvery substance within. She licks it from her fingers, shivering in delight at the taste. A gasp escapes her. And then another, and she finally tips the entire vial to her lips and swallows it down.

I resist the urge to look away.

There's something a little carnal about her response— as if she's on the edge of pleasure. That forked tongue darts out, sliding inside the vial until she's secured every last drop, and as I watch, she blooms before my eyes.

"A worthy memory," she rasps, crushing the vial in her fist. "Ask your questions, little queen."

"The Crown of Shadows was lost to mortal memory," I tell her, knees flexing, so that if she so much as moves toward me, I'm ready to flee. "But you're not mortal. And they say you remember everything."

"Is that what you truly wish to ask?"

I ignore her. "I want to know where the Crown of Shadows is."

A smile paints her curved lips. "Aye. I remember the fate of the world. I remember what these lands were like before you Bright Ones invaded from beyond the stars. I remember the trees, and the singing, and the way we danced in our Hallows and gave gift to the Old Ones there. And then your kind came and hunted the forests until we were forced to flee. They bound the power of the Hallows and killed half of our Old Ones. They—"

"Killed the Old Ones?" You cannot kill one of the Old Ones. You can only trap them. I thought that was why the Hallows were first bound—the only means the Alliance of Light had of locking them away.

"There were hundreds of our gods," she murmurs, eyes glittering with rage as she watches me. "Only the most powerful survived and waged war on the invaders. Some of them were locked away. Others were killed. And a rare handful were forced to hide."

As long as their people believe in them, the Old Ones do not die. Which means…. "Some of them still survive? Free?"

There's a smile on her face. "That's a secret for another day, little queen."

"Why would you tell me this?" This kind of information could be dangerous in the wrong hands.

"Tell me," she says, instead. "Why did you make a bargain with the Mother of Night?"

I see Thiago's desperate face, his hands chained behind his back as my mother orders his execution. "Because I was desperate."

"Your kind hate my kind. I don't believe you."

"Because I needed the power to break my mother's curse."

"*Lie*," she whispers. "Or only half the truth. Not even the most desperate of fae kind would turn to the Old Ones for help. We are the enemy. We are the vile creatures that haunt the night. We are death and despair and ruin, according to your stories. You knew the cost would be high. You knew there had to be answers elsewhere. So why did you do it?"

I turn away, pacing to the edge of the swamp. A sleek black head bobs up through the murk, merciless black eyes locking on me, before the selkie vanishes into the waters again.

"Why treat with the enemy?" The oracle pushes. "You know the dangers. It is forbidden by all your people."

My shoulders slump. "When I was a little girl, my childhood nurse used to read to me. There was a book. A collection of stories from the time of the wars. My mother had the book burned when she caught my nurse reading it to us, and she had nurse's eyes plucked and her tongue removed, so she could never spread such lies again."

"You sounded almost like your mother for a moment. The truth, Iskvien. From your lips."

I turn back to her. "The truth lies on the lips of the victor, does it not? And my mother's people wrote the history books. They burned the stories that didn't speak their truth or paint the world the way they want us to see it. I've always wondered whether those tales Nanny Redwyne read to us are true. The Old Ones are powerful and dangerous, but they could be bargained with. The creatures that existed before the fae arrived were not evil, merely cruel and capricious. And if you kept your wits about you, there's no reason the Old Ones couldn't help you. I wanted to know what the truth was. I believed those stories. I thought I could trust her."

"And the answer to that?"

"I made a mistake. Perhaps for once in her life, my mother spoke the truth."

She sniffs the air. "I think I know why you made that bargain, Iskvien. You practically reek of old magic. I think I know why you were drawn to those stories. You could sense it, couldn't you? You've always been drawn to the forest, the darker the better. You've always heard the whisper through the stones beneath your feet, the power banked in the ley lines. Blood calls to blood, little queen, and your blood has been whispering promises of power for years, hasn't it?"

"The Mother of Night used me."

"Aye," she agrees. "She uses you. She wants freedom for her and her captured brethren. You have the promise of two powerful bloodlines within you. The world trembles beneath your feet—"

"I don't want it." My fists clench. "I don't want this power."

"You can't run," she merely tells me. "And you can't hide. And you can't lock it away. What now, little queen?"

Time to face your fears.

"Now I find the Crown of Shadows and give it to that bitch," I tell her. "I will pay my dues. But she will have no more of me than that."

The oracle cocks her head, considering me.

"We will see," she says. "I have one last request before I answer your question."

"No. No more requests." I've played that game before and lost. Badly. "You've had your price. Now you owe me answers."

Her smile grows. "I ask for no price but this: Seek the prophecy that speaks of a savior who will break Unseelie. Read the true prophecy. And then come and find me if you wish to know more."

No matter which way I twist the words, I can't see a trap. But I know there is one. "You're trying to use me too."

"Aye. But I will admit it openly. A queen will walk this realm, Iskvien. She is coming, and all the world is aquiver with the promise of her awakening. She will right ancient wrongs. She will bring peace to the lands and tear down an entire thicket of lies. She will renew that which was broken and return glory to those who had it stolen from them."

"I am not… I am not that queen."

She merely tilts her head and considers me. "No. You are not that queen. Though you have the promise of it. But we shall see what the future holds. Read the prophecy. That is all I ask."

"And the crown?"

"Once there was a prince," she says. "A power-hungry male who wanted to cast down the queens who ruled over him. He despised the yoke of Maia's name. He raged against the injustices he saw as keeping him from his rightful throne. He had three sisters—all younger—and all of them ahead of him in line for the throne of his kingdom. And his hunger grew. Not just for the throne his mother sat upon, but for the thrones of all who ruled.

"He slew his sisters in a bloody coup. He took his mother's head and placed it on a spike atop his city walls. And then he turned his attention to other powers—other thrones. But the queens are tied to the lands, and so he knew he would have to seek a dark and dangerous power in order to overthrow them.

"He went north and he made a bargain with a creature there who had the gift of metalworking. Halvern the Dwarf made the five great relics; the Sword of Mourning; The Shield of Victory; The Mirror of Betrayal; and the Armor of Lorendil…, but some say the Crown of Shadows was his greatest feat.

"Bring me a fallen star and a thousand souls, Halvern said. I will use the star's metal to forge the crown and the blood to quench the metal. And so, the prince trekked far and wide to find a star, still burning from its flight through the heavens. And he gathered a thousand souls and led them to their doom.

"And Halvern produced his finest working: A crown so dark and bloody that it could smite any who opposed the one who wore it. A crown that could shake the lands themselves and crack the fault lines that quivered through them. A crown that could drink at the magic of the lands— the source of the ley lines powers—until they were dry.

"The king ruled for a thousand years, and though the earth trembled beneath his touch, he held power over it.

He sent thousands to his death camps and conquered kingdoms all across the continent. He yearned to rule them all. And though great armies fought, they fell, one by one, until a single kingdom stood against him.

"And the princess who lived in that kingdom went to her father and said, 'Kneel, father. Kneel before him, greet him with open arms, and then send me to end him.' For she was beautiful and brave and cunning. And she knew that the king would see her face and demand her for his bed. And when the treaty was signed, she went to him with a knife in her boot, a smile on her lips, and murder in her heart.

"But she had not counted on the king's power. Nor had she counted on his cruelty. 'Because you have knelt,' the king told her, 'you shall serve with my dogs.' And he had her chained and leashed to his throne. He took her knife. And he took her body. And he took her pride. But he had not counted on her fury. Hatred brewed like a seed in her belly, and even as she submitted, even as she screamed and begged for mercy, she plotted his ruin.

"Power grew like a seed in the princess's heart. She was fae, and while she had not yet been consecrated to the lands, she could feel it crying out beneath her, desperate for an end to this tyrannical king's rule.

"She made a deal with one of her enemies—another young female who had been captured by the king for his harem. They slit the king's throat while he was asleep, thinking his death would bring them glory, and her enemy used the king's blood to bind the princess to the crown. But the king had worn the crown for so long that he was not entirely mortal anymore. He crawled onto his throne as the throne room shook and burned, his crown in hand.

He set it on his head, even as the princess fought him for ownership of it.

"The Crown of Shadows is sentient, and the princess knew she could not hope to win it by force. It feeds on the emotions of its wearer and gnaws at their soul. And the king was old by this stage, a shadow of his former self. So she offered the crown something that it hungered for: She offered it a new host to feed upon. A heart full of bloody vengeance. And a soul that craved power. And the crown accepted."

The oracle falls into silence, her dark eyes locked upon me.

I can barely breathe.

Why would the Mother of Night want such a thing?

I don't realize I've whispered the thought aloud until the oracle replies, "Because the crown was created to feed upon the power of the lands without being forced to bond with it. It can sidestep certain… restrictions. And the Mother of Night's link to the lands was severed the second she was cast into her prison world."

I've felt her power. I would hate to face her with unrestricted access to it.

"So she needs the crown to tie herself to the magic of the lands and break her way free of the prison," I whisper.

The oracle remains quiet.

If I put that crown in her hands, then I have set her free. I have set them all free. But if I don't….

My hands lace over my abdomen in horror.

"Where is the crown now?"

"If you find the king, you will find the truth of the crown's whereabouts."

"I want a name," I tell her. "Who was he?"

"But you should already know the name," she says with a faint smirk. "It was your bloodline that ended his reign."

I shake my head slightly. *I don't*—

"Myrdal."

The name means nothing to me.

"King Myrdal of Mirthwood."

Again, nothing. "I've never heard of anyone by that—"

Of course not.

It drops whole and fully formed into my brain.

There's one name that was obliterated from history. One name that was ruthlessly burned from the history books. One name that earned any bearer that spoke it the loss of their tongue.

And suddenly, I see a castle choked with vicious thorns and roses. The king my mother stole her lands—and power—from. The king she wiped from memory, as if to destroy any hint of the man.

"The Briar King. Myrdal." I breathe the word, and it takes shape, as if to give him a name suddenly makes him real. He's always been a myth. A monster. A secret we never dared speak of.

And my mother was gifted to him? She was raped and brutalized and forced to heel at his boots like a dog? I can barely breathe. This doesn't exonerate her actions. Nothing ever will. But there's a part of me that feels grief for that princess—the young fae woman who sacrificed everything in order to bring down a monster.

I don't know her.

There's nothing left of her within my mother's hard carapace.

But... it explains so much.

347

"Yes. *That* king. Your mother took his life and his crown and his lands," the oracle whispers, leaning closer as if she can smell my sudden fear and wants to drink it in. "You want to find the Crown of Shadows? Then take the crown from Myrdal's head, and you will understand everything."

To get that crown means venturing right into the heart of my mother's kingdom.

Past armies. Past enemies.

Right beneath her nose.

CHAPTER 28

"No. Absolutely not," Thiago snarls.

I spent the entire trip home to Ceres thinking through my arguments, so I'm calm as I face him. "I know the ruins of Briar Keep. I know every inch of the land surrounding it. It makes sense if I'm the one who goes."

"You're with child."

"We only suspect that—"

"Suspicion is enough for me!" he yells, his voice echoing through the council chambers. "If your mother gets her hands on you and my child, then this war is done. She will win, because I will do anything to get you both back. I will crawl at her feet. I will slit my own throat. I will chain myself to her throne if she so demands it."

"But I won't be alone," I tell him, because I discussed this with Eris on the boat ride back to the Hallow. "Eris will be coming with me."

"*Eris?*"

"You were quite content to let her accompany me into

Unseelie to visit the oracle. Do you not trust her with my life?" I ask him.

His face reddens and he shoots a glare at Eris. "You're awfully silent. I take it my wife has your consent for this foolish plan?"

She shrugs. "We need the crown. And we can't enter Asturia in force. Nor can we enter in secret. The entire countryside is crawling with Asturian troops who have the faces of Evernight's prince plastered on every propaganda poster nailed to the tavern doors. Vi knows the lay of the land. It makes sense."

I take a deep breath. "Two riders might be glanced over, especially females. And if not, then... the Hallow at Briar Keep hasn't been used in centuries, but if anyone can use it, it's going to be me."

"No," Thiago says simply. "No."

"So we wait?" We cannot afford to wait. Once Asturia and Evernight officially clash, the borders will lock up tighter than Nanny Redwyne's drawers. "Eight months, Thiago! We have eight months to find it!"

He crosses his arms. "I have concerns with this story. Your mother got her hands on a powerful weapon and she just left it on this Briar King's head?"

The thought troubles me too. Why would my mother have left it there?

To mock him?

Is she still tied to it?

It makes no sense, for she'd keep it close by, wouldn't she? And yet, I've never seen anything like that in her possession, nor felt its malevolence.

"It fed on the king, and then turned on him when she defied him," I say. "Maybe she didn't wish to be bound to such a thing. But the oracle said I would understand everything once I took the crown from his head."

"I don't like this—"

"Nor do I," I counter. "But this is the best hope we have. *Please*. Please trust me to do this. I need you here. I need you to create a diversion so my mother's attention is focused on you."

He doesn't like it, but he's wavering.

"You want her to be your queen," Eris points out quietly. "You can't smother her. You can't lock her away."

"I'm not...." He breaks off with a curse and starts pacing. "I can't lose you, Vi. I can't. You're the only thing that helps me hold this at bay."

My heart feels like lead in my chest. "What aren't you telling me?"

Thiago falls into stillness. "It's reached my collarbone. It's broken through some of my wards."

I stop breathing. He doesn't need to say what.

Mother's curse.

"Then we don't have any more time," Eris snaps, pushing to her feet.

I feel like I want to be sick.

But Thiago finally nods. "Fine. I'll allow it. What do you need? What sort of diversion do you want?"

I cross to him and kiss him gently. "I want you to attack Clydain. Take a small handful of warriors, but don't get caught. Make it messy."

IT FEELS STRANGE TO BE BACK WITHIN ASTURIA'S FORESTS.

The massive oaks blot out the sky, but the undergrowth

is not as wild and untamed as the wyrdwoods that litter Evernight. Evernight feels like a wild kingdom, barely civilized, whilst truffle pigs have trampled the under-growth here in the forest and my mother's hunters have chased the deer to exhaustion. I used to love these forests, but I can feel the loss here, the way the wilds mourn for a time when they weren't so sorely misused.

Eris and I slipped through the Hallow near Thornwood and headed south three days ago.

Though we're not entirely alone.

"Is it dinnertime yet?" Grimm demands, shadow-hopping from tree to tree.

"No," both Eris and I drone.

"I could have sworn—"

"No."

I sigh. "We ate two hours ago. And our supplies are limited."

"Well, why don't you kill one of these pigs that seems to be roaming the woods?"

I exchange a long, slow glance with Eris. "Because these 'pigs' have tusks as long as my forearm and I value my skin?"

"We've been walking for days. I thought you needed to find this crown before the end of the year?"

"It's been three days," Eris says very precisely. "And this is not the sort of thing one rushes. Not all of us can walk through shadows."

"You could have taken the Hallow to Briar Keep," he snorts. *"We could have been there, captured the crown, and be enjoying a nice, delicious roast pig right about now in the dining hall of Ceres."*

"The Hallow at Briar Keep hasn't been used in

centuries." At first we tried to ignore him, but there's only so many hours of incessant meowing that one can ignore.

"Why?"

"Because Briar Keep is haunted," I mutter, shifting my pack into a more comfortable place. "The entire ruins are choked with thorns, and while many have slipped inside, very few of them return. It's not safe."

"Haunted—?"

"Perhaps you can investigate for yourself," Eris says sharply as we break through the trees. "Here we are."

Nothing has changed.

Eerie thickets of thorns cling to the rough stone walls, and little turrets peer through them at off intervals. A raven caws as we take slow, stealthy steps toward the keep, but the tress are strangely devoid of animals.

Eris's nostrils flare, and she moves forward with slow, careful footsteps before abruptly pausing.

"What is—?"

A sharp hand gesture silences me.

Nothing moves through the ruins. Nothing but wind shivering through the brambles.

But now I can feel it too.

We're not alone.

"Who is it?" I whisper.

Eris holds up a hand and one finger.

"Well, o Lord of the Shadows," I mutter, silently stringing my bow. "Surely if there's someone lurking in there, you'll be able to find them."

Grimm turns and saunters directly into a shadow. *"Don't get yourself killed. I'll investigate."*

He's gone for maybe fifteen minutes before Eris shrugs

off her pack. "The little bastard's probably chasing mice. I don't like this."

"You want to set a trap?"

She grins.

"Let me guess…. You want me to play the bait?"

Eris flashes a smile as she slowly draws her dagger. "Well, let's be honest…. Nobody is going to mistake me for any sort of damsel. But you and those big, pretty eyes?"

I roll said pretty eyes. "Fine. Let's go see what I can draw out of the forest. Watch my back."

"Always."

I WALK SLOWLY THROUGH THE EMPTY COURTYARD, LEAVES crunching underfoot, and every inch of me prepared for an ambush.

But when it comes, it's from the most unexpected source.

"Halt!" calls a voice, the familiar sound slicing right through me.

Maia's mercy. Every inch of me freezes, and I spin around to face my sister, cursing her under my breath. Andraste slips out from beneath an arch.

We face each other, and I can't stop my heart from racing.

Her gold-plated armor gleams in the burnished light of sunset. Braids sweep her hair back off her face, though the rest of it hangs in a tangle of elegant curls. It's like looking at a younger, kinder version of my mother.

"What are you doing here?" Andraste's face hardens. "You shouldn't be here. Mother will—"

"What? Curse me? Steal my memories? Lock me away in the oubliette? There's nothing she can do that she hasn't already done."

"You fool," she says bitterly. "You think those are the worst things she could do to you?"

"What are you going to do? Summon her?"

Andraste's always been better at swordplay than me— despite all of Eris's teaching. There's no way I can beat her. Not with cold iron.

But I draw my sword anyway.

Magic? Maybe. It was the one area she lacked, and though I don't dare rouse the power of the Hallow before I know exactly what danger lurks around Briar Keep, I can feel the ley line quivering beneath my feet.

"*Summon* her?" Andraste demands.

"Or deliver me to her in chains? Why are *you* here?"

There's something about her expression that alerts me. "I wouldn't deliver you to her in chains. I just wanted to talk to you. I wanted to… see you. And I'm alone."

"How did you know I was going to be here?"

"Thornwood sent a raven to the castle, and you're lucky my people were the ones who intercepted it. Some of his men recognized you in the woods. If Mother knew—"

"So she *didn't* send you?" Betrayal's not in my sister's nature. She's never once revealed a hint of insubordination. "You're trying to tell me you're here of your own volition? That you didn't tell the queen I was in the country?"

"If she'd sent me, I would be backed by an army. I know who walks at your side. I just wanted to talk to you."

"Talk? You knew Lysander was going to try and kill me and you led him right into that fucking tent," I snap.

"I tried to warn you! What was I supposed to do? Tell her no? At least if I did it myself, I could... manipulate matters."

"Yes, but you always did play the game far better than I ever have. You had some purpose in being the one to present Lysander to us, and you have some purpose in being here now."

"Because she's going *mad*," Andraste snaps.

I draw back.

"Ever since you married Evernight, she's been spiraling. I could see it happening, but I thought that if I just kept her distracted, then perhaps I could manage her moods. Perhaps she wouldn't be as destructive as I feared."

"You may as well have tried to hold back the tides."

"What was I supposed to do?" she snaps. "You left me. You married the *enemy,* and Mother lost her mind. You know what she's like. How could I rein her in? I've never had the power to match her—that was always you, wild and erratic, but burning like a wildfire with promise."

It takes me aback. "I've never—"

"Been able to control it," she snaps. "You nearly shook the castle down around our ears the night that Mother sent Nanny Redwyne away, and you were eleven."

And there it is, an elusive memory trickling through me.

—anger, screaming, the walls shaking, and guards grabbing Nanny Redwyne as they haul her away—

I suck in a sharp breath.

Fae children are gifted with magic, but they don't truly

come into their own until they're well into their teens. To display so much power at the age of eleven is an anomaly.

Or maybe it's not, because maybe it wasn't the fae half of my heritage that nearly tore the castle apart.

"Yes, you. The prodigy. Mother's little pet. The one she favored out of the pair of us until she began to fear you," she grates out, fists clenched at her side.

That doesn't sound like my recollection of events at all.

Or wait....

Maybe... it does. Because she loved me once. Mother loved me once.

And then all of a sudden, she didn't.

Andraste's face hardens. "I don't have anyone else to turn to. You know what the court is like. They'll eat each other alive the second they think there's a chance to get ahead. If I show one ounce of weakness...."

"Perhaps you should have thought of that before you struck a deal with Mother."

Andraste merely shakes her head with a tired sigh. "I had to, Vi. I had to fall in line with her."

"No, you didn't." Anger blooms. "If you had stood at my side—"

"She's have obliterated the pair of us, and you know it. We were both younger, and any power either of us has since gained would barely surmount what she could throw at us." She hesitates. "And there were... other reasons...."

We're getting nowhere. "Say what you came to say and then leave."

Andraste turns toward the arched gateway, raking one hand through her hair in an uncharacteristic sign of nerves. "I need help to try and prevent a war. Our people will suffer if this goes any further. It doesn't matter who wins, there will be mass casualties."

"War is coming, whether you like it or not. She crossed the line, not us. And there is no guarantee she'll win."

"When does Mother ever *lose*? Do you think she would march against you with only the Queen of Aska at her side? Think, curse you."

And so I do.

I test a theory. "She's made an alliance with Angharad."

Andraste's lips thin. "No. That would be too far, too much for her border lords to swallow. And she can't afford to lose Thornwood."

"But there is no other alliance she could make...."

"Except for the goblin clans."

The thought leaves me breathless, blood draining from my cheeks. The goblin clans have been kingless for centuries, though I've heard whispers there are several scions of the royal bloodline fighting for the throne.

"She's in negotiations with Urach of the Black Hand. She will back his claim for the throne in return for foot troops. She has more than one ally, Vi, and that ally is right at your unprotected flank."

I can picture them marching down through the gap in the mountains, hammering down upon an unsuspecting Evernight northern flank. The unseelie armies would never be allowed through the spine of the world—goblins have no liking for either of their fairer brethren—so the north has long been considered safe.

But there are no defenses against the clans.

They *are* our protection.

Evernight would be crushed between two powerful forces.

I have to get back to Thiago. I have to warn him.

"Why would you tell me this?"

It would be a swift defeat of Evernight.

Again, she looks away. "Because it doesn't end there. One kingdom was always enough for me. This is madness. This isn't just a skirmish. It isn't just a war. She wants to drag the entire south down, and if she succeeds, then the unseelie are poised in the north, salivating over the prospect of our five kingdoms tearing at each other like dogs. I just want to protect my people. I can't do this alone."

Asturians will die with this information. She's given us the means to turn the tide of an imminent defeat. But perhaps more of our people will die if she doesn't yield.

I slowly sheathe my sword.

Once we were allies. Once we were *sisters*. Is there any chance of either of us returning to that point?

"What do you intend?" I ask.

"Hold your generals back," she says. "I just need time. If our forces clash, then it's too late—"

"It's already too late. The only way we survive is if Mother dies."

Andraste takes a step back, rubbing at her throat, eyes troubled.

"Once you are on the throne," I tell her, "then there is the possibility of a truce with Evernight. There's a possibility we can hold the Alliance together."

"I don't have the means to kill her," she finally says.

"Maybe… maybe I do."

Our eyes meet.

"How did you do it?" she demands. "How did you get the power to defeat her at the Queensmoot? I've never felt such power before. I could feel it, shivering up through the earth itself—"

"I was desperate. And so I made a bargain with the Mother of Night."

"What sort of bargain?" For a second, she's my older sister, snapping at my stupidity. "Curse it, Vi. Have you lost your mind?"

"Not my mind, no."

"What did you bargain with? The Old Ones cannot be trusted."

I stare at her for long seconds. I don't know if I trust her. She's given me precious information, but as I said, she always did play the game better than I did.

Maybe I can play the game too. A little bit of information, though not all of it.... "She wanted my firstborn child—"

The blood drains from her face. "Vi!"

"But if I can give her the crown that sits on the Briar King's head, then the debt will be repaid."

Andraste shakes her head in horror. "And if you can't get the crown?"

I merely stare at her.

"No. *No!*" She rakes her hands through her braids again. "Gods, how could you be so stupid! How could you—"

"I was desperate!" I snap. "And there is still time. There has to *be* a child."

"This is my fault," she whispers, staring blankly at nothing. "This is all my fault. I thought.... I thought...."

Eris appears from the shadows, stalking slowly across the cobbles. "It's none of your business, Princess of Thorns. Vi." She gives me a look. "We need to get moving. She's stalling."

"I'm not stalling," Andraste whips her blade free, backing away from Eris warily. "I came alone."

"Really?" Eris curls her lip. "Then why is there a cloud of dust moving toward us? There's at least one squad of Asturian soldiers riding this way."

"*What?*" both Andraste and I say.

"It's a trap."

"Not by me!" Andraste strides to the archway as if she wants to see.

Eris is quicker. Hauling Andraste back into her arms, she sets a knife to her throat. "Drop the sword."

"Make me."

Eris presses the knife tight enough to draw blood, and my sister's sword clatters to the ground.

"Wait!" I reach for them. "Don't kill her," I tell Eris. "I need her."

"She's the enemy, Vi."

"I know." But… for a second. "Was any of it the truth? The goblins? The Alliance? Your intentions?"

Andraste's chin tilts higher as Eris tightens the knife. "All of it. You need to get out of here. Now! I swear I had nothing to do with this. Take the west trail. If they're coming from Hawthorne Castle, they'll expect you to flee directly north, toward the Thornwood Hallow."

I glance at the cloud of dust. "We can't leave. Not without the crown."

"Besides," Eris says with a smile. "Why would we flee when we've got such a pretty hostage?"

361

Andraste growls under her breath. "I can't be caught here!"

"You should have thought of that earlier." Eris withdraws the blade, hauling my sister's arms behind her back. She takes a thin leather cord from behind her belt and binds Andraste's wrists together.

"Vi!" Andraste looks to me. "If Mother knows I was here—"

I ignore her. The coincidence is just a little too uncomfortable for my liking. "Let's head inside the ruins. We can set her free in the forest on the way out."

"*Inside* the ruins?" Andraste gapes at me. "The keep is haunted by the Briar King. Only the outer towers are safe to enter. Fae who try to explore the ruins never come back out."

Eris hauls her to her feet. "It's all right, bitchspawn. I'm the scariest creature in these woods. Nothing's going to get the slip on me." And then she gives me a certain look. "And we can decide what we're going to do with her later. There's no need to set her free. Not just yet. She's your mother's heir. If we have her in our grasp, then your mother's not going to strike the first blow, is she?"

This is the sort of ruthless decision I need to make. I'm still acting as though Andi's my sister. "Fine. Let's go get the crown. We'll work out what to do with her once we're done here."

It all goes back to the start.

The Briar King sits on his dusty throne, his hollow skull pierced with brambles that twine through his empty eye sockets and out his mouth. It looks like he's screaming, and perhaps he was when my mother killed him with her thorns.

Each bleached hand lies on the arms of his throne, his fingers curled around the arms, but it's the crown on his head that draws my eyes.

Black as my mother's soul, when the light of my torch shines on it, it doesn't so much reflect the light as it absorbs it.

"What if there's a trap?" Andraste asks as Eris shoves her into the throne room.

"Then I'll send you in first to spring it," Eris says.

"Vi, I need to talk to you," Andraste says urgently. "Alone."

"There's nothing you can't say to me that Eris can't hear," I reply.

"Yes, there *is*," Andraste stresses.

"Permission to gag her?" Eris asks.

I stare at the Briar King, trying to work out if there's an easy way to approach him. "You're actually asking for permission?"

"Well, you are my queen."

I shoot Andraste a look. "No more talking, or I'll let her stuff a sock in your mouth."

Andraste glares back.

All lies still.

Grimm suddenly appears, sniffing around the base of the throne, his nose itching. *"It took you long enough."*

"Where have you been?" Eris demands.

"Investigating," he replies, and the spider webs clinging to his whiskers tell the truth of his tale. *"There's something in the ruins, and I haven't managed to work out what it is yet."*

"You're right." Eris shoves Andraste forward. "There *was* something in the ruins, and we had to deal with it."

"*Oh, her. She's harmless. It's not she who makes the hairs down my spine creep. This smells like a trap.*"

"A trap in particular, or is it the situation setting your hackles on edge?"

The grimalkin leaps up on the edge of the throne, its paws delicately avoiding the skeletal bones. "*The situation. I can't smell anything other than dust. But if the Crown of Shadows has the power I think it does, then it would hardly be unguarded.*"

"Crown of Shadows?" Andraste mutters. "It's just an old rusted crown."

Eris hauls her pack over her shoulder and tugs something from it, as Andraste backs away with a mutinous expression.

I circle the throne as she and Eris argue.

Just a long-dead king sitting there, pierced through with briars.

I slice through the thorns curling around the crown and lift it from his head. Nothing moves, but it feels as though the room somehow exhaled.

Grimm and I share a look.

And...

Nothing.

Rust crumbles in my hands, revealing part of the metal is breaking away. Iron? What sort of fae king would wear a crown of iron? The ache in his temples must have been horrific, and his skin would have burned. If I wasn't wearing gloves it would have blistered my skin.

Unless... this is not the Crown of Shadows.

Something clicks within the crown.

Sharp needles suddenly stab through the crown's grooves, slashing through my fingers. I cry out and drop the cursed thing, and it vibrates on the ground as if my blood has activated some long-dormant spell. Little mechanical clicks come from within it. Each prong realigns itself, turning upside down, until the bloody thing looks like it has eight legs. The hollow circlet that once sat upon the Briar King's head forms an armored carapace.

I back away.

Why does everything that is dark and unseelie have such a hankering for spiders?

The grimalkin hisses as the thorns in the room start to shiver and shake. Stone grinds in the walls, dust falling from the ceiling. And the Briar King's skeleton vibrates on its throne.

We need to get out of here now.

"Grimm!"

The furry meld of shadows leaps into my arms, clawing its way up onto my shoulder. *"Move, you cursed meat suit!"*

I leap from the dais, drawing my sword.

"What in the Darkness just happened?" Eris yells.

"It's a trap!"

But who set it?

The oracle said that if I took the crown from King Myrdal's head, then I would understand everything.

But none of this makes sense.

"Thief," hisses the Briar King, his hollow eyes turning to somehow lock upon me. Blue lights gleam in the center of his eye sockets like a pair of will-o'-the-wisps. A wight. I've roused a wight. "Now you shall pay the price for disturbing my slumber."

THE GROUND STARTS SHAKING AS THE BRIAR KING LIFTS A metal-clad hand, clenching the fingers of his gauntlet shut.

"W-what is that?" Andraste demands.

"All that remains of King Myrdal after Mother was through with him."

Eris spins around, her knife held in her fist and the whites of her eyes showing. "We need to leave. Now."

"The real crown has to be here somewhere! Distract it."

"Vi!" Andraste slices her ropes on Eris's drawn blade, which is a gutsy move at the best of times. "As much as I hate to agree with your... friend, this is not the time. Give me my sword!"

"No," Eris snaps.

"Give her the sword," I yell, because three swords are better than two.

Eris shoots me an incredulous look, then tosses Andraste's sword at her.

"Maybe the clue was in that thing!" Eris points at the spider-crown scuttling over the walls. "There has to be a reason the oracle sent you to find it."

"I'll get it."

I sprint across the stone flagstones, sliding beneath a whip of actinic blue fire as the Briar King stands. Snatching at the crown, I scrabble to my feet, and shove it in the bag slung over my shoulder.

Andraste lunges forward, slashing through one of the whip-like vines. Her blade sheers through the thick trunk, but the mess of thorns writhes toward her.

I leap over the thorns, grabbing Andraste's gauntleted wrist as I go. "Run!"

Together, the pair of us sprint toward the archway, where Eris is gesturing to us.

"I'll cover you!" Eris yells.

Stone columns collapse ahead of us, the arch crumbling across the entrance. I skid to a halt, throwing my hands up to protect my face.

When the dust clears, the entrance is completely covered.

"Curse it." I turn around breathlessly. There has to be some way out.

"This way," Andraste says grimly, yanking me toward a set of broken doors that lead further into the ruined keep.

Thorns lash out, and I leap over them, landing with a jarring thud and throwing myself forward into a roll. One slashes through my cheek, the sting like the hot kiss of a blade. "Eris!"

She clears the way, the sweep of her sword hacking through brambles and thorns.

The thorns don't touch her, I notice.

Instead, they recoil, as if not even they are certain what sort of magic stalks within their midst. But there are more of them, crawling over the walls and seeking to cut off our only path to freedom.

I drive my sword through the thorns, slashing and hacking. Sweat drips down my spine, and I can feel that cursed creature trying to break free of my bag.

Eris cuts an entire wall of thorns free, revealing a gaping tunnel. Andraste summons a faelight, and a thick layer of dust on the carpets stretches into infinity. Nothing has come this way for centuries, but I can't help staring into the dark and wondering if this is the *only* way out.

There has to be a way out.

There has to be—

There.

Something shivers, deep below me.

"I can feel the Hallow," I gasp, turning toward an ancient spiral staircase. "It's still alive."

Eris grabs my arm. "This Hallow has been forbidden for centuries. We don't know if it's even usable."

"Do you have a better idea?"

Behind her, a horrific rumble echoes through the stones.

"*Is it just me?*" Grimm asks, his fur rising along his spine, "*Or can anyone else hear that dreadful rasping sound?*"

I have no idea where he appeared from.

"It's not just you," Eris says, her face grim as she turns toward the throne room.

The doors slam open, the stones in the floors parting as if some enormous leviathan swims beneath them. The bleached skull of something monstrous tosses apart enormous blocks of slate as if they're mere pebbles. I catch a glimpse of an ancient eye socket, gleaming with the eerie blue light of a wight's magic.

"Is that a...." Andraste's voice trails off.

"Dragon," I whisper in horror, because the last of the great dragons died out centuries ago.

"Find that Hallow!" Eris screams, shoving me toward the stairs.

We sprint down the hallway as the creature shoulders its way through the floors behind us.

Down and down and down we go, boots hammering on the stone.

Creepy catacombs loom ahead of us.

Of course.

"This way!" I lunge through cobwebs, sweeping them aside with my sword.

A rat skitters past my boots—*please let it be a rat*—and then an enormous belch of blue flame rockets through the catacombs behind us.

Its heat blooms over my skin as I throw myself behind a stone statue of some headless armored prince. Knees stinging, I throw my arms over my face and belatedly shield. A bubble of air surrounds me, blue flame washing over the edges.

And then the flames die down.

I slowly lower my arms, gasping for breath. Little spot fires bloom all along the tunnel. An ancient pennant drips flame, and a channel of oil on the far side of the tunnel blazes with light.

The air tastes hot and ashy.

"Eris?" I yell.

Nothing.

"Andraste?"

My sister appears on quiet feet, jerking me upright even as she presses a finger to her lips. I'm so relieved to see someone alive—even her. I grab my sword from the ground, hissing as my hand closes around hot metal, though I dare not drop it.

"I don't know where Eris went," Andraste says, linking with me mentally. *"We have to get out of here."*

"Not without her."

The dragon is enormous, its skeletal tail lashing behind it as it lumbers around the corner of the catacombs. Once upon a time, it must have been as big as three houses, but all that remains are bones, bleached by the grave.

"*I have an idea.*" I point to the roof.

She understands instantly.

"*Distract it!*" She slips into the shadows.

"Hey, you!" I yell, stepping out of my hiding place and waving my hands.

The wight's head turns toward me.

"That's it, you big, ugly bastard. Focus on me!"

A gush of hot flame spews toward me and I scream, scrambling for cover and warding desperately.

Light spills through a crevice in the ceiling ahead of me. Another pair of columns have crumbled, leaving the straining roof supports collapsed against each other.

There's more than one way to kill a dragon wight.

I skid to a halt in the middle of the hallway and turn.

The enormous creature seems to sense me, its head swiveling toward me and its nostrils flaring with blue fire as if it prepares to attack again.

"Run, Vi!" Andraste calls from where she's scampering across the roof supports.

An enormous ball of blue flame shoots toward me. I'll never make it in time—

A scream dies in my throat as I slam my crossed wrists up in front of me, willing a shield of pure air to form around me. The heat dies. Sound fades. There's nothing but silence, and as I blink in shock, I see a gush of blue flames ripple over me.

And then the flames die down and the dragon lumbers toward me.

Blessed Maia. I lower my arms, smelling the stink of scorched leather from where my boot soles didn't quite fare as well. I mustn't have shielded completely.

But my sister strikes her hand against the supporting

columns that shield the roof, and cracks run through the stone as she unleashes her own magic.

The dragon freezes, looking up.

And the entire ceiling collapses upon it.

Eris appears out of the rubble, sprinting up its spine and grasping her massive sword in both hands. She leaps over falling stones, warding a vicious rock away from her as she lands on the dragon's skull.

"Die!" She drives her sword through its skull.

The wight screams, and the blue lights in its eyes flare hot for a second before its body starts collapsing.

"This way!" I gesture for her to follow me, even as the soles of my boots still steam.

Vines crawl through the nearest doorway, thick with bristling thorns. There are too many of them to cut through.

Grimm streaks beneath them, leaving me to follow. "*It's in here!*"

I slice through the closest briars, finding myself in a circular chamber. Eris staggers into me, but she's spitting curses because her sword lodged in the dragon's skull. I toss her mine.

Thirteen enormous stones line the walls. The dusty floor is cut with bronze glyphs that wink in the faelight I summon.

The Hallow.

"Vi?" Andraste pants at my side, blood dripping from a cut on her temples. "What are you doing?" She stills as she sees the state of the glyphs. Some of them have been defaced, and there's a skeleton resting with its back against the nearest wall.

At least one of the adventurers who came exploring has been accounted for.

"I can use the Hallow," I tell her.

She backs away, shaking her head. "No. This is forbidden. If the glyphs are shattered—"

"She can use it," Eris says with a snort. "Are you coming, bitchspawn?"

Andraste stares at me for a long moment. "No."

"You're not safe here!" I argue.

There's a horrible look in her eyes. "You called it the Crown of Shadows. But whatever that thing in your bag is, it's not the real crown."

The breath slams from my lungs. "How would you know that?"

Her gaze meets mine. "Because the Crown of Shadows sits on Mother's head."

Everything goes silent, leaving only a ringing in my ears. "*No.*" The Asturian royal crown is an elegant gold piece I've seen a thousand times. I've even touched it once, though Mother slammed the door of her dressing chambers open and demanded to know what I thought I was doing.

It didn't feel like it had any sort of power.

"It *is*," Andraste insists. "She told me that if anything ever happened to us—if your husband ever attacked the castle—then I needed to get the crown out safely. I needed to bring it to her, no matter *what* I had to do."

This must have been what she wanted to tell me in secret.

And what was it the oracle said?

That I would understand everything.... Not that I would have the crown in my possession.

Suddenly shouts echo through the halls. My mother's warriors. Andraste's attention jerks upward, and then she backs away. "Go. I'll cover you. I'll tell them it was me. That I set this entire affair off."

"What about Mother?" I ask sharply.

The expression melts off Andraste's face. "I've been lying to her for years. What's another lie? I'll tell her I was meeting a male for a secret assignation."

My eyebrows rise. "You've been lying to her for years? You?"

She hesitates and then tips her chin up. "We all have secrets, Vi."

"We never used to have secrets."

Andraste gives me a sad little smile. "Sometimes it's the only way to protect those we love. I hope one day you'll understand that."

What does that mean?

"Down here!" Someone yells.

"We need to go," Eris says, grabbing my hand.

"Come on, come on, come on." I slice my hand with the dagger, searching the columns for runes I might recognize.

Is this even going to work?

There. I see Valerian's glyph and dart toward it, before skidding to a halt. The rune is half-crumbled.

"Be ready," I yell at Eris. "This might be a rough ride."

And then the world turns inside out and plunges me straight into darkness.

CHAPTER 29

The plan is reckless. It's dangerous. It relies upon the fact that I can trust my sister to keep her mouth shut about our need for the crown, when the past has proven such trust to be worth so little.

It's barely been two days since the revelation at Briar Keep, and it's taken me every second of those two days to convince Thiago to risk this stealthy assault. Especially after he found nothing at Clydain except for an empty keep.

Eris, surprisingly, was the one who convinced him.

"I don't think the Princess of Asturia was lying," she told him last night. "I don't think she's telling the entire truth, but Andraste had multiple chances to turn Vi over to their mother and she didn't take it."

"If you were going to gamble my wife's life on such a statement," he said coldly, "would you throw the die?"

Eris hesitated, but she finally nodded. "Yes."

And Thiago closed his eyes and surrendered, though

this time, he's not going to allow me to risk this without him.

The eve of Imbolc dawns.

And with it my mother's spring celebrations, in which the entire aristocracy of Asturia will be invited into Hawthorne castle to celebrate. It's our best chance to get close to the crown.

It's our only chance.

Finn and I slip into Asturia by way of the Briar Keep Hallow and make our way toward Hawthorne castle. We hitch a ride with a drayman carting wine, and the slow pace makes my skin itch, even though I know it's for the best.

Imbolc is one of Asturia's most widely celebrated holidays—when summer slays winter. Every town and village we pass is setting up poles on their village greens, but the castle is where the grand celebrations will be held.

"Ready?" Finn murmurs as the drayman turns his mules toward the castle.

We call farewell as dusk starts to fall and slip from the cart before turning into the woods. Once there, I strip out of my woolen peasant gown and haul on the silk dress I had tucked in a bag hidden under my skirts.

The dress is the color of a bitten plum, though it lightens through the skirts until the very hem is almost silver. A feathered mask covers my face, and Thalia found an auburn wig for my hair. Every inch of me is bedecked for a festival, though my leather boots reach midthigh and there are two daggers sheathed in them.

I feel ready to face my mother for the first time in my life. Not as a beggar or a child desperate for her attention, but as a survivor. As someone who has something to protect. She won't take my love away from me, not this time.

And she won't ever get her hands on the child I'm sure is within me.

Minstrels stroll through the forests, plucking chords on their lutes as they tune them. A pair of winged demi-fey hang feathers in the trees, wearing miniature versions of red and gold livery. The air of excitement hangs in the air.

Imbolc was always my favorite holiday.

"Are you in?" Thiago murmurs, his thoughts sliding over mine like a gloved hand shielded in cool leather. He and Eris hide within the woods several miles north. Close enough for them to rescue us if anything goes awry, but not too close for someone to feel the resonance of their fae magic.

Finn's magic is strange enough that he doesn't feel like fae, and my connection to Evernight vanished the second we arrived at the Hallow. While some of my mother's guards might scan the resonance of their guest's magic, I was counting on the fact that I'll only rate as someone of middling talent.

"Nobody's questioned us," I reply, tucking my arm through Finn's elbow. *"The guards scanned us from a distance, but whatever part of me was born in this court must have felt familiar enough that no alarms were sounded."*

Finn takes my hand. "Are you ready, my love?"

His eyes twinkle, and I know he's merely teasing me—just as I know Thiago can hear every word he utters through our mental link.

"I'm going to kill him," whispers a dark voice in my head.

"Stop being so territorial," I whisper back. *"And get out of my head. I need to concentrate."*

The fae of my mother's court already dance beneath the trees of the royal hunting preserve. Music hums through the air; the harps my mother favors spilling soft sounds even as bards sing of cruel hearts and poisonous kisses.

"This way," I tell Finn, pushing him into the shadows of the trees. "If my mother follows her usual routine, she'll be by the lake. We'll skirt the banquet tables and enter the castle from the queen's wood while she's distracted with bringing in Imbolc."

I know the ritual.

Imbolc brings the start of the lambing season and stands between the summer and winter solstices. Bonfires are lit throughout the forest, and all the guests wear masks and heavy cloaks.

One of the fae guests will be crowned the Prince of Winter, and another will be crowned the Prince of Summer —forced to duel to represent the clash between seasons. Summer will win, of course, and then the Queen of Summer will be crowned by my mother—though of course the crown she is gifted with is the Crown of Summer, and not the Asturian royal crown.

No, that will be locked away in the castle, which means this is our best time to strike.

The castle will be lightly guarded. My mother will be distracted by the festivities, and I know her well enough to know that the smile she grants the new Summer Queen will be tight and jealous. She won't let the night's queen out of her sight, because my mother prefers all attention to be upon her.

It's a temporary honor, of course, though the Summer Queen will bless all of those who have married between seasons and kiss the foreheads of numerous babies.

And then the wine will be brought out.

Come midnight, everyone will sling off their cloaks, revealing gossamer gowns and tunics beneath, and the hedonistic part of the night will truly start.

This is our best chance.

The enormous oaks that guard the royal hunting preserve have been here for centuries. The Queen oak thrives in the heart of the forest, and some say it was planted by my mother herself when she bound herself to the land and took her naming rights as queen. Fae lanterns hang through the trees, illuminating everything in a soft glowing light.

It's beautiful.

I spent so much time in these woods as a child, playing hide and seek with Andraste. We used to carve little notes to each other in our secret language in the bark of the trees —a map of sorts to the heart of the queen's forest, where there's a little cavern we claimed for the two of us.

And then my mother found the carvings and banned us from the woods, furious that we'd desecrated sacred trees.

"Is everything all right?" Finn asks, clearly picking up on my mood.

"Old memories." I laugh a little at the irony. "They weren't all bad."

And maybe that's the hardest truth to swallow, because all the good memories I have belong to those moments I shared with my sister when we were both children. Young. Carefree. Foolish.

I can trust her, can't I?

Finn's gaze slides over the gathering. "Looks a little solemn for my tastes."

"That's because nobody's naked. Yet."

"Yet?" The corners of his lips kick up. "Do tell."

"We're not going to remain behind to see," I warn him. "One hour to get in and out. Don't get distracted."

"What could distract me?" His head turns as a lady in bright red shoots him a knowing wink.

"You're right. Eris is not here."

Finn shoots me a look somewhat akin to that of a deer catching the hunter's scent on the breeze. "And what is that supposed to mean?"

"Why don't you tell me?"

The mask shields his face, but his glare practically incinerates me.

"Ladies!" someone calls with a laugh. "And lords. And all who dwell in between. Let us bring in the summer. Let us sing to the sun and beg her for a good harvest!"

Every inch of me stills.

Mother.

I'd expected her to be holding court near the barrow mounds, where an enormous fae-made pool of water reflects the moon. It's her favorite place, deep in the heart of the queen's wood.

This is a disaster.

Though, if she captures me, at least I won't have to worry about the Mother of Night twisting me to her purpose or Angharad cutting the heart from my chest.

"Small wins," I whisper to myself.

"Pardon?" Finn mutters.

"Nothing."

"Let us bring in the summer!" a dozen other voices chorus.

The crowd parts even as my ribs constrict. And then a tall, elegant woman sweeps out of the shadows.

Gold feathers adorn her cloak, hiding all but the hem of her gown, and a ruff of them guard her throat. A crown nestles in her braided hair like hungry gold teeth stabbing into the sky. Someone's dusted ground gold along her cheekbones and painted her lips with it, though her eyes are shadowed with kohl.

I see every touch her brownie valet, Thistledown, has tried to make to present her as something she's not....

Queen of Summer.

A kind, benevolent monarch.

The power that brings this court into the season of growing.

Warm. Golden. A sun that shines so brightly, it obliterates all others.

And yet, somehow the effect fails. Gold has never looked so cold and merciless. Smiles slip as she passes by, though the clapping remains loud and emphatic.

One does not dare wield one's unease in front of the queen.

I kneel with the rest of them, hauling Finn to his knees and bowing my head so she won't see the shock on my lower face. It's been three months since I saw her last. Three months since I stood in that Hallow and faced her with all the power I could draw.

Does she know?

Does she suspect?

Did my sister tell her?

My palms feel clammy.

"Rise," Mother calls. "Rise and prepare to bring in the summer."

Two swords are brought forth as we all surge to our feet. One is made of hawthorne wood, and the other forged of spelled glass. Both have sharpened tips, though this is a mock battle and neither prince is supposed to be harmed. It's happened on occasion—purely through mischance—but it's said that a bloody start to summer's reign is a bad omen for the crops.

"Let Maia bless this court," my mother calls, lifting the hawthorne sword. "Bring forth her prince of summer. Bring forth our valiant knight, here to slay the icy cold!"

She flings the sword into the air, and it catapults end over end, until a gleeful blond knight snatches it with a cheer. He's captured by his friends and lifted onto shoulders, where he's brought forth into the center of the clearing.

"And his opponent?" My mother pauses, lifting the glass sword. "A prince of winter, with a heart of pure ice."

The tip of the glass sword circles the crowd, and a hint of trepidation grows within me. And then the sword pauses, pointing directly toward me.

Every inch of me goes cold.

"Vi?" Finn growls under his breath.

I have two knives. I can maybe ride the ley line from this distance. But we'll never escape—

"Come forth, my winter prince," my mother calls, and as the crowd claps and cheers, I realize it wasn't me after all. It's him.

Pure, fucking coincidence. Or maybe my mother's interest in any tall, broad-shouldered male she doesn't recognize.

I'm going to be sick.

He can't refuse. To refuse would bring certain scrutiny.

This is a fucking disaster.

"It's a mock battle. You're supposed to lose. Don't kill him!"

"Lose?" he asks incredulously.

"Yes." I push him toward the sword.

Finn staggers forward, his heavy black velvet cloak obscuring the breadth of his shoulders. A pair of laughing ladies tear it from him, and another pair lay hands to his shirt. Even behind the mask, I can tell his eyebrows just arched.

"*Vi?*" Thiago links with me as I pretend to clap and cheer, my heart rabbiting in my chest. "*What's wrong? I can sense your fear.*"

"*They've crowned Finn the Prince of Winter.*" I explain everything as succinctly as I can. "*Can he control himself?*"

Or am I going to need to rein in his Sylvaren tendencies?

"*I won't send him into a battle unless necessary, but a minor skirmish is fine. He's stricter with himself than he needs to be.*"

"*Once the fight is done, Finn will be overwhelmed with ladies. He'll have lost the battle, but he'll still be a prince for the night, and they'll all want to share in the attention.*"

"*So you're alone?*" Thiago demands.

I wince. "*You know the answer to that.*"

Finn shoots me a frustrated glance as the Prince of Summer attacks him. Every inch of him trembles with the urge to lunge forward and end this foolish fight, and I don't think he even knows how to lose.

"*Get out,*" Thiago says shortly. "*Finn can rejoin us later.*"

"*No.*" The castle is right there. "*This is our best chance.*

The castle won't ever be so unguarded again, and nor will my mother be parted from her crown!"

He's silent, but I swear he's cursing under his breath. *"Head directly toward the castle. I'll meet you there."*

"What? You can't come into the woods! My mother is here. She will sense your magic and —"

"Then maybe she and I can have the reckoning we've been dancing toward for thirteen years."

I can't breathe. This is my mother's seat of power. She's twice as dangerous here, where the woods yearn to answer her every whim.

"I'm not asking, Vi," he says with a silky whisper. *"Either you come back to me right now, or I will come for you."*

This is our only chance. I have to take the risk. *"Remind Finn that he's supposed to lose. And tell him not to bed any of the women wearing blue. They're naiads, and they'll try and drown him in a stream once they're done with him. Veil yourself and I'll meet you by the eastern walls. Do not use your magic unless necessary."*

PACING THE SHADOWS, I WAIT FOR THIAGO AS THE CLASH OF swords ring in the distance. The fight should have been over by now, and I hope against hope that Finn's Sylvaren blood hasn't roused.

Silence falls.

A shiver runs down my spine—the type of shiver that everything that has ever realized it is prey feels.

I slowly turn around as Thiago steps out of a patch of pure darkness, his face taut with predatory intensity.

I almost didn't sense him. His wards are woven so

tightly around him and his power that it's a wonder he can breathe.

Stalking toward me, he kisses me. Hard. One hand clasping the back of my skull, and the other caressing my jaw. And then it's over just as quickly as it began.

"How do we get in?" he asks.

"This way." I lead him around the castle wall.

There's a reason I chose this patch of the forest. Pausing beside a drape of ivy that coats the walls, I run my hands over the stone and search for the slight indentation I know is there. It gives a click, and then a section of the wall swings open.

"My sister and I used to sneak out when we were younger and watch them celebrate Imbolc."

"It's a surprise your mother kept you locked away from such rites. With her own carnal nature, I'd have expected her to push you toward them."

"No." I lead him into the dark. *"We would have been competition. Tonight is her night, and she likes to revel in the unabashed attention of her entire court."*

The wall swings shut behind us, plunging us into absolute blackness.

"Is it safe to summon a faelight?"

I spin one into being, and it comes to life easier than I can ever recall. Layer by layer, my mother's curse work is slowly being undone, and a little part of me thrills at how easy my fae magic is becoming to wield.

Silvery blue light cascades over the tunnel.

"Quiet," I tell him as we hurry through the darkness. *"This leads directly to the royal wing. Nobody knows it's here, but the guards have wolfhounds that guard the bailey, and if they hear us…."*

I don't need to add more.

It's a long way through a series of interlocking passages. From a glimpse of the unstirred dust on the floor, nobody's come this way in years.

Maybe Andraste stopped sneaking out after I married Thiago.

Finally, we're deep in the heart of the royal apartments. I pause beside a panel in the wall and plunge us into darkness again. "*My mother's chambers lie on the other side.*"

"*Of all the places I would prefer never to see the inside of.*" He nods, and I slowly, slowly ease the panel open.

The room is empty.

The curtains are thrown open, moonlight spilling across the room. My heart hammers as I place my first foot on the floor and pause, expecting blazing wards to ignite and alarms to scream.

There is nothing.

Exhaling hard, I slip into the room, and Thiago follows me like a thief in the night.

His gaze rakes over the sumptuous furnishings and elegant silks. From the sudden arch of his brow, I can tell it's not what he expected.

The wall is papered in a forest print, with little creatures peeking from behind the trees. The ceiling is a night sky, with dozens of sparkling little stars pulsating light. And the bed is scrolled gold, curling up into an enormous canopy, from which hangs delicate white silk.

"*This way,*" I tell him, crossing to the door at the furthest end of the room.

A tower adjoins my mother's chambers, and it's here where her most precious items are kept. There's a viewing platform at the top where she sometimes stares at the stars, but the room below it is locked and warded with the most dangerous spells she can summon. Only someone who shares her blood can enter that little treasury.

She used to invite me in there when I was a child, to view all her magical objects and curios. I would play with her necklaces and jewels, and she'd smile and drape one of her tiaras on my head.

I don't know where it all went wrong.

Slipping up the stairs, I nearly leap out of my skin when a riot of noise echoes through the night. Fireworks. They shatter in the night sky, casting a burst of light over our passage before plunging us into the shadows again.

The crown is always kept at the top of the tower.

I place my palm against the solid gold door, every inch of me shaking. "Know my blood," I whisper. "Let me in."

Heat wells against my skin, but it doesn't burn. It merely tastes me.

And then the door swings open.

She hasn't changed the wards. A tremble runs through me. I wasn't sure.

The treasury is just as I remember it. A dozen nooks are carved into the stone walls, and within each one rests a golden head. They have no faces, only slight indentations where the eyes and mouths should be, and I've always wondered if my mother knows how creepy they look. Sitting atop them is her collection of crowns and tiaras.

But it's the deepest nook at the far corner of the room that captures my attention.

I've never touched it.

This was the one crown Mother never let us near.

She wears it on her head every day, and I've even seen

her sleeping with it in her bed sometimes, like a child clutching its most precious toy.

I never, ever suspected.

"Don't touch it directly," Thiago warns, pacing toward it.

"I didn't intend to," I mutter, pulling on a set of thin leather gloves that I'd tucked behind my belt.

"Vi." There's something about his voice that warns me.

"What?"

I wave the faelight closer, and its then that I realize what's wrong.

A gold, faceless head sits within the nook, but there's nothing on its head. No crown. No wards. Merely an empty space where the crown should lie.

No. No! Where is it?

"A little thief," something whispers behind us. "Come in the night for a crown. How extraordinary."

Both of us freeze.

"I wonder…, should I alert the guards?" It's the door-knob that speaks. "Or should I call for my queen?"

"Run," Thiago says, shoving me toward the door.

It slams in my face, and I hammer at the beaten gold, before turning around with a frustrated hiss. Curse it. My heart rabbits in my chest as I face the inevitable truth. "It's a trap."

And the only one who knew we were coming was my sister.

The doorknob chuckles and then it starts screaming.

I shove Thiago in the chest. "Leave!"

I've seen him turn as insubstantial as shadow and know he can pass through solid stone if he has a mind.

"Do you honestly think I'm going to leave you behind? I've got a better idea. Why don't you come with me?"

I gesture to the door.

Thiago merely smiles. "I thought I'd make my own."

And then he turns and presses his fingers to the wall, and with a punch of raw power, stone explodes through the night.

"What part of 'do not use your magic' do you not understand?"

He can't face her. Not here. Not now.

Not with Mother's curse twisting him on edge.

We steal from the castle just as the guards sprint toward the tower behind us. Yells echo through the night and the portcullis slams down.

Too late.

We're already in the woods.

And while the ripple of our presence is clearly spreading through the castle, nobody in the woods seems to be aware of it.

"We can't run," I tell him, swallowing hard. "They'll be looking for someone who's running."

He could fly out of here, but can he carry me?

Or will there be archers in the trees?

Thiago slows, his hand sliding through mine. He tugs me into a crowd of laughing fae and steals a glass of elderberry wine from a servant's platter for me. "Then we don't run," he murmurs in my ear as he tugs me into his arms.

With the mask in place, he looks like the Lord of Darkness, breathed into fae form.

"What do we do?" Failure makes my breath catch. This was our one chance, and we lost it and….

"We dance," he tells me, his hand stroking my spine, "and we focus on getting out of here safely. Tomorrow, we will deal with the consequences."

I rest my head against his chest, dizzy with disappointment.

"This way," he says as he takes my hand and spins me into a dance.

There's a nonchalance to his actions, but I can see his eyes roving the night. A pair of guards come together at the edge of the clearing, but we are merely another couple in a sea of dancing fae.

The guard's jerk a couple apart, tugging their masks from their faces. With a curse, they move on, grabbing another couple from the dance. Ripples of surprise start stirring among the fae. Even drunk and merry, some of them are starting to realize this isn't normal.

"They're searching all the dark-haired couples," I breathe.

But as I speak, they wrench at a tall brunet dancing with a blonde fae woman.

"Any dark-haired male." Thiago's eyes narrow, and then he looks down at me. "Go. They won't stop you if you're not with me. Not with that hair. I'll slink into the shadows and follow you."

Pulse pounding, I fetch another glass of wine. He vanishes in a swirl of his cloak, and I push between a pair of gossiping fauns, making my way casually across the clearing. The prickle between my shoulder blades itches, but nobody stops me. Nobody cries out.

And then I'm in the trees once more, and there's a

shadow flitting along through the woods beside me, like an invisible wolf that follows at my heels.

"Finn's going to meet us by the lake," Thiago whispers in my head.

I head in that direction.

The dancers are thinning out now, and though I nearly trample a pair of entwined lovers as I stagger through a thicket, we're almost alone here.

Almost.

As I hurry around an oak, I see a tall figure picking her way through the middle of the clearing. The moonlight glimmers on her golden gown, and she clutches her skirts in hands that are bedecked with a half dozen rings.

I skid to a halt.

"The wards are not designed to rouse the guards," my mother says, her cold eyes locking upon me. "But they will wrap themselves around any intruders like spider silk, so I can track them at my leisure. Hello, little thief. Step into the light and show me who you are."

CHAPTER 30

"*Stay hidden*," I warn Thiago.

There's nothing but silence from his direction, but I know he's there.

The thought doesn't ease my nerves; this is what I've been trying to avoid at all costs. The last time these two were in the same vicinity, they nearly tore each other apart.

"Who are you?" she demands, flinging a hand toward me.

The mask is torn from my face, and the wig tumbles to the ground with it. My dark hair spills around my shoulders in an inky swirl, but as her winds rip at my skirts, I ward them away. I'm no longer entirely defenseless.

Her eyes flare wide with shock. "Iskvien?"

Good to know that when it comes to stealing her crown, I'm not even the first on her suspect list. She's blamed me for everything else my entire life, so I was half expecting it.

"Hello, *Mother*."

Armor jingles. Guards flood the woods, and torches

flare to life as they surround me. Dozens of them by the look of it. But my mother holds up her palm, warning them not to move.

"Where is he?" she demands.

"Where is who?"

"You know who I mean." Her voice drops into a snarl. "That filth you lay with."

Interesting. Her wards cling to me, but perhaps they slipped from his skin when he became naught more than shadows. "Perhaps I came to enjoy your Imbolc celebrations. Perhaps I missed life at the castle...." I can't keep a straight face. "Fine. That last one's a lie. There's not a damned thing I miss here."

"You mock me?"

The alternative is to try and strangle her with my bare hands. "Considering what you did to me, you should be relieved all I'm doing is mocking you."

"Seize her," Adaia snaps at her guards.

"I think not."

Wind stirs through the trees as I squat and press my fingertips to the ground. *There.* Far below us quivers the ley line, though the nexus point—the Hallow—is five miles to the north. Within its ringed stones I'd be invincible, but here, all I can do is pluck at the magic and feel it bubbling up through the ground as if the ley line has found a new nexus point.

Me.

Her eyes lock upon me. "I've been wondering how you did it."

"Surprise, Mother." I lift my head, feeling the wind stream through my hair as if something answers me. This is not Evernight, where I bound myself to the lands, but there's something there. A little tremor in the ground where my feet touch, as though *something* recognizes me. "You're not the only one with mysterious powers."

The guards rush toward me.

Throwing up a hand, I send them all flying with an explosion of flame. One slams into a tree. Another crashes in a cascade of metal.

She sends a howl of wind toward me, but it's the vines snaking over the grass that catch my attention as I stagger backward. One locks around my ankle, and I cross my arms and slash down sharply, parting her winds. Vicious thorns dig into my skin.

But the second my blood hits the earth, a tremor runs through the ground. Those thorns are suddenly mine, and I twist them back upon her, lashing them toward her with vicious speed.

My mother screams as she throws herself aside.

Scrambling to her hands and knees, she glares at me.

I hold my hands up. A faint light suffuses my fingertips. I can feel the lands whispering to me, calling out for succor. It's a little like the night I bound myself to Evernight. They yearn to be touched, yearn to uplift a queen—

"No!" my mother screams, and then she grabs a knife from her belt and throws herself at me.

I'm caught in the land's whispers, distracted by the thorns that beg me for command. A flash of light shears toward me, and only months of Eris's training forces me to react in time. Twisting beneath the blow, I roll her wrist over the top of my forearm and drive my fist into her ribs.

She collapses into an undignified heap at my feet.

Several of the guards draw sharp breaths.

Nobody has ever seen my mother stumble, and I recognize the danger all too late.

Mother looks up with a gasp, but there's murder in her eyes. I've seen her look at me with hate and rage, but never with this much cold. There's a moment where I still exist—the daughter who betrayed her, the daughter who turned against her—but then I see her visibly excise me from her life.

"You will *not* take my crown," she growls, and the color in her irises is smothered by a tide of black ink, until her eyes are fully black. "It is mine. As these lands are *mine*."

She forces herself to her feet, and that inky color steals through her cheeks until her face is mottled with black veins.

I can't help taking a step back.

This isn't my mother.

It's a monster in fae flesh, driven purely by vengeance.

How did I not see it?

"From the moment I felt you kicking in my womb, I knew you were a seed that should never have been given root. Everything about your begetting was a lie, and your birth *ruined* me. You were born to betray me, and I did not listen to my instincts," she hisses. "I told myself there must be some good in you. There must be some half of you that belonged to me, but all I can see is your father. You are a monster I should have drowned at birth."

For a second, I can't breathe.

It isn't true. I know it isn't true, and yet those words flay me from within.

Curling her fingers into claws, she spits a curse, and

then thorns rupture from the ground, stabbing for my throat.

I scream, but something sweeps the thorns out of the way. They wither and die, even as new ones keep stabbing through the soil, until I'm surrounded by a thicket of dry, brittle branches, poison still dripping from those inch-long thorns.

Adaia slowly lowers her hands, and this is the first time I've seen her fear.

The winds swirl again, but this time they carry his scent upon them. A dark shadow falls from the sky, landing with a thud in front of me.

And then Thiago is there, enormous feathered wings tucking in tightly against his body. His eyes are as black as hers are, and the barest hint of one of his darkyn tattoos creeps up his throat.

"Adaia." He slowly straightens. "I promised you a reckoning the last time we met."

"So you did." Her gaze slides to his wings. "No longer trying to hide your filthy nature, I see."

"Why pretend I care what you think of me?"

Little whispers stir through the grass. Thorns creeping like vines. She's trying to distract him.

"Watch out!" I call.

Thiago's lip curls, and then he flicks his hand and the thorns wither and die, crumbling into dust.

My mother stills. "You dare walk into my castle. You dare try and steal from me—"

"You had something I wanted."

A scream of rage escapes her. "You filthy, wretched *thief*. I will see you die for this!" Her fingers curling into claws, she strides toward him. Thorns rupture through the grass, reaching for him, but he's in the air, his massive wings thrusting down.

And that's when the world explodes.

Both of us are flung apart, and I hit the grass and roll to my feet, drawing my dagger. There's a ringing in my ears as my eyes fight to make sense of the world.

Fire rains down through the trees. Little sparks of ash streak through the sky like shooting stars. Somewhere to the right there's a bonfire—

"No!" my mother screams, pushing to her feet, her face stricken. "My oak. My *oak!"*

The queen's oak is burning, enormous flames licking toward the skies.

How did that—?

There's no time to lose in gaping.

"Run," Thiago says, shoving me into the trees. "There are hundreds of guards swarming out of the castle, and we need to get out of these woods!"

I SPRINT THROUGH THE TREES.

Thiago materializes out of the darkness, grabbing my arm. He's vanished his wings and looks completely seelie again. "This way!"

I told him not to use his magic here. Not to draw attention. "You set her *oak* on fire?" She's as bound to that tree as she is to the land.

"Not me!"

"Then *who*—?"

"I don't know. And we don't have time to find out. We need to—"

"I can't leave yet! She must have hidden the crown somewhere. She knew we were coming and she—"

"There'll be other chances, Vi." He shakes his head, glancing tersely at the fire. "We have to go. Now."

To leave without the crown makes my stomach knot. My mother knows what we want now, and she'll lock that crown away so fiercely that even the light will never get so much as another glimpse at it.

And without it….

I can't breathe. My feet won't move.

But they have to.

I let Thiago tug me into the forest, every step feeling as though my boots are made of lead. Torches flare through the trees, and he catches a glimpse of them and then draws me the other way. Toward the east.

Mother knows we need to get to the Hallow if we're to have any chance at escaping.

But torches gleam through the trees ahead of us too. More guards. They're coming from every direction.

"Do you trust me, Vi?" He wraps his arms around me.

"Of course, I do."

Darkness shrouds us both, and I wrap my arms beneath his and hug his shoulder blades as I recognize the whispers in the air around us. Something strokes my skin—

"Such a pretty girl," it whispers. "So sssoft and fleshy…. So delicioussss…"

Our eyes meet.

"I'm angry, and they call to me strongly when I give in to my emotions," he admits. And then his jaw locks and the whispers die away. "We'll have to fly."

"Can you even carry me?"

Wings appear beneath my hands, and then he spreads them as wide as he can. "Do you doubt me, my love?"

A soft gasp echoes behind us.

My head whips toward the sound, and there's Andraste, her mouth falling open in shock as she sees his wings.

"You," he says coldly, stepping toward her and dragging me with him.

"Stop!"

Thiago glances at me, his eyes completely black, but it's not the Thiago I know. There's a feral edge to his features. The darkyn prince who wishes to crush the world. "We can't trust her."

"Stop," I repeat, my hand pressed against his chest. "Let me talk to her. She wouldn't be here if she didn't have something important to say to me."

And I have something to say to *her*.

Every inch of him trembles, and he slowly lowers his head, his fingers curling into fists. "Make it quick."

Andraste's mouth forms a little O of horror. "It's true."

"That you betrayed us?" I shake my head. "I fall for it every time—"

"I didn't betray you."

"Really? We stole inside the castle but the crown *wasn't* there! She knew we were coming. She knew and—"

"It wasn't there," Andraste snaps, "because *I* took it." Brushing her cloak aside, she unties something from her hip and holds it in her gloved hand. "I was going slip away to the Hallow and send it through to you while she was distracted."

The crown.

Mother's crown.

It has no gemstones. Nor is it merely decorative. Seven sharp prongs stab away from a circlet of heavy gold, and as the light flickers over it, it feels as though something malevolent within the crown stares back.

"Here," she says, shoving it into my hands. "Take it."

"Why would you do this?"

She knows the consequences of betraying Mother. It was one thing to protect me at Briar Keep. Another to steal from our mother—and to deliberately sabotage the queen's plans.

Because while I didn't set that fire, there's only one other fae in the court who has the power to wield such flames. Fire runs through the Asturian matriarchal bloodline, and while it's one of the few fae gifts I can access, my sister wields it like a whip.

Andraste curls my fingers around the crown. "Take it. I can hear it whispering to me. Just take it. And get out of here. She's had the Hallows surrounded both here and at Briar Keep. She expects you to flee in that direction."

"But why?"

Her gloved hands are warm beneath mine as I take the crown.

I don't know if I imagine it, but there's a little shiver through my veins, as if some sort of power leaches through my skin. It's the crown.

"Because…."

"Because?"

"Because I am sorry. Because I can never take back any of my actions, my lies. And because…." Andraste looks at me with eyes wet with guilt. She shoots a glance over my shoulder toward Thiago and then presses something into my hand. "I don't want you to lose your child."

A little curl of paper.

"What are you trying to—?"

"Read it when you are safe," she says, shoving me toward Thiago. "Read it and know this: I am sorry. And I do not ask for forgiveness, only for understanding. I have tried to protect you as best I could. As I have tried to protect *her*. And I thought my silence was the best protection I could offer, for there are eyes and ears in every inch of this court. I did not dare reach out to tell you."

"To tell me what?"

Guilt darkens her eyes, but then another explosion of flame is set off nearby. My head whips toward the west. Toward the armory.

"Go," Andraste tells me. "I'll try and distract the guards."

Thiago hauls me into the trees, but I pause at the edge of the clearing and look back.

"*Goodbye,*" Andraste mouths, and a chill runs through me, because this time, I feel as though it's forever.

CHAPTER 31

The night is a blur.

Thiago flies us toward the north, finally setting me down somewhere near the Duke of Thornwood's lands —and the Hallow there. We arrive back in Ceres just as dawn breaks in the east.

I take three steps, and that's when I realize my thighs are slick, and it's not from desire. The dull pain that's been nagging at my back all day suddenly makes sense.

I stop halfway up the stairs in surprise.

"What is it?" Thiago asks, from behind.

"I...." I dash up the stairs into our chambers, and from there into the washroom. Stripping out of my clothes confirms the truth.

I'm not with child.

"Vi?" Thiago knocks on the door I slammed in his face. "What is it?"

"Give me a moment."

I clean up as best I can, and then slip into a robe that's hanging from the back of the door. A bath will have to wait. There's another nagging sensation in my chest, and this one won't be suppressed.

"What is it?" he repeats, when I open the door.

"My monthly finally came."

Expression drops from his face. "Ah."

And I wonder if we wear the same mask.

I was so certain I was with child, but the feeling that cuts through me is both of relief and loss. With the crown in our hands, there's no longer any threat from the Mother of Night, and I guess there's a little part of me that wanted a child.

His child.

Thiago opens his arms and I walk into them, leaning against him and closing my eyes.

"You're upset," he murmurs.

"No, I... I don't know what to think. I could almost imagine her." And the dreams. Every night the dreams. "It's a relief right now, but...."

"You wanted her."

"She felt real," I admit, curling into him. "She felt so real."

And to lose that feels like a little death inside me.

Thiago kisses the top of my head. "Go and take a bath. I'll send for some breakfast." He gives me a brief squeeze before he finally opens his arms. "You did it, Vi. You were right. We have the crown."

He heads for the door as I turn back to the wash chambers, but something stops me from entering.

I never checked the little message Andraste pressed into my hands. At first we were too busy running and fighting—and then flying—but now I can't help wondering what she was so desperate to tell me.

"I do not ask for forgiveness, only for understanding."

I find it in the inner pocket of my dress and unroll the little scroll of paper.

It's written in the language that Andraste and I invented when we were children—a series of dashes and swirls that only we could decipher. And it's been so long since I've seen it that it takes a moment for me to understand what I'm reading.

There was child, Vi. The fourth time you went away, you came back swollen with child. A little girl with your mouth. You named her Amaya—

Amaya.

The word strikes through me like a bell that's been rung.

Hammerstrikes of memory assault me.

And then I'm falling, falling, my hand clutching my head as another layer of curse work shatters and I'm swept into the past....

Pain. And desperation.

And fear.

"Push," snaps a hard voice. "Push."

I can't do it. I can't get through this. If I push, then my mother will take my baby away.

"*No!*" I scream, biting my knuckles. *Help me. Help me, please.* It's tearing me in two.

I need him. I need him so badly, and he's not here, and I'm so weak that I don't know if I have the strength to fight them all. *Thiago!* I throw the thought out into the night, but there's no answer.

And there won't be.

This little ruined keep of Clydain—which has been my home for the past six months—is far to the north of Asturia and warded by so many levels of magic that no one will ever hear me or see me again.

"Please... no." Another spasm of pain tears me into two, and my spine bows as I scream.

"You have to push!"

"Vi." Someone kneels beside me, taking me by the hand, and I clutch at them as if they're my last lifeline.

I can barely breathe, every iota of my being trying *not* to birth this baby. It's the only way I can protect her, and every inch of me contorts with pain.

But suddenly Andraste's face is next to mine. "If you don't push," she says, "your baby will die."

I burst into tears, gasping raggedly. "Please don't let her take my baby.... *Please.*"

My sister's face dissolves as the unbearable urge to push takes over. Gods, it hurts. Every panting breath feels like I'm being torn in two. But I beg her. I beg her with my eyes and the entire whole of my being.

"That's it!" the midwife encourages. "Bear down, Princess."

"I'll protect her as if she is my own," Andraste says, cradling me as I shake. "I promise, Vi. I'll never let anything happen to her." And then her voice drops, until it's only a whisper. "In Maia's name, Vi. I *will* protect her no matter what I must do."

It's the only thing I can hold on to as I scream and grunt and push.

And then suddenly the pressure is gone, and my body

collapses back in Andraste's arms as the baby slips free of me.

My baby. My baby. I try to raise my arm....

The midwife lifts her head from between my thighs, a little bundle in her arms. A cry splits the air, and sweet Maia, but my baby is breathing. My baby's breathing and blessed gods, she's so—

"Show me." A voice cuts through my haze, and then my mother swims out of the shadows.

Every inch of her is smothered in black, and the golden crown on her head seems to loom over all of us. She's never far from it.

"No." I tense, but Andraste's grip on my hands tightens.

"You were right. It's a little girl," the nurse says, her gaze drifting between my mother and me. She tilts the baby toward my mother.

A girl.

My mother takes the bundle in her arms, and every inch of dread I've ever felt sinks its icy daggers through my chest.

"Don't you dare touch her." I try to push up onto my hands, but my body spasms again.

"Hush now," my mother croons as my baby cries. "Look how beautiful you are."

I don't even know what she looks like.

"Give her back!" I scream, reaching for my baby. *No, please. Not this. Anything but this....* "Give her back!"

"She doesn't belong to you anymore," my mother says, lifting my baby and smiling down at her. "She is mine. Mine to raise as I see fit. Mine to mold. Mine to destroy if I so choose."

No.

I try to shove my way out of the birthing bed, but my limbs are so weak and I'm still shaking.

"Mother." Andraste appears at the queen's side, and rests a hand on my mother's arm. "May I see my niece?"

My mother offers my baby to my sister, and Andraste gathers her safely into her arms.

"Please." I reach toward them. Toward my daughter.

Andraste moves back to the bed, still cooing at the bundle.

"Andraste," Mother barks.

"She should see her," my sister snaps back, shooting Mother a fierce look. "Let her see her. You've won. Grant her this one small mercy."

I try to haul myself out of bed, but my body is still wracked with contractions. And I don't know if Adaia replies, because all I can see is the bundle in my sister's arms.

Andraste kneels on the bed beside me and eases back the linens.

My baby.

She's so little. So perfect. All scrunched up and red-faced and squalling. Her hair is matted to her skin with a thick waxy coating, and her face screws up as she cries. The second I touch her, she turns her snuffling mouth toward me, trying to latch on to my finger.

And my heart breaks in two.

I promised. I promised I'd protect you forever and I can't....

"Please," I beg Andraste.

Take her away. Get her out of here. Protect her.

And our eyes meet as if she hears me.

It's been a long time since she's heard me.

"What do you want to name her?" my sister whispers, and I know this is the only thing I might have.

"Amaya. Call her Amaya."

A slight variation in honor of his mother.

"That's enough," my mother says coldly.

"No, please." I grab for the bundle, that little finger still curled around mine. "*Please*."

Andraste hesitates, and for a second I think I might have a chance. Just one.

"Enough." My mother's voice is a whip crack. "Get that child out of here before I decide to see it drowned."

Andraste straightens, and as she wraps the linens around my daughter, her shoulders square for one defiant moment. "Amaya will be powerful," she says in a hollow voice. "She is born of your blood, Mother. And as much as you despise him, she's born of his blood too. Amaya will wield all the powers of the Evernight and Asturian royal lines, and if you harm her, then you will see your greatest weapon against the Prince of Evernight destroyed."

Greatest weapon?

"Don't you dare," I gasp.

"Raise her." My sister doesn't even look at me. "Raise her in seclusion so that no one knows of her birth. Train her to be strong and powerful. Love her." She pauses then, looking down at my baby. "And teach her the truth about her birth—that her father is a monster who stole her mother away and defiled her."

"No, no, no, no, no!"

They're not listening. Nobody is listening to me.

My mother steps closer, twitching the blankets aside and considering my daughter's fate. And then she smiles. "You always were my favorite child, my eldest. You're always thinking ahead. And you're right. I'm letting my anger rule me." She leans down and presses a kiss to my baby's forehead. "This baby is mine. And she will be the greatest weapon I can ever wield."

"*No!*"

Hands pin me down. The nursemaids. And just as I prepare to roll from the bed, another uncontrollable spasm assails me.

"You must push again, Princess," the midwife says as my vision blurs again. "This is your afterbirth. You've lost a lot of blood and you must push, or you might die."

I don't care.

"My baby, my baby, my baby...." But the door shuts behind my sister, and all I can see is her figure outlined in a halo of light before they're gone.

Forever.

And there's nothing I can do but scream.

"Vi? Vi!" Someone grips my shoulders as I kick and sob.

I blink out of the memory, every inch of me torn open and ravaged.

Thiago hauls me into his arms. "It's all right, it's all right. You're safe. I've got you."

But it's not all right....

She was there, and her little finger curled around mine as if I could keep her safe.... And I didn't. I didn't.

I don't know where she is.

I don't know what her life has been like, but I can imagine.

Tears stream down my face, but it's the rage in my

heart that can't be hidden. I always thought my mother had taken everything she could from me.

But I was wrong.

"I will kill her."

"Vi?"

I let the note fall into his hand, and Thiago's eyes race as he tries to read it.

"There was a baby. My mother stole my baby from me and then she cursed me to forget her. *This* is what she was hiding at Clydain."

I see the moment he understands. Horror shrouds his expression.

It was difficult enough when all I thought I had lost was him.

I reach for that little curl of paper. I only managed to read the first half before my memories broke through another layer of the curse.

There is more.

What mother will never know is this: I swapped the babies. I gave your daughter to the forest, to Old Mother Hibbert, so she will be safe. And the child that Mother has raised is an orphan with limited magic. It was the only way I knew to protect her. Amaya is in the north now. With the unseelie. I'm sorry. For not fighting harder. For not defying mother. For keeping such a secret. It was the only way I could see to protect Amaya at the time.

CHAPTER 32

Andraste

Sometimes the best disguise is to hide in plain sight.

Nobody will ever suspect I had a hand in tonight's events as I marshal the guards and try to put out the fire that still rages. To the court of Asturia, I'm the perfect princess heir. The one who kneels at her mother's side and hunts at her direction. The one who bowed her head when her sister fought.

But they'll never see the truth.

I am the knife at my mother's back, the knife she will never see coming.

I ease the doors to my chambers shut and rest my back against them with a sigh of relief. It's only now, in the sanctity of my own rooms, that I let my hands tremble.

To see that look in Vi's eyes—

She will never forgive me now that she knows the truth.

I want to vomit. I've held it in all night, but now—

Bile rises in my throat, and I rush to the wash chambers, sliding to my knees and gorging the contents of my stomach into the water closet. It's not enough. As I lie there shaking, my head resting on the seat, all I can feel is the numbness.

There's a beast inside me, and it wants out, ripping at my innards with sharp claws. But silence rings in my ears.

I am hollow, and all I want to do is lie here, but lying here means defeat, and maybe I could give in to it, but mine is not the only life that requires this subterfuge.

Amaya.

I see her little face and hear her cries echoing through the lonely forest. Some nights, in my nightmares, Old Mother Hibbert doesn't come, and I'm forced to flee with the baby, howling wolves nipping at my heels.

But some nights—the gentler nights—I see her smile at me as she leads me into a garden of strange flowers, where she points each one out to me and names them. She's a little girl in those dreams, and although she looks so much like my sister, she's sweeter than either of us ever were. Innocent. A child really, when neither of us were ever allowed to be children.

I will protect that with my last dying breath.

And if I don't get up, my mother will wonder why I'm so upset. And maybe she'll start questioning my whereabouts when her tree caught fire.

And from there, maybe she'll start questioning more of my actions.

Get up.

Clean up.

Hide the mess.

Gods, the mess. It's the push I need to be able to climb

my feet and force myself to reach for my toothbrush. The maids will be in soon, and I can't allow anyone to see me like this or smell the vomit. Mint drives the wretched taste from my tongue, and I scour my mouth raw until my gums bleed.

I clean everything, and then slip inside the rain shower, washing away the remnants of the night until the water has long run cold.

Clean. Dry. Half-dressed.

Empty.

By now Vi will know the truth, and there's no coming back from this.

It's the emptiness that slays me as I rake my hand over the foggy mirror. I promised myself I'd never do this again, but my eyes fall on the washbasin, and there's my dagger, neatly sheathed and tied to my belt.

I need this.

I need to feel. To bleed. To cut this poison from my veins so that it's no longer bursting inside my skin.

Vi. I keep seeing her face. And as I draw the knife and lift my gaze to my reflection, I feel sick again. Just once. Just once to get the feelings out, so I can go back to being the perfect princess.

Somewhere that no one will ever see it.

I don't even feel the knife slice across the smooth skin of my upper thigh, but the relief is instant. Pain screams through me, and it's all rising to the surface. I'm no longer hollow. No longer empty. It's all there, and I need more, and I use the knife again.

There's never any coming back—

"Andraste! Andi, stop!" Hands close around the knife,

jerking it from my grasp, and it's like waking up from a dream.

There's blood all over my hands. But all the pain in my heart is now in my skin, and I can breathe. The knot in my chest is finally gone, though when I look up into Edain's eyes, a new one forms.

Panic flares. "What are you *doing* in here?"

"Erlking's cock," Edain breathes, lifting my hands away from my thigh with an expression of horror. "What were you thinking?"

The fae heal swiftly. By morning there will be no sign of even a single mark. It will all be smooth, unblemished skin.

"I slipped." Even as I say the words, I realize how pointless it is. Each cut is long and straight and deliberate.

He knows.

Hot eyes rake over my face and then he's cursing under his breath as he tears his jacket off and rips strips from the sleeves. "What happened?"

I know he's not talking about the knife.

"What are you doing in my chambers?" I push him away, but he grabs my arm and shoves me back against the basin.

"If you leave this room, I'll tell your mother what you've done to yourself."

My gaze snaps to his. "You wouldn't."

But his lip curls, and he pushes me against the vanity as he tears the linen into thin strips. "Of course I would. Look at you. You're a mess. What happened out there in the woods?"

"I don't know. My sister was there with her husband, and—"

"I wasn't talking about Vi," he growls. "What happened to *you*?"

"Nothing."

"You're not just covered in blood for no reason." He reaches out to jerk the faucet on. The enchantments set over the royal apartments mean hot, fresh water at any time of day or night, but it takes a few moments for the spells to work. Steam begins to fill my washroom as Edain dips a cloth in the pooling water and then uses it to wipe some of the blood from my skin.

"This isn't necessary." I'm starting to become aware of the fact I'm wearing nothing more than a towel.

"Well, someone has to hide all the blood." There's a flash of his dangerous smile. "It's what I'm best at, isn't it?"

Bedplay. Wet work. All of it done in the shadows.

Not even my mother dares talk of Edain's talents with a knife and the way many of her enemies suddenly disappear. But I've seen him slip into her chambers unannounced, and I've seen the blood on his clothes and the emptiness in his eyes.

And then news will come of a mysterious death, and my mother will smile to herself in private and offer condolences in public.

"And what are you best at?" he murmurs, wiping the blood from my skin with strangely gentle hands. "The crown princess who stalks around this palace with such a flawless mask it's difficult to even catch a glimpse of the woman beneath it? A crown princess who spends hours each day drilling with the best of her guards, as if she's trying to fight an enemy she never names? A crown princess who murmurs caution in her mother's ear and tries to hide the horror in her eyes when her mother ignores her words?"

He may as well have slapped my face.

"*What?*"

He looks up. "Sometimes the mask slips. Sometimes I see you. The *real* you. And if you think I'm unaware of where your sympathies lie, then you should think again."

No. He can't know.

I capture his wrists, and for a second there's a part of me that wonders if I can get rid of the threat—

"Make me promise, Princess. Make me swear that I won't breathe a word of it." There's a savage heat in his eyes, as if he can read me like a book. "Because if there's one thing we both know, it's that you don't have the means—or the heart—to kill me."

Every inch of me thrums with the need to either fight or flee. The knife's still on the bench, the hilt slippery with blood, but it's close enough. "Nobody's invincible."

His hand cups my cheek, and then the rasp of his thumb strokes down my jaw. "I am." He leans closer, and then his other hand comes up to cup my face. "And you will lose if you even reach for that knife." His breath whispers against my ear. "Because you're not a killer, Princess. And I am."

I don't know how to take those words.

Because while they're a threat, his hands are gentle.

"But I'm not here to hurt you," he concedes, "and I'm not going to tell her, so stop looking at the knife."

"Then why *are* you here?"

Edain stares at me for a long, heated second. "It sometimes amazes me how blind you truly are. In that, you're

415

your mother's daughter. Adaia can't see what's right beneath her nose."

I blink. "Fuck you."

And he laughs. "Surely you can do better than that, Princess. Now sit the fuck down and let me see your wounds."

I don't want him touching me, but I have no choice. He captures my hips and lifts me onto the bench, and then he takes my knife and flips it until he captures the blade between his fingers before he slides it behind his belt.

Then his eyes dare me to do something about it.

Fine. I stare past him, at the wall. "What were you doing out in the woods?"

"Watching the game play out." He ducks his head and curses under his breath as he examines my thigh. "You're bleeding again. Don't move."

Watching the game play out.... It never occurred to me that Edain is the one I should be watching.

And once again he senses it as he swiftly cleans me up. "Try not to think too hard, Princess. You might strain a muscle."

My eyes narrow. "I think I liked you better when you weren't pretending to care for me."

His laugh is soft and silky. "You've never liked me, Princess. Because I am the mirror to your soul."

His dark hair falls into his eyes as he reaches around my thigh to bandage my wounds. The towel edges up. His breath shivers over my skin, and suddenly I realize I've never truly looked at him. Not the way I should have. Because it's clear he's been watching me, and while he's unearthed a few of my secrets, I don't know anything more about him than the peripheral.

All I know of him are shadows, shadows of the whole.

The reckless, petty, spoiled pet who whispers in my mother's ear.

The dangerous, charming seducer.

But he's not just a pretty fae male sprawled across a bed. He's a sheathed knife. Threatening. Unpredictable. The kiss of steel against your bared throat when you barely realized it was there.

Looking at Edain this close, his dark features barely a breath away, feels dangerous in ways I've never noticed before.

Perhaps I could tear his mask off and see what lies beneath those chiseled, urbane edges.

Perhaps we both wear nothing but masks.

We stare at each other for long seconds.

"I know what it looks like in the mirror when you hate yourself," he whispers. "You and I are two halves of a whole, Andraste." His thumb settles on my knee, stroking back and forth. "And you can glue the pieces back together and forge them into a shield, but there are fault lines in every inch of you."

I tense when his thumb moves higher, and he leans closer.

"You hate me," he whispers, his breath caressing my lips. "I see it every time you look at me."

"I don't hate you." It's a rare moment of understanding. "I pity you."

His thumb digs in a little, and his lashes half shield his eyes, but then he's stroking me again. His thumb questing higher, a question mark against my thigh. "Would you still hate me if I loved you?"

And then his lips brush against mine, and it's unbearably soft—even as his words knife through my heart.

Love.

Love is ruin. Love is pain. Love is loss.

Love is a lie.

And he mocks me with the sound of that word.

My nails dig into his forearms, but he laughs under his breath, and I can taste it. And then there's no more pretense that this is anything more than lust as the kiss turns hotter and more dangerous.

The shock of it makes me gasp, and then his tongue lashes mine. Somehow, I have a fistful of his robe, knuckles grazing the silky skin of his chest, though whether I meant to push him away or pull him closer is unknown, even to me.

I didn't think he'd do it.

And even now I tense in uncertainty.

If Mother caught us, she'd have both our heads.

There is no escape.

There is no hope.

There is only one lie after another, and my mother never knows. She never looks at me—her trusted daughter—the daughter that would never betray her, and ever suspects....

But I'm not the perfect daughter. I've never been the perfect daughter.

And the two of us are trapped in her net, desperately trying to keep our heads above the maelstrom that is my mother.

Just this once, I want to betray her.

My teeth sink into Edain's lip, and then I'm pushing

against him, the kiss turning deep and hungry. He senses everything I won't say.

Make it all go away.

And he does.

And gods, I can't breathe again, but this time it's for another reason entirely. This time I feel too *much*. He kisses me as if we're both trying to lose ourselves in each other, the slick slide of his tongue a lash against mine. His thumb digs into my uninjured thigh, inching higher.

"Make it hurt," I beg.

Make me feel.

He pushes away, both of us reeling a little and breathing hard.

We stare at each other.

The line that once held me safe from his advances has been crossed. Obliterated. And he did it deliberately.

Resting on his knuckles, he stares into my eyes as if he's trying to see through my soul. And then he laughs under his breath and shakes his head before he steps away. "No."

No?

"What do you mean?"

Edain turns around, the simple linen of his shirt clinging to his shoulders. "I mean no. I won't be the tool you can use to make yourself bleed again." Wiping a hand over his lips, he licks his fingers as if he can still taste me. "Kiss me when you want it to stop hurting, Princess, and I might think about it."

That's the problem.

I never want it to stop hurting.

Pain means life. Pain is an end to the nothingness. Pain

is a reminder that I'm still here. I'm still me. And sometimes, it's the only way to remind myself.

Edain sees it in my face. "I might be your mother's fucktoy, but I'm not about to become her daughter's toy too." He crosses to the window and twitches the curtains aside, staring out into the night. The distant fires highlight the stark lines of his face. "You're playing a dangerous game."

"Game?"

Edain allows the curtain to fall, and somehow it makes the room feel smaller. "You may have fooled the rest of the court, but you don't fool me." He turns around, his expression dark. "Your mother is beyond furious. I've spent all evening trying to talk her out of marching into Evernight with every warrior she can get her hands on. She's still fucking sobbing in the ashes of that tree."

My lashes lower. "A regrettable mistake. The prince of Evernight chose his target well."

"You and I both know the prince never went anywhere near that tree."

It's a dangerous accusation.

And I've never entirely known how much I can trust him.

Edain's father married my mother and then died in a hunting "accident" several years later. By the end of the week, Edain was in my mother's bed, and he's been there ever since.

"The gift of fire runs in your mother's line," he continues, his eyes glittering with an expression I can't quite name, "but your sister's never been able to master it the way you have. And the way that tree lit up, as though someone had packed it with explosive powder, makes me think magic was involved. So if it wasn't your sister, and it certainly wasn't your mother, then…."

"Are you trying to suggest *I* had something to do with it?" I load my voice with every ounce of haughtiness I can find, and this time, I hop off the bench and step toward him. "Do you hear yourself? I am the Crown Princess of Asturia. I am my mother's heir. And I have always been loyal to her. If you *ever* suggest such a betrayal by my hand, then I will be sure to—"

"What?" He doesn't back away. "Are you going to murder my father? Are you going to force me into your bed? Threaten to cut my throat if I don't behave?" The muscle in his throat bobs, and he captures my jaw in a merciless grip. "Do you know, right now, you look exactly like your mother's heir. Every inch of you."

I tear my face away. "Don't you ever touch me."

"Again," he says softly.

"*Ever*."

His hand tenses into a fist, but he paces away from me before spinning on his heel.

We stare at each other, like enemies daring the other to cross the undrawn line between us.

"Have a care," he finally murmurs. "Your mother is right on the edge. It seems someone stole her crown as well as setting her favorite tree on fire. She wants to burn things."

"Then I guess you had best prepare for a long night ahead."

Oh, that makes him angry.

"And *there* you are again." He shakes his head and turns for the door. "For a second, I almost thought you were something more than your mother's clone."

It's only once the door slams behind him that I find I can breathe again.

And I feel sick to my stomach, because as I lift my eyes to the mirror, I see exactly what he sees.

My mother's daughter.

Eaten hollow from the inside out.

"One thing," I whisper to myself. "You did one thing right."

It's not enough to balance the scales. It never will be.

But at least my sister has the crown she needs to save her daughter.

CHAPTER 33

Iskvien

We land in a Hallow in the snow, and Thiago freezes, his head cocked as if he's listening. Baylor and Eris fan out, swords held low, and Finn nocks an arrow loosely, prepared to draw on a second's notice.

I don't care if there's danger here.

My daughter is here.

And if anything gets between us, I will destroy it.

"Snow," Thalia growls under her breath, taking a step and sinking up to her boots. "Why does it always have to be snow?"

"Quiet," Baylor mutters.

She rolls her eyes. "Did you think I didn't ward us all the second we arrived? If there's anything out there, they won't see or hear us. All they'll see will be mysterious footprints appearing in the snow."

The last time we were in unseelie, Thiago said he didn't dare use his power here, and it's furled up tight and small within him, just in case there's another darkyn nearby.

My heart skips a beat as he and Eris share a look.

"Nothing," Eris finally says. "I can barely even hear the heartbeat of a pair of birds."

"The wards on Old Mother Hibbert's cottage are so old, they were crafted by the otherkin," Thiago murmurs. "You won't smell the children. You won't be able to hear them. Not even a heartbeat. She puts a spell on all her children, so they'll always be able to find their way back to the cottage, even on the darkest night." He turns to the south, peering intently into the forest. "It's this way."

"Even after all this time?" I ask as I follow him.

Thiago slogs through the snow, cutting a trail for me. "It's not a sound or something I can see. It's the call of the hearth. A beating drum in my heart that says, 'Home, home, home.' A feeling more than anything. And yes, even after all these years."

Eris frowns as she falls into step beside me. "There aren't any animals nearby," she says in a troubled voice.

"The cottage spells tell predators to move on," Thiago explains. "They won't know why, but they'll simply feel the urge to be elsewhere."

"Not even any birds, Thiago," she points out. "There are no mice squeaking beneath the snow, no owls fluffing their feathers in the trees. The world is simply silent and empty."

Finn sets a hand on the hilt of his sword. "Thanks, Eris. I wasn't quite feeling nervous enough about entering unseelie in the first place. Now my balls want to tuck tail and run."

Thiago shoots her a look, but he doesn't say anything.

She's said enough.

Something's not quite right here.

Even Grimm remains quiet, from his perch atop my shoulders.

It takes us nearly an hour of walking before Thiago holds up a hand. "The cottage is just ahead," he says. "The children aren't used to strangers. Strangers mean death here in the north, so don't make any sudden moves. I speak their language, so I'll tell them to take me to Old Mother Hibbert."

We all nod and stamp our feet.

I feel sick with nerves. I've been trying not to think of it all morning, but Amaya's within earshot. I don't know what to say to her. She doesn't know me—she doesn't know any of us—and all I can hope is that she's led a happy life until this moment.

What if she hasn't *led a happy life?*

I freeze, and Thiago squeezes my hand, as if he can sense what I'm thinking.

"*Soon,*" he whispers in my mind, and then he's pushing through a pair of fir trees, sweeping snow off the branches with his arm.

A little glade appears.

And there's a cottage in the middle of it, the kind of cottage that belongs in all the old fairy tales. It stands cold and silent in the forest, and Thiago slams to a halt as he sees it, his nostrils flaring.

"What's wrong?" I can practically feel his tension. "We're nearly there."

"You can see it?" he asks slowly.

I nod, and then I remember…. The wards keep prying eyes away. I'm not supposed to be able to see it.

"The fires are always burning," he breathes. "She always keeps the fires lit for the littlest ones, and there's more than a tongue-lashing for you if you allow them to fall cold." He takes a step toward the cottage. And another. "The lanterns burn with faelight, night and day, just in case one of the children loses their way in the forest. Something's wrong."

My stomach drops. My little girl….

"Can you sense anything?" I ask Grimm desperately.

"*Pain. And fear,*" the grimalkin replies quietly. "*And the stink of the Shadow Ways.*"

They came for her, I know it.

I should have paid more attention to my dreams. The fetch no longer had need of me, because they *had her*….

I'm not the only one with the blood of the Old Ones. I'm not the only *leanabh an dàn*. And Angharad only needs one; the right kind of sacrifice to break open the Hallow that guards the Horned One.

A breathless sob escapes me as Eris pushes past us, drawing her sword.

"I can smell blood," she says.

And that's when I start to smell it too.

"Amaya!" I yell, shoving past all of them, but Thiago grabs my arm grimly.

"Slowly, Vi." He turns to look at the cottage. "Because whatever did this may still be here."

THE CLOSER WE GET TO THE COTTAGE, THE MORE I SEE SIGNS of ruin.

Glass shards glitter in the window panes, and flames

have burnt one side of the house before they were seemingly doused. Someone's torn the shutters from the windows, and they hang from broken hinges.

There's a trail of blood leading through the snow. Footsteps churn the snow to slush, and all around the clearing branches lie broken and cleaved, as if someone threw enormous amounts of spell craft around.

Thiago wrenches open the door to the cottage, and nothing prepares me for the sight of a broken broom lying forlornly in the entry. There's blood on the floor. Blood on the walls. Smashed toys and an abandoned boot that looks far too small to be an adult's.

It's the boot that does me in.

"Amaya?" I'm choking on the word, my heart pounding so hard I swear I'm going to break a rib.

But there's no sign of any children.

I shove inside. "Amaya!"

Thiago pushes past me and slams into an invisible ward. He feels at it. "The blood wards." The words steal from his lips. "Old Mother Hibbert unlocked the blood wards."

"What does that mean?" I demand.

He flexes his fingers against them. "I can't get through. Nothing can get through. It was something Old Mother Hibbert always warned us about. If we were ever attacked, then we were to flee into the cottage and hide in the cellar while she fired the blood wards." He curses under his breath. "It was the last line of defense, and something she would only ever do if she thought the children were at grave risk."

"Then Amaya may be inside," I whisper, hope bleeding through me.

427

"If she's in the cellar, then she's safe. But Vi...." He swallows hard. "They'll last for twenty-four hours after Old Mother Hibbert's death. She's either dead or dying. We need to find her."

"This way," Grimm tells me, *"I can hear someone wheezing."*

And then he launches from my shoulder and flies over the snow as if he has invisible wings.

I stagger after him, careless of the others.

Grimm follows the blood trail through the snow, to where a patch of firs shiver under the weight of their frozen burden. There's a patch of multicolored skirts, and I find an old woman propped up with her back resting against the trunk of the fir, a bloodstained flask in her hand.

The ancient hag gulps and gasps, as if her lungs have been pierced. I walk toward her in a dream-like state, even as my mind sees everything.

"Don't... come closer," she hisses, and she curls her hand around a femur that looks like it was snapped in two.

I don't know why, but the sight of her ragged fingerless gloves breaks my heart a little.

She took my daughter in and raised her as her own, despite the fact she has so truly little. Ancient blue tattoos are engraved on her haggard cheeks, and her half-rotted teeth are stained.

"I'm not here to hurt you," I call, sweeping my cape off my shoulders. "Here." I squat beneath the firs and lay it over her legs. "We're friends. We're.... You have my daughter. You have my.... My Amaya."

The worry etched on her face eases, and she stares at me for a long, slow moment. "You're her, aren't you?"

I don't know what she means.

"Said they wanted... a princess. But if they couldn't... get the mother.... They'd take the child." She spits a bloodied mouthful onto the snow. "Wouldn't let her go.... Not one of my babies. That filth.... That filth. Swore I'd kill it...."

She laughs and shudders, and then coughs on blood.

"Where is she?" I whisper.

Tears streak down that weathered old face. "I c-couldn't... Couldn't stop 'em. All I had left in me... was this...."

They took her. The fetches took my daughter.

I knew.

A part of me knew the second I saw that broken door.

I rest my forehead against hers, squeezing her hand tightly. "I will get her back."

A shudder runs through her.

"Here," I whisper, reaching out with my magic. "Let me heal you a little."

"No." A hand grasps mine, surprisingly strong. "Ain't enough... left o' me."

Healing is a sharp-edged sword. I can use my magic to seal those ragged wounds, but I can't gift her with strength. All it will do is weaken her further as the magic draws on her body's reserves.

She's too far gone for me to bring her back. Too old. Too weak. Healing will kill her. But I hate feeling so helpless.

"Just find my sweet Amaya," she grates out. "Find my

little girl and bring her back." Grabbing hold of a set of keys hanging around her throat, she gestures for me to take them. "Give 'em… to Larina. House… belongs… to her now."

I take the keys and help her tip the flask to her lips, cradling her scalp as she tries to drink. My vision blurs. "How long ago?"

"Three… hours."

Three hours. We were so close.

She slumps into the snow, and the fight slowly leaches from her eyes. Too much. Too much blood, too much pain.

"Blessed be," I whisper, squeezing her hand.

Thank you for taking care of my daughter.

"Find… them." The pressure of her hand begins to falter. "Find my… my babies…."

"I'll find them," I promise her as her hand falls to the side and her head slowly lolls back. "I promise I'll find them all and I'll protect them. As you have."

And then her lungs give one last rattle.

Silence falls.

The only thing that breaks it is footsteps crunching through the snow behind me.

I tug my cloak up over the old hag's face, dashing the tears from my eyes. There is no time to mourn. No time to regret.

I will burn that fucking bitch alive, and all her fetches too.

"Vi?" There's a look of horror on Thiago's face as I shove to my feet, taking the keys with me.

"They took Amaya." My fingers unerringly find the bracelet that keeps me safe from the fetch's eyes, and I start to slip it from my wrist. "The fetch will have taken her back to Angharad, and they'll be preparing her for the ritual."

My voice sounds so cool and so far away.

"They'll be at the Black Keep." Eris stands behind him, and I realize they're all there.

"There'll be guards," Finn says, and for once his face is serious. "Angharad has packs of fetches and banes who serve her. The Black Keep…. The defenses alone…. I don't know how we'll get in. Or even if we can."

It was different when it was me they were after. I was merely prey trying desperately to escape my bloody end.

But they took my daughter.

They *took* my daughter.

This time, I'm not prey. This time, I'm the hunter.

I drop the bracelet into the snow, feeling a little tingle run down my spine, as if my magic gives a breath of relief to be unsmothered. There's no longer any fear left within me. Realizing the truth has scoured me down to my bones, and all I feel is empty.

Though there's a little spark of rage there, just waiting to be kindled.

"I can get in," I tell them.

After all, there's a Hallow there.

It's not just an Old One's prison.

"And then we'll kill them." I meet Thiago's eyes. "We'll kill them all."

And he nods.

I wait outside in the snow as Thiago leaves the keys for the eldest girl. He can't break the wards, but he can slide the keys through them, because they belong to the house.

It's just me and Grimm.

The others are sweeping the snow to make sure there're no other survivors out there—children who didn't make it back to the cottage in time, but who might have found shelter.

And the grimalkin's tail lashes back and forth, back and forth, as he sits there and watches me.

"Did you know?" I ask hollowly, my fists shaking with rage. "You say you see the future, and everything you have said to me…. Tell me you didn't know that I have a daughter out there who is all alone!"

For the first time, there's a hint of doubt in his eyes. "*I knew. It was not yet time for you to face your past.*"

"Who are you?" I demand. "Why are you taunting me?"

"*Haven't you not realized yet?*" he growls. "*I have lost my* child. *The child you will lead me back to.*"

The shock drives the heat from my face. "Amaya? Amaya is your bonded companion?"

He merely blinks at me.

"But why did you not say something?" I slide to my knees before him. "If you knew where she was—?"

But he's looking at me, and I feel that debt of knowledge sink into my bones like lead.

"*She is my child, and I promised I would protect her with my life,*" he tells me, his voice serious for once. "*And I would have given my life when the fetches came to get her. I saw it as clearly as I can see the grief on your face. It didn't matter how many times I tried to twist the future, it all came down to the same scene: I died, and they took my child anyway."*

"Then why are you here—?"

"There was one future that led me down a different path. A single future in which I could protect her, and that future meant I had to abandon her. I had to let her be taken and find the one person who could save her: Her mother. And don't think it didn't cost me. I abandoned her in the moment she needed me most, and I couldn't tell her why for fear it would interfere with my possibilities."

The one person who could save her….

I kneel back on my haunches, sick with grief. "We're going to rescue her?"

His green eyes hold the weight of the world. *"I don't know."* He hesitates. *"You are the* leanabh an dàn. *You twist fate, Princess. I see a thousand possibilities around you, but I don't see the end of our journey. I only see… a Hallow, an ancient god rising, and a princess sobbing as she rocks her daughter in her arms. I never see beyond that moment in time, but I do know this: You will find her. And you will hold her in your arms before tomorrow ends."*

"Vi?" Thiago murmurs, stepping out of the cottage and resting a hand on my shoulder. "What's he saying?"

I didn't realize I was the only one who could hear Grimm, so I swiftly fill him in.

"There is one last thing," Grimm tells me, and his eyes glow so golden I can't look away from them. *"If you set out for the Black Keep, then the Horned One will be freed from his prison. You will hold your daughter in your arms, this I promise, but in doing so, you will set about a chain of events that sees him freed."*

A punch of breath escapes me.

The only way the Horned One can break free is if powerful blood is spilled within his Hallow—if Angharad manages to complete her sacrifice.

"If we don't go, he will rise anyway. Her blood will be just as powerful as my own. But if there is a possibility we could rescue Amaya, then I will take it."

"If you get to her in time, then she will survive."

And I note how carefully Grimm phrased everything.

He said I would hold Amaya in my arms. He said the Horned One will rise. And Amaya will survive.

But he didn't say that I would walk out of there alive.

Maybe that's the price I must pay to keep her safe.

"Vi?" Thiago demands.

I slide my hand over his, squeezing gently. "If we go to Black Keep, then Amaya will be safe. She will survive." And I look up at him and don't tell him my suspicions. "Grimm says I'll hold her in my arms. We will have our daughter back."

I just don't say for how long.

CHAPTER 34

I close my eyes as Thiago carries me back to the Hallow, trying to open the line between myself and the fetch. I've seen through its eyes before, but I've been trying to fight the link between us for so long, that it's not until I touch the white hand mark on my arm—where it touched me once—that I manage to get through.

I thought I'd killed it when I blasted it with light, but it must have twisted into the Shadow Ways at the last moment.

I open my eyes to a dark hallway, and there's a weight dangling at the end of my hand.

"Let me go!" the little girl screams, sinking her white teeth into our hand.

Pain jars through me, and I can't stop him as he backhands her across the face. She slams into the wall, and I'm screaming in my head, trying to stop him from touching her, when he goes still.

He turns to look at the wall—toward my mortal body

—and then I'm no longer in his skin. Instead, we're staring at each other across the distance.

"You will die," I tell him, "if you ever touch my daughter again."

The fetch merely smiles and hauls Amaya to her feet.

"Too late, little bitch queen," he whispers. "She is bound for the Horned One now."

He makes a sharp cutting gesture, and the world drops away. I try to reach for her, my gaze meeting hers, but—

I jolt back to awareness in Thiago's arms, gasping for breath.

"She was so close," I whisper. "I saw her face. Her eyes. She has your eyes."

"We'll get her back, Vi."

Heat floods behind my eyes. I promised I would protect her. I promised that all she would ever know is love.

But there's no time for tears.

Only rage.

My mother never broke me. I won't allow this to do so either. Amaya needs me.

He slowly sets me on my feet.

"Take me to the Hallow," I whisper.

"We're not ready," he says. "Eris and Baylor are redistributing our packs and trying to—"

"Not to travel," I tell him. "I need to talk to the Mother of Night."

"Vi—"

"No." I turn and press my palm against his cheek, thumb stroking the stubble along his jaw. "I love you, Thiago. I do. But there is no more time for second guessing. I need to see *her*."

And this time, I do not go to bargain.

I CLOSE MY EYES AS I LIE IN THE SNOW IN THE CENTER OF THE Hallow.

"*Are you there?*"

My stomach plummets. The ground drops away.

And when I open them, I'm standing within the Mother of Night's prison world. Soft lights pick through the darkness, but the Mother waits for me, her hood in place and her dark eyes implacable as she rests her hands on the arms of her throne.

Rage beats within my chest like a flurry of bird's wings; some part of me feels empty and scraped raw. Perhaps my chest *is* nothing more than a cage, my ribs the bloody bars? Perhaps there is a bird in there, waiting to be released, though if it is, then it's a falcon, and its claws knot in my guts even as I think it.

"They took my daughter," I tell her.

She merely tilts her head. "Yes."

She knew. She knew all along when I first came to her, rash with promises.

We stare at each other.

"You have the crown in your possession," she says. "But you did not bring it with you."

"No, I didn't." I pace the circle of stone below her dais. "Did you know that my mother spent years stealing my memories from me so I would dance to her tune? I thought I found freedom with Thiago, but there you were, whispering in the shadows…, manipulating me just as she did.

"I'm tired of being manipulated. I'm tired of being a

pawn. I'm tired of having everything I've ever loved, everything I've ever hoped for taken away from me."

"You have more to lose."

"Is that a threat?" My voice roughens.

"It is merely an observation." She slowly shakes her head. "You are so young. So rash…. You made a bargain with me, Iskvien, and you have not paid the terms of it."

"It's not yet the end of the year. I owe you nothing."

There's an ancient sense of sadness in her eyes that I didn't expect. "If you go to the Black Keep, a part of you won't return."

And there it is….

Confirmation of everything I know in my heart.

I try to breathe through it, try to ignore it. I'm not ready to die. I want to see Amaya smile. I want to tell her how much I love her. But if there is one thing my mother has taught me, it's how to lock away your heart and focus on what's right in front of you. I swallow. Hard. "Worried about your crown? If we're all dead, then our bargain is broken. You get nothing."

"You are no match for the Horned One."

"But that's where you're wrong. I don't have to be." Striding up the dais, I rest both hands on the edges of her throne and lean forward, until I can almost taste her breath. "Because all I need is an Old One to counter his magic, and all my books say you were the only one with the power to stand against him. You want the crown? Then you will protect me from Angharad's magic and the Horned One's power. *If* I return from the Black Keep with my daughter, I will give you the fucking thing the second I arrive in Ceres. I will ram it so far down your throat that you can taste it."

Her black eyes remain unmoved. "You are growing in power. But you should be careful how you speak to me, Daughter of Darkness. Because we are not done yet."

"No? Well here is what I know…. You need me or you need my daughter in order to free yourself and your kind. Right now, Amaya is in danger. They're going to use her as a sacrifice to bring that bastard back. And I am going to rescue her. If you want to protect your asset, then you will do as I say."

I turn and walk away.

And with a click of my fingers, I tap into the power of the Hallow and step back into the real world.

It's becoming a little easier each time.

But I see the relief on Thiago's face as he drags me out of the circle and into his arms. "What did she say?"

"Nothing. But she'll protect me." I give a rough, bitter-edged laugh. "She has no choice."

I stare through the open arch of the Hallow at the full moon that floats through darkening skies. Not quite night, though the caress of it darkens the horizon. Soft footsteps pad through the snow behind me, and I know before I turn who they belong to.

"You," I say dully.

Grimm curls his tail around himself, staring at me. *"Well?"*

"Well, what?" I snap. "Have you not done enough?"

"For a creature with such large tapered ears, you do not seem to listen very well."

I've had enough. I rest my hand on the hilt of my

439

sword and stalk into the Hallow, where Eris is dumping weaponry in preparation for our trip to the Black Keep.

"Ask me again when the moon is full, your heart is torn in two, and you have no more hope remaining," he calls.

And my feet slow.

My heart beats with rage. The others are waiting at the Hallow for me. And my daughter—

But I slowly turn around. "You want me to ask how Maia defeated Sylvian *now*?"

He looks pointedly at the full moon.

"Fine." I stalk toward him. "Tell me, o wise one…. How did Maia defeat her sister-queen? How does any of this help me find my daughter?"

"Tell me about Charun."

I swear…. "I don't have time for this—"

"Yes, you do."

I gnaw on the inside of my cheek. "Charun was an ancient Hallow that was destroyed when Maia battled Sylvian."

"It was an origin Hallow," he corrects.

"Fine, it was an origin…."

And a stray thought occurs.

The origin Hallows are where the Old Ones are bound into their prison worlds. But Charun was never one of the prison Hallows—there was no Old One tied to that Hallow. It was destroyed thousands of years ago. And there were only thirteen Old—

Wrong, whisper my instincts. There were dozens of Old Ones that the otherkin worshipped. Pages and pages of them in Imerys's book.

The image of those three moons sear themselves in my mind's eye, and suddenly they're superimposed by the golden lines of three moons bound together—the symbol for the Daughter of the Three Moons.

Suddenly, there's a furry gray cat in my vision, staring at me smugly.

"*Behold,*" he mocks. "*The pieces fall into place.*"

"I don't understand what this has to do with anything. The Hallow at Charun served the Daughter of the Three Moons, who no longer exists. I'd thought the Mother of Night absorbed her into her mythos and stole her worshippers, but how does Maia fit in?"

Grimm leans closer. "*Do you think you are the first* leanabh an dàn?"

The world drops out from beneath me.

Of course not. The Mother told me that herself.

But….

He leans closer. "*Maia bound herself to the lands. She made herself the first bound queen. She began her life as fae, but by the time she ascended, she was so much more.*"

The lands…. Which were tied to the Old Ones and their powers of nature.

But how? How does Charun fit into anything?

And then my breath catches.

I see the obliterated Hallow, those runes blown out of the stone, and its power weak and ebbing. Something drained them. Something massive. Nearly two thousand years later and the Hallow has barely recovered, as though it will always be a shadow of itself.

"*Maia made a deal with the Mother of Night,*" the grimalkin patiently explains, "*when she went to fight Sylvian. She knew her armies and her own powers were barely a match for her sister-queen's, and so she made sure she was going to win. Maia didn't merely ascend to godhood, little princess.*"

She bound herself to the Daughter of Three Moons' Hallow and wrestled her power from her. And then she obliterated Sylvian and her armies. They say the light of her implosion swept from sea to sea."

"I still don't understand what this has to do with my daughter," I snap.

Grimm's eyes narrow. *"You are going to the Black Keep to rescue your daughter from Angharad, who plans to sacrifice her to the Hallow in order to break the Horned One free from his prison, are you not?"*

I can't breathe again. But I nod.

Grimm stalks forward on predatory paws. *"That is my child they plan to sacrifice, and while I am omnipotent, I cannot do this alone. If they raise the Horned One, then we are going to be facing an old god of unimaginable power."* His eyes flare gold. *"If we fail, then bind yourself to the Hallow and I will get the child out of there. Wrest his power from him. You have Maia's blood in your veins. You have the power of the Old Ones. It's our only hope."*

"I am not a—"

"God?" Grimm curls his lip. *"Well, neither was Maia. But every fae on the continent prays to that bitch at night, and I don't hear her complaining about it."*

BIND MYSELF TO THE HALLOW. WRESTLE WITH THE HORNED One. Steal his power.

I bite my lip as the others gather in the middle of the clearing.

I'm not powerful. I'm not a goddess. I'm just a woman who wants her daughter back.

And he was the most powerful of all the Old Ones.

Yes, something whispers in my mind, *but he is also trapped. If he is freed, he will be newly reawakened in this world. Weaker than he ever was. Hungry. Possibly vulnerable.*

I feel sick.

"Are you ready?" I ask as I stand in the middle of the Hallow.

Thiago slashes a knife over his forearm, drawing enough blood to power the glyphs that will take us north. He decided I should reserve my strength for the fight ahead. "Ready."

He looks at me, and I see the question in his eyes.

Am I ready?

I step forward and capture a fistful of his shirt, hauling his mouth toward mine. It's a kiss born of passion and desperation. A kiss meant to convey everything I feel for him.

I love you, I tell him with my lips.

And then we're both breathing hard, foreheads pressed against each other's. His hand slides through my hair, as if he too feels the weight of the future upon us.

"Thank you," I whisper. "For everything."

He gave me freedom when I could not see it for myself. He's offered me nothing but love, ever since the first moment we laid eyes upon each other.

"I am honored to be your wife."

His eyes narrow. "What are you planning, Vi?"

"Planning?"

His fist curls in my hair. "That sounds like goodbye. That sounds like you're plotting to do something foolish."

"We go to face Angharad and the Horned One. Is that not foolish enough?"

He looks at me.

I close my eyes and breathe him in. He's moonlight and darkness; smoke on the wind; the scent of burned cinnamon. My promise. My hope. My dream.

He's been there at my side at every step of the way.

And he deserves the truth.

"There's a possibility I could bind myself to the Horned One's Hallow," I whisper, "and wrest his power from him if he rises."

"He will not rise," Thiago growls. "I will not lose you. I will not lose Amaya. And if that bitch thinks she's going to harm either of you, then she knows not what she faces. We just have to get to Amaya and protect her. Angharad will have her bound within the Hallow. The second we're all within its circumference, use the Hallow to get us out of there."

It's a simple plan.

They're always the best.

I nod, and he kisses my forehead.

"Vi." One last kiss-roughened word. I look up, and Thiago's eyes turn sultry as he strokes my cheek. "Promise me you will get her out. Promise thrice."

To promise three times locks me into a vow I won't be able to break. "I promise—if I get a chance—that I will get her out of there." And then I repeat the words twice.

"Even if I—or one of the others—isn't within the Hallow."

My lips stutter over the words.

"Done," he whispers, and I feel the vow grab hold of me.

"On one condition," I add.

Thiago goes still.

"Promise me thrice that if you're the first to reach her and everything is going badly, then you will do the same."

His jaw tightens.

But he gives me his oath, and then we both lean against each other.

"It's time," Eris says behind us.

I break away from him, breathing hard. It's done. No matter what happens, Amaya will be safe.

Thiago tugs on the gauntlet that will conceal his powers. It makes his magic a mere whisper, and I can barely feel him through the bond we share, but his powers brew within him, and the second he needs to unleash his full strength, he can.

"Are we all ready?" Thiago calls.

"To serve the Darkness, I am ready," Finn replies.

"To serve the Darkness," Eris says with a nod.

"To serve the Darkness," Baylor growls, reaching over his head to draw his massive broadsword.

Grimm leaps up on my shoulders. *"I only serve myself,"* he sneers. *"But I'll accompany you to the end, if need be."*

"Let's go then." Thiago reaches out and smears his blood across the glyph that will take us to the Black Keep. The Hallow hums, the earth staring to vibrate beneath our feet. The Hallow snaps shut around us, spinning me into nothingness.

An instant that seems like forever.

And then I slam back into my body as we finally arrive in the foothills above the Black Keep.

Right into the middle of a pack of unseelie warriors armed with banes on leashes.

CHAPTER 35

There's blood on the snow. Blood on my clothes.

I can feel it hot on my cheeks and wet in my hair.

And even though they're dead—even though they're all dead—something inside me howls for more blood.

There's no way directly inside the Black Keep—the Hallow there is on an unconnected ley line that doesn't cross any others besides this one—so the nearest Hallow is here, in the foothills of the Dragon's Teeth mountain range. It's the main source of transport for Angharad's troops, and there were over twenty stationed here before we arrived.

I didn't know that until Eris tortured it out of one of the guards.

Thiago slowly lowers his sword, breathing hard. "Are they all down?"

Eris moves through the snow, stabbing her blade into bodies with ruthless efficiency. "Down and dead."

Blood still hums through my veins. It was a short and

brutal fight. We'd caught them by surprise, and by the time they'd drawn their weapons, we were upon them. The leader barely had time to scramble for his horn before Eris drew her sword behind her head and then heaved it at him from across the clearing.

She puts her boot on his head as I watch and yanks her blade free. The horn remains silent in the snow.

"Do you think anyone heard?" Thiago demands.

Baylor scans the hills, his nostrils flaring. "There's no sound of anyone nearby. And I can't scent anything."

"None of them are loaded with equipment to stay out here for the night, which means they'll be due to check in sometime in the next half day," Eris guesses. "Or another company will be coming to replace them, but I don't know how soon. And the Black Keep is only an hour away. There will be patrols out and about."

"Drag them out of the Hallow and strip them of their armor," Thiago says, "then cover their bodies with snow. We need all the delay we can get."

And then he turns and uses a blast of wind to stir the snow so that it covers the blood.

THE BLACK KEEP LOOMS BELOW US IN THE VALLEY, A CENTRAL spire soaring toward the heavens. Thick walls guard it, and steep cliffs slide away from it like skirts. There's only one way in; a long narrow bridge that arcs over nothingness toward it.

Now I know why Thiago insisted upon bringing the armor.

We strip off our outer clothes and fit ourselves into the

bloody assortment of armor we stole from the Unseelie. Everything is black—which hides the blood well—but there's a soaring white wyvern emblazoned on my chest, and another one on the shield I can barely lift. It's taller than I am.

"This isn't going to work," Baylor mutters. "Iskvien's too short to be mistaken for one of Angharad's warriors."

Thiago considers me. "He's right. Get dressed again. You can be our prisoner."

"You do realize it's freezing," I growl, dumping the shield with pleasure. "You could have realized this flaw in the plan before I removed my nice warm coat." I strip out of the black leathers and haul my own clothes on again.

"And now we just need some fog," Thiago whispers, staring at the valley. "Vi, can you see through our fetch's eyes?"

It makes my skin creep every time I try, but I need to know what's happening inside the keep. Grimm promised that no harm would come to Amaya until night falls—and the Black Keep is much further west than Old Mother Hibbert's cottage was. Though the sun is slinking toward the horizon, the moon hasn't bared her shimmering face yet.

Taking a deep breath, I slip the bracelet off and reach for the fetch that's bound to me.

—*chanting echoes through an enormous hall, and unseelie sway as they call for their dark god to rise. A little girl yanks at her chains, her teeth bared in fury as I step between the stones of the Hallow*—

I pull back and slam the bracelet on so that the fetch won't sense me. "She's alive."

Just scared and desperate.

"How soon can you call in that fog?"

"Give me twenty minutes," Thiago murmurs, his eyes distant as he stares across the gulf between us and the Black Keep. "Anything faster will draw attention."

I pace the ledge.

It surprises me how beautiful it is up here.

Despite the snow and the sheared-off mountains in the background, there's a purity to the world that makes my chest hurt. Ever since I bound myself to Evernight, I've been able to feel the land breathing beneath my feet, and though we're a long way from home, there's something stirring beneath me.

I reach down and stir the snow away from the ground with a wisp of wind before placing my palm flat on the ground.

Somewhere beneath the castle the earth bucks and twists…. It feels like the land is screaming, like it's trying to force solid stone to become diamond.

And then I find that pressure point.

"Who are you?" asks a little voice.

I rip my palm away.

And realize Grimm is watching me.

"You can hear her," he murmurs. *"She's always been gifted. She's always been drawn to the land. She is a natural queen who will rule this world if she's given the chance."*

I slowly press my palm back to the rock. I don't dare reply—I don't know who else is listening, or if they even can.

But I don't want her to feel alone.

"Amaya?" I breathe.

There's a sense of stillness as if she's listening to me. Wondering, perhaps.

"I am someone who loves you very much," I whisper, and I can sense her reaching for that thread of thought.

Somewhere inside that keep, my daughter stirs and places her palm flat on the stone beneath her, the chains jangling around her wrist.

And I gasp as I feel our palms touch.

"You're like me," she whispers.

I close my eyes and curl my fingers through hers. *"I'm like you."* I want to tell her that I'm coming for her, but I don't dare, just in case someone else hears. All I can give her is this…. *"You're not alone. You will never be alone."*

"I'm so frightened."

"Be brave." I squeeze her little hand, sending all my love down the bond between us.

And then there's the sensation of a sudden looming darkness turning toward me. I give Amaya one last squeeze, and then I tuck myself up small and quiet, severing my link to the lands.

Silence.

Nothing follows me down that link.

But I can almost feel a pair of eyes turning outward from the keep, as if that other entity knows that something's not right.

I don't know how long I've been gone, but fog blankets the valley.

The walls and towers of the keep are carved from obsidian that's been strengthened with spell craft, but with the sun no longer shining, it merely looks like a dull black castle now.

"Are we ready?" I ask.

Thiago lowers his hands.

And then he nods.

WE CROSS THE BRIDGE, THE OTHER FOUR MARCHING IN UNISON around me. My hands are bound loosely in front of me with rough rope, and the hood of my cape is drawn over my head.

"Halt," calls a rough voice, and a sentry strides through the gates. "Who are you?"

"Isbarrion of the Wyldwoods, come to rally to Angharad's banner," Thiago lies, his helmet obscuring most of his face.

"I've not seen you before."

Thiago stares at him insolently. "I've not been here before. We came to make a pledge to our queen, if she'll have us."

"Oh, she'll have you. War's on the winds." The sentry grins. "Vengeance is coming to those down south who thought to force us to our knees."

"I'd like to see that. Do you know where the royal sorcerer is? We were riding for the keep when we caught this one"—he jerks a thumb over his shoulder toward me —"by the lake. Thought she'd make a nice little gift for Isem, considering we're late. You know he likes them young and pretty."

The sentry glances at me. "The pet is busy."

"Careful where you say that," Thiago growls. "The walls have ears, and I've heard it said the sorcerer is always listening."

Their eyes meet, and maybe there's enough truth in that to disabuse the sentry of any uncertainty here.

Isem sits at Angharad's right hand, and I've met the pale little weasel several times; enough to know that to the common folk—the warriors in Angharad's armies—he's probably not well-liked.

The sentry spits. "They're in the Well of Tears. His Pastiness gave the order that they weren't to be disturbed."

"Guess there's time for me to have a little fun with my prize," Thiago leers, grabbing a handful of my backside, "until he's got time for me."

A horn suddenly cuts through the mountains behind us just as I try to slap his hand away.

I freeze, my head whipping around.

And then Thiago growls under his breath, still playing at being the guard who's drawn a shitty duty. "Now what?"

"Trouble," the sentry says, then curses under his breath. "Looks like none of us are getting any rest tonight. Take her to the dungeons and lock her in. Then you'd best get your ass back to the yard. That horn belongs to Vargas, and he was due to take over the watch at the Hallow." The sentry steps aside. "Let them in, boys. And send a runner up to the keep to fetch Urivel. Tell him they're calling for backup out there by the Hallow."

Thiago tugs on my ropes and jerks me into the keep. The others follow.

"Prize?" I growl.

"They're a little more primitive here in Angharad's court. This way," Thiago says, taking an abrupt left into the heart of the keep. He grabs me by the forearm. "Glare at me as though you want to bite my throat out."

That won't be difficult. "Did you have to grope me in front of that prick?"

"Yes, I did. He was trying to peer under your hood."

He shoves me past a trio of marching soldiers, barely even looking at them. I can't believe nobody's raised a cry yet, but Thiago moves as if he owns the castle. Of course, he always moves like that, but there's something about the set of his shoulders and the look on his face that makes it very clear he knows where he is and where he's going.

Nobody dares get in his way to question him.

"Do you know where we're going?" I gasp, scurrying to keep up with him, "Or are you simply guessing?"

"I know where I'm going."

I shoot him a look.

His lips press thinly together as he pushes me toward the left. "I came looking for my father once. I wanted to kill him, but he was riding at Angharad's side then, surrounded by an entire army of unseelie. I was much younger, and the only way to get close enough was to infiltrate her army and work my way closer to the keep. I served here for several months before I realized that even if I got close to him, I was never going to be able to kill him."

"Will... Amaya...?"

I can tell he hasn't thought of it. His brow furrows. "I hope not. I hope there's no piece of me inside her. Not like that. She deserves to know peace."

"Which way?" Eris asks as we reach a branch in the tunnel.

Thiago pauses and glances to the left. "This way. We're going down now. The Well of Tears is not far. I think it best if we keep our mouths shut from now on."

Torches line the walls of the Well of Tears, and banes prowl the open cavern. But it's the set of standing stones that have been hauled into an upright position by pulleys that captures my attention.

This is where the Horned One is bound.

And I can see from the cleave lines through the base of the stones that they fell at one stage. When the Alliance of Light came for the Horned One, he clearly didn't go easy. Power sheared through those stones, and someone's resurrected them and resealed them with melted brass.

The Hallow pulses.

But it's an odd beat.

An echo.

As if the power that flows through the stones meets that brass line and takes a second to skip over it through the rest of the stone.

Dozens of banes are chained to the walls. Another dozen or so unseelie warriors stand guard with their hands on their swords. They're not like the ones in the foothills. No, these ones wear black markings tattooed on their cheeks, and there's a hardness to their eyes and bodies that assures me they won't be easy to defeat.

But it's the sight of the three fetches standing between us and the Hallow that makes my heart pound in my ears.

"How are we going to get past them?" I whisper.

Grimm suddenly shimmers into the physical world, wending his way through my legs. "*Consider them mine, Princess. I'll make the Shadows so dangerous they won't dare fade into them.*"

And then he's gone again.

A guard turns, frowning at our sudden appearance.

"What are you doing down here? The queen is not to be disturbed while she—"

He suddenly sees the blood dripping from Thiago's short sword, and his tongue trips over itself. There were five guards outside, but Thiago dispatched them with ruthless efficiency.

The guard's eyes widen. "You're not—"

Thiago lunges forward, grabbing him by the helmet and yanking him onto the blade. A soft cry chokes out from the guard's mouth, but Thiago catches him as he slumps, and tries to ease him back into the shadows.

Too late.

Another guard notices. "What are you—?"

One of Finn's arrows suddenly sprouts in his throat. He goes down with a clatter, and every head in the Well turns sharply toward us.

"Well, fuck," Baylor growls, drawing both of his massive swords.

"Cover me," Eris yells at Finn, and then she's leaping over the edge of the stairs and landing in a crowd of unseelie.

"Vi!"

I turn at Thiago's yell, and he slashes his sword through the ropes that are bound loosely around my wrists. Tugging a dagger free, he tosses it toward me, and then he's turning, the arc of his sword gleaming as it slices through the throat of an unseelie warrior.

They attack us in droves, and there's no time to think. Only time to move. I duck the whine of a sword, grabbing the bastard's arm as he extends and stabbing my dagger into the vulnerable patch under his arm. A wheeze escapes him as I hit the lung, and then I draw it out and whip it across his throat.

Blood splashes my cheeks.

I kick his fallen sword into my hand and leap over his body, bringing both weapons up to block an overhead swing. The vibration jolts up my arms. But all my training has been against warriors both taller and heavier than I am. I deflect the blow to the side and spin low, onto my knees, the bite of my dagger slashing through a hamstring.

The fight is short and brutal, and some part of me relishes the blood.

I drive my sword straight through a guard's gut. *This is for Old Mother Hibbert.*

Another one lunges at me.

For all those children who ran in fear....

For me.

For Amaya.

It's that thought that nearly undoes me. *Amaya.* I turn for the Hallow once more, and this time I catch a glimpse of her, gaping at us as if she can't believe her eyes.

Bending low, I smack my palm against the stone floor, feeling the ripple of my blow vibrate through the floor toward her. *"Be brave,"* I tell her. *"We're coming for you."*

Amaya looks down at her palms, as if she heard me.

The room seems to vanish.

All I can see is her.

A little girl dressed in a pale white smock, her tiny wrists manacled to the middle of the Hallow, where she cowers from the banes that snap at her and the fetches that laugh as she begs.

Fear drains away.

I know what I must do.

"Cover me," I say, walking toward her.

As much as I yearn to smear blood across the floors, my fight doesn't begin or end with a sword.

"Vi!" Thiago snaps, but I'm already past his reach.

"Just get me to that Hallow."

I am going to get my daughter back.

He lunges forward, turning a blade that was meant for me. Another unseelie sprints toward me, but he goes down with an arrow in the throat. And then Eris is there, her sword held low as she guards my right flank.

"*Can you hear me?*" I call out to the Mother of Night.

There's no answer, but I can feel her presence over my shoulder, like thunder thickening the air on the horizon. The little hairs down my spine lift. And I give myself to the Hallow.

There's something wrong with it.

Not merely the way the stones were cut, but with the Hallow itself.

Every other Hallow I've met has been a conduit between the ley lines and myself, but this one doesn't give up its energy. It drinks it in, like a sucking chasm of nothingness that seeks to fill itself. It feels like reaching your arm into a bottomless pool of oil; thick and viscous and choking. I could drown in that pool if I let myself, and it would slowly haul me under, a clammy sucker mouth clamping over mine as it drinks the very oxygen from my veins.

Something watches me.

Something enormous in the dark.

A little flutter swims through my stomach, but there's a hand in mine, suddenly squeezing.

"*If you stare too long into the abyss,*" the Mother of Night whispers in my ear, "*then you risk capturing His attention. He is Darkness, Princess. True and utter Darkness, and you don't want that staining your soul.*"

I have to stare back if I want to have any hope of binding myself to the Hallow.

But she squeezes my hand again. "*Not this Hallow, Iskvien. If you bind yourself here—now—then all you will do is drink your own poison.*"

"How do I defeat him?" I cry.

"*You don't.*"

"They're going to kill her."

I can see Angharad now, her bare feet slapping on the stone as her black skirts whisk around her legs. She moves like a creature of the night, drawing the long thin dagger from her hip as she grabs Amaya's wrist.

Isem, her pet sorcerer, stands by the Hallow chanting.

"Please," cries a small voice. "Please don't hurt me."

And everything inside me goes still.

They're the first words I've ever heard Amaya physically say—and I know, with a mother's instinct, that they come from *her* mouth.

"That's enough." The voice trembles through the cavern, shaking rocks from the walls.

I lift my sword, but my hand pauses as Angharad hauls my daughter upright and puts a knife to her throat.

"Throw down your weapons," she commands with a cruel smile.

"Don't you touch her." The words are a growl from my throat. "If you hurt her, then I swear I will destroy you. I will destroy this entire fucking Hallow, so you can never resurrect him."

Reaching out, I summon the power through the Hallow.

The sensation of that dark presence is stronger, and its attention turns to me the second I link with the Hallow, but this time I push further. I slip past that leviathan waiting in its dark waters and plunge directly to the Hallow's core.

There.

There's the ley line.

And I know Angharad can feel the floor shivering beneath her feet, because she looks down in shock before slowly lifting her head.

Our eyes meet.

"It seems we are at a bit of an impasse." Angharad bares her teeth in a smile, and Amaya squeals with fright as the knife clearly cuts in.

"Stop!" I scream, holding that roiling power within my grasp but helpless to do anything with it.

"Throw down your weapons," Angharad commands again, and this time, it's not a suggestion.

"Thiago?" Eris asks.

"Do as she says."

Swords clatter as they strike the ground. It doesn't matter. We were never going to defeat her with steel.

A warm body brushes against my legs, more of a reminder than a creature fully formed.

"Grimm," I whisper.

"I will protect her with my life," he tells me before he fades into the shadows. *"Keep that bitch queen's attention on you."*

"You've been very elusive, Princess," Angharad calls. "Invisible even to my Heartless. I was starting to grow a

459

little vexed, but then my commander realized there was another little thread of light calling to him. A child who could sing to the Hallows. A child who walked the snowy north, shielded by an old hag and dozens of other children. It took him a long time to find her, but when he did, what a curiosity she was. A child of destiny with no mother or father. A child who had been abandoned. A child with the power to break the world."

"She wasn't abandoned," I snap, and this time, my gaze meets Amaya's. "My mother stole her from me, and if I had known for one second that Amaya was out there, I would have stopped at nothing to find her."

"Ah." Angharad leans low, resting her chin on Amaya's shoulder. "It's enough to bring tears to one's eyes. Your mother came for you, child. She loves you enough to spring my trap. But it will be too late." Angharad's voice rises. "Because the child's magic supersedes the mother's. My lord god desires a sacrifice of immense proportions, and now I have my heart set on—"

She suddenly screams as a set of teeth sinks into her hand, and a shadowy figure forms, his weight driving Angharad's hand away from Amaya's throat.

"Thiago!" He's closer than I am.

"Rouse the Hallow!" he snaps as he sprints toward them.

Amaya throws herself aside, but her chains haul her up short.

Angharad screams and stabs her knife into the shadow that tears at her hand. Grimm howls as he's flung aside, but he crawls to Amaya, hissing weakly as he glares at the queen.

"You filthy little cur!" Angharad screams.

Light blooms through my veins. The Hallow ignites. And the world around me turns to nothing more than shadows as I glow with so much light that every creature around us cries out and throws their arms over their faces.

The fetches scream, vanishing through the last traces of shadow.

A whine hisses past my ear, and I'm focusing so completely on the Hallow that for a second, I don't even feel it. But the slam of the arrow into my shoulder drives the breath from my lungs, and suddenly the Hallow is torn from my grip.

I scream as I hit the ground, losing my grasp on all of that power.

"Now!" Angharad bellows, and her fetches suddenly reappear and close ranks between us and the Hallow.

The pain makes me want to vomit.

But Thiago's inside that ring.

"*Go,*" I whisper to him. "*Get her out.*"

Grabbing the arrow by the shaft, I try to roll to my knees. Pain and darkness shoot through me. It's close to the bone, I think.

And then Eris is there, grabbing the shaft from my hands.

"Bite down," she says, shoving her leather glove between my teeth.

Stars swirl through a night sky in my mind as she snaps the arrow. I scream through the leather, saliva gushing from my mouth.

"We'll cut it out later," she says, slipping an arm under my shoulder and hauling me to my feet. "Focus on the Hallow."

Red light and shadows wage war within the Hallow

stones. Thiago takes a menacing step toward Angharad, tearing off his gauntlet. Suddenly every inch of our bond clicks into place, his magic rushing through the world. Darkness unfurls behind him like a pair of shadowy wings, and I can hear whispers—almost on the edge of hearing.

They're quiet tonight, his daemons.

Almost as if they know where we are and what we face.

But there's nothing but determination in his expression.

The world plunges into a primeval darkness. My heart stutters in my chest, a scream of fear trapped in my throat. I've never felt his power fully unleashed, but there's something large and dangerous within those shadows, a predator that makes even me want to flee....

A spark of red light burns within the darkness.

A spark of rage.

And then there's a whisper: "Where have *you* been hiding, my little darkyn?" And then Angharad laughs. "Of course. How did I not see it? She was such a beautiful queen. So powerful. So full of rage and defiance. Of course he would have sought to break her, but your mother clearly had one last little secret to keep."

The darkness burns away. Chains of red fire lash around Thiago's throat and chest, but he cleaves them with a single stroke of his hand.

"I wonder if your father knows of your existence?" Angharad muses.

His shadows lunge for her, swallowing her in a cloud of darkness. For a second I think she's gone, but then her laughter echoes through the cavern. A red collar forms around one of the shadows, and it screams with rage. Another collar glows. A second daemon is struck down, writhing on the floor at her feet.

Angharad straightens as the other three draw back. "Your father taught me many tricks, little princeling. But there are some things even he did not know." She spins red light to life in her hands. "When Death fell, they carved him apart with the fires of the Underworld." Hot light burns around her fingers. "It is the only thing the shades of Death's soul fear."

Lunging forward, the light in her hand's forms into a sword, and she sweeps it through the nearest shadow daemon.

The scream it makes almost shatters my eardrums. I clap my hands over my ears.

When it's finally, blessedly over, I see Thiago on his knees.

Four of his daemons writhe around his shoulders, but there's fear in them now. All those malicious little whispers are muted.

"If your father could see you now," Angharad spits, "he would tear your head from your shoulders for daring to pretend you're even a hint of what he is."

Thiago looks at me. Simply looks. "I am a million times the man my father is."

There's a thousand words in the narrow flicker of his eyes. Desperation. Determination. And love.

A father's love for the child he's never known.

"Don't," I whisper. *"Get her out of here."*

But it's too late.

He climbs to his feet.

Angharad laughs, light flooding from the crack at her

feet. She grabs a fistful of Amaya's hair and puts the knife to my daughter's throat. "Not another step closer, dark prince."

"You want your sacrifice?" he growls. "Then take me instead."

No. I start to climb down the slope, slipping and sliding desperately.

"This is a child of the *dan*," she hisses. "Her power is absolute."

"And I am a child of Death."

He's never said it. Not out loud. But the sound of his voice cracks through the cavern, and I swear that every single creature in the place sucks in a sharp breath.

Angharad straightens, dragging the knife from Amaya's throat. Amaya cries out, trying to bite her knuckles, but Angharad merely shoves her away and turns to face Thiago.

My little girl hits the floor, and just for a second, our eyes meet.

I'm coming. I'm coming to get you. Just hold on.

"Take me," he calls. "And let her go."

Angharad freezes, as if she can sense some piece of a trap.

"Lower your shields," she calls.

Thiago pauses, and then he's opening to her—to me, to the world.

His essence almost overwhelms me.

In a heartbeat I know every inch of him; the boy who ran gleefully through a snowy forest with dozens of other children even as he yearned to find his true family; the warlord who knelt before a queen after saving the life of her firstborn son before grimly lifting his face to hers and hoping she would see him, hoping she would recognize him; the prince who hid his identity from the world so he would never besmirch her; the son who begged her to keep breathing, forcing his hands to try and still the blood-flow even as she lifted a tremulous hand and gently stroked his face for the first and only time....

This has to be one of Thiago's tricks. He's just trying to get closer to her. But my heart quickens with sudden dread.

"*I'm sorry, Vi.*" It's a whisper, a caress of sadness. "*For not having the time to show you how much I love you. She's too close to Amaya.*"

He half turns to look at me.

No, no, no, no, no.

A scream tears from my throat as Angharad darts forward, quick as a snake. She drives her blade right into his chest, and power explodes out through him, the Darkness whirling around him in one frenzied burst as if, even at the end, they choose to try and flee rather than defend him.

"*Thiago!*"

He forces his gaze to mine, a soft smile on his lips as he wraps his arms around Angharad, crushing her close to him.

"*You were my hope. You were my light. You were the queen I always dreamed of serving. Thank you.*"

And then he's gone.

It's like a knife through my heart, death scything through him with a vicious surge of power. I scream as his vibrant eyes grow dim, and then his body is falling and—

He's gone.

The warm, constant presence in my mind vanishes as if

it was never there, wrenched from me by a merciless grip. There is no us. There is only me, left alone and shaken in the depths of my wretched body.

"Thiago!" I scream as I sprint toward his falling body.

He hits the ground, his head bouncing, and even from here I can hear the crack as the stone in the center of the Hallow splits.

The Hallow has its kingly sacrifice.

Power shivers through the walls, a blinding white light shooting through the cracks in the stone and spearing into the heavens. It forces me to slow, but I have to get to him, I have to see him, to try—

And then light erupts.

A wave of force slams me to the ground. Pure power. An enormous shadowy form made of smoke spills from the Hallow. I hear a roar of fury echoing through a voice so deep and guttural that it vibrates through my chest.

And I start crawling.

I will not let him die alone.

I will not let him die for nothing.

All I can see is the little girl curled in a fetal position on the stone, and she *needs* me.

Angharad smiles, standing in the precise center of the Hallow. The glow of power suffuses her, and when she opens her eyes, they're an eerie, emotionless black. "Come forth, my lord."

Hot golden sparks form in the shadow's enormous head, burning into vicious eyes. The brimstone reek of him almost makes me gag, and sparks shoot from the cloud until I'm crawling over a bed of embers.

Close. So close....

A man steps out of the shadowy beast, naked and shivering. He stumbles to his knees, the muscles in his thighs trembling. Dark hair cascades down his spine in a tangled mane, and when he lifts his face to the ceiling, my heart almost stops at the sight of his horrifically beautiful face.

"My love," Angharad whispers, going to her knees before him and capturing his face in her hands.

But as those eyes open and I see the burning coals where his pupils should be, I know it's not the lover she's tried to bring back from the dead, but the Old One that even the Mother of Night fears.

He blinks, and then those hot coals are gone and his irises are dark enough to steal the light from his pupils. "My love," he whispers, cradling her face and bringing their mouths together.

"Vi!" Eris screams behind me. "Come back!"

Not without my daughter.

I shove to my feet, gaze locking on Amaya. Shadows coalesce around Thiago's body, as if whatever lived inside him is finally free. I can't take them both. I can't—

But maybe my magic will—

And then the Horned One breaks away from Angharad's kiss and turns his soul-searing eyes upon me.

He smiles and flings his hand out, diverting the spill of raw power that gushes from the heart of the earth.

A ring of fire explodes out from the Hallow.

I scream, throwing my hands up—

A figure appears in front of me, arms splaying wide, and I see a pale, beautiful face within her hood. Firm arms wrap around me just as the wall of magic hits.

We're both doused in fuel and set aflame. Nothing could survive this. Not even—

"*Just breathe,*" the Mother of Night whispers, her body

467

shielding mine from the blast of power. *"Breathe, Iskvien. Ride the power. Ride the wave. Let it flow through you."*

Every inch of me feels stretched and broken, as if the magic is incinerating me from within. I scream on and on, the sound torn from a shredded throat.

"You cannot fight it," she says, pressing my face into my shoulder. *"This is* ala. *It is the energy within woven into a force that will destroy all that cannot contain it. It is the world beneath your feet. It is the heart of Arcaedia unleashed through a crack in the surface. To fight it will destroy you."*

And maybe I want such oblivion.

Maybe I want something to make the pain go away.

"He's gone," I sob as I curl into her embrace.

"Yes. He is gone from this world." A gentle hand slides through my hair, and the impression of her voice softens. *"But you are not. And nor is your daughter. You need to live, Iskvien. You need to survive—"*

So I can set her free.

"Oh, child." She laughs sadly. *"If you could only see the future that I can see."*

The flow of power finally slows to a trickle.

And I gasp when I see what has happened to her. The right side of her face is burned and bloodied. Little cinders spark in her flesh, and ash breaks away from her, floating to the ground.

That could have been me.

That should have been me.

She protected me.

But now she's falling, and as she hits the ground, she dissolves into nothing and all I hear is *"This one last favor I do for you. Get your daughter. And escape. You must escape, because the Horned One is free, and he will be hungry."*

I scrabble to my hands and knees as her presence winks out.

Thiago's gone, nothing but a dark smear in the shape of his body remaining on the slate floor. Enormous wings of blackened ash paint the floor around him, but as I watch, a gust of wind sends the ash flying.

I snatch at the ash, but it vanishes between my hands, and suddenly this is all real.

He's gone.

He's gone, and I want to scream at the sudden emptiness in my chest—that hole where my heart should be. Where he should be.

But he did not die just to see me collapse. And the Mother of Night did not suffer just to see me fail.

I push to my feet, staring at the vortex of power that streams into the sky.

Amaya.

Amaya is all that matters.

I step between the Hallow stones, and power rips and tears at me. *Ride it*, the Mother said.

And so I do.

The instant I let the power flood through me, the world changes. It's no longer a gushing current that strips the flesh from my bones. It's a song of life, it's the whisper of winds through the trees, the rumble of the earth, the sound of coursing water raging over jagged rocks. It is everything and nothing. It is life.

Arcaedia.

It feels like the time I bound myself to the land, and for a second I wonder if the fae queens realize that this binding is similar to what the Old Ones do with their Hallows.

Did we absorb their custom?

Or did we steal it?

For the first time in my life, I tune into the other side of my nature, and my blood allows me to go to her.

Amaya huddles on the floor, sobbing into her hands. Chains manacle her narrow wrists, but I set hands to them and I can see every single little molecule that comprises the iron. It burns a little—my fae blood is strong enough to flinch at the feel of it—but I simply break them apart in my hands.

"Amaya."

She looks up, and the sight of her eyes is another stab through the heart.

I have this, I remind myself. *I have this last little gift from him.*

"Who are you?" she cries, trying to shield her face.

"I'm your mother." The whisper is torn from my lips. Her hair's so soft, and my eyes drink in every little aspect of that face. "I'm here to rescue you. We came for you because we love you." There's doubt in her eyes, and I drag her against me with with my uninsured arm, wrapping her in a hug that I need just as much as she does. "I love you. And I have finally found you. And I will never let you go. *Never.*"

My daughter.

My *daughter.*

And if I don't dare look at that shadowy smear on the stone, then perhaps I can pretend my heart hasn't broken in two.

He's gone.

But I barely have time for tears.

Because we aren't safe yet, and if there is one thing my

husband would want— Would have wanted from me, it is for his daughter to be safe.

"My queen." The words come from Finn. He squeezes my shoulder, and I gape at him as he holds out a hand, gesturing for me to step aside so he can carry Amaya. "What do we do?"

Every wall in the castle shakes. Lightning tears through the sky.

But it's the sound of those words.

My queen.

Without their prince, they have nothing. And it hits me all over again. "Don't call me that."

I never want to hear that word again.

Baylor falls into place beside Finn, his expression grim. "We need to leave."

He's gone.

And even as that black hole stretches wide inside my soul, consuming me from within, I know I have to pull myself together.

Amaya. Escape. Home.

I have to try.

"Eris?" I call.

She stands on the edge of the Hallow, staring across the distance at Angharad.

"Eris." I fill my voice with all the command I can muster, and her head snaps toward me. "Come." I press a kiss to the top of Amaya's head as I prepare to use the Hallow's power to take us all to safety. "We have to leave."

And when we are finally safe in Valerian, then and only then will I be able to let out the trapped scream that is lodged in my throat.

EPILOGUE

ANDRASTE

Some lies are never spoken. Some of them infuse every pore of your body. You become the lie. You wrap yourself so tightly in it that no one ever knows the truth of your heart.

"The spell backfired," Mother says, letting the pendant spin on its chain. Light flashes through the ruby, casting red glints across her ruined face. This is the first morning she's been able to venture from her apartments, and the damage the loss of her oak did to her is written over every inch of her skin. "I couldn't understand why. How did they steal my crown when it is warded to my hand alone?"

Edain pauses where he's pouring us both a goblet of wine.

But every inch of me is controlled as I reach for one of the strawberries on the platter between us. "I don't know, Mother. Perhaps—"

"And then I thought… what if it recognized her blood

somehow? After all, you've lifted it from my head at times. You've placed it back in its cabinet and locked it away for the night. It knows you. It knows I allow you to touch it. But your sister?" Her cold gaze sweeps to mine, and everything within me goes still. "I made certain Iskvien could never, ever take what was mine without conse- quences. I wove a curse around that crown that would blight your sister's pretty face should she dare take it from its resting place. And yet, there was not a single blemish on her skin."

"Perhaps she circumvented the curse." I stare her in the eyes, trying to control my racing heart. "We don't know the extent of Vi's powers. What she did to you at the Queensmoot—"

"Ah, yes." Mother captures the spinning ruby in her hand, her fingers closing around it like a cage. "The Queensmoot. Where you knelt before me and begged for their lives."

"A decision I have since regretted."

Mother turns to Edain. "Tell me, my love. Do you think my daughter stole my crown?"

There's no hint of his usual cruel smile as he meets my eyes and offers me a goblet of bloodred wine. "Yes," he says. "I know she stole it."

But he doesn't say which one.

This time, there's no controlling myself. He kissed me, and nothing has been the same ever since. My fingers bump against his, and wine spills as I try to take the goblet from him.

"You never lie to me," Mother croons, taking his hand and drawing it to her lips. "So many others do, you real- ize? But you always tell me the truth, Edain."

And she suddenly laughs.

My gaze jerks to his.

"I always thought that blood was the only thing I could trust, but when you have a daughter who has betrayed everything you ever stood for, you learn to trust nobody." Mother smiles at him. "And so I made it impossible for you to lie to me, didn't I, my love? I *bound* you to me. I choked you with chains of spell work so thick that you can never speak an untruth. You are mine, heart and soul, Edain. And you must never lie to me."

"I will never lie to you." It's as if the spell is broken, as if he can move again. He captures her hand and looks her boldly in the eye. "You are my queen. You are my everything."

I can't help thinking of the way he bandaged my wounds so gently. Of the way he kissed me. I want to gag.

What has he said to her?

What has he done?

"Do you love her?" Mother whispers, plunging the both of us into a tense wariness. "I see you looking at my sweet Andraste sometimes, when you think I am not aware. I see the way your eyes hunger for her. Do you love her, Edain? Do you love my daughter?"

There's a long moment of silence, so long I almost think he's not going to answer her.

"Yes," he finally says.

Shock blooms through me. I can't move. I barely dare look at him.

Would you still hate me if I loved you?

My heart lodges in my throat. And when he looks at me, I see the truth written there.

"You didn't know." She sounds pleased at my horror as

she captures his face and digs her nails into his cheeks. "You didn't know, because you despise him, don't you? Kiss me," she says. "Kiss me as if I am your *everything*."

He leans down, his eyelids growing sleepy as she captures his face and kisses him.

And I can't look at them anymore.

"You see," Mother whispers, finally letting him go. "You're the only one I can trust, because I *made you that way*. Now tell me the truth. Who stole my crown, Edain?"

"Your daughter."

"*Which* daughter?"

I can't breathe. He stands so still, a violent trembling breaking through his shoulders as if he's trying to fight the hex she's wrought around him.

"Which daughter?" Her voice becomes low and dangerous. "Do you think I will not break you? Do you think I will not make you crawl for me? Make you beg?" She pushes to her feet as he goes to one knee, clutching at his throat. "Do you dare love her more than you love me?"

Every inch of his face goes red.

"Stop it." I can't watch this. "He doesn't love me. It's always been a game to him. We've never—"

"He loves me," she hisses. "He loves me *more*. And he will tell me the truth or I will rip it from his tongue."

There's a gagging lump in my throat. I've spent so many years hating him, so many years feeling numb to her cruelties, but there's something about this moment that itches beneath my skin.

He knows the risks.

He knows she'll kill him if necessary, but he's holding his tongue *for me*.

Nobody has ever tried to protect me.

476

And then he breaks, a scream tearing from his throat, his fingers clenching into his palms—

"Stop it!" I rise, casting the goblet aside with a splash. "Stop it. He's done nothing wrong."

"He will tell me the truth," Adaia says coldly, curling her fingers into claws. "I am his *queen*, and he will answer me or he will die."

Edain hits the carpet, clutching at his throat and thrashing. His wild eyes find me, and there's a look there that slays me to the core—

"I took it!" I yell. "*I* took your fucking crown!"

The words ring in the sudden silence.

But Edain rolls to his hands and knees, gasping for breath as if whatever held him immobile has now released.

I don't regret a thing. I never did and I never will. And I can't believe that I said the words, because she will *kill* me.

But maybe there is some sense of freedom. I don't have to pretend anymore. I don't have to lie. I don't have to swallow my own poison.

I am free.

"Why?" she whispers, but there's no shock in her voice. She knew.

And then she turns to me, and I know she's not asking why I took the crown.

"I gave you everything," she whispers, drawing herself up as I back away. "I nurtured you, raised you above your sister, let you at my breast like an asp...."

"You took her from me." The truth spills from my lips in a whisper. "You poisoned us against each other. You tore us apart."

"I gave you a choice. Only one of you could be my heir—"

"We were *children*! I loved my sister!"

"She was a lying, treacherous child who betrayed us all—"

"You forced her into the Prince of Evernight's arms!" I yell. "And you cannot even see the role you played in all of this! Vi ran away because of you!" A helpless laugh breaks through me. "And she's happy, Mother. She's finally escaped your poison, and perhaps she is all the better for it." I push closer. "You want to know why I took your crown? For *love*, Mother. Because no matter how hard you have tried, you have never quite been able to destroy that which beats in my heart. I love my sister. I would do anything for my sister. And I hope she is happy and free and that she will never see you again—"

The slap almost drives me off my feet. I stagger into the table and knock the entire platter of strawberries to the floor. The clang of it ringing on the marble tiles is enough to set my teeth on edge, but I force myself to straighten. Force myself to tilt my chin and stare her in the eye.

"Kill me and you lose your court," I tell her. "They will see your lack of power as if it is a mortal weakness. You can't even control your own family. Your daughters *hate* you." The urge to laugh is almost destructive. "But the court loves *me*. I've spent years cultivating my alliances, as you taught me. The people cheer when I ride through the streets and curse you when you do. The only reason you have been able to hold on to your crown in the past ten years is because I have been there to sway their opinion. I have begged your people to listen to their queen, and I have counselled your lords to put away their steel when you strike at one of their own." I step closer to her. "Without me, Mother, you are alone. And you are weak. And you are hated. So punish me as you like, but with Evernight at your throat and Stormlight snapping at your heels, you're surrounded by enemies. Don't make another one within your own court."

"You little slut."

I tense, prepared for the flaying lash of her magic—

But it never comes. Edain grabs my mother's arm, holding her power back. Their eyes meet, and I can see the moment where she decides to turn all her fury and rage upon him. "You *dare?*"

"If you kill her, then you lose the north."

It steals my mother's breath.

And mine too.

What is he doing?

Why would he dare confront her in such a mood?

But he's not the one she turns upon. She captures my face, the prick of her jeweled claws biting through my skin. "Don't ever think you have outplayed me. Do you think I wouldn't dare raise a hand against my precious child?" My mother straightens. "Guards!"

The doors bang open.

A half dozen of my mother's guards enter, garbed in gold-plated armor.

"Are the horses ready?" she snaps at Korman, the lieutenant in charge.

He's not my favorite. Indeed, as I search the faces of the guards, I realize none of them are ones I would trust. They're all mercenary, all loyal to my mother and her coin.

"Yes, Your Majesty."

"Horses?" I demand. "What horses?"

With a snap of her fingers, my mother locks invisible bands of force around me, clamping my arms to my body. She hauls me to my feet with a gesture, her face cruel and furious. "You're right. If I kill you, then my country will tear itself apart. Besides, a dead daughter serves no purpose, and I have allies to please. And luckily, one of them needs a bride."

"A *bride*?"

No!

Edain takes a step forward, but mother throws her arm toward him, and he goes to his knees, a shining golden rope clamping his arms to his ribs and another one gagging him.

"Do not dare," she snarls at him.

His eyes promise murder, but my mother isn't done yet.

"I will take your love and I will twist it into a thousand writhing snakes," she hisses at him, golden light filling her eyes.

A curse. My eyes widen.

"You will never touch another fae for as long as you live," she spits the curse, along with a mouthful of blood. "Your touch will burn, your soul will wither, and your flesh will beg for relief, but there shall be none to be found. Live a thousand years, Edain, and never know another's touch again."

The curse strikes its target.

Edain screams, his spine bowing as little golden thorns flare to life in his skin.

"Mother, stop!' I yell.

"It's too late, Andraste. You will never have him now.

Your heart may yearn, but your flesh will never meet," she croons. "Instead, you will serve another."

I kick against her magic, but the golden ropes only squeeze me tighter. "No!"

"Send her to the goblin king with my regards," my mother sneers. "Tell him he may do with her as he pleases, as long as he claims he married the bitch and fulfils his part of our bargain."

The goblin clans are merciless. They haven't had a king in years, though there is rumor that there is one born of an ancient lineage who could rule them, if he would dare try to unite them.

No, no, no, no, no! I kick and scream, but there's no escaping her guards. Iron gauntlets sear my flesh as they grab me, and I know this was planned. A solid fist of metal drives into my gut, the breath whooshing out of me. Another clips my cheek.

I'm on my knees, my hands wrenched behind me, there's no escape but—

A hand fists in my hair, wrenching my face higher so my mother can look me in the eye one more time. "I will be sure to tell my lords that when you volunteered to save Asturia, I wept with grief at the thought that I would never see my beloved Andraste again. May, my darling, please come in."

"What are you doing to Aunt Andi?" comes a tiny voice.

May.

The blood drains from my face as the little girl I exchanged for my niece hovers in the doorway, a stuffed bear hanging from her hand.

"Don't do this! She's innocent."

"You were the one who told me she would be the perfect weapon to destroy her father." Mother gestures May closer. "Do you like the castle, my darling? It's much better than that drafty old keep at Clydain, isn't it?"

She doesn't know.

A relieved breath escapes me.

But then I still.

If she discovers May doesn't share her blood, then she will kill her.

I did this.

I can't let her hurt the girl.

"Do you want to be a princess?" my mother purrs, as she kneels in front of my adopted niece. "You will be my new heir and the people of our kingdom will adore you."

May looks at me uncertainly, her long black hair tangling over her shoulders. "Why are you hurting her?" she whispers. "Please don't hurt her."

"You're a kind little girl," Mother purrs. "But you see what happens when those you are kind to betray you? You give them everything and they try and steal all your happiness away. I can't let them steal my happiness, May. They must be punished. Do you understand?"

There's only one way to protect May. I seek out Edain. "Protect her, please protect her. Tell Vi what happened here. I'll—"

"Send her north," Mother tells the guards, giving them a lazy nod as she sweeps toward the doors with May's hand in hers. "She's the goblin king's now. I have a new crown heir."

Dear Reader,

Thank you so much for reading Crown of Darkness. I hope you enjoyed it.

As for Iskvien and Thiago, please note: I write ROMANCE. HEA guaranteed.

Iskvien and Thiago's story continues in **CURSE OF DARKNESS**.

Books in series:

Promise of Darkness
Crown of Darkness
Curse of Darkness

Novellas in same series:

Seduced By Darkness

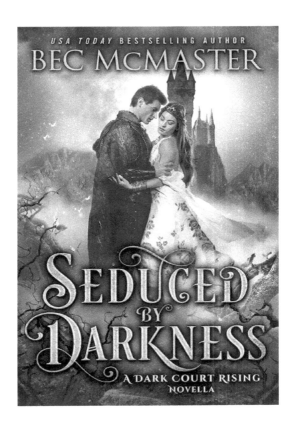

PREORDER NOW

He fell in love with the woman of his dreams, but he never realized what that love would cost him.

When a dark prince attends the Lammastide rites, he lays eyes on the woman he's been searching for his entire life.

The problem? She's his enemy's daughter.

A novella from Thiago's POV about his love story with Princess Iskvien. Author highly recommends reading AFTER Promise of Darkness.

AVAILABLE FEBRUARY 2021

Forged By Desire

Of Silk And Steam

Novellas in same series:

Tarnished Knight

The Clockwork Menace

LONDON STEAMPUNK: THE BLUE BLOOD CONSPIRACY

Mission: Improper

The Mech Who Loved Me

You Only Love Twice

To Catch A Rogue

Dukes Are Forever

From London, With Love

London Steampunk: The Blue Blood Conspiracy Boxset 1-3

London Steampunk: The Blue Blood Conspiracy Complete Series Boxset

DARK ARTS SERIES

Shadowbound

Hexbound

Soulbound

Dark Arts Box set 1-3

BURNED LANDS SERIES

Nobody's Hero

The Last True Hero

The Hero Within

The Burned Lands Complete Trilogy Boxset